D0468435

WRAPPED IN PLEASURE

NEW YORK TIMES AND USA TODAY
BESTSELLING AUTHOR

BRENDA
JACKSON
WRAPPED IN PLEASURE

ARABESQUE®

Recycling programs
for this product may
not exist in your area.

ISBN-13: 978-0-373-83177-7

WRAPPED IN PLEASURE
© 2010 by Harlequin Enterprises S.A.

The publisher acknowledges the copyright holder
of the individual works as follows:

DELANEY'S DESERT SHEIKH
© 2002 by Brenda Streater Jackson

SEDUCED BY A STRANGER
© 2010 by Brenda Streater Jackson

www.kimanipress.com

Printed in U.S.A.

CONTENTS

Dear Reader,

I am very happy to bring this book to you because with *Wrapped in Pleasure* I get to satisfy my readers' two most ardent requests—to reprint *Delaney's Desert Sheikh,* which is the first book in the Westmoreland series, and to write Sheikh Rasheed Valdemon's story. Rasheed was first introduced to readers in my book *Fire and Desire* from the Madaris series.

Rasheed Valdemon's story is a special one that my readers have been waiting for. Writing this story gave me the chance to bring together two of my most popular families, the Madarises and Westmorelands. From the moment I introduced Rasheed, I knew I wanted to write his story, but I needed a special heroine to make it happen. I have found that special woman in Johari Nafretiri Yasir.

I had no idea when I penned my first story for Harlequin's Silhouette Desire line that nearly eight years later the Westmorelands would still be a favorite among my readers. And I am happy to announce to those readers who may have missed those early Westmoreland books that the reprinting of Delaney's story is just the beginning. The others will follow in the order in which they were originally printed. Look for Dare and Thorn's story next month in a two-in-one book titled *Ravished by Passion.*

Happy reading!

Brenda Jackson

THE WESTMORELAND FAMILY

Scott and Delane Westmoreland

John (Evelyn)

② Dare (Shelly) A.J, Allison ⑥	③ Thorn (Tara) Trace ⑪	④ Stone (Madison) Rock ⑧	⑤ Storm (Jayla) Shaura, Johanna ⑨	⑦ Chase (Jessica) Carlton Scott ⑭	① Delaney (Jamal) Ari, Arielle
Jared (Dana) Jaren ⑫	Spencer (Chardonnay) Russell ⑬	Durango (Savannah) Sarah	Ian (Brooke) Pierce, Price	Quade (Cheyenne) Venus, Athena, Troy	Reggie (Olivia) ⑤
Clint (Alyssa) Cain	Cole (Patrina) Emilie, Emery	Casey (McKinnor) Corey Martin ⑩			

James (Sarah)

Corey (Abbie) Madison

① Delaney's Desert Sheikh
② A Little Dare
③ Thorn's Challenge
④ Stone Cold Surrender
⑤ Riding the Storm
⑥ Jared's Counterfeit Fiancée

⑦ The Chase is On
⑧ The Durango Affair
⑨ Ian's Ultimate Gamble
⑩ Seduction, Westmoreland Style
⑪ Spencer's Forbidden Passion
⑫ Taming Clint Westmoreland

⑬ Cole's Red-Hot Pursuit
⑭ Quade's Babies
⑮ Tall, Dark…Westmoreland!

Ponder the path of thy feet,
and let all thy ways be established.
—*Proverbs* 4:26

Acknowledgments

To the love of my life, Gerald Jackson, Sr.

To fellow author Olivia Gates whose help was immeasurable. Thanks for sharing information about your homeland in the Middle East and for giving me a better understanding of your culture.

DELANEY'S DESERT SHEIKH

Chapter 1

This was the first time he had been between a pair of legs and not gotten the satisfaction he wanted.

Jamal Ari Yasir drew in a deep, calming breath as he slid his body from underneath the table. Standing, he wiped the sweat from his brow. After an entire hour he still hadn't been able to stop the table from wobbling.

"I'm a sheikh and not a repairman, after all," he said with a degree of frustration, tossing the handyman tools back in the box where they belonged. He had come to the cabin to get some rest, but the only thing he was getting was bored.

And it was only the second day. He had twenty-eight to go.

He wasn't used to doing nothing. In his country a man's worth was measured by what he accomplished each day. Most of his people worked from sunup to sundown, not because they had to, but because they were accustomed to doing so for the good of Tahran. And although he was the son of one of the most influential sheikhs in the world, he had been required from birth to work just as hard as the people he served.

Over the past three months he had represented his country as a negotiator in a crucial business deal that also involved other nations surrounding Tahran. When the proceedings ended with all parties satisfied, he had felt the need to escape and find solitude to rest his world-weary mind and body.

The sound of a slamming car door caught Jamal's attention, and he immediately wondered who it could be. He knew it wasn't Philip, his former college roommate from Harvard, who had graciously offered him the use of the cabin. Philip had recently married and was somewhere in the Caribbean enjoying a two-week honeymoon.

Jamal headed toward the living room, his curiosity piqued. No one would make the turnoff from the major highway unless they knew a cabin was there—five miles back, deep in the woods. Walking over to the window, he looked out, drawing in a deep breath. Mesmerized. Hypnotized. Suddenly consumed with lust of the worst kind.

An African-American woman had gotten out of a late-model car and was bending over, taking something out of the trunk. All he could see was her backside but that was enough. He doubted he could handle anything else right now.

The pair of shorts she wore stretched tightly across the sexiest bottom he had ever seen—and during his thirty-four years he had seen plenty. But never like this and never this generous. And definitely never this well-defined and proportioned. What he was looking at was a great piece of art with all the right curves and angles.

Without very much effort, he could imagine her backside

pressed against his front as they slept in a spoon position. A smile curved his lips. But who would be able to sleep cuddled next to a body like hers? His gaze moved to her thighs. They were shapely, firm and perfectly contoured.

For an unconscious moment he stood rooted in place, gazing at her through the window. Reason jolted his lust-filled mind when she pulled out one large piece of luggage and a smaller piece. He frowned, then decided he would worry about the implications of the luggage later. He wanted to see the rest of her for now.

No sooner had that thought crossed his mind than she closed the trunk and turned around. It took only a split second for heat to course through his body, and he registered that she was simply gorgeous. Strikingly beautiful.

As she continued to toy with her luggage, his gaze began toying with her, starting at the top. She had curly, dark brown hair that tumbled around her honey-brown face and shoulders, giving her a brazenly sexy look. She had a nicely rounded chin and a beautifully shaped mouth.

He reluctantly moved his gaze away from her mouth and forged a path downward past the smooth column of her throat to her high round breasts, then lower, settling on her great-looking legs.

The woman was one alluring package.

Jamal shook his head, feeling a deep surge of regret that she had obviously come to the wrong cabin. Deciding he had seen enough for one day—not sure his hormones could handle seeing much more—he moved away from the window.

Opening the door, he stepped outside onto the porch. He was tempted to ask if he could have his way with her—once, maybe twice—before she left. Instead he leaned in the doorway and inquired in a friendly yet hot-and-bothered voice, "May I help you?"

* * *

Delaney Westmoreland jerked up her head, startled. Her heart began racing as she stared at the man standing on the porch, casually leaning in the doorway. And what a man he was. If any man could be described as beautiful, it would be him. The late-afternoon sun brought out the rich caramel coloring of his skin, giving true meaning to the description of tall, dark and handsome. Her experience was limited when it came to men, but it didn't take a rocket scientist to know this man was sexy as sin. This man would cause a girl to drool even with a dry mouth.

Amazing.

He was tall, probably six foot three, and was wearing a pair of European-tailored trousers and an expensive-looking white shirt. To her way of thinking he was dressed completely out of sync with his surroundings.

Not that she was complaining, mind you.

His hair, straight black and thick, barely touched the collar of his shirt, and dark piercing eyes that appeared alert and intelligent were trained on her, just as her gaze was trained on him. She blinked once, twice, to make sure he was real. When she was certain that he was, she forced her sanity to return and asked in a level yet slightly strained voice, "Who are you?"

A moment of silence passed between them before he responded. "I should be asking you that question." He moved away from the doorway and stepped off the porch.

Feeling breathless but trying like hell not to show it, Delaney kept her eyes steady as he approached. After all, he was a stranger, and there was a good chance the two of them were all alone in the middle of nowhere. She ignored the foolish part of her mind that said, There's nothing worse than not taking advantage of a good-looking opportunity.

Instead, she gave in to the more cautious side of her mind and said, "I'm Delaney Westmoreland and you're trespassing on private property."

The sexy-as-sin, make-you-drool man came to a stop in front of her, and when she tipped her head back to look up at him, a warm feeling coiled deep in her stomach. Up close he was even more beautiful.

"And I'm Jamal Ari Yasir. This place is owned by a good friend of mine, and I believe *you're* the one who's trespassing."

Delaney's eyes narrowed. She wondered if he really was a friend of Reggie as he claimed. Had her cousin forgotten he'd loaned this man the cabin when he'd offered it to her? "What's your friend's name?"

"Philip Dunbar."

"Philip Dunbar?" she asked, her voice dropping to a low, sexy timbre.

"Yes, you know him?"

She nodded. "Yes. Philip and my cousin, Reggie, were business partners at one time. Reggie is the one who offered me the use of the cabin. I'd forgotten he and Philip had joint ownership to this place."

"You've been here before?"

"Yes, once before. What about you?"

Jamal shook his head and smiled. "This is my first visit."

His smile made Delaney's breath catch in her throat. And his eyes were trained on her again, watching her closely. She didn't like being under the scope of his penetrating stare. "Do you have to stare at me like that?" she snapped.

His right eyebrow went up. "I wasn't aware I was staring."

"Well, you are." Her eyes narrowed at him. "And where are you from, anyway? You don't look American."

His lips lifted into a grin. "I'm not. I'm from the Middle East. A small country called Tahran. Ever heard of it?"

"No, but then geography wasn't my best subject. You speak our language quite well for a foreigner."

He shrugged. "English was one of the subjects I was taught at an early age, and then I came to this country at eighteen to attend Harvard."

"You're a graduate of Harvard?" she asked.

"Yes."

"And what do you do for a living?" she asked, wondering if perhaps he worked in some capacity for the federal government.

Jamal crossed his arms over his chest, thinking that Western women enjoyed asking a lot of questions. "I help my father take care of my people."

"*Your* people?"

"Yes, *my* people. I'm a sheikh, and the prince of Tahran. My father is the amir."

Delaney knew amir was just another way of referring to a king. "If you're the son of a king then what are you doing here? Although this is a nice place, I'd think as a prince you could do better."

Jamal frowned. "I could if I chose to do so, but Philip offered me the use of this cabin in friendship. It would have been rude of me not to accept, especially since he knew I wanted to be in seclusion for a while. Whenever it's known that I'm in your country, the press usually hounds me. He thought a month here is just what I needed."

"A month?"

"Yes. And how long had you planned to stay?"

"A month, too."

His eyebrow arched. "Well, we both know that being here together is impossible, so I'll be glad to put your luggage back in your car."

Delaney placed her hands on her hips. "And why should I be the one who has to leave?"

"Because I was here first."

He had a point, though it was one she decided not to give him. "But you can afford to go someplace else. I can't. Reggie gave me a month of rest and relaxation here as a graduation present."

"A graduation present?"

"Yes. I graduated from medical school last Friday. After eight years of nonstop studying, he thought a month here would do me good."

"Yes, I'm sure that it would have."

Delaney breathed a not-so-quiet sigh when she saw he was going to be difficult. "There's a democratic way to settle this."

"Is there?"

"Yes. Which do you prefer, flipping a coin or pulling straws?"

Her options made his lips twitch into an involuntary smile. "Neither. I suggest that you let me help you put your luggage back in the car."

Delaney drew in a deep, infuriated breath. How dare he think he could tell her what to do? She'd been the only girl with five older brothers and had discovered fairly early in life not to let anyone from the opposite sex push her around. She would handle him the same way she handled them. With complete stubbornness.

Placing her hands on her hips she met his gaze with the Westmoreland glare. "I am not leaving."

He didn't seem at all affected when he said, "Yes, you are."

"No, I'm not."

His jaw suddenly had the look of being chiseled from stone. "In my country women do what they are told."

Delaney flashed him a look of sheer irritation. "Well, welcome to America, *Your Highness*. In this country women have the right to speak their minds. We can even tell a man where to go."

Jamal's eyebrows shot up in confusion. "Where to go?"

"Yes, like go fly a kite, go take a leap or go to hell."

Jamal couldn't help but chuckle. It was apparent Delaney Westmoreland was potently sassy. He had learned that American women didn't hesitate to let you know when they were upset about something. In his country women learned very early in life not to show their emotions. He decided to try another approach, one that would possibly appeal to her intelligence. "Be reasonable."

She glared at him, letting him know that approach wasn't going to work. "I *am* being reasonable, and right now a cabin on a lake for a month, rent free, is more than reasonable. It's a steal, a dream come true, a must have. Besides, you aren't the only one who needs to be in seclusion for a while."

Delaney immediately thought of her rather large family. Now that she had completed medical school, they assumed she was qualified to diagnose every ache and pain they had. She would never get any rest if they knew where to find her. Her parents knew how to reach her in case of an emergency and that was good enough. She loved her relations dearly but she was due for a break.

"Why are you in seclusion?"

She frowned. "It's personal."

Jamal couldn't help wondering if perhaps she was hiding from a jealous lover or even a husband. She wasn't wearing a wedding band, but then he knew from firsthand experience that some American women took off their rings when it suited them. "Are you married?"

"No, are you?" she responded crisply.

"Not yet," he murmured softly. "I'm expected to marry before my next birthday."

"Good for you, now please be a nice prince and take my luggage into the house. If I'm not mistaken, there are three bedrooms and all with connecting bathrooms, so it's plenty big enough and private enough for the both of us. I plan to do a lot of sleeping, so there will be days when you probably won't see me at all."

He stared at her. "And on those days when I do see you?"

Delaney shrugged. "Just pretend that you don't. However, if you find that difficult to do and feel things are getting a little bit too crowded around here to suit you, I'd completely understand if you left." She glanced around the yard. "By the way, where's your car?"

Jamal sighed, wondering how he could get her to leave. "My secretary has it," he responded drily. "He checked into a motel a few miles away from here, preferring to be close by just in case I needed anything."

Delaney lifted a cool eyebrow. "Must be nice getting the royal treatment."

He ignored her chill and responded, "It has its advantages. Asalum has been with me since the day I was born."

Delaney couldn't help but hear the deep affection in his voice. "Like I said, it must be nice."

"Are you sure you want to stay here?" His tone was slightly challenging as his black eyes held her dark brown ones.

The question, spoken in a deep, sexy voice, gave Delaney pause. No, she wasn't sure, but she knew for certain that she wasn't ready to leave; especially not after driving seven hours straight to get there. Maybe she would feel different after taking a shower and a very long nap.

She met Jamal's dark gaze and almost shuddered under its intensity. A shiver of desire rippled through her. She felt it now, just as she had when she'd first seen him standing on the porch. At twenty-five, she was mature enough to recognize there was such a thing as overactive hormones. But then, she was also mature enough to know how to control them and not yield to temptation. Getting involved with a male chauvinist prince was the last thing she wanted, and she hoped getting involved with her was the last thing he wanted, as well.

She met his gaze and lifted her chin in a defiant stance and said, "I'm staying."

The woman was as stubborn as they came, Jamal thought as he leaned against the doorjamb in the kitchen. He watched Delaney as she unpacked the groceries she had brought with her. When she finished she turned around. "Thanks for bringing in my luggage and those boxes."

He nodded as his gaze held hers. Once again he felt that sudden surge of lust that made his body tighten and knew she had noticed his reaction. Nervously she licked her lips as she dragged her eyes away from his. It was obvious that she was also aware of the strong sexual chemistry arcing between them.

"If you're having second thoughts about staying…"

Her eyes filled with the fire he was getting used to. "Forget it."

"Remember it was your decision," he said evenly.

"I'll remember." She walked over to him and glared up at him. "And I would suggest that you don't get any ideas about trying to do anything underhanded to run me off. I'll leave when I get ready to leave and not before."

Jamal thought that the angrier she got the more beautiful she became. "I'm too much of a gentleman to behave in such a manner."

"Good. I'll take your word on that." She turned to leave the room.

He watched the sway of Delaney's hips until she was no longer in sight. His nostrils flared in response to the enticing feminine scent she had left behind, and the primitive sultan male in him released a low growl.

One thing was for certain; he would not be getting bored again anytime soon.

With a soul-weary sigh, Delaney ran her fingers through her hair and leaned against the closed bedroom door. A jolt of heat ripped from the tip of her painted toes all the way to the crown of her head. Jamal's gaze had been hot and hungry.

What had she gotten herself into?

The thought that she was actually willing to share a cabin with a man she didn't know was plain ludicrous. The only thing to her credit was the fact that while he had been outside getting the boxes out of the car, she had used her cell phone to call Reggie.

Born the same year, she and Reggie had forged a closeness from the time they had been babies, and over the years he had become more than just a cousin. He was sort of like her best buddy.

He had always kept her secrets, and she had always kept his. Since his interest had been in working with numbers, no one was surprised when he had established an accounting firm a few years ago after earning a graduate degree in Business Administration from Morehouse College.

After apologizing for the mix-up, Reggie had assured her that Jamal was legit. He had met him through Philip a few years ago. Reggie further verified Jamal's claim that he was a prince and had gone on to warn her that according to Philip, Jamal had very little tolerance for Western women.

She had ended the conversation with Reggie, thinking that she couldn't care less about the man's tolerance level, and had no intention of letting him dictate whether or not she would stay.

She deserved thirty days to rest and do nothing, and by golly, come hell or high water, she planned to enjoy her vacation.

Crossing the room, she plopped down onto a reclining chair. She glanced at the luggage on her bed, too tired to unpack just yet. Putting up the groceries had taken everything out of her. Jamal had stood there the entire time watching her.

Although he hadn't said anything, she had felt his gaze as if it had been a personal caress. And a few times she had actually looked across the room and caught him staring. No, *glaring* was more like it.

She knew his intent had been to try to unnerve her. But as far as she was concerned, he had a long way to go to ruffle her feathers. The Westmoreland brothers—Dare, Thorn, Stone, Chase and Storm—made dealing with someone like Jamal a piece of cake.

Her cheeks grew warm when she imagined that he was probably just as tasty as a piece of cake. Utterly delicious. A mouthwatering delight. Even now her body felt the heat. He had evoked within her the most intense physical reaction and attraction to a man she had ever experienced.

She shook her head, deciding she definitely needed to take a cool shower and not get tempted.

No matter how crazy her body was acting, she didn't need a man. What she needed was sleep.

Chapter 2

Delaney stood in the kitchen doorway and stared for a long moment at the masculine legs sticking out from underneath the kitchen table. Nice, she thought, studying the firmness of male thighs clad in a pair of immaculately pressed jeans.

Since arriving four days ago, this was only her third time seeing Jamal. Just as she'd told him that first day, she intended to get the sleep she deserved. Other than waking up occasionally to grab something to eat, she had remained in her bedroom sleeping like a baby.

Except for that one time he had awakened her, making a racket outside her bedroom window while practicing some type of martial art. She had forced her body from the bed and gone to the window to see what the heck was going on.

Through the clear pane she'd watched him. He'd been wearing a sweat top and a pair of satin boxing trunks that were expertly tailored for a snug fit.

She'd watched, mesmerized, as he put his body through a series of strenuous standing-jump kicks and punches. She admired such tremendous vitality, discipline and power. She had also admired his body, which showed an abundance of masculine strength. For the longest time she had stood at the window rooted in place, undetected, while she ogled him. A woman could only take a man like Jamal in slow degrees.

Deciding that if she didn't move away from the window she would surely die a slow and painful death from lust overload, she had made her way back to the bed and nearly collapsed.

"Dammit!"

Jamal's outburst got her attention and brought her thoughts back to the present. She couldn't help but smile. No matter how well he mastered the English language, a curse word coming from him didn't sound quite the same as it did coming from an American. Her brothers had a tendency to use that particular word with a lot more flair.

She walked over to the table and glanced down. "Need help?"

At first he froze in place, evidently surprised by her presence. "No, I can manage," was his tart reply.

"You're sure?"

"Positive," he all but snapped.

"Suit yourself," she snapped back. She turned and walked over to the kitchen cabinet to get a bowl for the cereal she had brought with her, ignoring the fact that he had slid from underneath the table and was standing up.

"So, what got you up this morning?" he asked, tossing the tools he'd been using in a box.

"Hunger." She put cereal into her bowl, then poured on the milk. Seeing the kitchen table was not available for her to use, she grabbed the cereal box and a spoon and went outside onto the porch.

Already the morning was hot and she knew it would get hotter, typical for a North Carolina summer. She was glad the inside of the cabin had air-conditioning. This was sweaty, sticky heat, the kind that made you want to walk around naked.

Her brothers would be scandalized if they knew she'd done that on occasion when it got hot enough at her home, which was one of the advantages of living alone. She released a deep sigh as she sat down on the steps thinking that with Jamal sharing the cabin walking around naked wasn't an option.

She had taken a mouthful of her cereal when she heard the screen door opening behind her. The knowledge that Jamal was out on the porch and standing just a few feet behind her sent every instinct and conscious thought she had into overdrive. Out of the corner of her eye she saw him lean against the porch rail with a cup of coffee in his hand.

"You've given up moonlighting as a repairman already, *Your Highness?*" she asked in a snippy voice, dripping with sarcasm.

He evidently decided to take her taunt in stride and replied, "For now, yes, but I intend to find out what's wrong with that table and fix it before I leave here. I would hate to leave behind anything broken."

Delaney glanced over at him then wished she hadn't. It seemed his entire face, dark and stunning, shone in the morning sunlight. If she thought he'd been classically beautiful and had dressed out of sync four days ago, then today he had done a complete turnaround. Shirtless, unshaven and wearing jeans, he looked untamed and rugged and no longer like a wolf in sheep's clothing. He looked every bit a wolf, wild and rapacious and on the prowl. If given the chance he would probably eat her alive and lick his chops afterward.

There was nothing in the way he looked to denote he was

connected to royalty, a prince, a sheikh. Instead what she saw was an extremely handsome man with solid muscles and a body that exuded sheer masculinity.

He lowered his head to take a sip of his coffee, and she used that time to continue to study him undetected. Now that he was standing, she could see the full frontal view. His jeans were a tight fit and seemed to have been made just for his body. Probably had since he could afford a private tailor. And even if she hadn't seen him doing kickboxing, it would be quite obvious that he kept in shape with his wide, muscular shoulders, trim waistline and narrow hips.

She imagined having the opportunity to peel those jeans off him just long enough to wrap her legs tight around his waist. And then there was his naked chest. A chest her hand was just itching to touch. She was dying to feel whether his muscles were as hard as they looked.

Delaney's heart began pounding. She couldn't believe she was thinking such things. She was really beginning to lose it. Incredible. Nothing like this had ever happened to her before. She couldn't think of one single man in all her twenty-five years who had made her feel so wanton, so greedy, so…needy.

The only need she had experienced with the guys she had taken the time to date in college and medical school had been the need to bring the date to a quick end. And her only greed had been for food, especially her mother's mouthwatering strawberry pie.

No longer wanting to dwell on her sex life—or lack thereof—she racked her brain, trying to remember the question she had intended to ask Jamal a few minutes earlier. The same brain that had helped her to graduate at the top of her class just last week had turned to mush. She collected her scattered thoughts and remembered the question. "What's wrong with the table?"

He raised his head and looked at her as if she was dense. "It's broken."

She glared at him. "That much is obvious. How is it broken?"

He shrugged. "I have no idea. It wobbles."

Delaney raised her eyes heavenward. "Is that all?"

"A table is not supposed to wobble, Delaney."

And I shouldn't be getting turned on from the way you just said my name, she thought, turning her attention away from him and back to her food. That was the first time he had called her by name, and her body was experiencing an intense reaction to it. His tone of voice had been low and husky.

Her eyes stayed glued to her cereal box as she ate, thinking that her fixation with Tony the Tiger was a lot safer than her fascination with Jamal the Wolf. The last thing she needed was a complication in her life, and she had a feeling that getting involved with Jamal would definitely rank high on the Don't Do list. She had no doubt he was a master at seduction. He looked the part and she was smart enough to know he was way out of her league.

Satisfied that she was still in control of her tumultuous emotions, at least for the time being, Delaney smiled to herself as she continued to eat her cereal.

Releasing a deep sigh, Jamal commanded his body to take control of the desire racing through it. Ever since he had begun business negotiations with the country surrounding Tahran for a vital piece of land lying between them, he had been celibate, denying his body and freeing his mind to totally concentrate on doing what was in the best interest of his country. But now that the negotiations were over, his body was reminding him it had a need that was long overdue.

He scolded himself for his weakness and tried to ignore the sexual urges gripping him. If he had returned home after

Philip's wedding instead of taking his friend up on his offer to spend an entire month at this cabin, he would not be going through this torment.

In Tahran there were women readily available for him—women who thought it a privilege as well as an honor to take care of their prince's needs. They would come to his apartment, which was located in his own private section of the palace, and pleasure him any way he wanted. It had always been that way since his eighteenth birthday.

There was also Najeen, the woman who had been his mistress for the past three years. She was trained in the art of pleasing only him and did an excellent job of it. He had provided her with her own lavish cottage on the grounds not far from the palace, as well as personal servants to see to her every need. At no time had he ever craved a woman.

Until now.

"Tell me about your homeland, Jamal."

Jamal arched a brow, surprised at Delaney's request. He shifted his gaze from his cup of coffee and back to her. Her honey-brown face glowed in the sunlight, making her appear radiant, golden. She wasn't wearing any makeup, so her beauty was natural, awe-inspiring. He swallowed hard and tried once again to ignore the urgent need pounding inside him, signals of desire racing through his body.

"What do you want to know?" he asked with a huskiness he almost didn't recognize.

Delaney placed her empty bowl aside and leaned back on both hands as she looked at him. "Anything you want to tell me. It must be an interesting place to live."

He chuckled at the curiosity in her voice, then stared down at her for several moments before he began speaking. "Yes, interesting," he said slowly, "and quite beautiful." She couldn't know that he had just referred to his country...as well as to her.

Fighting for total control, he continued. "Tahran is located not far from Saudi Arabia, close to the Persian Gulf. It's a relatively small country compared to others close to it like Kuwait and Oman. Our summers are intensely hot and our winters are cool and short. And unlike most places in the Middle East, we get our share of rain. Our natural resources in addition to oil are fish, shrimp and natural gas. For the past few years my people have lived in peace and harmony with our neighbors. Once in a while disagreements flare up, but when that happens a special regional coalition resolves any disputed issues. I am one of the youngest members of that coalition."

"Are both your parents still living?"

Jamal took another sip of his coffee before answering. "My mother died when I was born and for many years my father and I lived alone with just the servants. Then Fatimah entered our lives."

"Fatimah?"

"Yes, my stepmother. She married my father when I was twelve." Jamal decided not to mention that his parents' marriage had been prearranged by their families to bring peace to two warring nations. His mother had been an African princess of Berber descent, and his father, an Arab prince. There had been no love between them, just duty, and he had been the only child born from that union. Then one day his father brought Fatimah home and their lives hadn't been the same.

His father's marriage to Fatimah was supposed to have been like his first marriage, one of duty and not love. But it had been evident with everyone from the start that the twenty-two-year-old Egyptian beauty had other plans for her forty-six-year-old husband. And it also became apparent to everyone in the palace that Fatimah was doing more for King Yasir than satisfying his loneliness and his physical needs in the bedroom. Their king was smiling. He was happy and he didn't travel outside his sheikhdom as often.

King Yasir no longer sent for other women to pleasure him, bestowing that task solely upon his wife. Then, within a year of their marriage, they had a child, a daughter they named Arielle. Three years later another daughter was born. They named her Johari.

Arielle, at nineteen, was now married to Prince Shudoya, a man she had been promised to since birth. Johari, at sixteen, was a handful after having been spoiled and pampered by their father. Jamal smiled, inwardly admitting that he'd had a hand in spoiling and pampering her, as well.

He simply adored his stepmother. More than once during his teen years, she had gone to his father on his behalf about issues that had been important to him.

"Do the two of you get along? You and your stepmother?"

Delaney's question invaded his thoughts. "Yes, Fatimah and I are very close."

Delaney stared at him. For some reason she found it hard to imagine him having a "very close" relationship with anyone. "Any siblings?" she decided to ask.

He nodded. "Yes, I have two sisters, Arielle and Johari. Arielle is nineteen and is married to a sheikh in a neighboring sheikhdom, and Johari is sixteen and has just completed her schooling in my country. She wants to come to America to further her studies."

"Will she?"

He looked at her like she had gone stone mad. "Of course not!"

Delaney stared at him, dumbfounded, wondering what he had against his sister being educated in the United States. "Why? You did."

Jamal clenched his jaw. "Yes, but my situation was different."

Delaney lifted her brow. "Different in what way?"

"I'm a man."

"So? What's that supposed to mean?"

"Evidently it means nothing in this country. I have observed more times than I care to count how the men let the women have control."

Delaney narrowed her eyes. "You consider having equal rights as having control?"

"Yes, in a way. Men are supposed to take care of the women. In your country more and more women are being educated to take care of themselves."

"And you see that as a bad thing?"

He gazed at her and remembered her sassiness from the first day and decided the last thing he wanted was to get embroiled in a bitter confrontation with her. He had his beliefs and she had hers. But since she had asked his opinion he would give it to her. "I see it as something that would not be tolerated in my country."

What he didn't add was that the alternative—the one his stepmother used so often and had perfected to an art—was for a woman to wrap herself around her husband's heart so tightly that he would give her the moon if she asked for it.

Taking another sip of coffee, Jamal decided to change the subject and shift the conversation to her. "Tell me about your family," he said, thinking that was a safer topic.

Evidently it's not, he thought when she glared at him.

"My family lives in Atlanta, and I'm the only girl as well as the youngest in the third generation of Westmorelands. And for the longest time my five brothers thought I needed protecting. They gave any guy who came within two feet of me pure hell. By my eighteenth birthday I had yet to have a date, so I finally put a stop to their foolishness."

He smiled. "And how did you do that?"

A wicked grin crossed her face. "Since I never had a social life I ended up with a lot of free time on my hands. So I started doing to them what they were doing to me—interfering in their lives. I suddenly became the nosy, busybody sister. I would deliberately monitor their calls, intentionally call their girlfriends by the wrong name and, more times than I care to count, I would conveniently drop by their places when I knew they had company and were probably right smack in the middle of something immoral."

She chuckled. "In other words, I became the kid sister from hell. It didn't take long for them to stop meddling in my affairs and back off. However, every once in a while they go brain dead and started sticking their noses into my business again. But it doesn't take much for me to remind them to butt out or suffer the consequences if they don't."

Jamal shook his head, having the deepest sympathy for her brothers. "Are any of your brothers married?"

She stared at him, her eyes full of amusement at his question. "Are you kidding? They have too much fun being single. They are players, the card-carrying kind. Alisdare, whom we call Dare, is thirty-five, and the sheriff of College Park, a suburb of Atlanta. Thorn is thirty-four and builds motorcycles as well as races them. Last year he was the only African-American on the circuit. Stone will be celebrating his thirty-second birthday next month. He's an author of action-thriller novels and writes under the pen name of Rock Mason."

She shifted in her seat as she continued. "Chase and Storm are twins but look nothing alike. They are thirty-one. Chase owns a soul-food restaurant and Storm is a fireman."

"With such busy professions, how can they find the time to keep tabs on you?"

She chuckled. "Oh, you would be surprised. They somehow seem to manage."

"Are your parents still living?"

"Yes. They have been together for over thirty-seven years and have a good marriage. However, my mother bought into my father's philosophy that she was supposed to stay home and take care of him and the kids. But after I left home she found herself with plenty of spare time on her hands and decided to go back to school. Dad wasn't too crazy with the idea but decided to indulge her, anyway, thinking she'd only last a few months. I'm proud to say that she graduated three years ago with a graduate degree in education."

Jamal set his empty coffee cup aside. "For some reason I have a feeling that you influenced your mother's sudden need to educate herself."

Delaney chuckled. "Of course. I've always known she had a brilliant mind—a mind that was being wasted doing nothing but running a house and taking care of her family. You know what they say. A mind is a terrible thing to waste. And why should men have all the advantages while women get stuck at home, barefoot and pregnant?"

Jamal shook his head. He hoped to Allah that Delaney Westmoreland never had the opportunity to visit his country for an extended period of time. She would probably cause a women's rights revolution with her way of thinking.

He stretched his body, tired of the conversation. It was evident that somewhere along the way Delaney had been given too much freedom. What she needed was some man's firm hand of control.

And what he needed was to have his head examined.

Even now his nostrils were absorbing her feminine scent, and it was nearly driving him insane. As she sat on the steps, her drawn-up knees exposed a lot of bare thigh that the shorts she was wearing didn't hide.

"Do you have female doctors in your country?"

He looked at her when her question pulled him back into the conversation. It was the same conversation he had convinced himself a few moments ago that he no longer wanted to indulge in. "Yes, we have women that deliver babies."

"That's all they do?" she asked annoyed.

He thought for a second. "Basically, yes."

She glared at him as she pursed her lips. "Your country is worse off than I thought."

"Only you would think so. The people in my country are happy."

She shook her head. "That's sad."

He lifted a brow. "What's sad?"

She drew his gaze. "That you would think they are happy."

Jamal frowned, feeling inordinately annoyed. Had she given him the opportunity, he would have told her that thanks to Fatimah, a highly educated woman herself, things had begun to change. The women in his country were now encouraged to pursue higher education, and several universities had been established for that purpose. And if they so desired, women could seek careers outside of the home. Fatimah was a strong supporter of women enjoying political and social rights in their country, but she was not radical in her push for reform. She simply used her influence over his father to accomplish the changes she supported.

He moved from the rail. It was time to practice his kickboxing, but first he needed to take a walk to relieve the anger consuming his mind and the intense ache that was gripping the lower part of his body. "I'm going down to the lake for a while. I'll see you later."

Delaney scooted aside to let him walk down the steps, tempted to tell him to take his time coming back. She watched as he walked off, appreciating how he filled out his jeans from the back. There was nothing like a man with a nice-looking butt.

She pulled in a deep breath and let it out again. Every time he looked at her, directly in her eyes, sparks of desire would go off inside of her. Now she fully understood what Ellen Draper, her college roommate at Tennessee State, meant when she'd tried explaining to her the complexities of sexual chemistry and physical attraction. At the time she hadn't had a clue because she hadn't yet met a man like Jamal Yasir.

Standing, she stretched. Today she planned to explore the area surrounding the cabin. Then later she intended to get more sleep. For the past three weeks she had studied all hours of the day and night preparing for final exams and had not gotten sufficient rest.

Now that she could, she would take advantage of the opportunity to relax. Besides, the less she was around Jamal, the better.

Jamal kept walking. He had passed the lake a mile back but intended to walk off as much sexual frustration as he could. The anger he'd felt with Delaney's comment about the people in his country not being happy had dissolved. Now he was dealing with the power of lust.

He stopped walking and studied the land surrounding the cabin. From where he stood the view was spectacular. This was the first time since coming to the cabin that he had actually taken the time to walk around and appreciate it.

He remembered the first time Philip had mentioned the cabin in the Carolinas, and how the view of the mountains had been totally breathtaking. Now he saw just what his friend had meant.

His mind then went back to Delaney, and he wondered if she had seen the view from this spot and if she would find it as breathtaking as he did. He doubted she had seen anything, since she rarely left the confines of her bedroom for long periods of time.

Jamal leaned against a tree when he heard his cell phone ring. He unsnapped it from the waist of his jeans and held it to his ear. "Yes, Asalum, what is it?"

"I'm just checking, Your Highness, to make sure all is well and that you don't need anything."

He shook his head. "I'm fine, but I have received an unexpected visitor."

"Who?"

He knew that Asalum was immediately on alert. In addition to serving as his personal secretary, Asalum had been his bodyguard from the time Jamal had been a child to the time he had officially reached manhood at eighteen.

He told him about Delaney's arrival. "If the woman is being a nuisance, Your Highness, perhaps I can persuade her to leave."

Jamal sighed. "That won't be necessary, Asalum. All she does most of the time is sleep, anyway."

There was a pause. Then a question. "Is she pregnant?"

Jamal arched a brow. "Why would you think she is pregnant?"

"Most women have a tendency to sleep a lot when they are pregnant."

Jamal nodded. If anyone knew the behavior of a pregnant woman it would be Asalum. Rebakkah, Asalum's wife, had borne him twelve children. "No, I don't think she's pregnant. She claims she's just tired."

Asalum snorted. "And what has she been doing to be so tired?"

"Studying for finals. She recently completed a medical degree at the university."

"Is that all? She must be a weak woman if studying can make her tired to the point of exhaustion."

For some reason Jamal felt the need to defend Delaney.

"She is not a weak woman. If anything she's too strong. Especially in her opinions."

"She sounds like a true Western woman, Your Highness."

Jamal rubbed his hand across his face. "She is. In every sense of the words. And, Asalum, she is also very beautiful."

For the longest moment Asalum didn't say anything, then he said quietly, "Beware of temptation, my prince."

Jamal thought about all that he had been experiencing since Delaney had arrived. Even now his body throbbed for relief. "Your warning comes too late. It has gone past temptation," Jamal said flatly.

"And what is it now?"

"Obsession."

Chapter 3

After being at the cabin a full week, Delaney finally completed the task of unpacking and put away the last of her things. With arms folded across her chest she walked over to the window and looked out. Her bedroom had a beautiful view of the lake, and she enjoyed waking up to it every morning. A number of thoughts and emotions were invading her mind, and at the top of the list was Jamal Yasir. She had to stop thinking about him. Ever since their talk that morning a few days ago, he had been on her mind although she hadn't wanted him there. So she had done the logical thing and avoided him like the plague.

A bit of anger erupted inside of her. In the past she had been able to school her thoughts and concentrate on one thing. And with that single-minded focus she had given medical school her complete attention. Now it seemed that with school behind her, her mind had gotten a life of its own and decided Jamal deserved her full consideration.

She was always consumed with thoughts of him. Intimate thoughts. Wayward thoughts. Thoughts of the most erotic kind. She wasn't surprised, because Jamal was the type of man who would elicit such thoughts from any woman, but Delaney was annoyed that she didn't have a better handle on her mental focus. Even with medical school behind her, she was still facing two years of residency, which would require another two years of concentration. An intimate relationship with any man should be the last thing on her mind.

But it wasn't.

And that's what had her resentful, moody and just plain hot, to the highest degree. Deciding to take a walk to cool off—like she really thought that would help—she grabbed her sunglasses off the dresser. She stepped outside of her room only to collide with the person who had been dominating her thoughts.

Jamal reached out to grab her shoulders to steady her and keep her from falling. She sucked in a quick breath when she noticed he was shirtless. Dark eyes gazed down into hers making her knees go weak, and the intensity of her lust went bone deep.

The rate of her breathing increased when his hand moved from her shoulder to her neck and the tip of his fingers slowly began caressing her throat. She could barely breathe with the magnitude of the sensations consuming her. The chemistry radiating between them was disturbingly basic and intrinsically sexy, and it was playing havoc with all five of her senses.

The sound of thunder roared somewhere in the distance and jolted them. He slowly released his hold, dropping his hands to his side. "Sorry, I didn't mean to bump into you," he said, the sound a throaty whisper that hummed through every nerve in Delaney's body before flowing through her bloodstream. And from the look in his eyes she could tell he wasn't immune. He was as aware as she was of the strong sexual tension that held both of them in its clutches.

"That's okay since I wasn't looking where I was going," she said softly, also offering an apology and inhaling deeply to calm her racing heart. She watched as his gaze slowly raked over her. She was wearing a pair of shorts and a crepe halter top. Suddenly she felt more naked than covered. More tensed than relaxed. And hotter than ever.

"Delaney?"

With the sound of her name spoken so sensually from his lips, her gaze locked with his, and at the same time he began leaning down closer to her. It was too close. Not close enough. And when she felt the warm brush of his breath against her throat, she responded softly, in an agonized whisper, "Yes?"

"It's going to rain," he said huskily.

She saw flickers of desire darken his gaze. "Sounds that way, doesn't it?" she managed to get out with extreme effort. She licked her lips slowly, cautiously. She was no longer aware of her surroundings, and barely heard the sound of the first drops of rain that suddenly began beating against the rooftop. Nor did she feel the tartness of the cold, damp air that suddenly filled the room.

All of her thoughts, her total concentration, was on the imposing figure looming before her. And she didn't consider resisting when he gently pulled her to him.

Go ahead, let him kiss you, a voice inside her head said. *Indulge yourself. Get it out of your system. Then the two of you can stop acting like two animals in heat. All it will take is this one, single kiss.*

A deep, drugging rush of desire filled Delaney. Shivers of wanting and need coursed down her spine. Yes, that's all it would take to get her head back on straight. A sexual attraction between a man and woman was healthy. Normal. Fulfilling. She'd just never had time to indulge before, but now she was ready. Now, with Jamal, indulging was necessary.

That was her last thought before Jamal's mouth covered hers.

Jamal took Delaney's lips with expertise and desperation. The need to taste her was elemental to him. Relentlessly his tongue explored her mouth, tasting and stroking, slowly moving beyond sampling to devouring. And when that wasn't enough he began sucking, drawing her into him with every breath.

He slipped his hand behind her head to hold her mouth in place while he got his fill, thinking it was impossible to do so, but determined to try anyway. He was at a point where he was willing to die trying.

He had kissed many women in his lifetime but had never felt a need to literally eat one alive. Never had any woman pushed him to such limits. He had been raised in an environment that accepted sex and intimacy for what they were—pleasure of the most tantalizing kind and a normal, healthy part of life.

But something deep within him believed there wasn't anything normal about this. What could be normal about wanting to stick your tongue down a woman's throat to see how far it could go? What was normal about wanting to suck her tongue forever if necessary to get the taste he was beginning to crave?

He pressed his body closer to hers, wanting her to feel him and know how much he desired her. He wanted her to know he wanted more than just a kiss. He wanted everything. He wanted it all.

And he intended to get it.

Jamal's fingers were insistent as they moved down her body to come to rest on her backside, gently pulling her closer. His body hardened at the feel of the tips of her nipples pressing against his bare chest through the material of her top. The contact was stimulating, inflaming, arousing.

And it was driving him insane.

The area between his thighs began to ache and get even harder. Grasping her hips he brought her more firmly against him, wanting her to feel his arousal, every throbbing inch. He knew she had gotten the message when he felt her fingers tangle in his hair, holding him close as he continued to devour her mouth.

Moments later, another loud clap of thunder, one that seemed to shake the entire earth, broke them apart. Delaney gasped so hard she almost choked. She bent over to pull air into her lungs, and seconds later, when she looked up and met Jamal's hot gaze, she felt her body responding all over again.

One kiss had not gotten him out of her system. That thought made her aware that unless she backed away, she would be in too deep. Already she felt herself sinking, drowning, being totally absorbed by him.

She backed up and he moved forward, cornering her against the wall. "I don't think we should have done that," she said softly, unconvincingly. Her voice was shaky, husky.

Jamal was glad they had done it and wanted to do it again. "It's been a week. We would have gotten around to kissing eventually," he said in a low, raspy voice. His body was still radiating an intimate intensity, although they were no longer touching.

"Why?" she asked, her curiosity running deep. When she saw the way his eyes darkened, a part of her wished that she hadn't asked him. He was looking at her in that way that made certain parts of her body get hot. And at the moment she couldn't handle the heat and doubted that she ever would.

"Because we want each other. We want to have sex," he replied, bluntly and directly. Although the words sounded brusque even to his ears, it was the truth and when it came to satisfying his body he believed in complete honesty. In his country such things were understood, expected and accepted.

Delaney's body trembled with Jamal's words. He'd made having sex sound so simple and basic. She thought of all the guys she had dated in her lifetime. She'd never wanted to have sex before. But Jamal was right—she *was* tempted now. But a part of her held back.

"I'm not a woman who makes a habit of getting into a man's bed," she said softly, feeling the need to let him know where she stood, and determined not to let him know that for the first time she was rethinking that policy.

"We don't have to use a bed if you don't want. We can use the table, the sofa or the floor. You pick the place. I'm bursting at the seams ready."

Delaney glanced down and saw his erection pressing against his zipper and knew he was dead serious. She inhaled deeply. He had missed her point entirely.

"What I mean is that I don't sleep with a man just for the fun of it."

He nodded slowly. "Then what about for the pleasure of it? Would you sleep with a man just for the pleasure it would give you?"

Delancy stared at him blankly. Indulging in sex mainly for pleasure? She knew her brothers did it all the time. They were experts in the field. None of them had a mind to marry, yet they bought enough condoms during the year to make it cost-efficient to form their own company.

"I've never thought about it before," she answered truthfully. "When I think of someone being horny, I immediately think of men, more so than I do women."

"Horny?"

She shook her head, thinking he was probably not familiar with a lot of American slang. "Yes, horny. It means needing sex in a bad way, almost to the point where your body is craving it."

Jamal leaned down close to her mouth. "In that case, I'm feeling *horny*," he murmured thickly against it. "Real horny. And I want to make you feel horny, too."

"That's not possible," she whispered softly, barely able to breathe.

A half smile lifted one corner of his mouth. "Yes, it is."

Before she could say anything, his hand reached down and touched her thigh at the same time his tongue licked her lips, before slowly easing inside her mouth. Once there he began stroking her tongue with his, as if he had all the time in the world and intended to do it all day at his leisure.

Delaney's entire body shivered when she felt his fingers at the zipper of her shorts, and a part of her wanted to push his hand away. But then another part, that foolish part that thrived on curiosity, the one that was slowly getting inflamed again, wanted to feel his touch and wanted to know how far he would take it.

She held her breath when he lowered the zipper slowly and deliberately, easing her into submission. His breathing was getting just as difficult as hers, and her entire body felt hot all over.

And then he inserted his hand inside her shorts, boldly touching her through the flimsy material of her panties. He touched her in a place no man had ever touched her before, and with that intimate touch, every cell in her body ignited. He began stroking her, slowly, languidly, making her feel horny. Just as he said he would do.

Never had she experienced anything so mind-numbing, so unbelievably sensuous as one of his hands gently pushed her thighs apart even more while his fingertip gave complete erotic attention to that ultrasensitive, highly stimulated spot between her legs, while his tongue continued to suck on hers.

The combination of his fingers and his tongue was too much. She felt faint. She felt scandalized. She was feeling pleasure of the highest magnitude.

Another rumble of thunder with enough force to shake the cabin jolted Delaney out of her sexual haze and back to solid ground. She pushed Jamal away. Taking a deep breath she slumped against the wall, not believing what had just happened between them. What she had let him do. The liberties she had given him.

She had been putty in his arms.

A totally different woman beneath his fingers.

She appreciated the fact that evidently someone up there was looking out for her and had intervened before she could make a total fool of herself. Just as she'd thought, Jamal was a master at seduction. He had known just how to kiss her and just where to touch her to make her weak enough to throw caution to the wind. And she was determined not to let it happen again.

Forcing her gaze to his, she knew she was dealing with a man who was probably used to getting what he wanted whenever he wanted it. All he had to do was snap his fingers, ring a bell or do whatever a prince did when he needed sexual fulfillment.

Did he think she would fit the same bill while he was in America? The thought that he did angered her. She was not part of his harem and had no intentions of being at his beck and call.

Furious with herself for letting him toy with her so easily, she glared at him. "I plan to take a cold shower. I suggest you do the same."

He didn't say anything for a long moment, and then he smiled at her. It was a smile that extended from his eyes all the way to each corner of his lips.

"A cold shower won't help, Delaney."

"Why won't it?" she all but snapped, refusing to admit he was probably right.

"Because now I know your taste and you know mine. When you get hungry enough you will want to be fed, and when that happens I will feed you until your body is full and content. I will provide it with all the sexual nourishment it needs."

Without giving her an opportunity to say anything, he turned and walked away.

After pacing the confines of her bedroom for what seemed like the longest time, Delaney sat on the edge of the bed. She couldn't ever remember being so irritated, so frustrated…so just plain mad.

"I'll feel better once I get my head back on straight," she said, as she stood and began pacing again. How could one man have the ability to set a body on fire the way Jamal had hers still burning?

All she had to do was close her eyes and she could actually still feel the essence of his tongue inside her mouth or the feel of his hands…more specifically, his fingers, on her flesh. And she could still feel the hardness of him pressed against her stomach.

A silky moan escaped her lips, and she knew she had to leave the cabin for a while and take a walk. But the problem was that it was raining, and not just a little sprinkle but a full-fledged thunderstorm.

She touched a finger to her lips, thinking that it was too bad the thundershowers couldn't wash away the memories of her kiss with Jamal.

A part of her wondered what Jamal was doing right now. Was his body being tormented like hers?

She sighed deeply. She had to stay determined. She had to stay strong. And most important, she had to continue to avoid Jamal Ari Yasir at all costs.

Chapter 4

"Going someplace?"

Delaney stopped in her trek across the room to the door. She wished she had waited until she'd been absolutely sure Jamal was asleep before leaving to go to the store. After their encounter a few days ago, she had avoided him by staying in her room most of the time.

But she had been too keyed-up to hide out in her room any longer. Heated desire flowed like warm wine through all parts of her body, making her feel things she had never felt before. Restless. On edge. Horny.

The rain for the past two days had kept them both inside the cabin. And whenever she got too hungry to stay in her room, she would go into the kitchen to find him sitting at the wobbly table sketching something out on paper. His black gaze would pierce her, nearly taking her breath away, and although he didn't say anything, she knew he watched her the entire time she was in close range. Like a wolf watching his prey.

She sighed as her gaze moved slowly down the length of him. He was dressed in a pair of white silk pajamas. The first thought that entered her mind was that she had seen her brothers in pajamas many times, but none of them had looked like this. And then there was the white kaffiyeh that he wore on his head. Silhouetted in the moonlight that flowed through the window, he looked the epitome of the tall, dark and handsome prince that he was.

Inhaling deeply, she needed all of the strength she could muster to hold her own with him, especially after the kiss they had shared; a kiss that made her breathless just remembering it. And it didn't help matters that she was noticing things she hadn't noticed before; like his hands and how perfect they looked. The fingers of those hands were long, deft and strong. They were fingers that had once swallowed hers in a warm clasp while he had kissed her; fingers whose tips had touched her cheek, traced the outline of her lips, and fingers that had touched her intimately. Then there were his eyebrows. She had been so taken with his eyes that she had failed to notice his brows. Now she did. They were deep, dark, slanted, and together with his eyes were deadly combinations.

"Delaney, I asked if you were going somewhere," Jamal said.

She swallowed as she gazed across the room at him and nearly came undone when he nailed her with his dark, penetrating eyes and those slanted brows.

"I'm going to the store," she finally responded. "There are some items I need to pick up."

"At this time of night?"

Even in the dim light Delaney could see the frown darkening his face. She met his frown with one of her own. "Yes, this time of night. Do you have a problem with it?"

For a long moment they stood there staring at each other—challenging. Delaney refused to back down, and so did he. To her way of thinking he reminded her of her brothers in their attempts to be overprotective. And that was the last thing she wanted or would tolerate.

"No, I don't have a problem with it. I was just being concerned," he finally said. "It's not safe for a woman to be out at night alone."

The quiet tone of his voice affected her more than she wanted it to. And the way he was looking at her didn't help matters. Intentionally or not, he was igniting feelings she had been experiencing lately; feelings she had tried ridding herself of by staying in her room. But now she felt the slow pounding of blood as it rushed to her head and back down to her toes. She also heard the ragged pant of her breathing and wondered if he heard it.

"I'm used to living alone, Jamal," she finally responded. "And I can take care of myself. Because of my study habits, I'm used to going shopping at night instead of in the daytime."

He nodded. "Do you mind some company? There are some things I need to pick up, as well."

Delaney narrowed dark eyes, wondering if he actually needed something or if he was using that as an excuse to tag along. If it was the latter, she wasn't having any of it. "If I wasn't here, how would you have managed to get those things?"

He shrugged. "I would have called Asalum. And although he would be more than happy to do my shopping for me, I prefer doing things for myself. Besides, it's after midnight and he needs his rest."

Delaney was glad to hear that he was considerate of the people who worked for him. Slowly nodding, she said, "Then I guess it will be all right if you come along."

Jamal laughed. It was a deep, husky, rich sound that made

heat spread through the lower part of her body. She slanted him a look. "Something funny?"

"Yes. You make it seem such a hardship to spend time with me."

Delaney sighed, looking away. He didn't know the half of it. Moments later she returned her attention to him. "Mainly because I had thought I would be here alone for the next few weeks."

He grinned at her suddenly. It was so unexpected that her anger lost some of its muster. "So had I," he said huskily, slowly crossing the room to stand in front of her. "But since we're not alone and it was your decision to stay, don't you think we should stop avoiding each other and make the most of it and get along?"

Delaney fought her body's reaction to his closeness. It wasn't easy. "I suppose we can try."

"What do we have to lose?"

Oh, I can think of a number of things I have to lose. My virginity for one, Delaney thought to herself. Instead of responding to his question, she turned and headed for the door. "I'll wait in the car while you change clothes."

"Did you get everything you need?" Delaney asked Jamal as they got back into her car to return to the cabin. Once they had gone inside the all-night supermarket he seemed to have disappeared.

"Yes, I got everything I need. What about you?"

"Yes. I even picked up a few things I hadn't intended to get," she said, thinking of the romance novel she had talked herself into buying. She couldn't remember the last time she'd been able to read a book for pleasure.

They drove back to the cabin in silence. Delaney kept her eyes on the road but felt Jamal's eyes on her all the while.

"What kind of doctor are you?" he asked after they had ridden a few miles.

His question got him a smile. She enjoyed talking about her profession and was proud of the fact that she was the only doctor in the Westmoreland family. "I will be a pediatrician, but first I have to complete my residency, which will take another two years."

"You like working with children?"

Delaney's response was immediate. "Not only do I enjoy working with kids, I love kids, period."

"So do I."

Delaney was surprised by his comment. "You do?" Most men, especially a single man, wouldn't admit that fact.

"Yes. I'm looking forward to getting married one day and having a family."

She nodded. "Me, too. I want a houseful."

Jamal chuckled and gave her a curious look. "Define a houseful."

The words leaped from Delaney's mouth without thinking about it. "At least six."

He smiled, finding it amazing that she wanted pretty close to the same number of children that he did. "You are asking for a lot, aren't you?"

She grinned. That was what her brothers always told her. They were convinced it would be hard to find a man who'd want that many kids. "Not a whole lot, just a good even number to make me happy and content."

When the car stopped at a traffic light, Jamal glanced over at Delaney. He thought she was too beautiful for words. Even with a face scrubbed clean of makeup and a fashionable scarf around her head to keep her hair in place, she was definitely one nice feminine package, a right sassy one at that.

His thoughts drifted to Najeen. She would remain his

mistress even after he took a wife. That was understood and it would also be accepted. He knew that Western women tended to be possessive after marriage. They would never tolerate a husband having a mistress. But then, most American women fancied themselves marrying for love. In his country you married for benefits—usually heirs. His marriage would be no different. Since he didn't believe in love he didn't plan on marrying for it. His would be an arranged marriage. Nothing more. Nothing less.

He could not see Delaney ever settling for that type of arrangement with any man. She would want it all: a man's love, his devotion, and his soul if there was a way she could get it.

Jamal cringed inwardly. The thought of any woman having that much control over a man was oddly disconcerting. The possibility that a woman would demand such a relationship would be unheard of in his country.

"Think you can juggle a career and motherhood?" he asked moments later. He wondered how she would respond. Western women also tended to be less domesticated. They enjoyed working just as hard as a man. He smiled. The woman he married would have only one job—to give him children. She could walk around naked all day if she chose to do so. She would be naked and pregnant the majority of the time.

"Sure," Delaney said smiling. "Just like you'll be able to handle being a prince *and* a father, I'll be able to handle being a doctor and a mom. I'm sure it will be a little hectic at times but you'll be successful at it and so will I."

Jamal frowned. "Don't you think your child would need your absolute attention, especially in the early years?"

Delaney heard the subtle tone of disapproval in his voice. "No more than your child would need *yours* as his father."

"But you are a woman."

She smiled in triumph, pleased with that fact. "Yes, and

you are a man. So what's your point? There's nothing written that says a mother's role in a child's life is more important than a father's. I tend to think both parents are needed to give the child love and structure. The man I marry will spend just as much time with our children as I do. We will divide our time equally in the raising of our child."

Jamal thought about the amount of time his father had spent with him while he'd been growing up. Even when his father had been in residence in the palace, Jamal had been cared for by a highly regarded servant—specifically, Asalum's wife, Rebakkah. And although his father had not spent a lot of time with him, he had always understood that he loved him. After all, he was his heir. Now that he was older, he knew their relationship was built on respect. He saw his father as a wise king who loved his people and who would do anything for them. Being his father's successor one day would be a hard job and he hoped he was at least half the man his father was.

Delaney was fully aware that Jamal had become quiet. Evidently she had given him something to think about. The nerve of him thinking that a woman's job was to stay barefoot and pregnant. He and her father, as well as her brother Storm, would get along perfectly.

It was a long-standing joke within the family that her youngest brother wanted a wife who he could keep in the bedroom, 24/7. The only time he would let her out of bed was when she needed to go to the bathroom. He wanted her in the bed when he left for work and in the bed when he came back home. His wife's primary job would be to have his children and to keep him happy in the bedroom, so it wouldn't matter to him if she were a lousy cook in the kitchen. He would hire a housekeeper to take care of any less important stuff.

Delaney shook her head. And all this time she'd thought that Storm was a rare breed. Evidently not. When they had made Storm, the mold hadn't been broken after all.

She glanced quickly at Jamal and wondered how she had gotten herself in this predicament. When she hadn't been able to sleep, going to the store in the middle of the night for some things she needed had seemed like a good idea. But she hadn't counted on Jamal accompanying her.

She sighed as the car traveled farther and farther away from the city and back toward the cabin. She stole another glance at him and saw that he was watching her. She quickly returned her gaze to the road.

When they finally arrived back at the cabin, Delaney felt wired. Too keyed-up to sleep. She decided to start cutting back on the hours of sleep she was putting in during the day. At night, while the cabin was quiet, her mind had started to wander and she didn't like the direction it was taking.

She quickly walked past Jamal when he opened the door, intending to make a path straight for her room. The last thing she could handle was another encounter like the one shared before. The man was definitely an experienced kisser.

What he had predicted was true. She hated admitting it but her body was hungry for him. A slow ache was beginning to form between her legs, and heat was settling there, as well.

"Would you like to share a cup of coffee with me, Delaney?"

The sound of his voice, husky and sexy, like always, did things to her insides. It also made that ache between her legs much more profound. Sharing a cup of coffee with him was the last thing she wanted to do. She would never make it through the first sip before jumping his bones. "No, thanks, I think I'll go on to bed."

"If you ever get tired of sleeping alone, just remember that my room is right across the hall."

Delaney tightened her lips. "Thanks for the offer, but I *won't* keep that in mind."

He reached out and brought his hand to her face and caressed her cheek. The action was so quick she hadn't had time to blink. His touch was soft, tender, gentle, and her breathing began a slow climb. He leaned toward her and whispered. "Won't you?"

Delaney closed her eyes, drinking in the masculine scent of him. Desire for him was about to clog her lungs. Fighting for control, she took a step back as she opened her eyes. "Sorry, *Your Highness,* but no, I won't." She then turned and walked quickly to her room, thinking she had lied to him and that she *would.*

"Oh, my goodness." Delaney shifted her body around in the hammock while keeping her eyes glued to the book, not believing what she was reading.

She hadn't read a romance novel in nearly eight years and then the ones she'd read had been those sweet romances. But nothing was sweet about the book she had purchased last night. The love scenes didn't leave you guessing about anything.

She had awakened that morning, and while Jamal had been outside doing his kickboxing routine, she'd sat at the wobbly table and had eaten a bagel and had drunk a cup of orange juice. Jamal was still outside by the time she had finished. She had passed him when she had left to find a good spot near the lake to read her book.

She took in a deep breath, then returned to the book once more. A few minutes later the rate of her heart increased, and she wondered if two people could actually perform that many positions in bed.

Stretching her body and giving herself a chance to catch her breath, she admitted that reading the book had turned her on. In her imagination, the tall, dark, handsome hero was Jamal and she was the elusive and sexy heroine.

Rolling onto her back she decided she had read enough. There was no use torturing her body anymore. The next thing Delaney knew, she had drifted off to sleep with thoughts of romancing the sheikh on her mind.

She dreamed she was being kissed in the most tantalizing and provocative way; not on her lips but along her shoulder and neck. Then she felt a gentle tug on her tank top as it was lifted up to expose her bare breasts. It had been too hot for a bra so she'd not worn one, and now, with the feel of her imaginary lover's tongue moving over her breasts, tasting her, nibbling on her, she was glad that she hadn't. A rush of heated desire spread through the lower part of her legs as a hot, wet tongue took hold of a nipple and gently began sucking, feasting on the budding tip.

A name, one she had given to her imaginary lover, came out on a gasp of a sound. Her mind began spinning, her breathing became even more erratic and her body hotter. A part of her didn't want the dream to end, but then another part was afraid for it to continue. It seemed so real that she was almost tortured beyond control, just on the edge of insanity.

Then suddenly her lover lowered her top and ceased all action without warning. Her breathing slowed back to normal as she struggled to gain control of her senses.

Moments later, Delaney lifted her dazed eyes and glanced around her. She was alone, but the dream had seemed so real. The nipples on her breasts were still throbbing and the area between her legs was aching for something it had never had before—relief.

She closed her eyes, wondering if she could dream up her lover again and decided she couldn't handle that much pleasure twice in the same day. Besides, she was still sleepy and tired. As she drifted off to sleep she couldn't help remembering her dream and thought it had been utterly amazing.

Jamal breathed deeply as he leaned back against the tree. What had possessed him to do what he'd just done to Delaney? It didn't take long for him to have his answer. He had been attracted to her from the first, and when he had come upon her sleeping in the hammock wearing a short midriff top and shorts, with a portion of her stomach bare to his gaze, he couldn't resist the thought of tasting her. A taste he had thought about a lot lately.

Her breasts, even while she slept, had been erect with the dark tips of her nipples showing firmly against her blouse. Without very much thought, he had gone to her and had knelt before her to feast upon every inch of her body. But he hadn't gotten as far as he wanted before coming to his senses.

Just thinking about making love to her made him aroused to the point that his erection, pressing against the fly of his jeans, was beginning to ache. And when she had moaned out his name, he'd almost lost it.

A woman had been the last thing on his mind when he had arrived at the cabin. Now a woman, one woman in particular, was the only thing he could think about.

His body felt hot. It felt inflamed. He wondered if he should pack his things and ask Asalum to come for him. Maybe it was time for him to return to Tahran. Never before had he wanted any woman to the point of seducing her while she slept.

But he knew he couldn't leave. She had moaned out his name. He hadn't imagined it. She may deny wanting him while she was awake, but while she slept it was a different matter.

His libido stirred. He wanted to taste her again. In truth, he wanted more than that. He wanted to make love with her. And every muscle in his body strained toward that goal.

Chapter 5

Jamal was sitting at the wobbly table drinking a cup of tea when Delaney came inside for lunch a few hours later. She glanced over at him as she made her way to the refrigerator to take out the items she needed for a sandwich.

"I'm making a sandwich for lunch," she said, opening the refrigerator. "Would you like one, too?"

Jamal shifted in the chair as he looked at her. He didn't want a sandwich. He wanted sex. And as a result, he felt restless and on edge. Earlier in the week he had tasted her mouth, today he had feasted on her nipples. There wasn't much of her left to discover, but what there was sent his hormones into overdrive.

When he didn't answer, she turned away from the refrigerator and looked at him curiously. "Jamal?"

"Yes?"

"I asked if you wanted a sandwich?"

He nodded, deciding to take her up on her offer. He needed to eat something, since he would need all his strength later for something he would enjoy. At least that was what he was hoping. "Yes, thank you. I would love to have a sandwich." *I would love to have you.*

He continued to watch as she took items out of the refrigerator and assembled them on the counter. The enticing scent of her perfume was filling the kitchen and he found himself getting deeply affected by it. And it didn't help matters that he knew she wasn't wearing a bra under her top and that her breasts were the best kind to lick and suck. The moment his tongue had touched the taut nipple, the tip of it had hardened like a bud, tempting him to draw the whole thing in his mouth and gently suck and tease it with a pulling sensation. And the way she had moaned while squirming around on the hammock had let him know she enjoyed his actions.

He shifted his gaze from her chest to her bottom. Her backside had been what had caught his attention that very first day. It was also the main thing that had him hard now. She liked wearing shorts, the kind that showed just what a nice behind she had. Nice thighs, too. The shorts placed emphasis on the curve of her hips. He wondered what her behind looked like without clothes. He bet her buttocks were as firm and as lush as her breasts.

"Do you want mayonnaise on your bread?"

Her questions made him return his gaze to her face when she tossed him a glance over her shoulder. "No, mustard is fine," he answered, briefly considering pinning her against the counter and taking her from behind. He could just imagine pumping into her while pressed solidly against her backside.

He took another sip of his herbal tea. Usually the sweet brew calmed him. But not today and certainly not now.

"Be prepared to enjoy my sandwich," she was saying. "My

brothers think they're the bomb and would give anything for me to make them one. They have my special touch."

He nodded. He could believe that and suddenly felt envious of a slice of bread and wished he could trade places with it. He would love to have her hands on him, spreading whatever she wanted over his body, preferably kisses. She wouldn't even have to toast him since her touch would burn him to a crisp, anyway.

She glanced over his shoulder and smiled again. "You're quiet today. Are you okay?"

He was tempted to tell her that no, he wasn't okay, and if he were to stand up she would immediately see why he wasn't. But instead he said, "Yes, I'm fine."

Satisfied with his response, she turned back around to continue making their sandwiches. He leaned back in his chair. He watched her pat her foot on the hardwood floor while she worked. She was also humming. He wondered what had her in such a good mood. Unlike him, she must be sleeping at night and not experiencing sexual torment.

"Did you finish your book?" he decided to ask. She had been reading it all morning. The only time he noticed her not reading was when she'd fallen asleep on the hammock.

"Oh, yes, and it was wonderful," she said, reaching up in the cabinets to get two plates. "And of course there was a happy ending."

He lifted his brow. *So she had been reading one of those kinds.* "A happy ending?"

She nodded, turning around. "Yes. Marcus realized just how much Jamie meant to him and told her that he loved her before it was too late."

Jamal nodded. "He loved this woman?"

Delaney smiled dreamily. "Yes, he loved her."

Jamal frowned. "Then what you read was pure fantasy. Why waste your time reading such nonsense and foolishness?"

Delaney's smile was replaced with a fierce frown. "Nonsense? Foolishness?"

"Yes, nonsense and foolishness. Men don't love women that way."

Delaney braced herself against the counter and folded her arms across her chest. Her legs, Jamal noted, were spread apart. Seeing her stand that way almost made him forget what they were discussing. Instead his gaze moved to the junction of those legs and wondered how it would feel fitting his hard body there.

"And just how do men love women?"

Jamal's gaze left her midsection and moved up to her face. She was still frowning. Evidently she was no longer in such a good mood. "Usually they don't. At least not in my country."

Delaney lifted a brow. "People do get married in your country, don't they?"

"Of course."

"Then why would a man and a woman marry if not for love?"

Jamal stared at her, suddenly feeling disoriented. She had a way of making him feel like that whenever he locked on her dark brown eyes and lush lips. "They would marry for a number of reasons. Mainly for benefits," he responded, not taking his gaze off her eyes and lips. Especially her lips.

"Benefits?"

He nodded. "Yes. If it's a good union, the man brings to the table some kind of wealth and the woman brings strong family ties, allegiances and the ability to give him an heir. Those things are needed if a sheikhdom is to grow and prosper."

Delaney stared into his eyes, amazed at what he had just said. "So the marriages in your country are like business arrangements?"

He smiled. "Basically, yes. That's why the most successful ones are arranged at least thirty years in advance."

"Thirty years in advance!" she exclaimed, shaking her head in disbelief.

"Yes, at least that long, sometimes even longer. More often than not, the man and woman's family plans their union even before they are born. Such was the case with my father and mother. She was of Berber descent. The Berbers were and still are a proud North African tribe that inhabits the land in northwestern Libya. As a way to maintain peace between the Berbers and the Arabs, a marriage agreement between my mother, an African princess, and my father, an Arab prince, was made. Therefore, I am of Arab-Berber descent, just as the majority of the people of Tahran are. My parents were married a little more than a year when my mother died giving birth to me."

Delaney leaned back against the counter. At the moment what he was telling her was more interesting than making a sandwich. "What if your father, although pledged to your mother, had found someone else who he preferred to spend the rest of his life?"

"That would have been most unfortunate. And it wouldn't have meant a thing. He would still marry the woman he'd been pledged to marry. However, he could take the other woman he fancied as a mistress for the rest of his days."

"A mistress? And what would his wife have to say about something like that?"

He shrugged. "Nothing. It's common practice for a man to have both a wife and mistress. That sort of an arrangement is accepted."

Delaney shook her head. American men knew better. "That's such a waste, Jamal. Why would a man need both a wife *and* a mistress? A smart man would seek out and fall in love with a woman who can play both roles. In our country wives are equipped to fulfill every desire her husband may have."

Jamal lifted a brow. He could see her fulfilling every man's desire since he saw her as a very sensual woman. She would probably make a good *American* wife, if you liked the outspoken, sassy and rebellious type. She would keep a man on his toes and no doubt on his knees. But he had a feeling she would also keep him on his back—which would be well worth the trouble she would cause him.

He sighed, deciding he didn't want to talk about wives and mistresses any longer, especially when he knew how possessive American women were. "Are the sandwiches ready?"

Evidently, she wasn't ready to bring the subject to an end and asked, "The first day we met you indicated you were to marry next year."

He nodded. "Yes, that's true. In my country it's customary for a man to marry before his thirty-fifth birthday. And I'll be that age next summer."

"And the woman you're marrying? Was your marriage to her prearranged?"

Seeing she would not give the sandwich to him until her curiosity had been appeased, he said, "Yes, and no. My family had arranged my marriage to the future princess of Bahan before she was born. I was only six at the time. But she and her family were killed a few years ago while traveling in another country. That was less than a year before we were to marry. She was only eighteen at the time."

Delaney gave a sharp intake of air into her lungs. "Oh, that must have been awful for you."

Jamal shrugged. "I guess it would have been had I known her." Like I know you now, he thought, watching her eyes lift in confusion. The thought of anything ever happening to her…

"What do you mean if you had known her? You didn't know the woman you were going to marry?" Her mouth gaped open in pure astonishment.

"No, I had never met her. There was really no need. We

were going to marry. Her showing up at the wedding would have been soon enough."

"But…but what if she was someone you didn't want?"

Jamal looked at her, smiling as if she had asked a completely stupid question. "Of course I would have wanted her. She was pledged to be my wife, and I was pledged to be her husband. We would have married regardless."

Delaney inhaled slowly. "And you would have kept your mistress." She said the words quietly, not bothering to ask if he had one. A man like him would, especially a man who thought nothing of marrying a woman he had never met to fulfill a contract his family had made. He would bed his wife for heirs, fulfilling his duty, then bed his mistress for pleasure.

"Yes, I would keep my mistress." He thought of Najeen, then added, "I would never think of giving her up."

Delaney stared at him and his nonchalant attitude about being unfaithful. Her brothers, possibly with the exception of Thorn when he was in one of his prickly moods, were players, enjoying being bachelors to the fullest. But there was no doubt in her mind that when…and if they each found their soul mate, that woman would make them give up their players' cards. They would not only give her their complete love but their devotion and faithfulness, as well.

She was suddenly swamped by a mixture of feelings. There was no way she could get serious about a man like Jamal and accept the fact that he would be sleeping with another woman. She appreciated differences in cultures, but there were some things she would not tolerate. Infidelity was one of them. Violation of marriage vows was something she would not put up with.

Crossing the room with both plates in her hands, she set his sandwich down in front of him with a thump, glaring down at him. "Enjoy your sandwich. I hope you don't choke on it. I'm eating in my room, since I prefer not to share your company at the moment."

Jamal was out of his chair in a flash. He reached out and grabbed hold of her wrist and brought her closer to him. "Why?"

Her eyes darkened. "Why what?"

He studied her features. "Why did my words, spoken in total honesty, upset you? It's the way we do things in my country, Delaney. Accept it."

She tried pulling her hand free but he held on tight. "Accept it?" Her laugh was low, bitter and angry. She tilted her head back and glared up at him. "Why should I accept it? How you live your life is your business and means nothing to me."

Their faces were close. If they moved another inch their mouths would be touching. She tried to pull back, but he wouldn't let her. "If you truly mean that, then it would make things a lot easier."

Delaney tried not to notice that his eyes were focused on her mouth. "What do you mean by that?" she snapped, hating the fact that even now desire for him was spreading through all parts of her body. How could she still want him, after he admitted he would not marry for love and proudly boasted of having a mistress? A mistress he would never give up.

"If how I live my life means nothing to you, then it won't be an issue when we sleep together."

"What!"

"You heard what I said, Delaney. Western women tend to be possessive, which is one of the reasons I've never gotten too involved with one. You sleep with them once and they want to claim you forever. I've pretty much spelled out to you how my life will be when I will return to Tahran. I want you to fully understand that, before you share my bed. I make you no promises other than I will pleasure you in ways no man has pleasured you before."

Delaney shook her head, not believing the audacity of Jamal. He was as arrogant as they came. In his mind it was a foregone conclusion the two of them would sleep together. Well, she had news for him. It would be a damn cold day in July before she shared his bed.

She snatched her hand from his. "Let me get one thing straight, Prince." Her breath was coming in sharp, as sharp as her anger. "I have no intention of sleeping with you," she all but screamed, thumping him on his solid chest a few times for good measure. "I don't plan on being number three with any man, no matter the degree of pleasure. Your body could be made of solid gold and sprinkled with diamonds, I still wouldn't touch it unless it was mine exclusively. Do you hear me? I get exclusive rights from a man or nothing at all."

His gaze hardened as he stared at her. "I would never give any woman exclusive rights on me. Never."

"Then fine, we know where we stand, don't we?" She turned around to leave the room.

"Delaney…"

She told herself not to turn around, but found herself turning around, anyway. "What?"

He was frowning furiously. "Then I suggest you leave here. Now. Today."

Delaney inhaled deeply. Of all the nerve. "I've told you, Jamal, that I'm not leaving."

He stared at her for a long moment, then said, "Then you had best be on your guard, Delaney Westmoreland. I want you. I want you so badly I practically ache all over. I want you in a way I have never wanted a woman. I like inhaling your scent. I like tasting you and want to do so again…every part of you. I want to get inside your body and ignite us both with pleasure. Ever since you got here all I do is dream about having you, taking you, getting on top of you, inside of you and giving you the best sex you've ever had."

He slowly crossed the room to her. Ignoring the apprehension in her eyes, he lifted his hand to her cheek and continued. "For the two of us it all comes down to one word. *Lust.* So it doesn't matter who or what comes after we leave here. What we're dealing with, Delaney, is lust of the thickest and richest kind. Lust so strong it can bring a man to his knees. There is no love between us and there never will be. There will only be lust."

He stared deeply into her eyes. "Chances are when we leave here we will never see each other again. So what's wrong with enjoying our time together? What's wrong with engaging in something so pleasurable it will give us beautiful memories to feast on for years to come?"

His hand slowly left her cheek and moved to her neck. "I want to have sex with you every day while we're here, Delaney, in every position known to man. I want to fulfill your fantasies as well as my own."

Delaney swallowed. Everything he said sounded tempting, enticing. And a lesser woman would abandon everything, including her pride, and give in to what he was suggesting. But she couldn't.

For too many years she had watched her brothers go from woman to woman. She would shake her head in utter amazement at how easily the women would agree to a night, a week or whatever time they could get from one of the Westmoreland brothers, with the attitude that something was a lot better than nothing.

Well, she refused to settle for just anything. She wasn't that hard up. Besides, you couldn't miss what you never had, and although she would be the first to admit that Jamal had awakened feelings and desires within her that she hadn't known existed, she could control her urge to sample more.

With a resolve and a stubborn streak that could only match her brother Thorn, she took a step back. "No, Jamal, I meant what I said. Exclusive or nothing."

His eyes darkened and she watched his lips tilt in a seductive smile. "You think that now, Delaney, but you will be singing a different tune in the end."

His voice was husky, and the look in his eyes was challenging. She swallowed the lump in her throat. "What do you mean?"

His smile became biting. "I mean that when it comes to something I want, I don't play fair."

Delaney stared pointedly into his eyes; her heart slammed against her ribs, completely understanding what he meant. He would try to wear down her defenses and didn't care how he did it as long as the end result was what he wanted—her in his bed.

Well, she had news for him. Westmorelands, among other things, were hard as nails when they chose to be. They were also stubborn as sin, and some were more stubborn than others were. They didn't back down from a challenge. A light flickered in her eyes. The prince had met his match.

Delaney smiled, and her eyes were lit with a touch of humor. "You may not play fair, but you can ask any one of my brothers and they will tell you that when it comes to competition, I play to win."

"This is one game you won't win, Delaney."

"And this is one game I can't afford to lose, *Your Highness.*"

His eyes darkened as he frowned. "Don't say I didn't warn you."

She met his frown with one of her own. "And don't say I didn't warn *you.*" With nothing else to say, Delaney turned, and with her head held high she strutted out of the kitchen and headed to the porch to eat her sandwich alone.

Chapter 6

Jamal looked up when Delaney walked into the living room later that evening. War had been declared and she was using every weapon at her disposal to win. She was determined to flaunt in his face what she thought he would never have. Which he assumed was the reason for the outfit she had changed into. There was only one way to describe it—sinfully sensual.

It was some sort of lounging outfit with a robe. But the robe enticed more than it covered. He couldn't do anything but lean back in his chair and look at her from head to toe. A surge of raw, primitive possessiveness, as well as arousal of the most intense kind, rushed through him. He couldn't pretend indifference even if he wanted to, so there was no sense trying. Instead he tossed the papers he was working on aside and placed his long legs out in front of him and gave her his full attention, since he knew that is what she wanted, anyway.

He knew her game. She wanted to bring him to his knees

with no chance of him getting between her legs. But he had news for her. He would let her play out this little scene, then he intended to play out his.

The outfit she wore was peach in color and stood out against the color of her dark skin. The material was like soft silk, beneath a lacy robe that gave the right amount of feminine allure. The sway of the material against her body as she crossed the room clearly indicated she didn't have on a stitch of undergarments. The woman was foreplay on legs.

His groin throbbed as he watched her sit on the sofa across the room from him, real prim and proper and looking incredibly hot. Of its own accord his breathing deepened, making it difficult to pass oxygen through his lungs, yet he continued to torture himself by looking at her.

"So, what's up?" she asked in a deep, sultry voice.

He blinked when it occurred to him that she had spoken, and the sexy tone and the way she was looking at him made him aware of every male part of his body. "I can tell you of one thing in particular that's up, Delaney," he said smoothly. He may as well state the obvious since it had to be evident to her, even from across the room, that he had an erection the size of Egypt.

She didn't answer him. Instead she smiled saucily, as if she had scored a point. And he had to concede that she had. He wondered if she enjoyed seeing him sweat. He would remember just what she was putting him through when it was his turn to make his move. And when that time came he wouldn't let her retreat. She had started this, and he damn well intended to see her finish it. He intended to teach her a thing or two about tempting a desert sheikh.

The CD he had been listening to stopped playing, and a lingering silence filled the room. She watched him and he watched her. Inside he smoldered, his body was heating to a feverish pitch and from the look on her face she was savoring every moment.

"Do you want me to put on some more music?" he asked, slowly standing, not caring that she could see his obvious masculine display.

After taking it all in, seeing how big he was, she just nodded, unable to respond. The look on her face gave him pause, and he couldn't help but smile. Hell, what had she expected? Granted he'd been told by a number of women that he was very well endowed, but he thought surely she had seen a fully aroused male before.

Crossing the room he walked over to the CD player. "Is there anything in particular you would like to hear?" he asked huskily, in a quiet whisper. When she didn't answer he glanced at her over his shoulder.

She shrugged. He saw the deep movement of her throat as she swallowed before responding. "No. Whatever you decide to play is fine."

He picked up on her nervousness. Evidently, she didn't have this game of hers down as pat as she thought she did. With five brothers she should have known that a woman didn't stand a chance against a man with one thing on his mind. You play with fire, you got burned, and he was going to love scorching her in the process. By the time he lit her fire she would be ready to go up in smoke.

He put on Kenny G and it wasn't long before the sound of the saxophone filled the room. He turned around slowly and walked over to the sofa toward her. *Stalked* over to the sofa was probably a better word. He intended to see just how much temptation she could take.

Coming to a stop in front of her he reached out his hand. "Would you like to dance?" He saw the movement of her throat as she swallowed deeply again. Her gaze held his and he knew she was giving his question some thought.

He had an idea what her response would be. She had

started this and she intended to finish it. There was no way she would let him get the upper hand, even if it killed her. He smiled. He definitely didn't want her dead. He wanted a live body underneath him tonight when he made her admit defeat.

She slowly slid off the sofa, bringing her body so close to his that his nostrils flared with her scent. "Yes, I'll dance with you," she said softly, taking the hand he offered.

He nodded and pulled her into his arms. They both let out a deep rush of breath when their bodies connected. He closed his eyes, forcing his body to remain calm. She felt good against him, and when she leaned closer he groaned.

Neither of them said a word, but he could hear her indrawn breath each and every time his erection came into contact with her midsection, which he intentionally made happen a lot.

As Kenny G skillfully played the sax, he masterfully began his seduction to prove to Miss Westmoreland that she couldn't play with the big boys, no matter what her intent. When she rested her head against his chest, he opened his hand wide over her backside, cupping her to him as he slowed their movements even more.

He groaned again as he felt her lush bottom in his hand. He smoothly rubbed his hand over it, loving the way it felt. He decided not to speak. Words would only break the sensuous spell they were in. So he pulled her closer to his swollen erection, wishing they were in bed together instead of dancing, but grateful for what he could get, especially after she had been so adamant about him not getting anything.

When the music stopped playing, he didn't want to release her from his arms. And since she didn't take a step back he got the distinct impression she wasn't ready for the moment to end yet, either.

He knew what he had to do and what he wanted to do. And if tasting her led to other things, then so be it.

He leaned back slightly from her, which forced her head to lift from his chest. She met his gaze and he saw desire, just as potent, just as raw, in her eyes. He had to kiss her.

She must have had the same idea since without any protest her lips parted for him. A ragged moan escaped the moment he captured her mouth in his.

The movement of his tongue in her mouth was methodically slow and she reacted with a groan deep in her throat, which he absorbed in the kiss. He was an expert on kissing and used that expertise on her. He had been schooled in various places but found he had learned more during his stay in the Greek Isles than any other place. It was there he had mastered Ares, an advanced form of French kissing.

Some people preferred not using it because it could get you in such an aroused state, if you weren't careful things would be over for you before you even started. Only men with strong constitutions, those capable of extending the peak of their pleasure could use it. And it wasn't unusual for a woman to climax from the pleasure it gave her. Ares was developed around the belief that certain parts inside of your mouth, when stroked in the right way, gave you immense pleasure. He had never tried it on any other woman other than the person who had taught it to him at the age of twenty-one. It boggled his mind that he had never wanted to try it on Najeen, yet more than anything he wanted to experience it with Delaney. It was something about her taste that made it imperative for his state of mind.

Closing his eyes he took their kiss to another level. He could tell she noted the change but continued kissing him. Moments later he felt her arms reach up and encircle his neck as she became as much a part of their kiss as he did.

Moments later, startled, she pushed back out of his arms, her breasts rising and falling with every uneven breath she took. He wasn't through with her mouth yet. He'd barely started.

"Give me your tongue back, Delaney," he whispered in a low guttural tone. "Just stick it out and I'll take it from there."

She stared at him for a moment. Then, closing her eyes, she opened her mouth and darted her tongue out to him. Angling his head so he wouldn't bump her nose he captured it with his and drew it into his mouth. Slowly, gently, he set out to seduce her with the kiss he now controlled.

Delaney heard a soft moan from deep within her throat as she stroked her hands through Jamal's hair. She was in a state of heated bliss. She had no idea what he was doing to her but whatever it was, she didn't want him to stop. There were certain areas in her mouth that his tongue was touching that were driving her insane to the point that the heat between her legs was becoming unbearable.

She felt him rubbing against her and that combined with what he was doing to her mouth was too much. He sucked her tongue deep when she felt the first inkling of desire so strong it shot through her body like a missile and exploded within her.

She groaned, long and deep in her throat. Her body began to tremble. Every nerve ending seemed electrified. Her knees felt weak, her head began spinning and the last conscious thought that flooded her mind was that she was dying.

Delaney slowly opened her eyes and gazed up at Jamal. She was draped across him, sitting in his lap on the sofa. She blinked, her breathing was heavy, ragged. "What happened?" she asked in a whisper, surprised that she was able to get the words out. She felt so weak.

"You passed out."

She blinked again, not sure she had heard him correctly. "I passed out?"

He nodded slowly. "Yes. While I was kissing you."

Taking a deep breath, she closed her eyes, remembering. She may be a novice but she had the sense to recognize a climax when she experienced one. Her first and she was still a virgin. It seemed that every part of her body had become detached, as pleasure the degree of which she had never felt before had flooded through her. It had been just that intense.

She took another deep breath, closing her eyes, trying to gather her thoughts. She was a doctor, right out of medical school, and fully understood the workings of the human body. All through life she had aced all her biology classes. Under normal circumstances people didn't pass out during a kiss.

She frowned. But what she had shared with Jamal had not been a regular kiss. It had been a kiss that had made her climax all the way to her toes. She opened her eyes and looked up at him. He was studying her intently. "What did you do to me?" she asked breathlessly, as the aftereffects sent shivers through her body. Her mouth felt sensitive, raw, and his taste was embedded so deeply in the floor and roof of her mouth that she savored him every time she spoke.

He smiled and it was a smile that made her stomach clench in heat. "I kissed you in a very special way."

She licked her lips before asking, "And what way was that?"

"Ares. It's a very volatile form of French kissing."

Delaney stared up at him, unable to say a word. When she had entered the room earlier that evening she had thought she had everything under control. In the end he had brought out his secret weapon. But he had warned her from the very beginning that he didn't play fair.

"Is that the way you kiss your mistress?" she whispered, suddenly wanting to know, although she knew how she would feel when he gave her the answer.

His eyes darkened and a surprised look came into his face. "No, I've never kissed Najeen that way. Other than the woman who taught me the technique when I was twenty-one, I've never used it on anyone."

Delaney blinked. Now she was the one surprised. Not only had he given her the name of his mistress, but had admitted to sharing something with her he had not shared with any other woman. For some reason she felt pleased.

"You climaxed while I was kissing you."

Delaney's mouth opened in silent astonishment, not believing he had said that. A part of her started to deny such a thing but knew he was experienced enough to know she would be lying through her teeth. She searched her brain for a response. What could a woman say after a man made a statement such as that?

Before she could gather her wits he added, "You're wet."

She swallowed; the soreness of her mouth almost made the task difficult. She knew what he meant and wondered how he knew? Had he checked? She was sitting in his lap, draped over him in a position that was downright scandalous. Had he slipped his hand inside her clothes and fingered her the way he had done the last time? Evidently the question showed on her face. He responded.

"No, I didn't touch you there, although I was tempted to. Your scent gave you away. It was more potent and overpowering, which is usually the case after a woman has a climax."

Delaney stared at him, not believing the conversation they were having. At least, he was talking. She was merely listening, being educated and suddenly, thanks to him, was becoming aware of the intensity of her femininity.

He smiled again and as before her stomach clenched. He stood with her in his arms. "I think you've had enough excitement for one night. It's time for you to go to bed."

He began walking down the hall and she was surprised when he carried her into her bedroom instead of the one he was using. He gently placed her in the middle of the bed, then straightened and looked down at her.

"I want you, Delaney, but I refuse to take advantage of you at a weak moment. I will not have accomplished anything if you wake up in my arms in the morning regretting sleeping with me."

He sighed deeply before continuing. "As much as I want to bury myself inside of you, it's important to me that you come to me of your own free will, accepting things the way I have laid them out for you. All I can and will ever offer you is pleasure. What you got tonight was just a fraction of the pleasure I can give you. But it has to be with the understanding that my life is in Tahran, and once I leave here you can't be a part of it. I have obligations that I must fulfill and responsibilities I must take on."

He leaned down and cupped her cheek, his dark gaze intense. "All you can and ever will be to me is a beautiful memory that I will keep locked inside forever. Our two cultures make anything else impossible. Do you understand what I'm saying?" he asked quietly in a husky voice filled with regret.

Slowly Delaney nodded her head as she gazed up at him. "Yes, I understand."

Without saying anything else Jamal dropped his hand from her face, turned and walked out of the room, closing the door behind him.

Delaney buried her head in the bedcovers as she fought back the tears that burned her eyes.

Chapter 7

Delaney slowly opened her eyes to the brilliance of the sun that was shining through her bedroom window. Refusing to move just yet, she looked up at the ceiling as thoughts and memories of the night before scrambled through her brain.

She lifted her fingers to her mouth as she remembered the kiss she and Jamal had shared. Her mouth still felt warm and sensitive. It also felt branded. He had left a mark on her that he had not left on another woman. He had given her his special brand of kissing that had been so passionate it had made her lose consciousness.

Closing her eyes, Delaney gave her mind a moment to take stock of everything that had happened last night, as well as come to terms with the emotions she was feeling upon waking this morning.

Yesterday Jamal had pretty much spelled everything out to her. He had told her in no uncertain terms that he wanted her. But then in the same breath he had let her know that the time they spent at the cabin was all they would have together. He had obligations and responsibilities in his country that he would not turn his back on. He had a life beyond America that did not include her and never would. In other words, she would never have a place in his life.

As a woman who had never engaged in an affair, casual or otherwise, she had felt indignant that he would even suggest such a thing to her. But last night after he had left her alone in her bedroom, she had been able to think things through fully before drifting off to sleep.

Jamal's life was predestined. He was a prince, a sheikh, and his people and his country were his main concerns. He admitted he wanted her, not loved her. And he had stated time and time again that what was between them was lust of the strongest kind, and as two mature adults there was nothing wrong in engaging in pleasure with no strings attached.

What he offered was no different from what her brothers consistently offered the women they dated. And she had always abhorred the very thought of any woman being weak enough to accept so little. But now a part of her understood.

Things had become clear after Jamal had brought her into the room and placed her on the bed. And after listening to what he had said then, she had known: she was falling in love with Jamal. And now, in the bright of day, she didn't bother denying the truth.

Although her brothers were dead set against ever falling in love, a part of her had always known that she would be a quick and easy victim. Everyone knew that her parents had met one weekend at a church function and less than two weeks later had married. They claimed they had fallen in love at first sight and always predicted their children would find love the same way.

Delaney smiled, thinking of her brothers' refusal to believe their parents' prediction. But she had, which was one of the reasons she had remained a virgin. She had been waiting for the man she knew would be her one true love, her soul mate, and had refused to sell herself short by giving herself to someone less deserving.

Over the years she assumed the man would be a fellow physician, someone who shared the same love for medicine that she did. But it appeared things didn't turn out that way. Instead she had fallen for a prince, a man whose life she could never share.

She opened her eyes. What Jamal had said last night was true. When they parted ways, chances were they would never see each other again. Somehow she would have to accept that the man she loved would never fully belong to her. He would never be hers exclusively. But if she accepted what he was offering, at least she could have memories to treasure in the years to come.

She inhaled deeply, no longer bothered that there would not be a happy ending to her situation with Jamal. But until it was time for them to leave, she would take each day as it came and appreciate the time she would spend with him, storing up as many memories as she could.

She wanted him, the same way he wanted her, but in her heart she knew that for her, lust had nothing to do with it. Her mind and her actions were ruled by love.

"Are you sure you are all right, my prince?" Asalum asked Jamal as he gave him a scrutinizing gaze.

"Yes, Asalum, I am fine," Jamal responded drily.

Asalum wasn't too sure of that. His wise old eyes had assessed much. He had arrived at the cottage to deliver some important papers to His Highness to find him sitting outside on the steps, drinking coffee and looking like a lost camel. There were circles under his eyes, which indicated he had not gotten a good night's sleep, and his voice and features were expressionless.

Asalum glanced over to the car that was parked a few feet from where they stood. "I take it the Western woman is still here."

Jamal nodded. "Yes, she is still here."

"Prince, maybe you should—"

"No, Asalum," Jamal interrupted, knowing what his trusted friend and confidant was about to suggest. "She stays."

Asalum nodded slowly. He hoped Jamal knew what he was doing.

Delaney walked into the kitchen to the smell of rich coffee brewing. She was about to pour a cup when her cell phone rang. "Hello?"

"I just thought I would warn you that the Brothers Five are on the warpath."

Delaney smiled, recognizing Reggie's voice. "And just what are they up to now?"

"Well, for starters they threatened me with missing body parts if I didn't tell them where you were."

Delaney laughed. She needed to do that and it felt good. "But you didn't, did you?"

"No, only because I knew their threats were all bluster. After all, I'm family, although I must admit I had to remind them of that a few times, especially Thorn. The older he gets, the meaner he gets."

Delaney shook her head. "Didn't Mom and Dad assure them I was all right and just needed to get away and rest for a while?"

"Yeah, I'm sure they did, Laney, but you know your brothers better than anyone. They feel it's their God-given right to keep tabs on you at all times, and not knowing where you are is driving them crazy. So I thought I'd warn you about what to expect when you return home."

Delaney nodded. She could handle them. Besides, when she returned home they would provide the diversion that she needed to help get over Jamal. "Thanks for the warning."

"How are things going otherwise? Is the prince still there?" Reggie asked between bites of whatever he was eating.

"Yes, he's still here and things are going fine." Now was not the time to tell Reggie that she had fallen in love with Jamal. A confession like that would prompt Reggie to tell her brothers her whereabouts for sure. His loyalty to her only went so far. She decided a change of topic was due at this point.

"There is something I need to ask you about," she said, fixing her focus on one object in the kitchen.

"What?"

"The table in the kitchen. Did you and Philip know that it wobbles?"

She could hear Reggie laughing on the other end. "The table doesn't wobble. It's the floor. For some reason it's uneven in that particular spot. If you move the table a foot in either direction it will be perfect."

Delaney nodded, deciding to try it. "Thanks, and thanks again for keeping my brothers under control."

Reggie chuckled. "Laney, no one can keep your brothers under control. I merely refused to let them intimidate me. For now your secret is safe. However, if I figure they will really carry out their vicious threats, then I'll have to rethink my position."

Delaney grinned. "They won't. Just avoid them for the next three weeks and you'll be fine. Take care, Reggie."

"And you do the same."

After hanging up the phone, Delaney poured a cup of

coffee, then took a sip. She wondered if Jamal, who was an early riser, was outside practicing his kickboxing as he normally did each morning.

Glancing out the window, she arched her brow when she noted another car parked not far from hers, a shiny black Mercedes. And not far from the vehicle stood Jamal and another man. The two were engaged in what appeared to be intense conversation. She immediately knew the man with Jamal was Asalum. However, with his height and weight, the older man resembled more of a bodyguard than the personal secretary Jamal claimed he was.

Her gaze moved back to Jamal. There was such an inherent sensuality to him that it took her breath away. In her mind everything about him was perfect. His bone structure. His nose. His ebony eyes. His dark skin. And especially his seductive mouth that had kissed her so provocatively last night.

He was dressed in his Eastern attire, which reminded her that he was indeed a sheikh, something she tended to forget at times; especially when he dressed so American, the way he had last night. He'd been casually dressed in a pair of khakis and a designer polo shirt. Today he was wearing a long, straight white tunic beneath a loosely flowing top robe of royal blue. He also wore a white kaffiyeh on his head.

Delaney thought about the decision she had made. Feeling somewhat shaky, she took another sip of her coffee. She knew exactly what would happen once she told him that she had decided to take what he offered. There was no way he would ever know that she loved him, since she had no intention of ever admitting that to him. His knowing wouldn't change a thing, anyway.

She sighed deeply. She had to make him believe she no longer had any reservations about their future and she had accepted the way things would be.

No longer satisfied with watching him through the kitchen window, she decided to finish her coffee out on the porch the way she normally did each morning. She wanted him to see her. She wanted to feel the warmth of his eyes when they came in contact with hers. And she needed to look into them and know his desire for her was still there.

At the sound of the door opening, Jamal and Asalum turned. Delaney became the object of both men's intense stares but for entirely different reasons. Asalum was studying her as the woman who had his prince so agitated. Having been with His Highness all of his life, he read the signs. Jamal wanted this woman sexually, and in a very bad way. No other woman would do, so there was no need for him to suggest a substitute. He could only pray to Allah that Jamal didn't take drastic measures. He had never seen his prince crave any woman with such intensity.

Jamal's gaze locked with Delaney's the moment she stepped outside of the door. The first thing he thought was that she was simply beautiful. The next thing he thought was that she looked different today. Gone were the shorts and tops she normally wore, instead she was wearing a sundress that had thin straps at the shoulders. Her curly hair was no longer flowing freely around her face but was up and contained by a clip.

"I must be going, Your Highness," Asalum said, reclaiming Jamal's attention, or at least trying to. Jamal kept his gaze on Delaney as he nodded to Asalum's statement.

As far as Asalum was concerned that in itself spoke volumes. Shaking his head, he inwardly prayed for Allah's intervention as he got into the car and drove away.

Inhaling deeply, Delaney released the doorknob and walked to the center of the porch. Her gaze never left Jamal's and she read in his what she wanted to read. The dark eyes holding hers were intense, forceful and sharp; and the nerve endings in her body began to tighten and the area between her legs filled with warmth with the look he was giving her.

And when he began walking toward her, he again reminded her of a predatory wolf and gave her the distinct impression that he was stalking her, his prey. There was something about him that was deliciously dangerous, excitingly wild and arrogantly brazen. A part of her knew that no matter how far he went today in this game of theirs, she would be there with him all the way. In the end he would succeed in capturing her, but she would not make it easy. She intended to make him work.

When Jamal came to a stop in front of her, dark eyes held hers in sensual challenge. "Good morning, Delaney," he murmured softly.

"Good morning, Jamal," she responded in kind. She then looked him up and down. "You're dressed differently this morning."

A smile twitched his lips, and amusement lit his eyes as he looked her up and down, just as she had done him. "Yes, and so are you."

Delaney smiled to herself. She was beginning to like this game of theirs. "I thought today would be a good day to do something I haven't done since I got here."

"Which is?"

"To try out the hot tub on the back deck. It's roomy enough for two, and I was wondering if you would like to join me?"

Jamal raised a brow, evidently surprised by her invitation but having no intention of turning it down. "Yes, I think I will."

A tense silence followed. Delaney knew that he wasn't anyone's fool and saw her ploy as seduction in the making and was determined, as he'd done the night before, to turn things to his advantage. He didn't play fair.

She was hoping he wouldn't. In fact, she was counting on it.

"I'll go on out back," she said, her voice only a notch above a whisper. "My swimming suit is under my dress."

"And it won't take long for me to change clothes and join you," he said huskily.

She turned to leave, then suddenly turned back to him. "And one more thing, Jamal."

"Yes?"

"You have to promise to keep your hands to yourself."

A rakish grin tilted the corner of his lips, and a wicked gleam lit his eyes. "All right, I promise."

Delaney blinked, surprised he had made such a promise. She really hadn't expected him to. Without saying another word, she opened the door and went back into the house, wondering if he really intended to keep his promise.

Delaney was already settled in the hot tub when Jamal appeared on the back deck. She found it difficult to breathe or to look away. She finally let out a deep whoosh of air when she broke eye contact with him to take a more detailed look at his outfit.

The swimming trunks he wore were scantier than the boxer trunks he usually wore for kickboxing. Everything about him oozed sex appeal, and she felt inwardly pleased that for the next three weeks he belonged only to her.

"The water looks warm," Jamal said, breaking into Delaney's thoughts.

She smiled up at him. "It is."

Tossing a towel aside, he eased onto the edge of the tub. She watched his every move, mesmerized, as he swung into the water and took the seat in the hot tub that faced her. He sank lower, allowing the bubbly, swirling water to cover him from the shoulders down.

"Mmm, this feels good," he said huskily, closing his eyes and resting his head against the back of the tub.

"Yes, it does, doesn't it," Delaney said, raising a brow. Was he actually not going to try anything? He seemed perfectly content to sit there and go to sleep. He hadn't even tried taking a peek at her swimming outfit beneath the water. If he had, he would have known that she was wearing very little. On a dare from one of her college roommates, she had purchased the skimpy, sheer, two-piece flesh-tone bikini, although she had never worn it out in public.

Feeling frustrated and disappointed, she was about to close her own eyes when she felt him. He had stretched out his foot and it had come to rest right smack between her legs. Before she could take a sharp intake of breath, he had tilted his toes to softly caress her most sensitive area. She closed her eyes and sucked in a deep breath as his foot gently massaged and kneaded her center in tantalizing precision, slowly through the thin material of her swimsuit.

But he didn't plan to stop there. He lifted his foot higher to rest between her breasts. Then with his big toe leading the pack, he caressed the right nipple through the thin material of her bikini top, and when he had her panting for breath, he moved on to the other breast.

When all movement ceased, Delaney opened her eyes to find Jamal had covered the distance separating them and was now facing her in the tub.

"I don't need hands to seduce you, Delaney," he whispered softly yet arrogantly, his lips mere inches from hers. "Let me demonstrate."

And he did.

Leaning toward her he used his teeth to catch hold of the material of her bikini top to lift it up. Growling like the wolf she thought him to be, he sought out her naked breasts with a hunger that nearly made her scream in pleasure. Using his knee he shifted her body so that her breasts were above water. His tongue tasted, sucked, devoured each breast, and she became a writhing mass of heated bliss.

Moments later a moan of protest escaped her lips when he leaned back. She slowly opened her eyes to find him staring at her with raw, primitive need reflected in his eyes.

Her breasts, tender from the attention he had given them, rose and fell with every uneven breath she took. As she continued to look at him, he smiled hotly, boldly, and she knew he was not finished with her yet.

Not by a long shot.

She held her breath when he leaned toward her again and with the tip of his tongue traced the lines of her lips before traveling the complete fullness of her mouth. Automatically her lips parted, just as he'd known they would, and he slipped his tongue inside.

A shudder of desire swept through her, and she wondered what madness had possessed her to forbid him to use his hands. Improvising, Jamal was using his tongue to seduce her as effectively as he would have used his hands. Jamal was an expert kisser and he was using that expertise on her, showing her just how much he enjoyed kissing her. And by her response he knew just how much she enjoyed being kissed.

Moments later he ended the kiss and pulled back. A sexy smile tilted the corners of his lips. "I want to see you naked, Delaney."

His words, murmured softly in the most sensual voice, touched Delaney deeply and sent a surge of emotions through her body. Once again he was able to shake up passion within her that she hadn't known existed—passion she wanted to explore with him.

Moaning, she leaned toward him. She was free to use her

hands even if he wasn't. Feeling bold she circled her arms around his neck and kissed him again. Already used to each other, their tongues met, mingled and began stroking intimately.

When she finally lifted her mouth from his, she drew back, looked into his eyes and whispered thickly, "And I want to see you naked, as well."

His eyes darkened even more. "When you are nude will I be able to use my hands?" he asked in a deep, husky tone.

She smiled and instead of answering she asked a question of her own. "When you are nude will I be able to use *my* hands?"

His voice lowered to a growl when he answered. "You can use anything you want."

Her smile widened. "And so can you."

Chapter 8

Jamal was nearly at his wit's end as he watched Delaney towel herself dry. The swimming suit she had on was too indecent, too improper and too obscene for any woman to wear, but he was getting a tremendous thrill seeing her in it. His already ragged pulse had picked up a notch, and his breath was becoming so thick it could barely pass through his lungs.

She would be arrested and jailed if she wore anything so scandalous in his country with the pretense of going swimming in it. The material was so sheer he had to widen his eyes to make sure he wasn't seeing naked skin. And both pieces clung to her curves in the most provocative way, nearly exposing everything. Everything he wanted. Everything he had dreamed about. Everything he craved. And everything he intended to have.

He frowned. She was deliberately driving him mad.

"Like what you see, *Your Highness*?"

And she was deliberately provoking him.

Awareness joined the arousal already flaring in his eyes. He crossed his arms and looked at her assessingly, eager for her to strip. "Yes, I like what I see, but I want to see more." She was inflaming him one minute and frustrating him the next. He knew this was a game to her, a game she intended to play out until the end…and win. She may be amused now but when this was over he would be the one cackling in sensuous delight.

"Anxious, aren't you, Jamal?"

There was no reason for him to lie. "Yes."

She grinned, tossing the towel aside. "I think we should go inside."

He lifted a dark brow. As far as he was concerned here was just as good a place as anywhere. "Why?"

Delaney silently considered his question, sending him a sidelong glance. Did he actually think she would strip naked out in the open? "Because I prefer being inside when I take off my clothes."

Jamal favored her with a long, frustrated sigh. "It doesn't matter where you are as long as you take them off, Delaney. I'm holding you to your word."

"And I'm holding you to yours." She turned to go inside.

Following behind, close on her heels, he crossed the deck and quickly reached out and opened the back door for her.

She looked back over her shoulder and smiled. "Thanks, Jamal. You are such a gentleman," she said in a low, throaty voice.

Jamal smiled. He hoped she thought that same thing a few hours from now. A true gentleman couldn't possibly be thinking of doing some of the things that he planned to do to her. He would try to be a *gentle man* but beyond that he couldn't and wouldn't make any promises. As soon as they were inside with the door closed he said, "Okay, do it."

Delaney shook her head thinking Jamal must have a fetish for a woman's naked body. But she knew the reason he was challenging her and was so anxious to see her naked was because he really didn't believe she would go through with it. He thought she was stringing him along. After all, she had told him she played to win. She glanced around. "Be real, Jamal. I can't strip naked in a kitchen."

He frowned at her. "Why not?"

She shrugged. "It's not decent."

Jamal couldn't help but laugh. "You're worried about decency dressed in an outfit like that?"

"Yes."

Jamal rolled his eyes heavenward. "It's not like you have a whole lot to take off, Delaney. You're stalling."

"I'm not stalling."

"Then prove it."

"All right. I'd feel better taking off my clothes in the bedroom."

Jamal nodded, wondering what excuse she would come up with once he got her into the bedroom. Although he was frustrated as sin, he had to admit he was getting some excitement out of her toying with him, however he much preferred that she toyed with him in quite a different way. This game of hers had gone on long enough.

"Okay, Delaney, let's go to the bedroom."

"I'll need a few minutes to get things ready," she said quickly.

Jamal could only stare at her. Surely she had to be joking. What was there to get ready? She was half-naked already. Before he could open his mouth to voice that very opinion, she said, "Just five minutes, Jamal. That's all I'm asking." She turned and rushed off, not waiting for his response.

"Five minutes, Delaney, is all you will get," he called after her. "Then I'm going to join you, whether you're ready or not."

Delaney glanced around the room. She was ready.

Because her bedroom was on the side facing the mountains, at this time of the day it was the one with the least amount of sunlight, which was perfect for the darkened effect she needed. The curtains in the room were drawn and lit candles were placed in various spots in the room. Already their honeysuckle scent had filled the midday air.

She had removed the top layer of bedcovering and the two pillows from the bed; arranging them on the floor and adorning each side with the two tall artificial ficus trees in the room.

She smiled. Everything was set up to make the room resemble a lovers' haven, and as far as she was concerned it was fit for a prince...or a wolf in prince's clothing. It was time the hunter got captured by his game.

She turned when she heard the gentle knock on the door. Taking a deep breath, she crossed the room. Taking another quick glance around, she took another deep breath and slowly opened the door.

Jamal swallowed with difficulty and somehow remembered to breathe when Delaney opened the door, wearing a short, shimmering, baby-doll-style nightie that was sheerer than her bikini had been. Where the swimming suit had left a little to the imagination, this outfit told the full story.

Completely white, the material was a sharp contrast to her dark skin, and he could easily make out certain parts of her body, clearly visible through the transparent chiffon material. The first question that came to his mind was, why would a woman who thought she would be spending a month alone in a cabin out in the middle of nowhere bring such intensely feminine apparel? He would have to ask her that question later…but not now. The only thing he wanted to do now, other than get his breathing back on track, was to touch her.

But first he needed to think…and then he conceded that his brain had shut down. He was now thinking with another body part. He forced his gaze to move to her face. She was looking at him, just as entranced with him as he was with her. He had changed into a silk robe and from the way it hung open it was obvious he wasn't wearing anything underneath.

The look of desire in her eyes made a deep, heated shudder pass through him, and when she took a step back into the room, he followed, closing the door behind him. He quickly took in his surroundings: the drawn curtains, the candles and the bedcovers and pillows strewn on the floor.

He then gave Delaney his full attention. Reaching out, he placed a finger under her chin. "Take it off, Delaney," he whispered, holding her gaze. "No more excuses, no more games. You have succeeded in pushing me to my limit."

Delaney stared at him, unable to do anything else. Through the haze of passion she saw him, really saw him, and knew that he might not love her, but she had something he desperately wanted. And from the way he was breathing and the size of the arousal he wasn't trying to hide, she had something he urgently needed.

A ray of hope sprang within her. He may be predestined to marry another woman, and he may have a mistress waiting for him in his native land, but now, today, right at this very moment, *she* was the woman he wanted and desired with an intensity that took her breath away.

"Take it off."

His words, Delaney noted, had been spoken…or a better word would be *growled*…through clenched teeth and heated frustration. She would bet no woman had ever given him such a hassle to see her naked. The one thing he would remember about her was that she hadn't been easy.

Reaching up to ease the spaghetti straps off her shoulders, she gave the top part of her body a sensuous wiggle, which prompted the gown to ease down past her small waist, over her curvaceous thighs and land in a pool at her feet.

She met Jamal's gaze when she heard his sharp intake of breath. She watched as his eyes became darker still, and saw how he was focusing entirely on her naked body, seemingly spellbound by what he saw. His eyes roamed over her like a lover's caress, the deep penetration of his gaze blazing a heated path from the tips of each of her breasts to the area between her legs. Then he reached up and released the clip on her hair, which tumbled around her shoulders.

A thickness settled deep in her throat, and her chest inhaled tightly a faint whisper of air. She thought she would always remember this moment when she had openly displayed herself to him, the man she loved. He was seeing her as no man ever had.

"Now it's your turn," she managed to say in the silence that had settled between them. She watched as he slowly pushed the robe from his shoulders, then stood before her proud, all male, intensely enlarged and naked for her. The glow from the candles reflected off his brown skin.

"I want you, Delaney." His whispered plea penetrated the room. "I want to take you in all the ways a man can take a woman. And I promise to give you pleasure of the richest, purest and most profound kind. Will you let me do that? Will you accept me as I am, accept the things that cannot be and accept that this is all we can have together?"

Delaney stared at him, knowing what her answer would be. This wasn't a cold day in July, and he wasn't coming to her exclusively. Yet she would go to him willingly, without shame and with no regrets. She lifted her head proudly as she fought back the burning in her eyes, inwardly conceding yet again that she loved him. And because she loved him, for whatever time they had left to spend together she would be his, the sheikh's woman, and he would be hers, Delaney's desert sheikh.

She met his gaze, knowing he waited for her response. As much as he wanted her, if she denied him he would accept her decision. But she had no intention of denying him. "Yes, Jamal, I want to experience the pleasure you offer, knowing that is all I can and will ever get from you."

For a moment Delaney could have sworn she saw regret, deep and profound, flash in his eyes just before he reached out and gathered her in his arms, sealing his lips with hers.

An insurmountable degree of passion flared quickly between them the moment his tongue touched hers, and the only thing she could do was revel in the fiery sensations bombarding her. His skin felt hot pressed against hers, and when his hand began caressing her backside, instinctively she got closer, feeling him large and hot, intimately pressing against her.

The kiss seemed to go on and on, neither wanting to break it, both wanting to savor every moment they spent together and not rush toward what they knew awaited them. The more they kissed the more fire ignited between them. They began devouring each other's mouths with a hunger that bordered on obsession. His tongue was familiar with every inch of her mouth, every nook and cranny, and it tasted and stroked her to oblivion.

When breathing became a necessity that neither could any longer deny, Jamal broke off the kiss but immediately leaned her back over his arms and went to her breasts. Delaney didn't think her mind or senses could take anything more, with the way his mouth and tongue felt locked on her breasts.

Displaying an expertise that had her weak in the knees, he paid sensual homage to her breasts, lavishing them with gentle bites and passionate licks. The scalding touch of his tongue on her nipples flooded her insides with heat so intense she thought she would burn to a crisp right there in his arms.

"Jamal…"

He didn't answer. Instead he picked her up in his arms and carried her to the area she had prepared for them on the floor. He quickly glanced around the room and saw what she had tried to do. She had attempted to turn a section of her bedroom into an exotic, romantic haven.

Whispering something in Arabic, then Berber, he eased down on the floor with her in his arms, suddenly feeling a deep tightening in his chest when full understanding hit him. She was giving herself to him on a level that was deeply passionate, erotically exotic and painstakingly touching.

Quickly forcing the foreign emotions he felt to the back of his mind, he took her lips once again. While holding her mouth captive to his, his fingers sought out every area of her body, flicking light touches over her dark skin, trailing from the tip of her breasts, down to her waist and naval and along her inner thigh before claiming the area between her legs.

Delaney broke off their kiss, closed her eyes and shuddered a moan when she felt Jamal's fingers touch her intimately, stroking, probing, caressing. She struggled to breathe, to maintain control and to not drown in the sensations he enveloped her in.

She opened her eyes and looked at him. His gaze was locked on hers, and she could tell from the taut expression covering his dark face that he was one step from sexual madness. The erection she felt against her hip was big and hard, and she didn't think it could possibly get much bigger or harder. Nor did she think she could take much more of what he was doing to her.

"I want you in a way I have never wanted another woman, Delaney," he murmured seductively as his fingers continued to stroke the very essence of her. "I want this," he said hot against her ear, pushing his fingers deeper inside of her so she would know just what "this" was.

Delaney could barely breathe. Her only response was a shuddering moan.

He slowly moved his fingers in and out, relishing the tiny purrs and moans she made, knowing he was giving her pleasure.

A sudden tremble passed through his body, and he knew at that moment he couldn't last any longer. He had to get inside of her. Shifting his body to where she lay under him, he sat back on his haunches and looked down at her, glorying in the beautiful darkness of her skin, the magnificent curves of her hip, the flatness of her stomach and the rich sharp scent that was totally her.

Her gaze was holding his, and he saw desire so profound in her eyes he almost lost it. He had to connect with her and sample the very essence of the gift she was offering him. "Are you protected, Delaney?" he asked in a voice so low he wasn't sure she had heard him.

She shook her head. "No, I…"

Whatever it was she was going to say she decided not to finish it. But that was all right, he would protect her. Standing, he quickly crossed the room to gather his robe off the floor. He had placed packs of condoms in the pockets. After putting one on he returned to her and knelt back in place before her, pausing to admire her lying there, waiting for him. Unable to help himself he leaned down and captured her lips again, in a passion that shook him to the core and made everything inside of him feel the need for her.

He tasted her richness as his tongue stroked hers to a hunger that matched his, tantalizing them into a feverish pitch. Breaking off the kiss he whispered something in Arabic as he slid her body beneath him, his gaze locked to hers. A part of him knew that he would always remember this moment as he fitted his body over her, parting her thighs.

His erection was like a radar and guided him unerringly to his destination, the part of her it desperately wanted, probing her entrance before slowly slipping inside, wanting to savor the feel of entering her body. Her heated muscles that encompassed him were tight, almost unbearably so, and held him as he inched his way forward.

He watched as she drew in a deep breath as her body's silkiness sheathed him, and he kept moving forward slowly, until he came to an unexpected resistance. He frowned, then stared at her, not believing what he had come up against, but knowing it was the truth.

"You're a virgin," he whispered softly. Amazed. Dazed. Confused.

She suddenly lifted her legs to wrap around his waist, holding him captive. Meeting his astonished gaze, she whispered sassily, "And your point is, *Your Highness?*"

Jamal couldn't help but smile, although this was not one of those rare times he usually did so. He was always a very serious person when having sex with a woman. He frowned when it suddenly occurred to him that he was doing more with Delaney than merely having sex. With his full concentration on her he responded, "My point is that I don't do virgins."

She reached up and placed her arms around his neck, lifted her chin and met his stare. "You'll do this one, Prince."

He held her gaze, feeling angry because he knew she was right. There was no way he could retreat. "Why didn't you tell me, Delaney?"

She shrugged and whispered softly, "I didn't think it was such a big deal."

His face became hard as granite. "It *is* a big deal. In my country I would be honor-bound to marry any woman I deflowered."

"Then it's a good thing we're not in your country, isn't it?" She could see the dark storm gathering in his eyes.

"But what about your family? They would expect me to do the right thing."

Delaney's eyes widened when she immediately thought of her brothers. They wouldn't give him a chance to do the right thing. They would take him apart piece by piece instead. "My family has nothing to do with this. I'm a grown woman and make my own decisions. Women in this country can do that, Jamal."

"But—"

Instead of letting him finish whatever he intended to say, she deliberately shifted her body, bringing him a little deeper inside of her. She smiled when she heard his sharp intake of breath. She had him just where she wanted him.

Almost.

"Stop that!" he said, frowning down at her. "I have to think about this."

"Wrong answer, Prince. There's no time to think," she said, as the feel of him throbbing inside of her sent her senses spinning and heat flaring in all parts of her body. She writhed beneath him and felt him place his hands on her hips to hold her still.

"Delaney, I'm warning you."

She stared at him, at the hardness of his face, the darkness of his eyes and the sweat that beaded his brow. He wanted her but was fighting it.

It was time to end his fight. She wanted her memories and she intended to get them.

She lifted her body to capture his mouth and before he could pull back, her tongue skated over his lips. When he let out a deep moan she slipped inside, stroking his tongue into sweet surrender, the way he had done her mouth several times. She knew that once she had his mouth under her control, the rest would be history. There was no way he would not concede.

He groaned deep in his throat and grabbed her wrists, but he didn't release her. Nor did he break their kiss. Instead he became a willing participant, a prisoner of desire of the hottest kind. She knew he was still fighting her, trying to hold on to his last shred of will, his ingrained inclination to do the right thing. But she was beyond that and wanted him beyond it, too.

She felt his hands release her wrists and move to her hips, lifting her to him, and with one hard thrust, he had completely filled her.

Delaney gasped at the first sensation of pain, but it subsided when he slowly began moving inside of her. He broke off their kiss and held her gaze in the fiery darkness of his. "I brand you mine," he growled, nuzzling his nose against her neck as he rode her the way he had dreamed of since that first day, with an urgency that bordered on mania. His hands that were locked at her hips lifted her, held her in place to meet his every thrust.

Delaney closed her eyes, drowning in the pleasure he was giving her. Her fingers dug deeply into his shoulders, and her legs were wrapped tightly around his waist. She opened her eyes to see him looking at her, almost into her soul, and she whispered in a voice filled with quivering need, mind-stealing pleasure. "If you brand me, then I brand you, too, Jamal."

Her words sent Jamal's mind reeling and he knew she *had* branded him. Closing his eyes, he reared his head back, feeling his body connect to her, becoming a part of her, lured to a place he didn't want to go but found himself going anyway. In the back of his mind he heard her whimpering sounds of pleasure as his body continued to pump repeatedly into hers, taking her on a journey he had never traveled before with any woman. And when he felt the tip of her tongue softly lick the side of his face, tracing a path down his neck, he knew then and there he would always remember this but the memories would never be enough.

"Jamal!"

He felt her draw in a shuddering breath. He felt her body quiver tightly around him, clenching him, milking him and elevating him to the same plane she was on. He inhaled deeply, his nostrils flaring when the scent of her engulfed him, surrounded him. Sensations he had never experienced before took control, flooding him to the point where he couldn't think; he could only feel.

He released a huge, guttural groan when the world exploded around him and forged them tighter in each other's arms, as extreme sexual gratification claimed their bodies, their mind and their senses.

And for the first time in his entire life, Jamal felt mind-boggling pleasure and body-satisfying peace. He knew then and there that he would never get enough of this woman.

Chapter 9

Jamal stirred awake as the flickering candles cast shadows in the room. He glanced down at the woman he still held in his arms. She was getting much-deserved rest.

After making love that first time, they had both succumbed to sexual oblivion, quickly falling asleep, only to wake up an hour or so later just as hungry for each other as they had been before. He had been concerned that it was too soon again for her, but Delaney took matters into her own hands, straddling him and seducing him to the point where he had finally flipped her underneath him and given her what they both wanted.

Once again he had experienced something with her he had never experienced before, and knew when they separated he would never find peace. She would always be a clinging memory for the rest of his days.

In the past after having slept with a woman, he would quickly send her away, then shower to remove the smell of lingering sex. But the only place he wanted Delaney was just where she was, in his arms, and he didn't want to shower. In fact, he wanted to smother in the sexual scent their bodies had created.

He looked down at the way they were still intimately locked together, their limbs tangled and their arms around each other as if each was holding the other captive, refusing to let go. He reached out and stroked a lock of hair back from her face thinking how peaceful she looked asleep. She had the same blissful expression on her face that she had the night she had passed out from him kissing her.

He inhaled deeply. He had made love to other Western women, but nothing had prepared him for the likes of Delaney Westmoreland. She was a woman who could hold her own with him. She called him Your Highness with a haughtiness that was outright disrespectful for a man of his stature and distinction. She didn't hesitate to let him know she couldn't care less for those things, and that in his country he might be an Arabian prince but to her he was just a man. No more, no less. Other women gave in to him too easily and were quick to let him have his way. But that wasn't the case with the passionate, provocative and smart-mouthed Delaney.

And then there was the fact that she had been a virgin. Never in a thousand years would he have considered such a possibility, not with the body she had and especially with her nonconservative views. The woman was definitely full of surprises.

He shifted when he began to harden inside of her. As much as he wanted her again, he needed to take care of her. The best thing for her body right now was a soak in a tub of hot water.

"Delaney?" He whispered her name and gently nudged her awake. She lifted sleep-drugged eyes up at him, and her lips, swollen from his kisses, eased into a smile. That smile pulled at something inside of him. It also made him become larger. He saw her startled expression when she felt her body automatically stretch to take him deeper.

He had to find a way to stop this madness. His body was becoming addicted to her. He moved to pull out, but she tightened the leg she had entangled with his. Frowning, he looked down at her. "You need to soak in a tub of hot water," he rasped softly, trying to reason with her and gain her cooperation.

She shook her head. "No. Not now, maybe later." The sound of her voice came out in a sultry purr.

He tried ignoring it. "No, now. Besides, I need to put on another condom before we do this again. If I don't, we run the risk of an accident happening."

He figured that explanation would work on her good sense. It didn't.

He felt the muscles of her body holding him inside of her tighten. He closed his eyes to pull out of her, but the more he tried the more her muscles held him.

He glared down at her, despising himself for wanting her so much. She was torturing him, and she damn well knew it. "Do you know what you're asking for?"

She met his gaze. "Yes," she murmured softly, while her body continued to milk him into a state of mindless pleasure. "I'm asking for *you,* Jamal."

"Delaney…" Her words were like a torch, sending his body up in flames. He captured her mouth with his at the same time his body thrust deep inside of her, giving her just what she had asked for.

"Mmm, this feels good," Delaney said, leaning back in the hot tub.

After they had made love, he had gathered her naked body

up in his arms and taken her outside and placed her in the hot tub then got in with her. "It will help relieve the soreness," Jamal said slowly, looking at her. He had decided to sit on the other side of the tub, at what he considered a safe distance away. He couldn't trust himself to keep his hands off her.

"I'll survive a little soreness, Jamal. I am not a weak woman."

He chuckled, thinking that was an understatement. "No, Delaney, you are definitely not a weak woman. You're as strong as they come."

Delaney quirked a brow, not knowing whether he meant it as a compliment or an insult. She knew he was used to docile women; women who were meek and mild. She doubted it was in her makeup to ever be that way.

She glanced around. The sun had gone down, and dusk was settling in around them. "Are you sure it's all right for us to be out here naked? What if someone sees us?"

"I don't have a problem being seen naked."

Delaney lifted eyes heavenward. "Well, I do."

Jamal leaned back and closed his eyes. "This is private property, you said so yourself. And besides, they can look at you all they want, but they'd better not touch."

Delaney stared at him. "Getting a little possessive, aren't we?"

Jamal slowly opened his eyes and met her stare. "Yes." His attitude about that was something he couldn't quite understand. He had never been possessive of any woman, not even Najeen. That thought didn't sit too well with him. Deciding to change the subject, he said, "Tell me about this job of yours as a doctor."

Delaney spent the next half hour telling him about how she had to go through a period of residency where she would work at the hospital in a pediatric ward.

"Is this hospital a long way from your home in Atlanta?" he asked as he shifted his body below the water line some more.

"Far enough. It's in Bowling Green, Kentucky, so I'm leasing an apartment for the two years I'll be working there." She didn't add that she needed that distance away from her brothers.

When she had first left home for college she made the mistake of going to a school that was less than a two-hour drive from Atlanta. Her brothers nearly drove her crazy with their frequent impromptu visits. The only people who enjoyed seeing them had been the females living in her dorm who thought her brothers were to die for.

For medical school she had decided on Howard University in D.C. Although her brothers' trips to see her weren't as frequent, they still managed to check on her periodically just the same, claiming their parents' concern was the reason for their visits.

"After your residency do you plan to open up your own medical office?" Jamal asked.

"Yes, it's my dream to open up a medical office somewhere in the Atlanta area."

Jamal nodded. "And I hope your dream comes true, Delaney."

She knew he meant that with all sincerity and was deeply touched by it. "Thanks."

Later that evening they ate a light meal that the two of them prepared together. He noticed she had slid the table closer to the window and that it wasn't wobbling. She told him of her conversation with Reggie, who had told her that the problem had not been with the table but with the floor.

"So as you can see, Jamal, things aren't always as they seem to be."

He had lifted a brow at her comment but said nothing.

She smiled. He knew she had been trying to make a point

about something, but from his expression it was quite obvious he didn't get it. Delaney felt confident that one day he would.

After dinner she sat in the living room watching television while he sat on the opposite end of the sofa sketching on something. It was the same papers that he had occasionally worked on since she had arrived.

"What are you doing?" she asked curiously when he had finally placed the documents aside.

He reached out his arms to her and she covered the distance and went to him. He placed her in his lap while he showed her what he had been working on. "This is something I plan to build in my country. It will be a place my people can go for their necessities."

She studied the sketch, admiring the structural design. "It's sort of like an open market."

He smiled, glad she had recognized it for what it was. "Yes. It will be similar to the places you refer to in your country as a one-stop shop. Here they will be able to buy their food, clothing and any other miscellaneous items they might need. I also want it as a place for them to socialize while doing so, to come together. Although the majority of my people are like me, both Arab and Berber descent, and are in harmony for the most part, there are those who every once in a while try to cause friction between the two ethnic groups."

Delaney lifted her head. "What sort of friction?"

He smiled at her, feeling her genuine interest. "It's a feud that's dated back hundreds of years. The reason my mother and father married to begin with was to unite the Arabs and the Berbers, producing me, an heir of both heritages. The disagreement is about what should be recognized as the official language of our nation. Right now it's Arabic and has been for hundreds of years, but a group of African-born descendents believes it should be Berber."

Delaney nodded. "You mainly speak Arabic, right?"

"Yes, but I am fluent in both. When I become the king, my biggest challenge will be how to get everyone to embrace both languages, since both are a part of my country's heritage."

Delaney studied his features. "What are your views on the matter, Jamal?"

He smiled down at her. "I understand the need for both sides. There is a need to teach the Berber language and preserve and promote the Berber culture. However, since Arabic is the official language, everyone is duty bound to speak it. But I'm not for Arabization being imposed on the Berbers who reside in isolated regions and who want to keep their heritage intact, just as long as they remain loyal to Tahran and its leadership. The needs of all of my people are important to me."

Delaney nodded. A thought then struck her. "Speaking of needs, what about medical care? How do your people get the medical care they need?"

He looked at her as if surprised by her question. "We have hospitals."

She twisted in his arms, the concern in her features evident. "But what about those people living in smaller cities who can't make it to a hospital? Don't you think you may want to consider having a clinic just for them?"

Jamal lifted a brow. "In a market?"

She shook her head, smiling. "Not necessarily in the market but adjacent to it. I believe this entire idea has merit as a way to get people out and about in an open marketplace-type setting. But think of how convenient it would be to them. It might prompt more people who need it to seek medical care."

Jamal nodded, thinking she had a point. He had often approached his father with concerns of the need for more medical facilities. Keeping his people healthy was another way of keeping them safe. He looked down at the plans he had designed. "And where do you suggest this facility be placed?"

Delaney's smile widened. She was pleased that he had asked her opinion. For the next hour or so they discussed his designs. She had been surprised when he told her that although his master's degree from Harvard had been in business administration, he had also received a bachelor degree from Oxford in structural engineering.

That night when they retired to his bedroom, he again told her of his intent to not touch her anymore that day. He just wanted to hold her in his arms.

"Why did you change your mind about us?" he asked her quietly, holding her close, loving the feel of her softness next to him.

Delaney knew she could not tell him the truth. She did not want him to know that she had fallen in love with him. There was nothing to gain by doing so. "I took another look at things, Jamal, and decided that I wasn't getting any younger and it was time I did something about being a virgin."

He was surprised. Women in his country remained virgins until they married. "You had a problem with being a virgin?"

She heard the censure in his voice. "No, I didn't have a problem with it, but then I didn't want to die a virgin, either."

He took her hand in his, letting his fingers curl around hers and ignoring the sexual rush just touching her invoked. "There were never any plans in your future to marry?"

"Yes, but no time soon. I wanted to establish myself as a doctor before getting serious about anyone."

Jamal nodded. He then thought of another question that he wanted to ask her. "What about your lingerie?"

She lifted a brow. "My lingerie?"

"Yes."

"What about them?"

He cleared his throat. "They are the type a woman normally wears to entice a man. Why would you bring such sleeping attire when you had planned to be at this cabin alone?"

Delaney smiled, understanding his question. She enjoyed going shopping for sexy lingerie and feminine undergarments. Her bras and panties were always purchased in matching sets, and she tended to be attracted to bright colors and for the most part shied away from plain-looking white underthings.

"I like looking and feeling sexy, Jamal, even when there's no one there to notice but me. Whenever I buy lingerie and underthings, I buy what I like for me with no man in mind."

"Oh."

"Now I have a question for you, Jamal," Delaney said softly.

"Yes?"

"Why would you bring all those packs of condoms with you when you had planned to be here alone?"

He grinned sheepishly at her. "I didn't bring them. I purchased them after I got here."

"When?" she asked lifting a curious brow.

"The night you and I went to that all-night supermart," he said, studying her features and wondering how she felt knowing he had planned her seduction even then. He reached out and touched her chin with his finger. "Are you upset?"

"No," she said as a smile curved her lips. "I'm not upset. I'm glad you did have the good sense to buy them."

Long after Delaney had fallen asleep, Jamal was still awake. For some reason the thought of another man sleeping with her, holding her in his arms the way he was doing bothered him. It also disturbed him that one day there would be a man in her life who would see her in all those sexy lingerie and underthings that she liked buying for herself.

When he finally dozed off to sleep, his mind was trying to fight the possessiveness he felt for the beautiful woman asleep in his arms.

"I take it that you enjoyed the movie," Jamal said when he pulled Delaney's car to a stop in front of the cabin.

She smiled, showing perfect white teeth and very sensuous lips. "What woman wouldn't enjoy a movie with Denzel Washington in it?"

He searched her face, amazed at the tinge of jealousy he was feeling. "You really like him, don't you?"

"Of course," she responded, getting out of the car and walking up the steps to the door. "What woman could resist Denzel?"

Jamal frowned. "And you would go out on a date with him if he were to ask you?"

Delaney stopped walking and turned around. She studied Jamal's expression, seeing his frown and clenched teeth. As she continued to observe him, she had a sudden flash of insight when something clicked in her brain. He's jealous! Of all the outrageous...

She inwardly smiled. If that was true it meant, just possibly, that he cared something for her. But then a voice within her taunted, *Not necessarily. It could also mean that now that he has slept with you he sees you as a possession he wants to keep and add to the other things he owns.*

"Yes, I would go out with him," she finally answered, and saw the frown on his face deepen. "However, I don't plan on losing sleep waiting for such a miracle to happen. Besides, I doubt he would ask any woman out on a date since he's a married man." She quirked a brow. "Why do you want to know?"

He walked past her and said, "Curious."

She fell silent as she followed him to the porch. When she had awakened that morning he had already left the bed and was outside practicing his kickboxing. By the time she had made coffee and placed a few Danish rolls in the oven he had come inside. They had enjoyed a pleasant conversation, then he had suggested that they take in a midday matinee at the movie theater.

She knew his intention had been to get her out of the cabin for most of the day so he wouldn't be tempted to touch her again. He wanted to give her body time to adjust to their making love before they did it again, although she had tried convincing him that her body had adjusted just fine. She sighed deeply. It was time for her to take matters into her own hands.

Jamal's hands tightened like fists at his sides when he stood aside to let Delaney enter the cabin. He didn't understand why an irrational stab of envy had consumed him, making him angry, since he was familiar with Western women's fascination with movie actors and sports figures. But it rubbed him the wrong way to include Delaney in that number.

Closing the door behind them, he watched as she tossed her purse on the sofa. He had admired her outfit the moment she had emerged from the bedroom wearing it. She certainly knew how to dress to show off her attributes to the maximum. The short blue dress stopped way above her knees and showed off her curves and shapely legs. Her high-heeled sandals were sexy enough to drive him to distraction.

Then there was that lush behind of hers that always kept his pulse working overtime. He was just dying to touch it, run his hand all over it. He took a deep, fortifying breath as he let his gaze trace her legs from the tip of her polished toes, past her ankles, beyond her knees and up to her thighs that met the hem of her dress. He couldn't help but think about what was under that dress. He shook his head. How had he thought he could go a whole day without making love to her again?

"How does soup and a sandwich sound, Jamal?"

Jamal swallowed. His low reserve of willpower was pitiful. It took every ounce that he had to move his gaze away from her legs and focus on her face. "That sounds good and I'd like to help."

She smiled. "You're getting pretty handy in the kitchen. You seem to enjoy being there."

Jamal's brows furrowed. Not really, he wanted to say. She was the one who enjoyed being in the kitchen. He merely enjoyed being wherever she was. "Things are not always as they seem to be, Delaney."

She studied him for a long moment, then turned toward the kitchen. He followed, trying his best not to notice how the soft material of the dress hugged her hips as she walked ahead of him.

"Do you want to chop the veggies for the soup?"

His mind clicked when he heard a sound. He thought he heard her speak but wasn't sure. "Did you say something?"

She stopped walking and turned around. Her eyes smiled fondly at him as if he was a dim-witted human being. The way he was lusting after her, he was certainly feeling like one. "I asked if you wanted to chop the veggies for the soup I'm making."

"Oh, sure. Whatever you need me to do. I'm at your disposal."

"Are you always this generous to the women you sleep with?"

Jamal tensed, not liking her question and wondering how she could ask such a thing. While he was with her he didn't want to think about other women. "I'm considered a very generous man to a lot of people, Delaney," he said, holding her gaze, refusing to let her bait him.

She nodded and continued her walk to the kitchen.

Jamal sighed. He knew there was an American saying that…if you can't stand the heat stay out of the kitchen. He muttered a low curse. He was following the heat right into the kitchen.

Delaney stopped stirring the ingredients she had already put in the pot and glanced over at Jamal. He was standing at the counter slicing vegetables. "How are you doing over there?"

He lifted his head from his task, and his gaze met hers across the room. "I'm just about finished."

"Good. The vegetables will be ready to go into the pot in a few minutes."

He swallowed hard. "It smells good. I bet it will taste good, too."

She gave a casual shrug. "There's nothing like something smelling good and tasting good," she said before turning back around.

Jamal was doing his best not to remember how good she smelled and how good she tasted. He also tried not to remember other things. Like the feel of her beneath his hands as he held her hips firmly, lifting her as he had entered her; how her eyes would darken each time he thrust into her, pulled out and thrust into her again. And the sounds of pleasure she made, and how her body would tighten around him, holding him deep inside of her, milking him bone-dry. At least trying to.

Jamal diced mercilessly into a tomato, furious with his lusty thoughts and knowing his control was slipping. Taking a deep breath he gathered the chopped vegetables in a bowl and on unsteady legs slowly made his way across the room to Delaney.

She turned and smiled at him, taking the bowl he offered.

"You did a good job," she said, dumping the chopped vegetables into the steaming pot. "Now all we have to do is wait for another boil and then let things simmer awhile."

Jamal nodded. He knew all about boiling and simmering. He came damn close to telling her that he was already doing both from the feminine heat she generated. For the past thirty minutes he had tried to distract himself from watching her move about in the kitchen. Every move she made had turned him on. When she had reached up into the cabinets looking for garlic salt, her already short dress had risen, showing more leg and thigh and making sweat pop out on his brow. The sight had been pure temptation.

He took a step closer to her. "So what kind of soup are you making?"

She chuckled good-naturedly. "Vegetable soup."

The lower part of his body throbbed from the intensity of his need. He forced a smile. "That was simple enough to figure out, so why couldn't I think of that?"

Delaney placed the lid on the pot, turned the dial to simmer and looked up at him. "Maybe you have your mind on other things." She stepped away from the stove and walked over to the sink.

He followed her. He should have been expecting this, her being one step ahead of him. He wouldn't put it past her to have set him up. "So what do you think I have on my mind?" he asked, looking at her intently.

She shrugged and met his gaze squarely. "I'm not a mind reader, Jamal."

"No," he said, raking his gaze over her body. "Only because you're too busy being a seductress."

"No, I'm not."

"Yes, you are. Do you think I don't know what you've deliberately been doing to me for the past half hour?"

For a long moment neither said anything as their gazes clashed. Then Delaney asked in a deep, sultry voice, "Well, did it work?"

Jamal took a step closer as he muttered under his breath. He reached out and brought her body tightly against him, letting her feel how well her ploy had succeeded. "What do you think?"

She moaned softly and shifted her stance to spread her legs, wanting the feel of the hard length of him between them. Even through the material of their clothing there was simmering heat. Her eyes were half-closed when she said, "I think you should give your body what it wants and stop trying to play hard to get."

He lowered his head and licked her lips, slowly, thoroughly. "I was trying to spare you and give your body a chance to adjust."

Delaney's breath quickened with the feel of his tongue licking her lips as if he was definitely enjoying the taste. "I don't want to be spared, and my body doesn't need to adjust. The only thing it needs is you," she said quietly, shivering inside as his tongue continued to torment her. "I want to be made love to and satisfied. I want you inside of me, Jamal. Now."

The only thing Jamal remembered after that was taking her mouth with an intensity that overwhelmed him as he picked her up in his arms. He wanted her now, too. Quickly crossing the room, he set her on the table and pushed up her dress to her waist and lifted her hips to pull her panties completely off.

Like a desperate man he tore at the zipper of his jeans and set himself free just long enough to push her legs apart. Pulling her to him he then entered her. "Oh, yes," he said, throwing his head back when he felt her heat clutch him, surround him.

"You make me crazy, Delaney," he said, squeezing his

eyes shut and placing a tight hold on her thighs, savoring how she felt. He didn't want her to move. He just wanted to stand there, between her legs, locked inside of her.

"Don't move," he ordered when he felt her body shift. "Just let me feel myself inside of you for a minute. Let me feel how wet you are around me and how tight." He wondered how a body so wet could hold him so snugly.

He inhaled her scent. It was like an aphrodisiac, making his sexual hunger all the more intense. "Lie back," he whispered hoarsely, and held on to her hips while she did so. When she was flat on her back on the table he leaned in and pulled her closer to him, going deeper inside of her. He opened his eyes when he felt her thighs quiver and stretch wide to wrap her legs around his waist.

What little control he had left vanished when he leaned down and caught her mouth with his. He closed his eyes and began making love to her with the intensity of a madman, a wolf mating, someone engaging in sex for the last time before facing a firing squad; he was just that greedy, besotted, possessed. He didn't think he could go another single day without getting some of this. All of it. And for a quick crazy moment he thought of taking her back to Tahran with him—against her will if he had to—just to keep her with him forever.

Forever.

He opened his eyes and muttered an Arabic curse then he mumbled an even worse one in Berber, not believing the path his thoughts had taken. Nothing was forever with him—especially a woman. But as he arched his back to go even deeper inside of Delaney, he knew that with her he had a different mindset. His body had a mind of its own. It wanted to devour her, every chance it got. Sexual intensity flared throughout his body, and he thought nothing could and would ever compare to this.

And moments later when she screamed out her climax, he sucked in a deep whiff of her scent at the same time that he exploded deep in her feminine core. It was then that he realized he wasn't wearing a condom. Too late to do anything about it now, since he had no intention of pulling out, and he continued to pour his seed deep within her as his body responded to the pleasure of their lovemaking.

He clenched his teeth as he drove into her hard, wanting to give her everything that was his, everything he had never given another woman. Finally admitting at that moment that what he was sharing with Delaney Westmoreland went beyond appeasing sexual appetites.

She had somehow found a way to erode his resolve and raw emotions. All his defenses were melting away, the dam around his heart had crumbled. When he realized what was happening to him, shock reverberated through his body, only intensifying his climax.

Then another emotion, one stronger, more powerful, ripped through him. Up to now it had been a foreign element, but at that moment he felt it, from the depths of his loins to the center of his heart.

Love.

He loved her.

Chapter 10

The next week flew by as Jamal and Delaney enjoyed the time they were spending together. Jamal was awakened before dawn one morning by the insistent ringing of his cell phone. He automatically reached for it off the nightstand next to the bed, knowing who his caller would be. "Yes, Asalum?"

He felt Delaney stir beside him; her arms were tight around him, and her naked limbs were tangled with his. Last night they'd had dinner outside on the patio, preferring to enjoy the beauty of the moon-kissed lake while they ate. Then later in his bed they had made love all through the night.

Something Asalum said grabbed Jamal's attention. "Say that again," he said, immediately sitting up. "When?" he asked, standing, and at the same time he grabbed for his robe.

He turned and met Delaney's curious gaze. "I'll contact my father immediately, Asalum," he was saying into the phone. He let out a heavy sigh. When he disconnected the call he sat down on the edge of the bed and pulled Delaney into his arms. Before she could ask him anything he kissed her.

"Good morning, Delaney," he whispered huskily, close to her ear when he finally released her mouth. He cradled her gently in his arms.

"Good morning, Prince," she said smiling up at him. Then her dark brow puckered in concern. "Is anything wrong?"

Jamal shifted positions to lean back against the headboard, taking Delaney with him. "I won't know until I talk to my father. Before I came to this country I had been involved in important negotiations involving several countries that border mine. The usual issues were under discussion, and after three months everyone left satisfied. But according to Asalum, the sheikh of one of those countries is trying to renege on the agreement that was accepted by everyone."

Delaney nodded. "So in other words, he's causing problems and being a pain in the butt."

Jamal chuckled, appreciating the way Delaney put things. "Yes, he is."

Delaney placed a quick kiss on his lips before slipping out of his arms and getting out of the bed. "Where are you going?" he asked, when she began gathering up her clothes off the floor. Seeing her naked was making his body stir in desire.

She turned and smiled at him. "I'm going to take a shower. I know you have an important call to make and I want to give you complete privacy to do so."

He grinned, looking her over from head to toe. "And without any distractions?"

She chuckled. "Yeah, and without any distractions." She gave him a saucy look. "You're welcome to join me in the shower after you finish your call." She then left his bedroom, closing the door behind her.

* * *

Jamal didn't finish the call in time to join Delaney in the shower. After talking to his father he discovered the situation was more serious than he had thought and he was needed in Tahran immediately.

He had placed a call to Asalum with instructions to make the necessary arrangements for his return to the Middle East. All his life he had known what was expected of him when duty called, but this was the first time he had something important in his life that meant everything to him.

He hadn't told Delaney how he felt because the emotions were new to him and he wasn't sure it changed anything. She was who she was, and he was who he was. Love or no love, they could never have a future together. But could he give her up?

He knew that somehow he had to let her go. She could never be his queen, and he loved her too much to ask her to be his mistress, especially knowing how she felt about the subject. And then there was that other problem his father had conveniently dumped in his lap. The old sheikh of Kadahan wanted Jamal to marry his daughter as soon as it could be arranged. The thought of marrying, which a few weeks ago he would have merely accepted as his duty, now bothered him to no end. He felt angered at the prospect of having any woman in his life other than Delaney. And he did not appreciate the pressure his father was putting on him to return home and consider marriage to Raschida Muhammad, princess of Kadahan, at once, just to make her father happy.

Jamal shook his head. And why the sudden rush for a wedding? Why did Sheikh Muhammad feel the urgency to marry his daughter off? Jamal had posed the question to his father, and the only answer he got was that the old sheikh's health was failing and he wanted to make sure his daughter, as well as his people, were in good hands should anything happen.

Jamal refused to believe Sheikh Muhammad had serious health problems. He had spent three months with the man while negotiating that contract, and Sheikh Muhammad had still been actively bedding his French mistress when Jamal had left to come to America.

He tightened his fists at his sides, wondering what the hell was going on. He suddenly felt as if he was headed for the gallows and wished there were some other eligible sheikh the princess could marry. For once he did not want to be the sacrificial lamb.

He inhaled a deep breath. There was nothing left to do but to return to Tahran. It seemed that life had landed him a crushing blow. He felt frustrated and shaken. He was about to leave the only woman he truly loved to return home and marry someone he cared nothing about. A part of him died at the thought, but he knew what he had to do.

He also knew he owed it to Delaney to let her know that he was leaving and the reason why. She deserved his honesty. Chances were that news of his engagement would go out over the wire service, and he didn't want her to find out about it from the newspapers.

It took several moments for him to compose himself, then he left his bedroom to find Delaney.

She was nowhere to be found in the cabin, so he walked toward the lake looking for her. It was a warm, sunny day and birds were flying overhead. A part of him wished he could be that carefree, with no responsibilities and only the commitments that would make him happy. But that wasn't the case. As his father had not hesitated to remind him a few minutes earlier, he was a prince, a sheikh, and he had responsibilities and obligations.

Jamal stopped walking when he saw Delaney. She was

sitting on the dock with her legs dangling over the edge, letting her toes play in the water. A light breeze stirred her hair about her face. She tossed it back in place, then leaned back on her hands to stare up at the birds; the same flock he had seen earlier.

Leaning against a tree, he continued to stare at her. He smiled. Seeing her sitting there, peaceful and serene, was the most beautiful sight he had ever seen, and he wanted to keep it in his memory forever. And knew that he would.

A battle was raging within him, love versus responsibility. Deep in his heart he knew which would win. He had been groomed and tutored to take on responsibilities all his life. But this thing called love was new to him. It was something he had never experienced, and for the first time in his life he felt lost, like a fish out of water.

A shiver passed through him. He loved her with a passion he hadn't known was possible, yet he had to let her go because duty called.

He forced himself to walk toward her, and when he got to the edge of the dock, he whispered her name and she turned and met his gaze. The look in her eyes and the expression on her face told it all. She didn't know the why of it, but she knew he was leaving.

And from the way her lips were quivering and from the way she was looking at him, she didn't have to say the words, because he immediately knew how she felt. The silent message in her eyes told him everything, just as he knew the silent message in his was exposing his very soul to her. For the first time it was unguarded...just for her.

They had both played the game and won...but at the same time they had both lost. He hadn't played fair and she had played to win and in the end they had gotten more than they had bargained for—each other's hearts. But now they were losing even more—the chance to be together.

"Come here," he whispered softly, and she stood and came into his arms willingly. He held her like a dying man taking his last drink, pulling her to him and holding her close, so close he could hear the unevenness of her breathing and the feel of her spine trembling. But at the moment all he wanted to do was hold her tight in his arms, close to his aching heart.

They stood that way, for how long he didn't know. He stepped back and looked at her, wondering how he would survive the days, weeks, months and years, without her. Wondering how a woman he had met only three weeks ago could change his life forever. But she had.

He swallowed the thick lump in his throat and said, "Duty calls."

She nodded slowly as she studied his features. Then she asked, "It's more than the business with the sheikh of that other country, isn't it?"

He met her gaze. Deep regret was in his eyes. "Yes. I've been summoned home to marry."

He watched as she took a deep breath, saying nothing for a few moments. Hurt and pain appeared in her features although he could tell she was trying not to let them show. Then she asked in a very quiet voice, "How soon will you be leaving?"

He thought he could feel the ground under his feet crumble when he said, "As soon as Asalum can make the necessary arrangements."

She tried to smile through the tears he saw wetting her eyes. "Need help packing, Your Highness?"

A surge of heartache and pain jolted through him. This was the first time she had called him Your Highness without the usual haughtiness in her voice. He reached out and clasped her fingers and brought them to his lips. In a voice rough with emotion, tinged with all the love he felt, he whispered, "I would be honored to accept your help, My Princess."

He pulled her into his arms and covered her mouth with his, zapping her strength as well as his own. The inside of her mouth was sweet, and he kissed her the way he had kissed her so many other times before, putting everything he had into it.

Without breaking the kiss he gathered her up into his arms and carried her over to the hammock. He wanted and needed her now. And she had the same wants and needs as he did, and began removing her clothes with the same speed he removed his. He then gathered her naked body in his arms and placed her flat on her back in the hammock. Straddling her, he used his legs to keep the hammock steady as he entered her body, almost losing it before he could push all the way inside. His entire body filled with love as he sank deeper and deeper into her. All his thoughts were concentrated on her.

For a moment, like the hammock, he felt his life was hanging by cords, but when she wrapped her legs around his waist and looped her arms around his neck, he knew she was all he would ever need and was the one thing he could never have.

But he would have these lasting memories of the time they had spent together. They were memories that would have to last him a lifetime. He began moving, thrusting in and out of her, his hunger for her at its highest peak, knowing this may very well be the last time he had her this way. Over and over again, he withdrew, then pushed forward again, wanting her and needing her with a passion.

Under the clear blue sky, with the sunshine beaming brightly overhead, he made love to his woman with an urgency that overwhelmed both of them. The muscles inside of her squeezed him, as he pumped into her relentlessly.

In the deep recesses of his mind he heard Delaney cry out as completion ripped through her, once, twice and a third time, before he finally let go, letting wave after wave of sensations swamp his body, and he shuddered deep into her, filling her fully.

He dug his heels into the solid ground to hold the hammock in place as he held her hips in a tight grip, experiencing the ultimate in sexual pleasure with the woman he loved.

Jamal and Delaney heard the sound of Asalum's car when it pulled up in the driveway. The older man had phoned earlier to say a private plane had arrived to take the prince back to his homeland and was waiting for them at the airport.

After making love outside they had come inside and showered together, only to make love again. She had sat on the bed and watched him dress in his native garb, trying not to think about the fact that one day soon another woman would be the one to be by his side.

When he had finished dressing, looking every bit a dashing Arab prince, a handsome desert sheikh, she helped him pack without a word being exchanged between them. There was nothing left to say. He had to do what he had to do.

Delaney inhaled deeply. She had known this day would eventually come, but she had counted on another week with him. But that was no longer possible. It was time for him to return to the life he had without her to marry another. She looked up and saw him watching her. She had been determined to make their parting easier but now…

"Will you walk me to the porch, Delaney?"

"Yes." She felt tears gathering in her throat. Crossing the room to him, she stood on tiptoe and kissed him on his lips. "Take care of yourself, Jamal."

He reached out and stroked her hair back from her face— a face he would remember forever. "You do the same." He inhaled deeply and said, "There were times when I wasn't as careful with you as I should have been, Delaney. If you are carrying my child, I want to know about it. I've left Asalum's number on the nightstand next to your bed. He knows how to reach me at any time, day or night. Promise you will call and let me know if you carry my heir."

Delaney looked up at Jamal, questions evident in her eyes. He knew what she was asking. "It doesn't matter," he said softly. "If you are pregnant, the child is mine and I will recognize it as such. Your child will be *our* child, and I will love it…just as much as I will always love you, its mother."

Tears streamed down her face with his admission of love. It had not been his intent to tell her how he felt, but he couldn't leave without letting her know their time together had meant everything to him, and without letting her know that he had fallen in love with her.

"And I love you, too, Jamal," she whispered, holding him tight to her.

He nodded. "Yes, but this is one of those times when love is not enough," he said hoarsely. "Duty comes before love."

Asalum blew the horn, letting them know it was time for him to leave. Delaney walked him to the door, then stood silently on the porch as she watched his trusted servant help him with his luggage. When that had been done Jamal turned and looked at her after taking a small box Asalum had handed to him.

Walking back to her he presented the box to her. "This is something I had Asalum make sure arrived with the plane. It is something I want you to have, Delaney. Please accept it not as a gift for what has passed between us, because I would never cheapen what we shared that way. But accept it as a token of my undying love and deep affection. And whenever you need to remember just how deeply I love you, just how much I care, take a look at it," he said, opening the box for her to see.

Delaney released a sharp intake of breath. Sitting on a surface of white velvet was the largest diamond ring she had ever seen. It was all of eight or nine carats. But what really caught her eye was the inscription on the inside of the wide band. It read—"My Princess." "But…but I can't take this."

"Yes, you can, Delaney. It belonged to my mother and is mine to give to the woman I choose."

"But what about the woman you must marry, and—"

"No, she is the woman being given to me. In my heart you are the woman I love and the woman I would choose if I could. This is mine and I want to give it to you."

Delaney shook her head as tears began clouding again in her eyes. "This is too much, Jamal. It is so special."

"Because you are too much, Delaney, and you are so special. And no matter who walks by my side, remember that things aren't as they seem to be. You are the one who will always have my heart."

He leaned and tenderly kissed her one last time before turning and walking to the car. He looked over his shoulder before getting inside, and waved goodbye.

She waved back, then stood rooted to the spot, watching the car drive away. She once remembered him saying that he didn't like leaving anything behind broken.

Evidently, it didn't include her heart.

She stood until the vehicle was no longer in sight. It was then that she allowed the floodgates to open, and she gave in to the rest of her tears.

The sun was low on the horizon by the time Delaney finished her walk. The cabin held too many memories, and she hadn't been ready to go there after Jamal left, so she'd taken a stroll around the cabin. But she had found no peace in doing that, either.

Every path she took held some memory of Jamal.

Already every cell in her body missed him, longed for him and wanted him. There was so much she'd wanted to say and wished she had said, but none of it would have mattered.

He had chosen duty over love.

Delaney's heart sank, yet a part of her both understood and accepted. She had known all along that things would end this way. There had been no other way for them to end. Jamal had been totally honest with her from the very beginning. He had not given her false hope or empty promises.

He was who he was. A man of honor. A man whose life was not his own, so it could never be hers.

She sighed when she reached the porch, remembering how they had often eaten breakfast while sitting on the steps enjoying the sun. She also remembered a particular time when he had said something to make her laugh just moments before claiming her mouth and kissing her in a way that had melted her insides.

Inhaling deeply, Delaney knew there was no way she could stay at the cabin any longer. She walked up the steps after making the decision to pack up her things and leave.

Delaney had just closed the last of her luggage when she heard a car door slam outside. Thinking, hoping, wishing that Jamal had returned for some reason, she raced out of the bedroom to the front door. When she opened it, she swallowed deeply, recognizing her visitors.

Five men were leaning against a sports utility vehicle, and each man had his arms crossed over his chest and a very serious look on his face. Delaney sighed as she studied them.

Dare stood every bit of six-four and was the most conservative of the five. As a sheriff he demanded respect for the law, and those who knew him knew he meant business and not to call his bluff. Thorn stood an inch or so taller than Dare and was considered the prickliest of the five. He was moody and temperamental when it suited him. And he was the daredevil in the family, the one who took risks by racing the motorcycles he built. Chase was basically easygoing when the others weren't around. He stood six-two and relished the success of his soul-food restaurant that had recently been named one of the best eating places in the Atlanta area. Stone was the most serious of the five, or at least he tried to be. His height fell somewhere between Chase's and Dare's. He enjoyed taking trips to different places, doing research for his books. So far all ten novels had appeared on the *New York Times* bestseller list. Last, but not least, was Storm, Chase's twin. He was as tall as Chase and had dimples to die for. It had always been his dream to become a fireman, and now because of a recent promotion, he was a proud lieutenant in the Atlanta Fire Department.

Even Delaney had to admit they were a handsome group, but at the moment she wasn't in the mood to be intimidated by the likes of the Westmoreland brothers. "You guys are a long way from home, aren't you?" she asked, moving her gaze from one to the other.

Of course it had to be the prickly Thorn who spoke up by saying, "What the hell are you doing out here by yourself in the middle of nowhere, Laney?"

Before she could answer, Dare chimed in. "I see another set of tire tracks, you guys. It looks like Laney wasn't here by herself, or she had a visitor."

Delaney raised her eyes heavenward. "Always the cop, aren't you, Dare?" She sighed. "Why the show of force? Didn't Mom and Dad tell you I was okay and wanted to be left in seclusion for a while?"

"Yes, they told us," Stone said easily, but eyed her suspiciously as if she would be the perfect villain for his next book. "But we had to check things out for ourselves. And who did that other car belong to?"

Delaney refused to answer. In fact, she had a question of her own. "How did you find me?"

Storm laughed. "Dare put your picture out over the FBI wire service as a most-wanted fugitive and we got a tip."

At her frown, Storm held up his hand and said, "I was just kidding, Laney. For goodness sakes, cut the 'I will kill you dead if that's true' look. Chase took a peek at the folks' caller ID and got your new cell number. The telephone company was able to trace where the roaming fees were being charged. Once we had that pinpointed the rest was a piece of cake."

Delaney shook her head. "Yeah, I bet it was, like none of you have anything better to do with your time than to hunt me down. I am twenty-five, you know."

Stone rolled his eyes. "Yeah, and the cost of milk was two-fifty a gallon yesterday, so what's your point?"

Delaney glared at the five of them as she came down off the porch. "My point is this. I can take care of myself, and if you start trying to get into my business, I will do the same for yours."

Four of the men looked uneasy. Of course it was Thorn who took her threat in stride. "You're welcome to mess things up with me and the woman I'm presently seeing. She's the clingy type, and I've been trying to get rid of her for weeks."

Delaney glared at him. "If your mood hasn't run her off then nothing will." She inhaled deeply, knowing her brothers were hopeless. They would never treat her like the adult she was. "Well, since you're all here, you may as well help carry my stuff to the car."

Chase lifted a brow. "You're leaving?"

"Yes."

"You never said whose car those tire tracks belonged to," Dare reminded her.

Delaney turned to go into the house, knowing her brothers would follow. She decided to tell them the truth since she knew they wouldn't believe her, anyway. "The car belonged to a prince, a desert sheikh from the Middle East," she tossed back over her shoulder.

She smiled when she heard Storm say to the others, "And she thinks we're stupid enough to believe that."

Chapter 11

Jamal gazed out of the window of the private plane as it landed at the Tahran airport. Any other time he would have thought it was good to be home, but tonight was an exception. His heart still ached for Delaney.

What was she doing? Was she thinking of him the way he was thinking of her?

"It is time to disembark, My Prince."

He lifted his gaze and met Asalum's concerned frown. Only someone as close to him as Asalum could know the pain he was feeling. He turned his head to look back out of the window, not saying anything for the longest time, then he said quietly, "I'm no longer filled with obsession, Asalum."

Asalum nodded. "And what is it now, Your Highness?"

"Depression."

Asalum shook his head. That much he had already concluded. The loss of the American woman was having a powerful effect on the prince.

Jamal slowly stood. He had noted the long, black limo parked on the runway. As usual his father had sent an entourage to welcome him home. With a grim set of his jaw he walked off the plane.

Within less than an hour's time he arrived at the palace. Sitting high on a hill it looked like a magnificent fortress, commanding its own respect and admiration, and had served as home for the Yasir family for hundreds of years.

After going through the massive wrought-iron gate, the limo had barely come to stop when a beautiful, young dark-haired woman raced from the front of the house into the courtyard.

"Jamal Ari!"

Jamal smiled for the first time since leaving America and watched his sister come to a stop next to the car, anxious for him to get out. A few moments later he found himself standing next to the car and embracing his sister, Johari.

"It's so good to have you home, Jamal Ari. I have so much to tell you," she said excitedly, pulling him through the huge wooden door she had come out of.

Jamal shook his head. If anyone could pull him out of his despairing mood, it would be Johari.

Later that night Jamal heard a soft knock on his door. He had claimed complete exhaustion, and his father had agreed to put off their talks until the next morning. Jamal had escaped to his private apartment in the palace, the entire west wing that was his. Rebakkah, Asalum's wife and the woman who had been his personal servant since birth, had brought him a tray of food a while ago that sat untouched on the table. He had no appetite to eat.

He opened the door to find his stepmother, Fatimah,

standing there. A beautiful woman with golden-brown skin and long, black wavy hair that flowed to her waist, she had retained her petite figure even after giving birth to two children. It seemed she never aged and was just as radiant at forty-four as she had been when she had come into his and his father's lives twenty-two years ago. He was not surprised to see her. Like Asalum, Fatimah knew him well and she knew when something was bothering him.

She stepped into his apartment and turned to face him. Concern was etched in her dark eyes. They were beautiful eyes that were all seeing, all knowing. "What is it, Jamal Ari?" she asked softly, studying him intently. "You are not yourself. Something is bothering you, and I want you to tell me what it is so I can make it better."

Jamal leaned against the door. He couldn't help but smile. When he was younger it seemed Fatimah had always been able to do that—make things better. Even if it pitted her against his father. She had never been outright disobedient, but she had definitely let the king know how she felt about certain things.

"I don't think you can make this one better, Fatimah," he said quietly. "This is something I have to work out for myself."

Fatimah looked at him for a long moment, then nodded, accepting his right to request that she not interfere. *For now.* "Well, whatever has you in such a sour mood will soon be forgotten. I sent word to Najeen that you had returned."

A frown covered Jamal's face. "Najeen?"

Fatimah's feminine chuckle bathed the air. "Yes, Najeen. Have you forgotten who she is?"

Jamal walked away from the door. He didn't want to see Najeen or any woman for that matter. The woman he wanted to see was millions of miles away. "Najeen will no longer be my mistress," he said softly.

Fatimah raised a dark brow. "Why? Do you have another?"

"No." He sighed deeply, not in the mood to explain. But seeing the surprised look on Fatimah's face he knew that he should. "I will be sending Najeen away, back to her homeland where she will be taken care of in the comfort she has become accustomed to until she takes another benefactor," he quietly decreed.

Fatimah nodded as she studied him. Her distress level rose. He was acting in a most peculiar way. "Is there a reason for your decision?"

His lashes lifted and his dark eyes met her even darker ones. Fatimah saw anxiety in their depths. She also saw something else that alarmed her. "Jamal Ari? What is it?"

He crossed the room to the window. The view outside was magnificent, but for the first time he didn't appreciate it. "While in America I met someone, Fatimah. A woman who stirred me in a way no other woman has. A Western woman who initially fought me at every turn, a woman who is just as proud and stubborn as I am, someone who was my complete opposite on some things but then my total equal on others. And…"

Silence. Across the room Fatimah watched his profile. She saw the way his hands balled into fists at his sides; the way his jaw hardened and the sharp gaze that was looking out the window without really seeing anything. "And what?" she prompted, hoping he would continue.

Slowly, he turned to face her and she saw the torment in his features. "And someone I fell helplessly and hopelessly in love with."

Fatimah's heart took a lurching leap of surprise in her throat. "A Western woman?"

He met her gaze thinking, *my* Western woman. From the moment Delaney had gotten out of the car that day she had arrived at the cabin, a part of him had known she would be his. He just hadn't known that he, in turn, would become hers. "Yes," he finally responded.

Fatimah studied him. "But you've never liked Western women, Jamal Ari. You always thought they were too modern, headstrong and disobedient."

A smile forced its way to his lips when he thought of Delaney. In her own way she was all those things. "Yes, but I fell in love with her, anyway."

Fatimah nodded. "So what are you going to do? You love one but are planning to wed another?"

Jamal inhaled a deep breath. "I must do what I must do, Fatimah. I am duty bound to do what is needed for my country."

"And what about what is needed for your heart, Jamal Ari?" she asked, crossing the room to him. She had taken him into her heart as her son the moment she had seen him many years ago. "Your heart is breaking. I can sense it."

"Yes," he said, not bothering to deny it. "A good leader's decisions should not be ruled by love, Fatimah. They should be ruled by what is in the best interest of his people. My feelings matter not."

Fatimah looked at him, aware of the coldness settling in him. The bitterness, as well. She smiled sadly. For as long as she had known him, Jamal Ari had always had a mind and a will of his own. Yes, he was as dedicated to the people as his father, but still, he did exactly what pleased him, which usually had been fast cars and beautiful women. But now for what he considered to be the good of his people, he was willing to bend his mind and his will. And in doing so he was slowly destroying himself.

"Your father once thought that way, Jamal Ari, but now he thinks differently," she finally said, hoping to make him see reason before it was too late. "And I hope you will open your mind to do the same. Love is a powerful beast. It can bring the strongest of beings to their knees."

Without saying anything else, she turned and walked out of the room. The door closed stiffly behind her, bathing the room in dead silence.

That night Jamal dreamed.

Delaney was with him, in his bed while he made love to her. Not caring that he wasn't using protection of any kind, his body repeatedly thrust into hers, glorying in the feel of her beneath him, of him being inside of her. In the darkness he could hear her moans of pleasure that combined with his own. He could actually feel the imprint of her nails on his back and shoulders as she gripped him, her fingers relentlessly pressing deeply into his skin. He felt his body moving closer to the edge and knew what he wanted more than anything. He wanted to impregnate her with his heir, just in case she wasn't pregnant already. He could envision a son with dark, copper-colored skin and a head of jet-black curls and eyes the color of dark chocolate.

His hand reached up and cupped her cheek, bringing her lips to his; lips he now hungered for all the time; lips he would tease into submission. They were also lips whose touch could arouse him to no end, drive him literally insane; lips belonging to a mouth he had branded.

He then gave his attention to her breasts as they thrust firmly and proudly from her body, taunting him to taste, which he did. He loved the feel of them against his tongue, wished he could love her this way forever and never have to stop. Around her he always felt primal, needy, lusty.

So he continued to make love to her, holding her tightly in his arms and whispering his words of love.

Thousands of miles away Delaney was in bed having that same dream.

Her body felt stretched, filled and hot. Her breasts felt

soul-stirringly tender from Jamal's caress, and she could feel him loving her in a way she had become used to: determined, forceful. And very thorough.

His touch felt so right, and she felt a simmering sense that relief was near. She moaned a low, needy sound when a shiver passed through her body, and she gloried in the feel of being made love to this way. Then she exploded into tiny pieces.

Sometime later she opened her eyes, letting them adjust to the darkness. Rejoining reality she found that she was in bed alone. She curled her body into a ball as the waves of passion subsided, sending tremors through her.

She lay there, too shaken to move. Her dream had seemed so real. It had been as if Jamal had actually been with her, inside of her, making love to her. Taking a deep breath she swung her legs down to the floor and eased out of bed.

Going into the bathroom she washed her face in cool water, still feeling the heat of her dream. She inhaled deeply, glad she had returned to her apartment and not done as her brothers had suggested and gone to her parents' home.

She needed time alone—time to deal with everything. Her brothers had relented and had given in to her request for privacy. But she knew their placidness wouldn't last long. For the moment they were humoring her.

Glancing up at the mirror, she studied her red, swollen eyes. After her brothers had left, indicating they would be back to check on her within a few weeks, she had lain across the bed and cried.

She knew she couldn't continue on this way. Jamal was gone and wasn't coming back. She had to get on with her life, and the best way to do that was to go to work. She was not supposed to report to the hospital for another two weeks, but she wanted to go to work now. She would call the chief of staff to see if she could start earlier than planned.

The best thing to do was to keep her mind occupied. She had to stop thinking about Jamal.

Jamal got out of bed drenched in sweat as chills from the night air touched his body, making him tremble. His dream had seemed so real. He inhaled deeply. There wasn't the lingering aroma of sex, that special scent that he and Delaney's mated bodies generated.

He momentarily closed his eyes, memorizing her scent and visualizing in his mind the nights he had been pleasured by her body in reality and not in a dream. He could never forget the sight of her lying on her back…waiting for him. Her legs were shapely, long and sleek, and her breasts, there for him to touch and taste, and he had thoroughly enjoyed doing both. But what took his breath away to just think about it was her rear, perfectly rounded and curvy, making him hard each time he saw it.

The memories were making his body hard, and his breath was ragged. A part of him cursed the fate that had taken him away from Delaney. He acknowledged he would have left eventually, anyway. But knowing that had made every moment with her precious as time had clicked away. The time they had spent together had not been nearly long enough.

He reached for his robe from a nearby chair and put it on, then walked across the room to the door leading to the balcony. Stars dotted the midnight sky and softly lit the courtyard below. With its numerous lush plants, beautiful flowers and exotic shrubs, the courtyard had always been his favorite place to hide out as a child. But no matter how well he thought he could hide, Asalum would always find him. He smiled at the memory, breathing in the scent of gardenias and jasmine.

He then smiled at the thought of what Delaney would think if she ever saw the palace. A part of him could see her feeling right at home here. There was no doubt in his mind that with her Western views she would be a breath of fresh air. Her liberal way of thinking would no doubt scandalize some, but her caring would capture the hearts of others. The same way she had captured his.

Just thinking about her was torment. He straightened slowly and sighed. After he met with his father in the morning he would leave for Kuwait to meet with the other members of the coalition to reach another agreement with the Sheikh of Caron.

Then he would travel to Ranyaa, his estates in northern Africa. And there he would stay until the marriage arrangements had been worked out. He didn't want to be around anyone any more than necessary. He wanted to be left alone…to drown in his misery.

Chapter 12

Delaney returned the squiggling baby to its mother. "She seems to be doing a whole lot better, Mrs. Ford. Her fever has broken, and her ears no longer look infected."

The woman shook her head, smiling. "Thanks, Dr. Westmoreland. You have been so nice to my Victoria. She likes you."

Delaney grinned. "I like her, too. And to be on the safe side, I'd like to see her again in a few weeks to recheck her ears."

"All right."

Delaney watched as the woman placed the baby in the stroller and left, waving goodbye before getting on the elevator. She sighed deeply. During the three weeks since she had started working she was getting used to being called Dr. Westmoreland. Her heart caught in her chest each time she heard it. All of her hard work and dedication to her studies had paid off. She was doing something she loved and that was providing medical care to children.

Someone behind her chuckled, and she half turned and saw it was Tara Matthews. Tara was a fellow resident pediatrician whom she had met when she began working at the hospital. They had quickly become good friends.

"Okay, what's so funny?" she asked Tara, smiling.

"You are," Tara said, shaking her head, grinning. "You really like babies, don't you?"

Managing a chuckle, Delaney said, "Of course I do. I'm a pediatrician, for heaven's sake. So are you, and I have to assume you like babies, too."

Tara took the stethoscope from around her neck and placed it in the pocket of her doctor's scrubs. "But not as much as you do. I wished I had a camera for the look of awe on your face when you were holding Victoria Ford. You were in hog heaven. And that's with every baby you care for."

Delaney chuckled, knowing that was true. "I already told you that I'm the only girl with five brothers and I was also the youngest. By the time I came along there weren't any babies in my family. And my brothers have declared themselves bachelors for life, which means I won't be getting any nieces or nephews anytime soon."

Tara folded her arms under her breasts and nodded. "And for me it was the complete opposite. I'm the oldest of four and I had to take care of my younger sister and brothers, so I can hold off having any children of my own for years to come."

Delaney laughed. She really liked Tara and appreciated their friendship. Like her, Tara had moved to Bowling Green without knowing a soul, and the two of them had hit it off. They lived in the same apartment building and carpooled to work occasionally, and on the weekends they would go shopping and to the video store, then stay up late for hours talking and watching old movies. Being the same age, they shared similar interests, and like her, Tara was unattached at the moment, although Delaney couldn't understand why. With her dark mahogany complexion, light brown eyes and dark brown hair, not to mention her hourglass figure, Tara was simply gorgeous. Delaney knew that a number of doctors had asked her out and she had turned them down without blinking an eye.

But then so had she.

It wasn't uncommon for the single doctors to check out the new unattached female residence physicians. Although Delaney had been asked out several times, like Tara, she had declined the offers. Usually in the afternoons when she left work, unless she and Tara had made plans to do something together that night, she went home, took a shower and went to bed.

And each night she dreamed of Jamal.

"Tara to Delaney. Tara to Delaney. Come in, please."

Delaney laughed when she realized Tara had been trying to get her attention. "I'm sorry, what were you saying?"

"I asked if you have any plans for tonight."

Delaney shook her head. "No, what about you?"

"No, none. Do you want to check out Denzel's new movie?"

Wincing, Delaney sucked in a deep breath. Tara's question reminded her that she had already seen the movie…with Jamal. She closed her eyes as she tried to blot out the memory.

"Delaney, are you all right?"

Delaney snapped her eyes back open and met Tara's concerned stare. "Yes, I'm fine." She took in another deep breath of air. "I've already seen the movie, but if you really want to go I can see it again."

Tara looked at her for a moment before saying, "You went with him, didn't you?"

Delaney took a deep breath. "Him who?"

"The guy you won't talk about."

Delaney didn't say anything for the longest time and then

she nodded. "Yes, and you're right, I don't want to talk about him."

Tara nodded and reached out a hand to touch Delaney's arm. "I'm sorry. I didn't mean to pry. I have no right."

Delaney shook her head. "No, you don't." A smile softened her features when she added, "Especially since you're harboring secrets of your own."

A gentle smile tilted the corners of Tara's lips. "Touché, my friend. One day, after I've taken one sip of chardonnay too many, I'll spill my guts."

Delaney's expression became serious. "And one day when my pain gets too unbearable and I can use a shoulder to cry on, I'll tell you about him."

Tara nodded, understanding completely. "Good enough."

"I can't marry Princess Raschida," Jamal said, meeting his father's deep stare. He had arrived back at the palace after having been gone three weeks. It had taken all that time for him to make decisions he knew would change his life forever. But there was nothing he could do about that. Delaney was the woman he wanted, and she was the woman he would have…if she still wanted him.

King Yasir held his son's gaze. "Do you know what you're saying?" he asked, pushing himself up from the wing chair he had been sitting in.

Jamal stared into the face of the man who had produced him, a man loved, respected and admired by many—a man Jamal knew would do anything for his people and a man who, in addition to everything else, believed in honor.

"Yes, Father," he answered quietly. "I know what I'm saying and I also know what this means. I truly thought I could go through with it, but now I know that I can't. I'm in love with someone else, and there is no way I can marry another."

King Yasir looked deep into his son's face. He had known when Jamal arrived home three weeks ago that something had been troubling him. Subsequently, Fatimah had shared with him what that something was. But he had turned a deaf ear to the thought that his son was in love with a Western woman. But now, seeing was believing. Jamal looked tormented and his features were those of a man who was hurting and whose very soul had been stripped away. With all the arrogance and lordliness Jamal was known to have, King Yasir was shocked that a woman had brought his son to this.

"This woman you love is a Western woman, is she not?" he asked gruffly.

Jamal continued to meet his father's gaze. "Yes," he said calmly.

"And you're willing to walk away from a woman of your people and marry someone not like you, of your faith and nationality?"

Chin up, head lifted and body straight, Jamal answered stiffly, "Yes, because, although not like me, she is of me. She is a part of me just as I am a part of her, Father. Love has united us as one."

The king's eyes darkened. "Love? And what do you know of love?" he declared. "Are you sure it's not your libido talking? Lust can be just as strong an emotion as love," he persisted.

Jamal walked closer into the room to face his father. "Yes, I'm aware of that, and I do admit I was attracted to her from the moment I first saw her. I even thought it to be lust for a while, but it is not. At thirty-four I know the difference. I have had an ongoing affair with Najeen for a number of years, yet I've never thought about falling in love with her."

"You wouldn't have. You knew her position in your life. She was your mistress. If a man of your status were to fall in love it should be with his wife."

"But things don't always happen that way, Father, as you well know. Look at the number of other dignitaries who are besotted with their mistresses. And to answer your question as to what I know about love, I can honestly say that I know more now than I did some weeks ago," he concluded heavily. "I know love is what has me willing to stand before you now and plead for your understanding that I marry the woman who has my heart. Love is what has me in total misery, torment and depression. Love is also what has kept me functioning regardless of those things."

He took a deep breath and continued, "Love is what I see whenever you and Fatimah are together, and love is what has me willing to abdicate my right to succession if I have to."

Shock was reflected in his father's face. "You will give up the right to be my heir—the crown prince, the future king—for this woman?"

Jamal knew his words had caused his father pain, but they had to be said to make him understand just what Delaney meant to him. "Yes, Father, I would. Fatimah was right. Love is powerful enough to bring even the strongest man to his knees. I love Delaney Westmoreland, and I want her for my princess."

"But does this woman want you? What if she refuses to accept our ways? What if she refuses to change, and—"

"I don't want her to change," Jamal said vehemently. "I love her just the way she is. I believe she would be willing to meet me halfway on certain things, and in my heart I also believe she will love our people as much as I do. But Delaney is not a woman who will bend because a man says she has to."

"This woman is disobedient?" the king asked, troubled, astounded.

"No more so than Fatimah was when she first came here. If I remember correctly there was some rumbling among the people when you married an Egyptian princess instead of one of your own. But over the years they have come to love and respect her."

King Yasir didn't say anything for a long moment, because what Jamal had just said was true. Fatimah was loved and admired by all. Finally he released a long, deep sigh. "Sheikh Muhammad isn't going to be happy with the news that you refused to marry his daughter. He may declare that our sheikhdom lacks honor. Are you willing to abide with that, Jamal?"

Jamal shook his head. That was the hardest thing he had to contend with. "I will talk to the sheikh and if I have to I will agree to scour the entire countryside and find a replacement that pleases him. But I will not marry his daughter."

The king nodded solemnly. He then picked up documents off his desk. "Finding a replacement might not be necessary. Fatimah brought something to my attention a few weeks ago, gossip that was circulating among the servants. It seems that the servants in the Muhammads' household had been whispering, and even with the distance separating our sheikhdoms, the wind carried some of those whispers here. Rebakkah felt it was her duty to make her queen aware of what was being said."

"And what was being said?" Jamal asked, watching lines of anger form in his father's face.

"Word that Princess Raschida is with child, which is the reason Sheikh Muhammad is in such a hurry to marry her off."

Jamal was taken aback. "I would have married her, not knowing this, and the child would not have been my true heir?"

"Yes," the king answered in a disgruntled voice. "Evidently they were hoping no one would be the wiser since she is in her very early stages."

Jamal became furious. "I can't believe Sheikh Muhammad would do such a thing."

"He was trying to save both himself and his daughter from embarrassment, Jamal. But I agree that what he had planned was dishonorable." He gazed down at the papers he held in his hand. "This report tells everything. When Fatimah brought me word, I had my men look into it, discreetly. It seemed that the princess has been involved in a secret affair—right under her father's nose—with a man who is a high-ranking official in his army."

"Well, the man can have her!" Jamal was appalled at how close he had come to being taken in. And here Delaney could be—and for some reason he believed that she was—pregnant with his legitimate heir.

"I think you should know, Father," he said, drawing his father's attention, "there is a possibility that Delaney carries my child."

His father's eyes widened. "Do you know that for certain?"

Jamal shook his head. "No. I haven't had any contact with her since I left America. I can only cite my beliefs on male intuition or possibly a revelation from Allah. But I plan to go to her and find out. I also plan to ask her to marry me and return with me as my bride."

"And if she doesn't want to do that?"

"Then I will convince her otherwise. Whatever it takes."

King Yasir nodded, knowing just how persuasive Jamal Ari could be when it suited him. "I much prefer that you marry someone from our country, Jamal, however, you are right, I do understand love doesn't recognize color, national origin or religion."

"Do I have your blessings, Father?"

The king slowly nodded his head. "Yes, although I am certain you would still marry her without my blessings. However, before I can fully accept her as the woman who will one day stand by your side to rule our people, I must meet her and get to know her. That is the best I can do," he quietly conceded.

Jamal nodded. "And that is all I ask, Father. You are more than fair."

King Yasir hugged his son in a strong display of affection, which Jamal returned. After the king released him from his embrace, Jamal turned and walked out of his father's study.

"Delaney, are you sure you're feeling all right?" Tara asked for the third time that day. "I hate to be a nuisance but you don't look well."

Delaney nodded. She didn't feel well, either, but then she wouldn't be feeling well for a number of days to come. She had missed her period and an over-the-counter pregnancy test she had taken that morning confirmed she was carrying Jamal's child. She planned to keep her word and let him know, but decided to wait until after her first appointment with the doctor in a few weeks.

A baby.

The thought that she was carrying Jamal's baby made her extremely happy, and if it wasn't for the bouts of morning sickness she had started having a few days ago, she would be fine. At least as fine as a woman could be who was still pining over the man she loved. Each day she had checked the international news section of the paper for word of his engagement or marriage. So far she hadn't seen anything.

Lovingly she caressed her stomach. Jamal had planted a baby inside of her. His baby, a part of him that she would love as much as she loved him.

"Delaney?"

Delaney looked up and met Tara's concerned stare. She was not ready to share her news with anyone yet. "I'm fine, Tara. I've just been busy lately, preparing for my brothers' visit. I have to get ready, both mentally and physically, for them. They can be rather tiring and taxing to one's peace of mind."

Tara chuckled. "When do you expect them?"

"Sometime later today. They had to wait for Storm to get off work before driving up. And I really appreciate you letting a couple of them stay at your place. There is no way all five of them will fit in my tiny apartment."

"Hey, don't mention it, and I'm looking forward to meeting them."

And there was no doubt in Delaney's mind that her brothers would definitely want to meet Tara. She couldn't wait to see their reaction to her, as well as her reaction to them. Tara was a woman who didn't tolerate arrogance in any man, and the Westmoreland brothers were as arrogant as they came.

On a private plane bound for America, Jamal sat back in the seat, relaxed. Asalum, using his connection with certain international security firms, had been able to obtain a residence address for Delaney in Bowling Green, Kentucky. Jamal planned to go straight to her home from the airport as soon as the plane landed.

He smiled at the thought of seeing her again. Inside of him the yearning to hold her in his arms was so intense it pulled at his inner strength. He laid his head back against the seat. They had been in the air eight hours already, and according to the pilot they had another four hours to go before they arrived in Kentucky.

Asalum appeared with a pillow. "For you, Prince."

Jamal took the pillow and placed it behind his head. "Thank you, Asalum." He looked up into the older man's world-weary and rugged face. "I'm no longer feeling depression."

Asalum couldn't hide his smile. "And what are you feeling now, My Prince?"

Jamal grinned heartily. "Jubilation."

Chapter 13

Tara leaned against the closed bathroom door. Concern was etched on her face as she heard the sound of Delaney throwing up on the other side. "Delaney? Are you sure you're going to be okay? That's the second time you've thrown up today."

Delaney held her head over the toilet thinking it was actually the third time. And all this time she thought morning sickness was just for the morning. "Yes, Tara, I'll be fine, just give me a second."

At that moment she could hear the sound of the doorbell. *Oh, my gosh! My brothers are here!* "Tara, please get the door. More than likely it's my brothers, and no matter what, please don't tell them I'm in the bathroom sick."

Tara smiled. "Okay, I'll do my best to stall them, but only if you promise to see Dr. Goldman tomorrow. Sounds like you might be coming down with a virus." She turned and crossed the room when the doorbell sounded a second time.

Opening the door, Tara's breath caught and held at the sight of the four men standing there. Then just as quickly she regained her composure. It took some doing. Delaney's brothers were definitely good-looking and oozing in raw sexuality. Dressed in jeans and T-shirts that advertised the Thorn-Byrd motorcycle, they all had massive shoulders, solid chests and firm thighs.

She cleared her throat. For the longest moment no one spoke. They just stood there staring at her in a way that made her glance down to make sure her T-shirt wasn't transparent or something. She decided it was time to say something. "You're Delaney's brothers?"

A crooked smiled tipped up the side of one of their mouths. He seemed to be a little older than the rest. "Yes, I'm Dare. And who are you?" he prompted curiously, not taking his eyes off her.

"I'm Tara Matthews, Delaney's friend, neighbor and fellow physician," she said, reaching her hand out to him. He took it and held it, a bit longer than she thought necessary, before shaking it. The others did the same when Dare introduced them. She took a step back. "Please come in. Delaney is in the bathroom."

Tara closed the door behind them thinking they appeared bigger than life. All of them were well over six feet tall. "I thought there were five of you," she said when they still gazed at her curiously.

The one whose name was Stone and whose smile was just as sexy as the one called Dare spoke up. "Our brother Thorn had a last-minute appointment and is flying in. He'll get here in the morning."

Tara nodded as she leaned back against the door while the four men continued to look at her. She started to ask them if anyone had ever told them it wasn't polite to stare when Delaney entered the room.

"I see you guys made it okay." Delaney shook her head when they didn't take their eyes off Tara to acknowledge her entrance into the room. They were behaving like any typical male animals that had an irresistible female within their scope.

"Yeah, we made it," Chase said smiling, but not at her, since his gaze was still on Tara.

Delaney bit her lip to keep from laughing. Most women fawned over Chase's killer smile, but Tara didn't appear the least flattered. In fact, it appeared she was beginning to get annoyed at her brothers' attention, if her frown was any indication. "Hey you guys, let up and give Tara a break. She's my friend."

Storm finally released his gaze from Tara and met Delaney's glare. "What are we doing?" he asked innocently.

"The four of you are checking her out like she's a piece of fried chicken just waiting to be eaten." She then glanced around the room. "Where's Thorn?"

"Not in our side," Chase said, finally breaking eye contact with Tara and turning to Delaney and smiling. His response was the usual one the brothers had given over the years whenever someone asked them about Thorn.

"So where is he?" Delaney asked again, hating it when they gave her their smart responses.

"He had a last-minute appointment, some very important customer he had to take care of, so he'll be flying in tomorrow morning," Dare said, finally turning to look at her and leaving his brothers to finish their appraisal of Tara.

"And how long are you guys staying?" Delaney asked. She didn't want to run the risk of being sick around them.

Dare smiled. "Trying to get rid of us already, Laney?"

Delaney frowned. If she'd had her choice they would never have come. She loved her brothers to death but they could get on her last nerve at times. She didn't want to think about how they were going to handle the news of her pregnancy. "No, I'm not trying to get rid of you, as if it would do me any good even if I were. I just wanted to know for sleeping-arrangement purposes. As you can see this place is rather small, and Tara has graciously offered to put two of you up at her place during your visit."

As she had known it would, that statement got her brothers' attention. All eyes returned to Tara, who merely shrugged and said, "It's the least I can do for a friend, but it seems that I need to put some ground rules in place."

Dare gave her a sexy smile. "Such as?"

"I expect you to be good."

Storm smiled and Tara and Delaney didn't miss the byplay gaze that passed between the brothers. "We're always *good*," he said slowly.

Tara lifted a brow and crossed her arms over her chest. "What I mean is *good* as in good behavior. You're to behave like gentlemen and treat me just like a member of the family."

Chase chuckled. "That's going to be a real challenge since you aren't a member of the family."

Tara laughed. "But I get the distinct feeling that the four of you like challenges."

Storm shook his head, grinning. "Thorn is the one who likes challenges. We prefer things to be made easy for us."

Tara laughed again as she came to stand before them in the center of the room. "Sorry, I don't do easy. Nor do I do hard, just to set the record straight in case you might be curious. I'm not looking for a serious relationship nor am I looking for a nonserious one. In other words, I'm not into casual affairs. I'm single and although I'm a die-hard heterosexual, I'm not interested in a man at the present time. Do we understand each other, guys?"

Dare nodded and smiled. "Yeah, you're definitely a challenge, so we'll leave you for Thorn."

Before Tara could open her mouth and give him the retort Delaney knew was coming, the doorbell sounded. Giving Tara a quick glance, she grinned and said, "Hold that thought," then crossed the room to answer the door.

She opened the door and drew in a breath so sharp her heart missed a beat and a wave of dizziness swept over her. "Jamal!"

Jamal took a step inside and closed the door behind him. Without saying a word and without noticing the other people in the room he pulled Delaney into his arms and kissed her. Automatically Delaney molded her body to his and placed her arms around his neck and kissed him back.

The intimate scene shocked the other five people in the room; four in particular.

"What the hell is going on!" Dare's voice bellowed, almost shaking the windows and causing Jamal and Delaney to abruptly end their kiss.

"No!" Delaney shouted when she saw the murderous expressions of anger on the faces of her brothers when they began walking toward her and Jamal. She leaned back against Jamal, blocking him, and felt him stiffen behind her before he gently eased her to his side.

Her four brothers stopped then, looking Jamal up and down as if he was someone from another planet instead of someone dressed in his native Arab garb.

Likewise, Jamal sized them up. He immediately knew who they were. The gaze he gave each one of them was dispassionate, but his features were fierce, sharp, lethal. He was letting them know he would protect Delaney, even from them if he had to.

"I can explain," Delaney said quickly, trying to defuse her brothers' anger before the situation got too far out of hand.

"You can explain things after he's taken care of," Stone said furiously. "Who the hell is this guy? And what is he doing kissing you like that?" And then, noticing Jamal's arms firmly around Delaney's waist, he met the man's dark stare. "And take your damn hands off of her."

"Stone, stop it!" Delaney all but screamed. "The four of you are acting like barbarians, and you're an officer of the law, Dare, for heaven's sake. If you give me a chance I can explain things."

Delaney stopped talking when suddenly a wave of dizziness and queasiness swept over her and she leaned against Jamal. His sharp gaze left her brothers and concentrated on her, turning her quickly into his arms. "Are you all right?" he whispered in concern.

She muttered a barely audible response, saying softly, "Take me to the bathroom, Jamal. Now!"

Reacting with unerring speed, Jamal picked her up in his arms and followed Tara out of the room, leaving the Westmoreland brothers too shocked by the whole scene to speak.

As soon as Jamal placed Delaney on her feet in the bathroom and locked the door behind them, she sank weakly to her knees in front of the commode and threw up for the fourth time that day. When she had emptied her stomach completely for what she hoped would be the last time, she flushed the toilet and tried standing, only to find herself engulfed in powerful arms.

Jamal picked her up and walked over to the counter and sat her on it. He then took a washcloth and wet it and wiped it over her face. Moments later he placed her back on her feet and while he held her around the waist, giving her support, she stood in front of the sink and brushed her teeth and rinsed out her mouth.

After that, he picked her up and sat her back on the counter and stood in front of her. "The prince is already causing problems, I see," he said softly, as he tenderly wiped her face again with the damp cloth.

Delaney gazed up at him, still amazed that he was actually there with her. Breath slowly slipped through her teeth as she gazed at him. If it was possible, he was more handsome than before. The dark eyes that were looking at her were gentle yet intent, and his chin was no longer clean shaven but was covered with a neatly trimmed beard that made him look as sexy as sin.

She inhaled deeply. She had so many questions to ask, but what he had just said suddenly came back to her. "What did you say?" She needed him to repeat it to make sure she had heard him correctly.

He looked amused but answered her, anyway. "I said the prince is already causing you problems." And this time he placed a gentle hand over her stomach.

She met his gaze. "How did you know I'm pregnant?"

His smile widened. "I had a feeling that you were. I've been dreaming about you every single night since we've been apart, and the dreams were so real that I would wake up in a sweat and sexually spent. And each time we made love in my dreams, I flooded your womb with my seed, which reminded me of the times I had actually done so at the cabin. I believe the dreams were Allah's way of letting me know of your condition."

Delaney nodded and looked down at his hand on her stomach. "Is that the reason you're here, Jamal? For confirmation that I'm having your baby?"

He lifted her chin. "No. I'm here because I was missing you too much to stay away and couldn't think about marrying another woman. So I told my father I loved you and wanted you as the woman in my life."

Delaney's eyes widened. "But what about the princess from that sheikhdom who you were to marry?"

Jamal stiffened. "It seems the princess needed to marry quickly since she was secretly with child from someone else. It was her dishonorable intent to try and pass the child off as mine."

"And what about Najeen? Was she well?"

Jamal lifted a brow, knowing what Delaney was trying to ask him in a roundabout way. He decided to rest her concerns in that area. "I didn't see Najeen. The first night I returned I told my stepmother to make sure she returned to her homeland. She is no longer my mistress."

Delaney reached out and touched his cheek, remembering how he had once said he would never give his mistress up. "Do you regret sending her away?"

He met her gaze and smiled. "The only thing I regret is leaving you, Delaney. I was so miserable without you. The only thing I had to survive on were my dreams," he said, his voice soft and husky.

She smiled. "And I had mine, too. And when I discovered I was pregnant I was so happy."

"How long have you known?"

"I had an idea when I missed my period last week, and then when I started experiencing bouts of sickness throughout the day I thought I'd better check things out. I took a pregnancy test this morning which pretty much confirmed things. I've made an appointment to see the doctor in two weeks." She traced her fingertips softly around his features, especially his lower lip. "How do you feel about me being pregnant, Jamal?"

He grinned. "The thought that you carry my child inside of you makes me extremely happy, Delaney. I didn't intentionally get you pregnant, but I was more lax with you than I have been with any other woman, so I think subconsciously I wanted you, and only you, to have my heir."

Happiness flooded Delaney. "Oh, Jamal."

"And you are the woman that I want for my princess, Delaney. Please say that you will marry me and come live with me in Tahran. There are a number of Americans in your military and private businesses living close by in Kuwait, and if you get homesick we can always come back here to visit at any time. We can even live in your country half the year and in mine the other half if that pleases you. I see my father being king for a long time, which means I won't I have to live permanently in Tahran for a number of years to come."

He leaned over and kissed her lips. "Say yes you will marry me so I can be yours exclusively."

Delaney knew there was no way she could refuse him. Her love for him was too great, and she knew she wanted to be with him for the rest of her life.

"Yes, Jamal. I will marry you."

Filled with joy of the richest kind, Jamal leaned in closer, and captured her lips with his, feeling a jolt of desire shoot down his spine at the contact. His hand moved to the back of her neck, and he ran his fingers through the thick, glossy curls before holding her neck firmly in place to let his mouth make love to hers, wanting to consume her.

He wanted to be reunited with her taste, and he focused his attention on the bone-melting kiss he was giving her. His tongue explored inside her mouth as he licked everywhere before taking her tongue in his and sucking on it in a way he knew would make her scream.

But he didn't want her to scream, or else he would have to hurt her brothers when they broke the door down to see what was going on. So he gentled the kiss, not quite ready to end it. He wanted to taste her some more. He needed to make sure this was the real thing and not a dream.

Jamal continued to let his tongue mate with hers, reacquainting himself with the pleasures he could find only with her.

"What the hell is going on in that bathroom?" Dare asked in a loud, sharp voice as he paced the floor. "I can't believe we're out here and not knocking the damn door down to find out for ourselves what's happening."

Tara glared at him, the same way she had been glaring at the other three since that man had taken Delaney into the bathroom and locked them in. "You're acting just like Delaney wants you to act, calm and civilized, and not like barbarians. She has a right to privacy."

"Privacy hell, she was sick," Stone implored. "And why is he in there taking care of her instead of one of us? We're her brothers."

Yes, but he is the father of her child, Tara wanted to tell them, now that she had figured things out. She sighed deeply. The least she could do for her friend was to keep her brothers under control. "While the four of you are waiting, can I get you to help me with something? I need help with this piece of exercise equipment I'm trying to put together."

They looked at her as if she was crazy. "Nice try, Tara, but we're not moving until we know for sure that Laney is okay," Dare said, smiling at her.

Tara shrugged. "All right. I'm sure it won't be too much longer before they—"

Everyone stopped talking when the bathroom door opened. Everyone who had been sitting down shot up out of their seats. "Laney, are you all right?" Storm asked with a worried look. He glared at Jamal when he saw the man's hand was back around his sister's waist. "I thought you were told about your hands," Storm said, filled with hostility.

Delaney actually chuckled. "Storm, that is no way to talk

to your future brother-in-law." Before anyone could recover from what she had just implied, she said, "I never got around to making introductions. Everyone, this is Sheikh Jamal Ari Yasir of Tahran. We met last month at the cabin and fell in love. Before we could make plans for our future he had to leave unexpectedly to return home. Now he's back and has asked me to marry him and I've accepted."

Mixed emotions went around the room. Tara screamed out her excitement, and the Westmoreland brothers stood frozen in shock.

"Marry?" Chase finally found his voice enough to ask, almost in a shout. "Are you nuts! He's not even from this country. Where in the hell will the two of you live?"

Delaney smiled sweetly. "Although we plan to spend a lot of time in America, we will mainly live in Tahran, which is located not far from Kuwait. All of you are welcome to visit anytime."

"You can't marry him!" Stone stormed.

"She can and she will." The room suddenly became quiet when Jamal spoke to everyone for the first time. The tone of his voice reflected authority, certainty and invincibility. "I appreciate all the care and concern you have shown to Delaney for the past twenty-five years and I find your actions nothing but admirable. But as my intended bride, the future princess of Tahran, she now becomes my responsibility. At the exact moment that she consented to marry me, she fell under the protection of my country. My father, King Yasir, has given his blessings and—"

"Your father is King Yasir?" Dare asked in total amazement.

Jamal lifted a brow. "Yes, do you know him?"

Dare shook his head, still semishocked at everything. "No, of course I don't know him, at least not personally, anyway. But a few years ago while I was in the Marines stationed near Saudi Arabia, I got the honor of meeting him when I was in charge of security for a political function he attended. That meeting left me very impressed with the way he carried himself and the care, concern and love he bestowed on his people."

Jamal nodded. "Thank you. I will pass on to him your compliment." He then studied Dare a moment before asking, "So you have resided in the Middle East?"

"Yes. I was stationed there for two years and I must admit the entire area is beautiful and the Persian Gulf is simply magnificent."

Jamal smiled, pleased at the compliment given to his homeland. "You must visit there again. Delaney and I will have private quarters in the palace and as she has indicated, all of you are welcome to visit."

"Damn," Storm said. "An actual palace?" He grinned. "That day when you told us those tire tracks belonged to a prince, we thought you were fooling." He laughed. "Nobody on the squad is going to believe my sister actually nabbed herself a real-live prince. John Carter walked around with his chest poked out when his sister flew to Tampa and married a professional football player. Just wait until I tell them that Laney is going to be a princess."

Chase frowned at his brother, then turned his full attention to Delaney. Uncertainty and concern were etched in his features. "Are you sure this is what *you* want, Laney? I have to know that this is what *you* want, no matter what *he* wants," Chase said, looking at Jamal. "Is marrying this guy going to make you happy? What about your career in medicine?"

Delaney glanced around the room at her brothers. The deep love and concern she saw in their eyes touched her. Although she had whined and complained about their overprotectiveness through the years, deep down in her heart she knew they had behaved in such a manner because they loved her and had cared for her well-being.

"Yes," she whispered softly, yet loud enough for all to hear. She glanced up at Jamal before turning back to everyone. "I love Jamal, and becoming his wife will be my greatest joy." As well as being the mother of his child, she decided not to add. Her brothers had to adjust to the idea of her getting married. She didn't want to complicate matters with the news that she was pregnant, as well. "And as for my career in medicine, I'm sure it will come in handy in some capacity in Tahran."

"I'm so happy for you, girlfriend," Tara said, smiling brightly and going over to Delaney and giving her a fierce hug.

Storm laughed. "Well, I guess that's that."

Dare shook his head solemnly. "No, that's not that. Thorn doesn't know yet. And, personally, I don't want to be around when he gets in tomorrow and finds out."

Chapter 14

That evening Delaney left her brothers in Tara's care while she and Jamal went out to dinner. Although he had invited everyone to join them, she was grateful they had declined, so she could spend an evening alone with him.

However, they had indicated to Jamal, engaged or not engaged, they expected her to sleep in her bed and *alone* tonight. They had made it clear that until there was a wedding they intended to protect their sister's honor. It had been hard for Delaney to keep a straight face at that one. And eye contact across the room with Tara indicated that her friend had figured out her condition and would keep her secret and would do everything she could to help keep the Westmoreland brothers busy until she returned—which Delaney intended to be rather late.

She nervously bit her bottom lip when she thought about Thorn. He could be rather irrational at times and was more overprotective than the others. She would have to talk to him privately just as soon as he arrived in the morning.

"Are you ready to leave, Delaney?"

Jamal's question broke into her thoughts, and she lovingly gazed across the table at him. Earlier that day, after getting nearly everything straightened out with her brothers, he had left to change clothes and had returned two hours later to take her to dinner.

Tonight he was dressed like a Westerner and looked absolutely stunning in a dark gray suit, white shirt and navy-blue tie. She smiled, thinking he was certainly a very handsome man. His dark eyes held her seductively in their gaze and had been doing so all night. "Yes," she said softly. "But it's early yet. You aren't planning to take me straight home, are you?"

He stood and walked around the table to pull her chair back for her. "No. I thought you might be interested in seeing the town house I've purchased to live in while I'm here."

Delaney raised a brow. "You've purchased a town house? But you just arrived today."

He nodded. "Asalum is most efficient when it comes to handling business matters. He took care of all the details and made the necessary arrangements from the jet while we were flying over here."

Delaney shook her head. She doubted she would ever get used to such extravagance. "Must be nice."

He chuckled. "It is nice, as you will soon see." He took her hand in his as they walked out of the restaurant. "And there is another reason I want to take you to my town house."

Delaney had a good idea just what that other reason was but wanted him to tell her, anyway. "And what reason is that, *Your Highness?*"

Jamal leaned down and whispered in her ear. Even with the

darkness of her skin, she actually blushed, then smiled up at him. "Um, I think something like that can be arranged, Prince."

Back at Delaney's apartment the Westmoreland brothers and Tara were involved in a game of bid whist. Tara excused herself from the next game and went into the kitchen to check on the cookies that she had baking in the oven.

They had ordered pizza earlier, and with Stone's complaint of not having anything sweet to eat, she had taken a tube of frozen cookie dough from Delaney's freezer and had baked a batch of chocolate chip cookies.

Tara smiled, inwardly admitting that now that she was getting to know them better, she liked Delaney's brothers. Although she thought their overprotectiveness was a bit much, it was definitely a show of the love they had for their sister.

She was taking the tray of baked cookies from the oven when Delaney's doorbell sounded. She hoped it wasn't one of the neighbors complaining that too much noise was coming from the apartment. Storm had a tendency to groan rather loudly whenever he lost, which was frequently. She smiled, thinking he was definitely a sore loser.

Back in the living room, Chase got up from the table to open the door. He snatched it open, wondering who would have the nerve to interrupt their card game.

He winced when he saw the person standing there. Damn, all hell is about to break loose, he thought frowning. "Thorn! What are you doing here? We weren't expecting you until the morning."

Thorn Westmoreland shook his head and looked questioningly beyond Chase to the table where his other brothers sat playing cards. At least they *had* been playing cards. Stone had stopped and sat unmoving, like a "stone" right in the middle of dealing out the cards, and both Dare and Storm looked at him as if he was a Martian.

He frowned, wondering what the hell had everyone spooked. Entering the apartment, he walked into the center of the room. "What the hell is everyone staring at? Do I have mud on my face or something?"

Dare, regaining his wits, returned to shuffling the cards. "We're just surprised to see you tonight."

"Yeah," Stone chimed in. "We weren't expecting you until the morning."

Thorn threw his overnight bag on the sofa. "Yes, that's what I heard, twice already. First from Chase and now you guys. So you're all surprised I showed up tonight. What's going on?"

Chase closed the door and walked across the room to reclaim his seat at the table. "What makes you think something is going on?"

"Because the four of you are looking guilty as sin about something."

Dare chuckled. "That's just your imagination, bro." As usual everyone was trying to decipher Thorn's mood and until they did, they weren't making any waves. And they definitely weren't going to say anything about Delaney's engagement. "I take it you got that customer satisfied."

"Yeah, and got a free flight here on his private jet." Thorn glanced around the apartment. "Where's Laney?"

Storm threw out a card. "She went out."

Thorn frowned and checked his watch. It was almost midnight. "She went out where?"

"She didn't say," Stone said, studying his hand.

Thorn's frown deepened. "When is she coming back?"

"We don't know exactly," Chase said, watching his brother, knowing that at any minute they would start seeing smoke come from his ears. It didn't take much to set Thorn off when he was in one of his foul moods. Usually this kind of mood meant he was overdue for getting laid, but it was Thorn's own fault for being so damn nitpicky when it came to women.

Thorn slowly walked over to the table. "And just what do you know, *exactly?*"

Dare chuckled. "Trust us, Thorn, you don't want to hear it. At least not from us. Just have a seat and sit tight until Laney comes home. Or better yet, pull up a chair and join the game. My truck needs a new engine so I need to win some money off you."

Thorn slammed his fist hard on the table, sending cards flying. When he was sure he had everyone's attention he proceeded to say, "I don't know what's going on but I have a feeling it involves Laney. And you guys know how much I hate secrets. So which one of you is going to spill your guts?"

Dare stood. So did Stone, Chase and Storm. Usually it took a combined effort to make Thorn see reason and cut the moody crap. "We aren't telling you anything so sit down and shut up," Dare said through clenched teeth.

At that moment Tara came charging out of the kitchen. She had heard enough. Thorn Westmoreland had some nerve, barging in here at this late hour and causing problems. Just who did he think he was?

Thorn caught her in his peripheral vision the moment she flew out of the kitchen. She stopped walking when he turned and stared at her.

Tara swallowed, wondering why the air had suddenly left the room, making it almost impossible for her to breathe. Her gaze held the muscular, well-built man who stood so tall she had to stretch her neck to look up at him. Dressed in a pair of jeans—and wearing them in a way she'd never known a man to wear them before—he utterly oozed sexuality and sensuality, all rolled into one. He was without a doubt the most gorgeous hunk of man she had ever laid eyes on.

He was staring at her, and his stare was burning intimate spots all over her body, branding her. She blinked, not appreciating the fact that any man, especially this man with his foul mood, could have this effect on her. She didn't have time for such foolishness. Sexual chemistry was too much bother, too time-consuming. Her job and her career came first. Physical attraction, love, sex, babies...and all the other stuff that went with it...was definitely a low priority on her totem pole.

She inhaled deeply, thinking that the best thing to do would be to say her peace and get the hell of out there, on the fastest legs she had. Once she was safe in her apartment, she would try and figure out what was happening to her and why.

With a deep frown she resumed walking until she stood directly in front of Thorn. She placed her hands on her hips and glared at him. "How dare you come here causing problems? Just who do you think you are? The Mighty Thorn? All we need is to give the neighbors a reason to complain. So why don't you do like you've been told and sit down and shut up!"

Taking a deep breath, she then turned her attention to the other four brothers. "I put the cookies on a plate in the kitchen. Help yourselves." After glaring one last time at Thorn, she quickly crossed the room and walked out the door, slamming it behind her.

Thorn forced his gaze away from the whirlwind who had told him off. He slowly turned and looked at his brothers, who for some reason were staring steadfastly at him...with smirks on their faces. "Who the hell is that?"

Dare chuckled as he crossed his arms over his chest. "*That*, Thorn, is *your* challenge."

* * *

The same sexual tension that had totally consumed Jamal and Delaney from the moment he had picked her up for dinner increased by umpteen degrees once he had her settled in the warm intimacy of the Mercedes sports car he was driving. Every look they exchanged was hot.

Delaney knew that each time he stopped for a traffic light he took his eyes off the road and turned his gaze to her. Then there was the hand that he simply refused to keep on the steering wheel—the one he preferred to use to caress her legs and thighs instead. And the short dress she had on made her body all that more accessible. It barely covered her thighs.

Her brothers' jaws had almost dropped when she'd walked out of the bedroom wearing it, but thank goodness they hadn't said anything. The look Jamal had given her had been totally different from her brothers' and she had hurriedly ushered him out of her apartment before anyone noticed what seeing her in it had done to a certain part of his body.

"Open."

Jamal's husky command filled the quiet stillness of the car's interior. Delaney couldn't help but notice his hand had worked its way up her inner thigh. Knowing just what he meant for her to do, she slowly opened her legs while studying his profile intently. His eyes were still on the road but she detected his breathing had shifted from steady to unsteady.

Her eyes fluttered shut when she felt the tenderness of his fingers touch the center of her panty hose between her legs. Boy, she had missed his fingers. Her dream was nothing compared to the real thing. The man was filling her with a purely sexual rush.

Her breathing became heavy when the tip of his finger worked insistently until it poked a hole in her panty hose, to get to just what it wanted. Tonight her panty hose was serving as both panty and hosiery, so once he found his way past the silky nylon all that was left was bare flesh, and his finger found her hot and wet.

"I can't wait to get you home, Delaney," he whispered softly, as his busy fingers continued to touch her, tease her and explore her fully. Her body shivered at the intimate contact, and she felt herself getting hotter and wetter. He felt it, too.

Her mind and thoughts concentrated on what he was doing to her when his fingers began a rhythm that made her arch her back against the seat. She opened her legs wider, which made her dress rise higher on her thighs, thankful that the people riding in the car next to them could not see what was happening inside theirs. Her mouth opened, then closed, along with her eyes, unable to get any words out, just moans…excruciating moans.

"When we get to my place, Delaney, I won't be using my finger. Do you know what I'll be using?"

She slowly opened her eyes and looked at him and saw they had come to a traffic light. He leaned over and whispered hotly in her ear, and the only thing she could think to say was, "My goodness."

Her breath suddenly became shaky and her body began shivering when he began rubbing inside of her harder, increasing the rhythm. The palms of her hands pressed hard against the car's dashboard when everything inside of her exploded, reeling her into a climax. Her body continued to shudder violently.

"Jamal!"

Her head went back and she moaned one final time as pleasure consumed her, slowly leaving her sated, breathless and feeling weak. Once she could get her breathing under control she found the strength to glance over at Jamal. She was too overwhelmed to even feel embarrassed at the fact that he had made her climax in a car while he had been driving with one hand.

"Are you okay, My Princess?"

"Yes," she replied weakly. At some point they had arrived at their destination when she noted he had brought the car to a complete stop in front of a massive group of elegant buildings. As she met his gaze, his lips tilted into an intense sexual smile. He slowly leaned over and placed a light, yet passionate kiss on her lips. "No matter how real my dreams seemed at night, whenever I woke up I could never conjure this."

"What?" she asked softly, barely able to speak.

"The scent of you having a climax. It's a scent that is purely you, private, individual and totally sensual. I wish like hell I could bottle it." He leaned over and kissed her again. "Stay put. I'm coming around the car to get you," he said when he finally released her lips.

She watched as he got out of the car and came around to her side and opened the door. Undoing her seat belt he scooped her up into his arms and, as if she was a precious bundle, he held her gently to him and carried her inside his home.

Jamal took Delaney straight to the bedroom and placed her on his bed. "I'll be right back. I need to lock the door."

Delaney nodded, closing her eyes, feeling blissful yet totally drained. Moments later she slowly reopened her eyes and glanced around. The bedroom was huge, probably big enough to fit two of her bedrooms in. She had noticed the same thing about the other parts of the house when he carried her through to the bedroom. She sat up, and when she noted her dress had risen up past her hips, tried tugging it back down.

"There's no need to pull it down since I'll be taking it completely off you in a second."

Heat filled Delaney's cheeks when she met Jamal's gaze across the room. He was standing in the doorway removing his jacket, which was followed by his tie. Her gaze stayed glued to him, while she watched him undress. She continued to look at him, thinking he was such a fine specimen of a man and that he was hers.

"Jamal?"

"Yes?"

"How soon do you want to get married?"

He smiled as he pulled the belt out of his pants. "Is tonight soon enough?"

She returned his smile. "Yes, but I'd like you to meet my parents first."

He nodded. "Only if you won't let them talk you out of marrying me."

Delaney didn't blink, not once when she said, "No one could do that. I love you too much."

Jamal had taken off all his clothes except for his pants. She remembered the first time she had seen him without a shirt and how her body had responded to the sheer masculinity of him. And her body was responding to him now.

He walked over to where she sat in the middle of the bed. "And I love you, too. I hadn't realized just how much until I had to leave you. Being without you was hard on me. You totally consumed my every thought. There were days when I wondered if I would make it without you."

Delaney looked at Jamal. She knew an admission like that had probably been hard for him to make. "I will make you a good princess, Jamal."

He sat on the edge of the bed and reached out and pulled her into his lap. "Mmm, will you, Delaney?" he asked, smiling. "Are you willing to salaam me each and every time you see me?"

She lifted a dark brow at him. "No."

"Well, then, are you willing to always walk two paces behind me?"

"No. Nor will I hide my face behind some veil," she decided to add.

Jamal couldn't keep the amusement out of his gaze. "You won't?"

"No, I won't."

"Mmm. Then will you be obedient and do *everything* that I say?"

She didn't give that question much thought, either, before quickly shaking her head. "No."

He chuckled as he looked at her. "All right, Delaney, then what *will* you do to make me a good princess?"

She shifted positions in his lap so that she was sitting facing him, straddling his hips. She placed her arms around his neck and met his gaze intently. "On the day I become your desert princess, you will become my desert sheikh. And I will love you more than any woman has ever loved you before. I will honor you and be by your side to do what I can for your people who will become *my* people. I will obey you to a point, but I will retain my right to disagree and make my own decisions about things, always respecting your customs when I do so."

Her gaze became intense when she added, "And I will give you sons and daughters who will honor you and respect you and who will grow up strong in our love and the love of their people. They will share two cultures and two countries, and I believe they will always love and appreciate both."

She inhaled deeply when she added, "And last but not least, I will be your wife *and* your mistress. I will take care of *all* your needs and make sure that you stay extremely happy and never regret making me your princess."

For the longest moment Jamal didn't say anything. Then he kissed her. First softly, then tenderly and finally hotly as his mouth slanted over hers, tasting her fully. He broke off the kiss and slowly stood with her in his arms, her legs still wrapped around his waist.

Placing her on her feet, he pulled her dress over her head, leaving her bare, except for her panty hose and chemise, which he quickly removed. When she stood before him completely naked, he removed his pants and boxer shorts, desperately wanting to be inside of her, with his body stroking hers.

Gathering her into his arms, he placed her back in the middle of the bed and joined her there. "How soon can I meet your parents?" he asked her, pulling her into his arms.

"I'm scheduled to be off this weekend so we can go to Atlanta then. I plan on calling them in the morning and telling them our good news."

"Even the news about the baby?"

"No, I want them to get used to the idea of me getting married and moving away before I tell them they will also become grandparents."

Jamal nodded. "I told my father there was a possibility you were carrying my heir."

Delaney raised a brow. "And what did he say?"

Jamal smiled. "Not much at the time but I could tell that the thought pleased him. He will enjoy being a grandfather as much as I'm going to enjoy being a father."

He then placed his body on top of hers, supporting himself on his elbows. "But right now I want to hurry up and become a husband. Your husband, Delaney."

He leaned down and kissed her, wanting to take their kiss to another level like he had that night in the cabin. After tasting her mouth for a few moments, he pulled back. "Stick out your tongue to me."

She blinked, then did what he instructed, knowing what was coming.

"Don't worry," he said huskily. "I won't let you pass out on me again."

When he captured her tongue in his mouth, she gasped for breath at the intensity of his tongue mating so sensually with hers. She moaned with pleasure when he touched those certain places in her mouth that gave her the greatest sexual gratification. The pleasure was so intense, she began to writhe beneath him and he placed his hands on her hips to keep her still.

He finally let go of her mouth and went to her breasts and paid the same homage there, nibbling, sucking and laving her with his tongue.

"Oh, Jamal."

The sound of his name from her lips was like an aphrodisiac, making him want to taste her everywhere. So he did. The scent of her spiraled him on to new heights, new territory and for both of them, a new adventure.

"I can't get enough of you, Delaney," he whispered against her hot flesh before easing his body upward to enter her. The tightness of her surrounded him, stroking the already-blazing fire within him.

"My Princess," he whispered softly as his body began pumping into her as he held her gaze, forcing her to look at him with each and every stroke into her body.

She wrapped her arms around him and targeted his mouth. "My Sheikh," she whispered before thrusting her tongue inside, intent on taking ownership and making love to his mouth the same way and with the same rhythm that he was using on her body.

Delaney released his mouth to look at him. Each time he

thrust into her, his neck strained and the tension etched in his face showed the degree of strength he had. Each time he pulled out her thighs trembled as flesh met flesh. Then suddenly he pushed deeper, nearly touching her womb, holding himself still inside of her, refusing to pull out.

He lowered his face to hers and came close to her lips and kissed her in such a way that made both their bodies simultaneously explode in ecstasy, as he filled her completely with the essence of his release making the three weeks they had spent apart well worth the reunion.

He strained forward, lifting her hips to receive him as their bodies exploded yet again, making them groan out when yet another climax struck.

And moments later, completely sated and totally pleasured, they collapsed in each other's arms.

A few hours later Jamal leaned forward over Delaney, breathed in deeply to inhale her scent, before kissing her awake.

He leaned back and watched as she opened her eyes slowly and smiled at him. "You can wake me up anytime, Your Highness."

Jamal chuckled and ran a finger along her cheek. "It's time for me to take you home. I did promise your brothers that I would have you back at a reasonable hour."

Delaney reached down and caressed him, and her smile widened. "And of course you will want to make love again before you take me home, right?"

"That had been my plan." He grinned, placing his body over hers. "I will love you forever, Delaney."

"And I will love you forever, too. Who would have thought that what was supposed to be a secluded vacation would bring us together? And to think we didn't even like each other at first."

Jamal leaned down and kissed her lips tenderly. "You know what they say, don't you?" he asked, tracing a path with his tongue down her throat.

"No," Delaney whispered, just barely. "What do they say?"

He smiled down at her. "Things are not always as they seem to be." He kissed her again, then said, "But the love that we share is everything we will ever want it to be and more."

Epilogue

"Another marriage ceremony?" Delaney asked Jamal as they captured some stolen moments in the palace courtyard. All around them, the atmosphere of the desert was hot and humid, yet the fragrance of jasmine and gardenias permeated the air, creating a seductive, erotic overtone. "This makes the fourth."

Their first wedding had been a beautiful garden wedding on her parents' lawn three weeks ago in Atlanta. The second ceremony had taken place last week when they arrived at the palace, with the king, queen and other dignitaries and their wives present. The third had been in the town square, arranged by the people of Tahran as a way to welcome the prince and his chosen princess.

A smile tilted the corners of Jamal's lips. "But think of how much fun we have with the wedding nights that follow each one."

Delaney reached out and placed her arms around her husband's neck, leaned up and kissed his lips. "Mmm, that is true."

She then turned in his arms so her back pressed against his front while his hand splayed across her stomach where their child rested. She didn't think she could ever be as happy as she was now.

Upon her arrival at the palace last week, she was immediately summoned to hold a private meeting alone with Jamal's father, King Yasir. At first the king had presented himself as the fierce, dictatorial ruler, and had relentlessly interrogated her about her views and beliefs.

She had answered all of his questions, honestly, truthfully and respectfully. In the end he had told her that her sharp tongue and tough stance reminded him of Queen Fatimah, and that he knew she would have no problem being understood, respected and loved. He had hugged her and accepted her into the family.

Jamal's sisters, Johari and Arielle, had also made her feel welcome and said they did not consider her as their brother's wife but as their sister. But it was Queen Fatimah who had endeared herself to Delaney's heart forever by meeting with her and sharing some of the things she had come up against as a foreigner in her husband's land and how she had set about changing things, in a subtle way.

She had even suggested that Delaney give some thought to using her medical knowledge to educate the women of Tahran about childhood diseases and what they could do to prevent them. As well, she suggested Delaney could practice medicine in the hospital the two of them would convince the king he needed to build.

"Ready to go back inside, Princess?" Jamal asked, leaning down and placing a kiss on her forehead.

"Is there another dinner party we must attend tonight?" she asked, twisting around to face him, suddenly captured by his dark gaze. Her body began feeling achy, hot and hungry. She wondered if there would ever be a time she would not be sexually attracted to her husband.

"No. In fact I thought that we could spend a quiet evening in our apartment," he said reaching down and tracing a finger along her cheek.

"That sounds wonderful, Jamal," she said smiling. They hadn't found a lot of time to spend alone except at night when they finally went to bed. She enjoyed the nights he made love to her, reminding her over and over again just how much she meant to him and just how much she was loved. She would fall asleep in his arms at night and be kissed awake by him each morning.

"Everyone should fall in love, shouldn't they, Jamal?" she asked smiling.

He grinned. "Yes, but I bet you would never convince your brothers of that."

She nodded, knowing that was true. "But they were happy for us, even Thorn, once he got used to the idea that I was indeed getting married."

Jamal shook his head, grinning. Thorn Westmoreland had taken great pleasure in being a thorn in his side. "Yes, but look how long it took him to come around. I almost had to call him out a few times. I've never known anyone so stubborn, man or woman, and that even includes you. I don't envy the woman who tries to capture his heart. I doubt such a thing is possible."

I wouldn't be too sure of that, Delaney thought. She

An Important Message from the Publisher

Dear Reader,

Because you've chosen to read one of our fine novels, I'd like to say "thank you"! And, as a special way to say thank you, I'm offering to send you two more Kimani™ Romance novels and two surprise gifts – absolutely FREE! These books will keep it real with true-to-life African American characters that turn up the heat and sizzle with passion.

Please enjoy the free books and gifts with our compliments...

Glenda Howard

For Kimani Press

Peel off Seal and Place Inside...

We'd like to send you two free books to introduce you to Kimani™ Romance books. These novels feature strong, sexy women, and African-American heroes that are charming, loving and true. Our authors fill each page with exceptional dialogue, exciting plot twists, and enough sizzling romance to keep you riveted until the very end!

KIMANI ROMANCE ... LOVE'S ULTIMATE DESTINATION

Your two books have a combined cover price of $13.98, but are yours **FREE!** We'll even send you two wonderful surprise gifts. You can't lose!

Two Kimani™ Romance Novels
Two exciting surprise gifts

YES! I have placed my

Editor's "thank you" Free Gifts seal in the space provided at right. Please send me 2 FREE books, and my 2 FREE Mystery Gifts. I understand that I am under no obligation to purchase anything further, as explained on the back of this card.

PLACE
FREE GIFTS
SEAL
HERE

168 XDL E4K4   368 XDL E4K4

FIRST NAME	LAST NAME

ADDRESS

APT.#	CITY

STATE/PROV.	ZIP/POSTAL CODE

Thank You!

BUSINESS REPLY MAIL
FIRST-CLASS MAIL   PERMIT NO. 717   BUFFALO, NY

POSTAGE WILL BE PAID BY ADDRESSEE

THE READER SERVICE
PO BOX 1867
BUFFALO NY 14240-9952

NO POSTAGE
NECESSARY
IF MAILED
IN THE
UNITED STATES

couldn't help but recall how Thorn kept looking at Tara at her wedding when he thought no one was watching. Tara had been her maid of honor, and all her brothers had been openly friendly to her, treating her like a member of the family. But for some reason Thorn had kept his distance. She found that rather interesting.

"What are you thinking, sweetheart?"

"Oh, just that it wouldn't surprise me if there is a woman out there who can capture Thorn's heart. In fact, I have an idea who she is."

Jamal raised a curious brow. "Really? Who?"

Her mouth curved into that smile that he adored. "Um, you'll find out soon enough."

Later that night, after making love to his wife, Jamal slipped from the bed, leaving Delaney sleeping. Putting on his robe, he left the confines of their apartment and walked down the stairs to the courtyard to find a private place to give thanks.

A half hour later on his way back to his apartment he met Asalum lurking in the shadows, always on guard to protect his prince.

Asalum studied Jamal's features. "Is all well with you, Your Highness?"

Jamal nodded. "Yes, my trusted friend and companion, all is well."

Silence filled the space between them, then a few moments later Jamal asked, "Do you know what I'm feeling now, Asalum?"

A smile curved the older man's lips. He had a good idea but asked anyway. "And what are you feeling, My Prince?"

Suddenly Jamal began to laugh. It was laughter of happiness, joy and contentment, and the rapturous sound punctured the silence of the night and echoed deep into the courtyard.

Moments later Jamal spoke when his laughter subsided. "Exultation."

* * * * *

SEDUCED BY A STRANGER

Prologue

"Sheikh Jamal Ari Yasir is on the line, Your Highness."

Turning from the hotel window, Sheikh Rasheed Valdemon nodded before moving across the suite to pick up the phone on the desk. It was the call he'd been expecting. "Has she been found, Jamal?" he asked immediately upon placing the receiver to his ear.

"No, she has not, Monty."

"Damn," Rasheed muttered. That single word was an American form of swearing, an expression of anger, irritation and contempt. However, at this particular moment, for him it represented infuriation to the nth degree.

Sheikh Jamal Ari Yasir of Tahran was the brother of Rasheed's missing fiancée and a man he had always considered a good friend. Both he and Jamal were heirs to the thrones of their native sheikhdoms, and had met in their teens while attending a private boarding school in France.

During those days Rasheed had been called Monty by his friends.

"Jamal, are you sure that she disappeared of her own free will and there was no foul play involved?" Rasheed asked with concern in his voice.

"Yes, Monty, I am sure. Right after she outsmarted her bodyguard and got away from him, she did take time to call Fatimah, my stepmother, to let her know she was safe but needed time to herself. She indicated a need to 'have fun' and would deal with the consequences later."

Rasheed took a deep breath. How dare Johari Nefretiri Yasir, the woman that he had been destined to marry since her birth twenty-four years ago—a marriage that had been arranged by their grandfathers to bring about an allegiance between their two countries—deliberately disappear here in the United States so she could delay her marriage to him and just for the frivolous reason of *having fun?*

For the past two years Johari had been attending Harvard University and now that she had graduated a week ago, she was to return to her native land of Tahran to begin planning for their wedding, which was to take place at the end of the year. Although they were to marry, he and his fiancée had never met. Such a thing was not unusual in their countries. In his opinion, meeting the day of the wedding would have been soon enough.

"Rasheed? Are you still there?"

His mind had been drifting and he forced himself to focus. "Yes, Jamal."

"I want to assure you that she will be found."

Rasheed knew Jamal's words to be true. Johari would eventually be found. But when? Based on Jamal's sister's behavior, Rasheed had sufficient grounds to call off the wedding. It was unlikely that many people would begrudge his decision to sever all ties between them. Considering everything, both families would understand and support such a move on his part since Johari's actions and conduct were not befitting the woman who would sit by his side as the future queen of Mowaiti.

"Monty, my family and I will understand if you decided to—"

"No, Jamal. I am committed to marrying your sister. Our grandfathers deemed it would be so and it will be," he quickly cut in to say.

"Are you certain?"

Was he certain? Rasheed breathed in deeply once again, knowing this was his way to bow gracefully out of the arranged marriage if he chose to take it. After all, he was thirty-nine years old and the thought of having to deal with a twenty-four-year-old whose idea of having fun was roaming around the United States unprotected, unsupervised and un-chaperoned was a bit daunting and something he really wasn't looking forward to. But his father, King Amin Valdemon, was ready for the heir apparent to take his place of leadership and preferably with a queen.

Since puberty Rasheed had enjoyed his choice of women, regardless of race, culture, ethnicity and nationality. And he took pride in the number of mistresses he'd accumulated over the years. They were women schooled in the art of pleasing a man, which made him a little apprehensive about acquiring a bride who lacked the skills and aptitudes he'd grown accustomed to. It was a good thing that in his country retaining his mistresses was acceptable even with a wife.

"Monty?"

His attention was once again drawn back to his conversation with Jamal. "Yes, Jamal. I'm certain that when this is over I will marry your sister." He paused for a moment and then said, "However, there is one stipulation."

"And what is that?"

"I want you to agree to allow me to use my own resources to locate her and once I have, I want you to let me handle things my way…and without any interference from anyone."

There was a long pause and then, "All right, Monty, considering the circumstances, I will grant you what you've asked, and will advise my father and stepmother of such."

Rasheed was only vaguely aware of hanging up the phone and moving across the room to retrieve his cell phone out of his jacket. He was well aware of how much Jamal cared for his youngest sister and for him to agree with Rasheed's stipulation meant a substantial amount of trust. But then Rasheed *had* given Jamal his word that a wedding would take place regardless.

Rasheed would decide on how to deal with Johari once he found her. But first, he had to find her and he knew who could discreetly accomplish that task. He punched into his cell phone the number he knew from memory. Earlier that day, he had parted ways with Alex Maxwell after they had both attended the wedding of Luke Madaris and Mackenzie Standfield.

The phone was picked up on the third ring. "Hello?"

"Alex, this is Sheikh Rasheed Valdemon. There is someone I want you to find for me."

Rasheed fixed a smile to his lips, satisfied because he knew that Alex was the one person capable of tracking and finding his runaway fiancée.

Chapter 1

"How do I look?" Her nerves energized with excitement, Johari Yasir turned from the full-length mirror to face Celine Humphrey. The two had met during Johari's first year at Harvard and had been best friends since.

Cel, who was sitting cross-legged on the bed while flipping through a magazine, glanced at Johari and breathed deeply in frustration. "It's too nice a dress for you to wear the day that you take your last breath, which is precisely what's going to happen when your family finds you. I can't believe I let you talk me into helping you get away from Saud."

Johari couldn't help but grin at the thought of how she had pulled a fast one over on the man who had been her bodyguard since her eighteenth birthday. "I've spoken to my mother to let her know I'm fine. And I've spoken to Arielle, as well," she said of her older sister. "I would call Delaney if I thought Jamal wouldn't try to have the call traced." Delaney was her brother's wife, whom she had gotten very close to over the past eight years.

Johari turned back to the mirror and looked at her reflection. Her outfit, a tiered green lace minidress, was both stunning and flirtatious. It was just one of the many articles of clothing she had purchased earlier that day. It gave the appearance she wanted as an independent woman who was ready to go out on the night and have plenty of adventure.

"I can imagine what your mother said, but tell me anyway," Cel said.

Johari turned back around to Cel and released a long sigh. "Of course Mom wanted me to come home. She thought she would make me feel better by reminding me that there is a twenty-four-year age difference between her and my father, and that they didn't meet until the day of the wedding either, yet they get along beautifully and love each other madly."

Johari paused for a second and then added, "Mom tried her best to assure me that I have nothing to fear in marrying Sheikh Rasheed Amin Hashim Valdemon just because he's fifteen years older. She is confident I will eventually have the same type of marriage she and my father share."

"But you don't think so?"

"No. My father does not have any mistresses. The same thing can't be said of the man I'm to marry. It is rumored that he has several and has been quoted in the press that he intends to keep them even after he's married. That's something I can't accept."

"What about your sister? Didn't you say that she had an arranged marriage, too?"

"Yes, but Karim gave up his mistress before he married Arielle without her having to ask him to do so."

"Have you asked to at least meet with your fiancé before the wedding to discuss your concerns?"

"What good would it do since it won't change anything? Regardless of my feelings, the ceremony will go on so I've decided if I'm going to be stuck in a marriage with a man who I'll be sharing with others, then I want to enjoy some of what life has to offer now."

"What will happen when he discovers you're still in the United States running around and partying and not back in Tahran planning your wedding like you're supposed to be doing?"

Johari shrugged. "There's no reason for him to know. I told Mom I was merely extending my time in this country for another two weeks. The sheikh does not have to know I'm doing so without my bodyguard. At the end of the two weeks I will then contact my family to let them know I'm ready to come home and they will send their private plane for me. Once I'm back in Tahran, I will start planning my wedding like a dutiful fiancée, which should appease everyone."

"But what will happen if—"

Johari threw up her hands. "Please, Cel, no more questions. The only thing I want is for you to get dressed so we can go out tonight and get on the dance floor. Hurry. I only have two weeks before the walls come crashing down and I intend to live it up before that happens."

Cel rolled her eyes as she eased off the bed. "You only have two weeks if your brother's men don't find you first. I wouldn't want to be in your shoes when they do."

Johari tossed her hair back from her shoulders and smiled. "Don't worry. They *won't* find me. I've done a very good job at covering my tracks."

Rasheed walked into the Manhattan night club and found his future wife dancing on top of a table. He stopped dead in his tracks, not because of her outlandish behavior, but mainly because the woman had to be, without a doubt, the most beautiful creature he had ever seen.

Young and vibrant, she had eyes the color of black pearls that could only be found in the Persian Gulf; skin that reminded him of the golden sands of the Sahara; lips that were perfectly shaped; and long black wavy hair that flowed past her shoulders. A pair of dangling earrings swung from her ears and a matching necklace hung around a graceful, beautiful throat.

As Rasheed intently studied Johari, he suddenly felt a tight lump in his throat, and decided there was something about her that had the ability to scramble his hormones and heighten his senses. And judging by all the men gazing at her with lust in their eyes, he knew he wasn't the only one entranced by her beauty.

He hung back, near the club's entrance. An instinct that had him ready to defend his fiancée's honor if he had to roared within him but he forced it back. He also tried to rein in a degree of desire that he hadn't felt in a long time, something that was working its way through his system. He had experienced a strong sexual attraction for a woman before, but not this quick, immediate and deep.

As far as he was concerned, she hadn't needed to dance on a table to get attention. Her looks and her figure would have demanded it anyway. When the tempo of the music increased a beat, she moved in such a provocative way that he found himself holding his breath. She tossed her head back, came close to the edge of the table but knew when to maneuver a few steps backward, never losing her balance while still keeping up with the rapid beat of the music. Her dress was short, way too short, and showing way too much thigh with the movements she was making. He began wondering just what was under that dress. A bra? There was a slim chance. A slip? He doubted it. Panties? For the love of Allah, he hoped so. One sure thing about it, if her aim was to have fun then she was certainly enjoying herself. That much was showing on her face. It looked radiant. Simply glowing. And it was as beautiful as any one face could possibly be. Never had he met a woman whose features were so gut-stirringly striking.

Moving away from the door he glanced around, trying to find an empty table, and when he didn't see one he headed for the bar. He took a seat at the same time the music came to an end, and noticed Johari was helped off the table by some anxious brute. A young Wall Street type who was probably looking for nothing more than a one-night stand.

Rasheed's jaw clenched. Not on his watch and not with his fiancée.

The same protective instinct he had experienced earlier flared again within him and he forced it back down as he erased the frown on his face. As the youngest daughter of a king, Johari Yasir's behavior should be befitting that of royalty—stately, decorous and dignified. With the outfit she was wearing, the dance she'd just performed, and the male attention she was getting, not to mention the way she tossed her head back, sending a mass of black wavy hair flying around her shoulders, how could the male patrons resist her? At that moment, Johari let out one hell of a sensuous laugh that reverberated through the club. With her head tilted back, Johari was the picture of a young woman whose behavior was wild, reckless and apparently out of control.

"What can I get you tonight?"

Rasheed tossed his drink order to the bartender over his shoulder as he continued to watch Johari, who had thanked the man and was now walking over to the table where another woman was sitting. At least she had had the good sense not to come to the club alone.

"Here you are, mister."

He thanked the bartender for his drink, stood up to retrieve his wallet from his pocket to pay his bill and then eased back on the stool. He took a sip of his drink while trying to decide the best way to handle Johari and the situation she had placed him in. He could simply approach her, tell her who he was and then let her know, in no uncertain terms, that she would be leaving with him, calmly, kicking, screaming or otherwise.

However, he had visited the United States on enough occasions, had even lived here for a few years while he, Jamal and a number of his international friends had attended Harvard, so he knew to cause a ruckus by forcing her against her will would be considered unlawful. Although he knew he would be justified because by agreeing to his stipulation her family had virtually transferred her well-being to his care and control.

His limo, which was being driven by his bodyguard and trusted servant, Ishaq, was parked out front, ready to whisk him and Johari to the airport where his private plane sat on the tarmac ready to fly wherever he instructed his pilot to take them. He could return her to her family with instructions that they keep her under lock and key if they had to.

He smiled at the thought and glanced back across the room. He met her gaze the same exact time she met his. And at that moment his reaction to her was once again astounding. Despite his best efforts he couldn't stop the sudden pounding in his chest or the heat that began forming in the pit of his stomach. Conversation was all around him, but everything was blocked out as his total concentration was on the woman who had totally captivated him.

He was hypnotized by the beautiful dark eyes holding his. They were virtually strangers, yet there was something about the look they were giving each other that was far too intimate.

He found it puzzling yet at the same time intriguing. It was only when her friend said something to her, capturing her attention, that she finally broke eye contact with him to look away.

After a few brief moments Rasheed's decision had been made. Johari knew the identity of the man she was to marry only as Sheikh Rasheed Amin Valdemon. Therefore, he would introduce himself as Monty. His surname would be the one he had begun using a couple of years ago while doing business in this country after he'd become an honorary member of the Madaris family.

When she glanced back over at him and their eyes met once again, a slow smile touched his lips. Since his rebellious fiancée wanted to have some fun he intended to make sure she got just what she wanted. But she would be having it on his terms.

"Is there any reason you keep looking at that man sitting at the bar, Jo?"

Johari pulled her gaze away from the sexy stranger with the dark piercing eyes, skin the color of almond, and straight black hair that flowed loosely around his shoulders. He had to be the sexiest man she had ever seen.

Barely catching her breath, she couldn't help but smile. "He is absolutely gorgeous," she whispered. "Every woman here is staring at him. You would be too if you weren't so in love with Gary."

Cel rolled her eyes. "I might be in love but I'm not blind. I checked him out when he walked in." She returned Johari's smile when she said, "I agree. He's absolutely gorgeous."

Johari leaned closer over the table. "So tell me, who is he? This is New York. Do you think he's a movie star?"

"Possibly, although I don't recall seeing him in any movie I've ever watched. I would remember, trust me," Cel said, quickly glancing over at him. "And look how well dressed he is. All the way down to his Italian shoes. Hmm, I think he's an international playboy."

Johari couldn't help but look over at the bar again. He was still staring at her as he sipped his drink. Although the man had an extremely handsome face, there was something about him that hinted at a degree of ruthlessness as well as a level of hardness and intolerance. There was a glint of danger that lurked in the depths of his eyes. What Johari found really unsettling was that she was drawn to him nonetheless. She found such aspects of his character intriguing and totally captivating, mainly because she believed he could also be gallant and charming if he chose to be. And as if to prove that particular point, he picked that moment to smile at her.

It was a slow, sexy smile that curved his lips and as his eyes bored into her, her body reacted in a way she couldn't understand; a way she had never experienced before. Her heart began pounding against her ribs. Goose bumps were forming on her arms and she felt a definite stirring in her stomach. His gaze scanned over her body, analyzing every part of her. For some reason she felt he had a clear view of those regions that were fully clothed. It was as if her little short dress was invisible, and her body was totally naked to his eyes.

Johari thought Cel was right about him being a playboy. Lover of women. International jet-setter. Possibly a billionaire businessman. Thanks to her brother, she knew his type. There was something about him that reminded her of Jamal during his pre-Delaney days. She bet this man could have any woman he chose, wasn't that easily impressed, and possessed the power to render any woman senseless.

Johari's gaze was dragged away from the stranger's when a waitress came to the table to refill her and Cel's drinks. She glanced over at her friend to find Cel watching her. "What?"

A concerned frown marred Cel's forehead. "I'm having second thoughts about flying out in the morning and leaving you here in New York alone."

Johari smiled. Cel would be meeting Gary in Florida, where the two would be cruising to the Bahamas. "I'll be fine and I promise to stay out of trouble."

Cel tore her gaze from Johari to glance over at the man sitting at the bar. "Even with him?" she asked, returning her attention to Johari. "He's still watching you and that can only mean one thing."

Johari lifted a brow. "What?"

"He wants you."

Something stirred within Johari at the thought. She stared at Cel. "He wants me?"

Cel nodded slowly "Yes, he wants you in his bed. I know that look, Jo." Cel glanced back over her shoulder and then looked at Johari and said, "Yes, he definitely wants you. I can feel the heat."

Johari didn't want to admit that she could feel the heat, as well, and now that Cel had fully explained what his interest implied, she could actually feel blood gushing fast and furiously through her veins. Why? Why would the thought of being seduced by a stranger fill her mind with such naughty thoughts?

The answer was quick in coming. Mainly because she had been sheltered all her life. She had lived in a beautiful palace under heavy guard, with chaperones all around and a multitude of bodyguards. As the youngest daughter of King Ari Yasir she had been pampered, spoiled and allowed her indulgences. But she'd also been well protected, shielded and unexposed to certain things. She had attended private girls' schools until the age of sixteen and then she had attended an all-female university in Dubai. At twenty-four she was still a virgin, an expectation by her family and the man she was to marry. Well, as far as she was concerned, the man she was to marry—with all his mistresses—didn't deserve her virginity!

"What are you thinking about, Jo?"

She glanced over at Cel. "I was just thinking about how I'm expected to come to my future husband's marriage bed as a virgin, yet possibly now even as we speak, he is somewhere in some woman's arms since he is not governed by the same rules that I am. He can sleep with anyone he chooses before we marry...or even *after* we marry if he were inclined to do so, and he probably will. I will merely be a wife, someone to bear his children. He will treat me with a degree of respect that is due a wife but he will never love me."

Cel shook her head. "That's really sad. I couldn't imagine marrying a man that I didn't love or who didn't love me."

"It is my duty. It is expected."

"Yes, and that's where our cultures differ," Cel said, taking a sip of her drink. "My duty to Gary, if that's the word you want to use, is no different than his duty to me, and as far as expectation goes, I expect him to be as loyal to me as I will be to him."

"And by loyal you mean to only sleep with you during the entire lifetime of your marriage?" Johari asked for clarification.

"Of course." Cel then smiled and said, "But then as a woman and as his wife, I'm going to do everything in my power for him to have everything he needs at home so he wouldn't think about straying. I will give him all the pleasure he will ever need."

Johari pushed her hair behind her ear as she stared across the table at Cel. Her friend's steady boyfriend of three years, Gary Akins, was a very handsome man and was a graduate of Harvard Law School. There was no doubt in Johari's mind that Gary was as deeply in love with Celine as she was with him and expected a wedding in the very near future.

"So, do you think my future husband would appreciate a woman who is well trained in the art of pleasure more than a woman who knows nothing at all?" Johari decided to ask.

Cel shrugged. "I'm not sure, but a lot of guys swear that they prefer experienced women over virgins in their beds, but a man with such an important title as a sheikh might look at things differently. He may feel a sense of entitlement. The only sheikh I've ever met is your brother. Not only was he handsome but his presence seemed overpowering. I also happened to notice that whenever he would come to the school and visit you, he seemed aloof to other woman, and after seeing his wife I can understand why. She is beautiful, and for him to only have eyes for her leads me to believe that she keeps him happy in the bedroom."

Johari couldn't help but smile. She would be the first to admit Delaney's presence in her brother's life had certainly shaken things up a bit. But everyone in Tahran loved and respected her for that reason. Jamal was an exceedingly happy man and it showed even after almost eight years of marriage.

"I was wondering if I could join you ladies?" The speaker had a deep, masculine voice, filled with strength and sensuality, and his English was perfect.

Johari and Cel glanced up. The handsome stranger was no longer sitting across the room at the bar but was standing beside their table.

Chapter 2

There had not been any doubt in Rasheed's mind that he would wed Johari Yasir, for better or for worse. But now that he was standing beside her chair and staring deep into the darkness of her eyes, there was no doubt in his mind, any time spent with her would be for the better. She was beautiful. Stunningly so.

From the confused look in her eyes, he could tell that she was mystified by the depths of their attraction to each other, which meant she was still very much an innocent at twenty-four. But then on the other hand, she had a willfulness, a wild streak that most women in his country wouldn't think of exhibiting. The very thought that she had defied her parents' wishes to return home, had tricked her bodyguard and was sitting in a nightclub in the heart of Manhattan and without so much as a chaperone, and dressed in a way that invited male attention, was not acceptable.

When seconds ticked by, with neither woman responding to his request to join them, but just sat staring at him, he was beginning to wonder if they had heard his request when the African-American woman blinked and then said, "Yes, you may join us. My name is Celine, but everyone calls me Cel. And this is my friend—"

"Jo," his fiancée quickly said. And he didn't miss the subtle eye exchange between the two women.

"Nice to meet you, Jo and Cel. And I am Monty," he said, following their lead and providing only his first name. He proceeded to take a seat at their table and then glanced between the two ladies. "Are you tourists or natives?" he asked.

"Tourists," Cel said. "We're in town taking in the sights and doing some shopping. What about you?"

His smile widened. It was evident that Celine had made herself the spokesperson for the two. "I'm in the city rather frequently so I have a town house here," he said.

"You're a businessman?"

That question had been asked by Johari. He glanced over at her to respond and the words got caught in his throat. There was a pure lushness in her lips, a sensual full-ness that any man would take pleasure in arousing. Once a woman's lips became aroused the rest of her soon followed suit. Not every man knew the true tricks of the tongue, but he did and wouldn't hesitate to use those tricks to his advantage.

"Yes," he said, forcing the word from between lips he would love to connect to hers, and the thought of her as the one he had been promised to marry and had every right to kiss sent a hot surge of desire through his entire body. "I'm a businessman."

"So you're familiar with all the exciting places?" Johari asked with enthusiasm in her voice.

He couldn't help but chuckle. She was really hung up on

having a great time. "Yes, Jo. In fact, I can take the two of you right now to a club known for its spectacular nightlife."

Her beautiful eyes lifted with more than a tinge of excitement. "Really?"

"Yes. And if you're interested, I have a private car outside that can take—"

"We're interested, but we prefer getting there on our own," Cel quickly cut in to say. "Just tell us where it is."

Celine didn't fully trust him, but he wasn't bothered by it and thought it was a good thing she had her guard up. A part of him appreciated how protective she was on Johari's behalf. "I can tell you where it is located. However, you won't be able to get in without me. It's a private club."

Celine lifted a brow. "How private?"

He knew why she was asking, and again he appreciated her for doing so. "Nothing illegal. The people who are there prefer to be discreet and keep to themselves."

Celine was staring at him and he could tell she still wasn't convinced, so he said, "I tell you what. I'll give you the address and the two of you can catch a cab. I'll meet you there and make sure you're admitted inside."

He saw the looks being passed between the two women and said, "I understand if you're hesitant about going and—"

"No, we'll go," Johari said. Cel, he saw, merely rolled her eyes in frustration.

He smiled. "Okay, and do you want to catch a cab or would you like to join me in my private car?"

"We'll catch a cab," Cel said quickly, not giving Johari the chance to even open her mouth.

"All right," he responded. "It's Club Chandler, located in the Trump International Hotel Towers."

"Trump Towers?" Celine asked, in a voice that said she was truly impressed.

"Yes," he said, pushing his chair back and standing. "I'll meet you there."

"Now I'm really having doubts about leaving you alone in New York," Cel said once they were settled in a cab and on their way to the New York's Upper West Side where Trump Towers was located. "If I hadn't been with you tonight there's no telling where you would be now. That man just said the key words and you were ready to take off."

Johari rolled her eyes. "I didn't bring you along to replace Saud, Cel. I would not have gone with Monty until I was sure he was not a bad person."

Cel stared at her for a moment before asking, "And how were you going to determine that? He's smooth and debonair, that's for sure, and that chauffeur-driven limo confirms he's got money. But still, I'm not all that certain how he got his wealth."

"He told us that he's a businessman," Johari said, looking out the window at the brightly lit buildings they passed. New York was a beautiful city and she had chosen it because her friends at Harvard said it was the place to go to visit and have a great time. She only had two weeks and she wanted to enjoy each and every single day.

"But he conveniently didn't say what type of business he was in. *And* he didn't give us his last name."

"Nor did we give him ours," Johari reminded her friend.

Cel reached over and shook Johari's shoulder to get her attention from looking out the window. "I've been living in his country a lot longer than you have, Jo, and I—"

"You are too suspicious of everyone."

"I just want to be cautious," Cel said.

"And I just want to have fun," Johari implored.

Cel didn't say anything for a moment, and then she opened her purse, pulled out her pair of designer sunglasses and slipped them over her eyes, smiled and said, "Okay, Cyndi Lauper, I get it. The girl just wants to have fun."

At Johari's confused look, Cel gave her a hug and said, "I'll explain it to you later."

"Thanks for taking care of this for me, Keith. And remember, tonight I am Monty to everyone."

Rasheed clicked off his cell phone after talking to the manager of Club Chandler. He then punched in numbers to make another call. A few moments later a male voice came on the line. "Hello."

"I have located your sister, Jamal."

"Praise Allah. Where was she?"

"In New York City, but don't ask me what she was doing when I found her," Rasheed said, shaking his head, remembering. "Trust me, you don't want to know."

There was only a slight pause before Jamal responded. "I'll let my parents know she's been found. Thanks, Monty."

Rasheed then proceeded to make several more phone calls. Fifteen minutes later he was placing his cell phone back in his jacket as his limo moved through the streets of New York, competing with the yellow cabs for the right of way. Unknown to Johari and Celine, one of his men was following their cab in case they decided to change their minds about meeting him at the club. Rasheed had no intention of letting his future wife go missing again.

Whenever Johari spoke, although she had fairly good English, she still carried a Mideastern accent. He liked the sound of her voice. There was something about it that made everything primitive within him respond to it.

When they had walked out of the club to hail their cab, he hadn't missed noticing just how tall, stately and elegant Johari was. Without really trying she had somewhat of a refined air about her, a certain sophistication that was paired with a sensuality so gripping he still was at a loss as to why the magnitude of it affected him so much.

"All is well, Your Highness?"

Ishaq's question interrupted his thoughts. Ishaq's grandfather, Swalar, had served Rasheed as his valet since Rasheed's thirteenth birthday. At the age of seventy, Swalar had retired and his grandson had taken his place almost four years ago. Just like his grandfather, Ishaq was loyal and was employed as both Rasheed's valet and bodyguard.

"Yes, Ishaq, all is well. However, when you and I are in the company of Johari Yasir I want you to skip the *Your Highness* and refer to me only as Monty."

"Yes, Your Highness. Will we be remaining in this country for long?"

Rasheed leaned back against the leather cushions of the car seat and then said, "I'm not sure. I'll have an idea of just how long after tonight."

"Monty Madaris! It's good seeing you again."

"Thanks, Keith, and let me introduce my special guests." Rasheed proceeded to introduce Johari and Celine as merely Jo and Cel.

He glanced around the huge private club. For a Wednesday night there was a huge crowd. Most were celebrities. There were also some wealthy businesspeople and notable creative types from the artistic community. But all were there only by special invitation. The media was not allowed, which afforded an even higher level of comfort and privacy.

"There's a table over there with a beautiful view of the city at night," he said, leading the way and acknowledging the many greetings he received while doing so.

"I can't believe this place," Celine said excitedly. "I could have sworn I saw Hugh Jackman sitting over there."

Rasheed smiled. "Maybe you did. A number of celebrities are in town this week for the premier of Sterling Hamilton's latest movie on Friday night. It appears some people decided to arrive early."

Johari's eyes widened. "The movie actor Sterling Hamilton?"

"Yes. He owns this club."

"He does?" both women asked simultaneously, clearly stunned.

His smile widened. He wasn't surprised Johari had heard of Sterling due to his international appeal. "Yes, it's named after his daughter and is just one of the many business ventures he's involved in," he said.

Johari glanced around and when her gaze returned to his, she smiled and said, "The decor reminds me of a restaurant I once visited back home."

He lifted a brow. "Back home? Are you not from the United States?" he asked. He figured providing that information had been a major slip on her part, one she realized too late.

He saw the nervous look exchanged between the two women before Johari answered. "No."

"And what country are you from?" he asked, as if wanting to know was nothing more than mild curiosity.

"One that is far away," Johari said, looking everywhere but at him.

He nodded and, as if her vague response had satisfied any interest on his part, he then asked, "So what do you think of New York City so far?"

As he'd expected, Celine did most of the talking, with

Johari only adding bits and pieces along the way. That was fine with him since it gave him a chance to study Johari. Green had never been one of his favorite colors on a woman…until now. He'd always preferred his mistresses to wear colors that reflected, preferably red. But there was something about Johari and her green dress that was very pleasing to his eyes. It could have been that the top part of her lace dress was designed in such a way that it displayed the upper swell of her breasts, showcasing her ample cleavage. Full, firm and perfectly shaped, they were perfectly proportioned and could ripen any man's imagination.

Her breasts provided temptation beyond belief and fueled something deep within him. It didn't take much to imagine taking the twin mounds into his hands, placing his mouth to them, using his tongue to lap away at her nipples in such a way that would make her cry out at the pleasure he would stir inside of her.

"Monty, it's good seeing you here tonight."

Rasheed pulled in a deep, calming breath before standing to greet his friend, Roderick Long, well-known former NBA star. "It's good seeing you, too, Rod."

Rod glanced at the two women sitting at Rasheed's table. "Some men have all the luck. Two beautiful women. May I get an introduction?"

Rasheed laughed. "Yes, you certainly may. Jo and Cel, this is an old friend, Roderick Long."

Cel, Rasheed noticed, had managed to close her mouth, which had dropped open when Rod had approached their table. From Johari's expression it was evident that she didn't have a clue as to who Rod was.

Rod reached out and shook both women's hands; first Johari's and then Cel's. "It's nice meeting the both of you, and Cel, would you care to dance?"

Cel seemed surprised by the invitation but recovered quickly enough to say, "Yes, thanks." She stood and Rasheed and Johari watched as she was whisked away without giving either of them a backward glance.

Rasheed smiled. Thanks to Keith and Rod, everything was going according to plan. He needed to have time alone with Johari, without her overprotective friend hovering over them, analyzing his every word.

He glanced over at Johari and could tell she was somewhat nervous about being alone with him. "Would you like to dance, as well?" he leaned over to ask her. "But before you answer I need to give you one stipulation."

Confusion clouded her dark eyes. "And what stipulation is that?"

He leaned in closer and whispered, "In this club you aren't allowed to dance on the tables."

Johari laughed before burying her face in her hands in shame. She then peeked out at Rasheed through spread fingers. "I can't believe I actually did that, but I got carried away. The music stirred something in my heart, and I did what came naturally."

"Why is having a good time so important to you, Jo?"

She dropped her hands from her face, glanced up at him. Who was this man with hard, piercing eyes one minute and gentle, caring eyes the next? And why did she wish she could bare her soul to him? Trust him. Tell him every single thing? It was a foolish notion to even consider such a thing. But for some bizarre reason it seemed as if she had known him her whole life.

"Jo?"

She blinked, suddenly realizing she was simply staring at him while he waited for an answer to his question. She could feel her heart thumping fiercely in her chest and knew that although she couldn't tell him everything, she could at least tell him this much. "In two weeks I will be returning home to my country."

He nodded, didn't say anything for a few moments and then asked, "How long have you been in the States?"

"Two years."

Johari knew Monty was an intelligent man who was well aware that for whatever reason, she was being vague and withholding certain information from him. She didn't expect him to fully understand, but that didn't matter as long as he accepted it. She studied his face, saw his curious expression but hoped he didn't pry further. Already she had placed herself at risk by revealing a few details. There was no doubt in her mind that even at this moment men her brother had employed were diligently searching for her, determined to find her and take her home. They were probably embarrassed that she was able to elude them for so long. A few of her friends from Harvard had gotten word to her that they had been questioned already, some of them more than once.

He stood. "Read to go?"

She lifted a brow. "Go where?"

The corners of his lips lifted in a smile. "To the dance floor, but not the same one Cel and Rod are using."

She glanced around the club and then looked back at him. "Is there another dance floor?"

"Yes. It's on a private balcony with a beautiful view of Central Park. Come on, I'll take you there," he said, holding his hand out to her.

Johari nervously gnawed her bottom lip as she studied his eyes for a second and then his outstretched hand. She met his gaze again and asked, "What if Cel comes back looking for me? She will get worried."

"I'll leave word with Keith as to where we will be." He continued to hold her eyes and then he said in a soft, husky tone, "Trust me to take you dancing and bring you back when you are ready to return. All I want to do is to give you a few moments of enjoyment."

Johari's heart continued to pound in her chest and then she placed her hand in his, felt the strength of his larger one encompassing hers. There was something about his touch that sent heat through her, making her fully aware of him and all his masculine sexuality. The fingers gripping hers were long, firm and strong.

He gently pulled her out of her seat and, still holding tight to her hand, led her through the throng of people and straight to where his friend Keith was standing. "If Cel and Rod ask where we've gone, please let them know we're up on the balcony."

Keith nodded with a smile. "Sure thing, Monty."

Still holding her hand, Monty led her out through a side door. She didn't pull back in hesitation or offer any words of protest. He had told her where they were going and she trusted him to take her there and bring her back just as he said he would do.

The moment they stepped onto the elevator and the door closed on them Rasheed drew in a deep breath. He was not sure just how he felt about Johari trusting him so easily.

He frowned, thinking they had met just hours ago, so there was no way she could be absolutely certain that he was not someone intent on doing her harm. Yet here she stood beside him with her small hand still firmly held by his larger one.

She was staring straight ahead as the elevator moved slowly upward, but his gaze flickered downward to her outfit. He would bet the sum of all his investments that she had never dressed so provocatively before. His thoughts were drawn back to hours earlier when he had walked into that club to find her actually dancing on the table. He could just imagine what Jamal's reaction would have been if their places had been switched and he had witnessed his sister displaying such outlandish behavior. Didn't she know that her family was honor-bound to let her fiancée know of her behavior while in this country? Her rebellious conduct was definitely not something that they could sweep under a Persian rug and easily dismiss.

And to think that this was the woman he was supposed to marry. The woman that he *would* marry.

The thought of that only made Rasheed sigh and shake his head. The sound made her glance up at him. She smiled faintly and he saw something he could very well do without seeing in her. Trust.

"Are we almost there, Monty?"

Her question, spoken in an accent he loved hearing, invaded the quietness of the elevator and disturbed his already unsettled mind. "It's the next floor," he said, and before he could get the words totally out of his mouth, the elevator came to a stop and the door swooshed open.

Tightening his hand in hers, he walked off the elevator with her by his side while wondering if she had any idea that he was taking her to his penthouse. If she didn't know before, she knew now, he thought, when they stopped in front of a set of large double doors. He let go of her hand while he fished the key from his pocket.

"This is where you live when you are in New York?" she asked, her voice silky and inquisitive, and filled with more wonder than caution, reminding him of the trust she had placed in him.

"Yes, I brought you here to dance in private," he said, taking the lock off the door.

What he didn't say was that he had done so because he

only wanted her to dance *with* him and dance *for* him. The thought of another man holding her in his arms was something he wasn't ready to accept. That was strange in itself since he'd never experienced being so possessive of any woman. His only reasoning for that was with a fiancée his emotional attachment could be expected to be different.

He gazed over at her and decided to calm her fears just in case she was doing a good job of hiding them. "If for some reason you don't feel comfortable about being here alone with me, Jo, we can leave and go back."

She held his gaze for a moment as if to consider his words. And then without saying anything she reached out, turned the knob and opened the door. Then, giving him another faint smile, she walked inside.

Chapter 3

Johari stood in the middle of Monty's New York home and turned around, taking in the large and spacious, beautifully decorated room—including all the exquisite paintings that hung on the wall, the marble flooring and the lovely Moroccan rug she was standing on. She didn't have to touch the furniture to know it had been hand-carved and built from the finest-quality materials. This home was a stunning representation of his taste as well as his wealth.

She turned to him. He had followed her inside his penthouse and was leaning against the closed door. He looked breathtakingly handsome and just looking at him almost made her forget the question she'd been about to ask. "You have other homes beside this one?"

"Yes," he said, moving away from the door to walk toward her. She even found his walk attractive—his strides were confident, sexy and so vastly different than the hurried, lazy, untutored walk of the guys she'd met at the university. The guys who had been her age. She couldn't help wondering Monty's age and guessed it to be in the mid-thirties.

"I have another home in Los Angeles. I also have homes in Brazil, London and Dubai."

She winced at the last since it was too close to her home for comfort. The only thing separating Dubai from her homeland was the Persian Gulf. "Dubai?"

"Yes," he said, coming to a stop in front of her. "I purchased it more out of necessity than anything else since my company is involved in a lot of construction there."

She was well aware of all the construction that had now transformed Dubai from the sleepy port town to the most populous. It was the fastest growing city on the Arabian Peninsula and credited most of its growth to tourism, trade and real estate, but the biggest boom came from tourism.

The only other neighboring country that could claim such growth was Mowaiti, which was benefiting largely due to the revenues from petroleum and natural gas. She didn't want to think about Mowaiti since that country's prince was the man she was to marry.

Her curiosity was piqued, so she felt now was a good time to ask, "And what type of business are you in, Monty?"

"I'm a business negotiator, representing several wealthy Americans wanting to do business abroad. I visit the country, scope out the land, so to speak, and help them make decisions as to whether they should invest their capital in such ventures."

She nodded. "And Dubai? What interest do you have there?"

"A group of the men I represent are building a hotel there." His eyebrows arched upward and he said, "I thought you wanted to dance."

She wondered if that was his way of saying he had answered enough of her questions, as many as he intended in order to appease her curiosity. She tilted her head back and smiled up at him. "I do and you have a beautiful home."

"Thank you and I will take you to the balcony now."

She followed as he escorted her from the living room through several other spacious rooms. Each one had wall-to-wall windows that provided a beautiful view of New York City's skyline. She couldn't help but admire the decor and when he opened a pair of French doors that led to a huge balcony, she almost lost her breath when she stepped out onto the mosaic tile floor.

There were several huge balconies surrounding the palace in Tahran where she'd lived, but what was so spectacular about this particular one was that it stretched out to include a lap pool. And just like Monty had said, there was a miniature dance floor that opened to a covered minicourt.

She looked upward, to see the beautiful June sky and then leveled her gaze to see beyond in the distance the glistening waters of the Hudson River. City lights lining Central Park beckoned below. Every single element combined with a magnificent force to provide such a majestic and panoramic view.

She turned to Monty to find he was looking at her. Her skin felt heated from the intense look she saw in his eyes. But his piercing gaze did not scare her. She actually felt safe with him.

"It's beautiful, Monty," she said simply. Truthfully.

The smile that touched his lips stirred something within her stomach. "Thank you. Because I travel quite a bit, I don't get to spend as much time here as I'd like."

"And the dance floor? Is there a story behind it?"

He shrugged. "I'm told that this place was once owned by a world-renowned ballerina who had the dance floor installed.

I considered removing it several times but never got around to doing so. Now I'm glad I didn't."

He took a step toward her. "Enough about this place," he said, bestowing a charming smile on her once again; one that had her heart literally pounding in her chest. "I brought you here to dance, so excuse me while I put on some music. Anything in particular you'd like to dance to?"

She shook her head. "A mixture of tunes would be nice."

"All right."

He then excused himself to walk the few feet to where a console had been built into the wall. With the press of a button the lights dimmed and music began playing. A fast song with an electrifying beat. Automatically Johari began tapping her feet as she felt the energy flow through her body. She loved dancing and unbeknownst to her parents, some of the young girls who lived on the grounds of the palace had taught her how to belly dance. And on more than one occasion she would join them when they rehearsed for their upcoming performances for her parents.

She closed her eyes as she kicked off her shoes, thinking there was just something about dancing that she found totally exhilarating, mystifying. She imagined herself back in her homeland, surrounded by the jewel-colored walls in the palace while dancing. In a room that was her private sanctuary, where she would dance to the rhythm for hours on end.

Her movements went on and on, taking her dance from an art form to an expression, a mode of nonverbal communication that had a language all its own. The music flowed within her and she became one with it. This dance was different from the one she'd done earlier on the table. Even then she had held back, but now she was letting go, feeling free, enjoying her audience of one. Dancing her heart out. For one particular man.

Moments later the music stopped and the movements of her body along with it. She breathed in deeply before opening her eyes and looked across the room. He was there, standing in the shadows watching her. He had given her space. He had let her dance. He had granted her a moment of bliss. She couldn't help but throw her head back and laugh, happy for the opportunity to unwind in a way she found so invigorating.

She held his gaze, while feeling emotions she had never felt before. She pulled in a deep, calming breath and whispered. "Thank you."

Rasheed thought he should be the one thanking her. He continued to stare at her. He had been totally mesmerized throughout her entire dance. At one point he thought that she would shimmy out of her clothes. Her movements had been precise, filled with sensuality, and had conjured up an unstoppable and unquenchable desire in his core. He knew it wasn't her intent, doubted that she was even aware that the dance she had just performed was a mating dance.

In motions he could define only as a combination of a belly dance, ballerina twirls, booty-shaking and hip rolling moves, she had rendered him totally spellbound. Thanks to her short, sexy dress he had seen a pair of creamy thighs, long luscious legs and a gorgeous pair of bare feet. She had perfect body structure and he detected strength as well as an elegant refinement in every bone in her body.

His heart had begun pounding in his chest at the intensity with which her dance touched him, stirred something primal and elemental deep within him. And he knew he would have answered the call if she had intentionally thrown it out there. Innocent or not. Her dance had had that sort of an effect on him.

He pushed a button to play another song. This time he

would slow things down a bit. And this time he would participate.

With labored breathing, Rasheed moved toward her and when he got within a few feet, he offered her his hand. She glanced at it, inhaled deeply before moving forward, covering the distance separating them.

Her movement across the floor to him, even in bare feet, had been graceful, so much to the point he marveled at her smooth execution. The moment Johari took his hand, Rasheed gently pulled her into his arms. Her body seemed to know it belonged to him; it meshed with his so fluidly and with a precision that was so perfect, he automatically felt his gut tighten at the contact.

He wrapped his arms around her in an appropriate manner, fighting the urge to run his hands across the center of her back and even lower to cup her curvaceous backside.

The scent of her perfume hung in the air, tantalized his nostrils, and made him wonder about things that he shouldn't. It wasn't that he didn't have the right to think of them, because he did. He just preferred not doing so at the moment. It was taking all his willpower to keep his mind on the fact that she was not just any woman he wanted in his bed. She was the woman who had been chosen to share his name, take his seed into her body and bear his children.

He couldn't argue with the fact that she was a puzzle, one he didn't necessarily need to figure out since he understood her motive in doing what she'd done. He had rebelled once or twice in his lifetime. But although he might understand her actions, it didn't necessarily mean he agreed with them. The reason he saw her as a puzzle was because there were so many things about her that should not be affecting him, yet they were and he needed to know why.

Such as, why did the thought of tasting her lips, feasting on them in a way that would brand them totally his, fill him with such emotion and intensity? Why did inhaling her perfume want to make him strip her naked, and why did the feel of her in his arms tempt him to do more than just dance with her?

With his chin resting on the crown of her head, he closed his eyes as their bodies began swaying in time to the music. The slow beat of the song was vastly different from the fast-paced one of earlier. But this rhythm was what he needed right now. He needed to know how well they fit together, how so much blatant, raw sensuality floated from within her while at the same time she was shrouded with such an angelical air.

He couldn't help the smile that crept onto his face at the thought of her having even one strand of an angelic hair on her head, especially after that hip-shaking, body-rolling dance she'd done. And her determination to have fun at any cost, even at the risk of angering her family and a fiancé, would also put her angelic status at risk.

Rasheed opened his eyes at the same moment that he drew in a ragged breath. Her cheek was resting against his chest and it felt warm, at home, and so right. Knowing if they remained in this same spot too much longer there would be no way he could control his desire for her, he increased their movements when the tempo of the music picked up somewhat. He pulled away from her slightly to waltz her around the dance floor when the rhythm smoothly advanced.

She laughed at the unexpected move and he savored the sound of her laughter in a way that obliterated all thoughts from his mind except one. And when the music made another transition, one that returned to the ultraslow beat of before, he tightened his hold on her hand and pulled her back to him, back into his arms, close to his body.

She gasped when she detected his aroused state but there was no way he would apologize for it. No, he was fighting everything within him to stay in control of the situation where she not only looked but also felt utterly compelling.

His gaze drifted downward to her mouth and those lips that he longed to taste. They had the ability to make him lose his breath just from looking at them and were sending a rush of heated desire through every part of his body. And when the music finally drifted to an end, a surge of sensuous sensations shattered within him and it was too late to even consider stopping what he was about to do.

He lowered his mouth to hers, fully convinced that, as her fiancé, he had every right to do so. And when his lips touched hers, when he felt how they quivered beneath his, when he was introduced to her taste and sensed her innocence, he no longer saw it as a right but as a privilege.

Rasheed wanted to believe that his longer-than-usual drought without sex was the reason he was latching onto her mouth like a man starving to taste the sweetness of her lips, to mate hungrily with her tongue, brand it, introduce his to hers. But he knew the moment he inserted his tongue into her mouth, immediately caught hold of hers and began sucking gently, that he would claim whatever excuse was out there. And when he heard a moan from deep in her throat, he wrapped his arms around her and drew her closer to absorb her warmth, accept her sensuality and make known—as much as he could and only to himself—that she was his. Totally. Irrevocably. Absolutely.

And his tongue, the one that was licking and tasting every corner of her mouth in heated bliss and slow, deliberate exploration, was boldly staking a claim at the same time as it was giving her an introduction. It was hers, the only male tongue that would ever go inside her mouth, and he wanted her to get used to it. Its daringness, its heat and its texture. His tongue could be rather tender at times, raunchy and brash at others. And on its really naughty days his tongue, she would discover, could steal the very breath from her body and make her whimper with a need that only he would be able to satisfy. And more often than not, his tongue had a mind of its own. A mind to please with an intent to deliver.

Knowing he could stand there and kiss her all night, ply her lips until her mouth was tender, he forced himself to pull back, pull away. The disappointment on her face when he did so was simply priceless.

She was gazing up at him with astonishment and then he watched as she drew in a ragged breath as the magnitude and the power of what they'd just shared threatened to overcome her. When she began shivering he reached out and pulled her closer into his arms.

This was the woman he had looked upon marrying with disdain, and with a degree of regret that made him inconsolable. When his father had summoned him to the palace and said he wanted him to be wedded by his fortieth birthday, which meant he would have to take her as a wife by the end of the year, it seemed he would finally become the ultimate sacrifice for Mowaiti.

He was a man who had been single a long time. He was set in his ways and he enjoyed women. Experienced women. And the very thought that he would have to marry a woman who was young, inexperienced and didn't possess any of the skills and aptitudes on the ways to please a man had nearly driven him into a depressed state.

His life, as he'd known it, was taking a turn for what he considered the worse. He had left the country to visit Whispering Pines, the huge ranch in Texas owned by his good friend and occasional business partner, Jake Madaris. Rasheed had needed the time alone to accept the changes that would take place in his life and had stayed in seclusion at Whispering Pines for a little more than a week.

He glanced down at Johari and pulled in a deep breath, not certain as to what to say now. This was not supposed to be happening to a man of his stature, distinction and eminence. His reaction to a fiancée, one who had been promised to him for twenty-four years, baffled him. He was well aware that some men thought highly of their wives, some even fancied themselves in love, but he knew such a thing wasn't possible for him.

He had no intention of ever truly settling down with one woman or falling in love with one for that matter. Such a thing was not even a consideration. He enjoyed his mistresses immensely. He liked the attention they gave him, the pleasure they delivered to him. He was hard-pressed to believe one woman was capable of replacing all of that…no matter how sweet her lips tasted.

What he needed to do, and what he would do, was to focus mainly on seducing Johari to his will. She would discover that he was a force to be reckoned with, and a defiant, rebellious, wild and reckless wife was one that he would not tolerate.

He shifted his attention back to her when she slowly pushed out of his arms, tilted her head back and looked at him. He saw the considering frown settle first on her forehead before slowly moving down her face then to her lips. Lips he had just thoroughly kissed. Intimately claimed.

"We should not have done that, Monty."

Her words, spoken in a soft, panic-filled voice, gave him pause. "And why not?" He wondered if she had failed to notice that although she had taken a step back, his arms remained wrapped around her waist in a very possessive hold.

She stared at the buttons on his jacket before lifting her gaze back to him. "Because I am promised to another."

His brow lifted in mock surprise. "You're engaged?"

"Yes."

He freed one hand from around her waist to lift her hand. After glancing at it, he looked back at her. "No ring?"

"In my country such a thing isn't needed."

"Maybe it should be," he decided to say. "In this country unless a woman wears some visible sign of a man's intent, she is not off-limits."

"But that is not how things are where I am from."

"And where are you from, Jo? You never did say," he countered.

She shivered again just seconds before saying, "And I can't say. It matters not."

Her eyes once again returned to the buttons on his jacket, but this time he reached and lifted her chin so their eyes could meet. "Keep your secrets, just as long as you know that no matter how much you might regret kissing me, I don't regret kissing you."

He then checked his watch. "Come on," he said, taking her hand and holding it firmly. "I need to get you back to Club Chandler before Cel summons the NYPD."

Chapter 4

"Have breakfast with me in the morning, Jo."

Johari glanced over at Monty. He was standing with his back against the wall in the elevator that was returning them to Club Chandler.

"I don't think that is wise," she said in a low voice. She wondered if he'd been able to tell that the kiss they had shared moments ago had been her first. She also wondered if all men kissed that way—with an ability to demolish a woman's senses, make them want to explode from the heat of passion. Her mouth still tingled from his intense kiss, and she could swear their lips had produced fiery sparks.

"If you're nervous about being alone with me, then let's invite Cel to dine with us."

His words pulled her thoughts back in and she shook her head. "That's not it, Monty. If I were nervous about being alone with you I wouldn't be alone with you now. And as far as Cel being invited, that's not possible because she is flying out in the morning."

He lifted a brow. "She's leaving New York?"

Too late Johari wondered if she'd said too much and figured if she had there was no way to retract it. "Yes. She's meeting her boyfriend in Florida to go on a cruise to the Bahamas."

"So you will be here in this city alone?"

Johari swallowed. She could say that she wouldn't be alone, that her fiancé would be flying into the city to join her. But for some reason she couldn't bring herself to do that. "Yes, I will be alone."

"So will I. Is there any reason we can't spend tomorrow together?"

A rush of sensations tore through her veins. She could think of several reasons and the way her body was reacting to his very presence was one of them, definitely topping the list. "I told you that I'm promised to someone."

"Yes, but I would think we can spend time together as just friends. Besides," he said, drawing out of the shadows where he was leaning against the panel wall to come stand before her, "I would hate for you to miss out on experiencing more excitement before returning home. I have the ability to take you not only around this city but anywhere else you'd like to go in the world."

Johari tried downplaying her body's reaction to his closeness as she attempted to take in what he'd just said. "Anywhere in the world?" she asked, looking at him with stunned eyes.

"Yes. Because of my business I have a private plane."

She nodded. Her family owned several private planes and she frequently went with her parents on trips. But as usual they were accompanied by heavy guards and chaperones.

There had never been a time when she was allowed to just go off and enjoy anything and anyplace by herself. The thought of doing so now was tempting.

She doubted Monty knew just how tempting it was. She studied him, saw the darkness in his eyes, felt heat radiating from him, then she quickly concluded that maybe he did know. She wondered what he thought would be in it for him. What he would get out of spending time with her? It was quite obvious he was a man who had been around. A man used to certain things. Money. Women. Sex.

"Why, Monty?" she decided to ask. "Why would you do that for me when you know there is nothing that I can do for you?" There, she'd asked, hoping she couldn't have made things any plainer than that.

"But there is something you can do for me. You can keep me company for as long as you can. You remind me of what it's like to be carefree. You want to do something that I haven't done in a long time and that is to just enjoy life."

He chuckled and said, "I've been told by a lot of people that I work too hard, don't have enough downtime for myself."

Johari nodded. She could believe that. Her brother had been the same way until he'd decided to take a month off and do nothing. That was when he had met Delaney.

She glanced up at Monty and decided to ask another question, one she'd been curious about since meeting him. "How old are you?"

A curve of a smile touched his lips. "How old do you think I am?"

She studied his features. His eyes, she thought, were full of intelligence way beyond whatever years she would guess. And she had reason to believe he possessed a razor-sharp mind. His features were magnificent, surpassed any woman's fantasy, the substance of any woman's dream. He was extremely handsome and didn't look any older than Jamal, but then her brother carried his age of forty-two well. "Um, around thirty-five or thirty-six?" she finally said.

He laughed. "I'm whatever age you want me to be. And that's all I'll say on the matter."

She smiled. "You're not curious as to my age?"

"Not enough to ask. In this country a man knows better."

She couldn't help but chuckle. "So I heard."

When the elevator came to a stop and the door opened, he took her hand as they stepped out into the hall. He turned to her. "So, will you meet me for breakfast in the morning around nine? There is a nice café on the corner of Fifth Avenue and Park. I will send my car for you. And then after breakfast we can start our day."

She gnawed on her bottom lip for a few moments. She didn't want him to send his car for her because she was not ready to let him know where she was staying. Succumbing to the desire to see him again, spend time with him, she nodded. "Yes, but I will take a cab and meet you there. And please don't mention anything in front of Cel. She would worry."

He gave her a satisfied smile. "I promise not to say a word."

Relief rippled through her. She didn't want Cel to not enjoy her cruise for agonizing over Johari's safety. "There is another promise I'd like you to make if we are to spend tomorrow together."

"What promise is that?"

"You will remember that I have a fiancé."

A smile touched his lips. "Although I wish I could forget, I promise that I will not."

Two hours later Rasheed was back in his condo and reliving in his mind all that had transpired that night. He and Johari had returned to the club to find it was still in full swing.

Cel had eyed him suspiciously but hadn't asked either of them any questions. And less than an hour later, she and Johari had thanked him for such a wonderful time but felt it was time for them to leave. He had offered to let his driver take them to their hotel, but they had declined. He had, however, made sure they had gotten safely in a cab. Once the yellow taxi had pulled away from the curb he had nodded to the driver in the dark-colored car who'd automatically followed close behind.

Shoving his hands into his pants pockets, he walked outside on the balcony, the same one Johari had danced on earlier. Moving closer to the very spot where she'd stood, where she had danced, he glanced around. He could still feel her presence as well as the heat she had left behind. Then there was her lingering scent. It was her scent that was gripping him, inside and out, making him remember how sexy she had looked in that dress and how well the material had fit her curves. And it was that dress, her scent, along with the memory of her taste that had him looking forward to seeing her in the morning.

Her taste.

It was as if his tongue had known her. Had been waiting. Had gotten possessive. And had greedily taken. He considered himself a very skillful kisser, but the first taste of her had nearly snatched his senses, rendered him mindless. And when she had touched her tongue to his, not sure if it was the proper thing to do, exposing her lack of experience, he'd been fascinated beyond belief in knowing that had been her first kiss.

And when he'd angled his head and deepened the kiss, every bone in his body shared in the pleasurable experience. And not once did she resist. She had returned the kiss, as best she knew how, and instead of boring him, her inexperience plunged him into a world filled with so much passion and pleasure, the concept of her being able to accomplish such a feat was still wearing on his brain.

He drew in a calming breath when he thought of the phone call he'd received moments ago to say that Johari and Cel had arrived at their destination safely.

Turning, he walked back inside the condo. It was late and time for him to take a shower and go to bed. Things had been rather interesting tonight and he looked forward to seeing Johari for breakfast in the morning.

Johari eased out of bed, hoping the noise would not awaken Celine. In bare feet she slid open the glass door to walk out onto the balcony. After she had slid the door shut behind her, she looked around, thinking this balcony was nothing compared to the one she had been on earlier. The one she had danced on for Monty.

Monty.

She still didn't know his age, since he'd been evasive about it, and then there was the question of his nationality. If he was American, and she leaned toward believing that he was because of his mastery of the English language, then he was of mixed ancestry, which was obvious with the shade of his skin. But then he could very well be of Greek, Italian or Turkish descent.

She pulled in a deep breath. There was so much about him that she didn't know.

Likewise, there was a lot he didn't know about her.

She did, however, know that his last name was Madaris, thanks to the man at the club. And on the cab ride home Cel did tell her the little bit of information she was able to get out of Roderick Long. Monty was a wealthy businessman with a strong connection to the Madaris family from Texas. And according to Cel, the Madaris family name was incredibly popular in Texas, especially Jacob Madaris, who was married to a movie star named Diamond Swain.

Also, she and Cel had compared notes in regard to what Monty did for a living and Rod had verified the information about his occupation that Monty had shared with her. He owned a very successful company representing wealthy businessmen in the global market.

Her thoughts then shifted to the kiss she and Monty had shared that night. At first, the intrusion of his tongue into her mouth had shocked her, but when he had basically locked their mouths, she got carried away by his sensuous skills, and had no choice but to become a willing participant. Sensations she had never experienced before took over her mind and parts of her body and she had no regrets of her involvement. Even now while reliving the memories, the nipples of her breasts, which were pressing against her nightgown, felt hard, sensitive. And although maybe she shouldn't, she felt excited about meeting Monty for breakfast in the morning.

She yawned, at once feeling sleepy, and hoped that when she returned to bed she would immediately drift off and not be tortured with dreams of her and Monty doing things they had no business doing.

Covering her mouth when a second yawn escaped, she returned inside and then moved slowly toward her bed, hoping morning would arrive quickly so she could gaze into Monty's eyes once again.

The next morning Rasheed sat in the plush café keeping a watchful eye on the door, wanting to make sure he saw Johari when she arrived. He had gotten a call from his man a few moments ago to say she had left the hotel and was en route to the café in a cab and would be arriving any second.

He leaned back in his seat and smiled when he thought

about the call he had placed earlier to Christy Madaris Maxwell. Since Christy was only a couple of years older than Johari, and since he figured his idea of *fun* would be vastly different than what Johari's would be, he had asked Christy for suggestions on what activities Johari might find to her liking. Christy thought spending a day at Coney Island would be enjoyable.

He could make no excuses that his definition of *exciting activities* leaned more toward the sexual side and could think of a number of spine-tingling things he would love doing with Johari. The thought of licking her from head to toe—especially savoring the area between her thighs—certainly sounded very delightful and pretty much topped the list. Performing such an act would definitely provide a form of entertainment for him he hadn't had in a while.

He was convinced his state of abstinence was the reason a deep pulse was throbbing in his middle section, behind the zipper of his pants. Kissing her was like a match being tossed into a barrel filled with dry leaves. And his dreams last night hadn't been much better. He had actually dreamed of making love to her and in his dream he had enjoyed it a lot more than any of the times with his mistresses. To envision such a thing had him wondering how much wine he'd drunk last night before finally going to bed.

Whatever other thoughts were filtering through his mind suddenly dissolved when Johari walked into the door. His mouth fell open and he could only sit there and stare. Last night he had thought she was beautiful. But now in the brightness of daylight, beneath the rays of the sun, she literally took his breath away.

There was an early-morning glow to her features and for some reason he felt the smile on her lips was meant just for him. And gone was the minidress from last night. Today she was wearing a pair of jeans and a blouse, and she looked absolutely stunning.

He stood when she moved toward his table. Ignoring the lust-filled looks from the other men who had stopped eating to gape at her luscious curves encased in formfitting jeans, she walked with the ease of someone who had an ingrained sense of grace and style. A sense of pride filled his chest knowing the woman that they were feasting their hungry eyes on belonged totally to him.

When she reached his table she nervously licked her lips, and the body part behind his zipper that had been throbbing all morning in anticipation of seeing her again and inhaling her scent suddenly wanted to misbehave.

"Good morning, Monty."

He thought, just like her looks, her voice had a breathtaking quality, as well. And there was a silkiness to it that flowed across his skin, had desire taking refuge in several of his body parts. "Jo. You look beautiful this morning," he said, responding to her greeting while inwardly frowning at the thought that he was behaving like an anxious suitor. "And thanks for joining me."

"Thank you for your invitation."

When she took a seat he did likewise. The waitress who'd known he was waiting on someone brought over menus. "Thank you." He then glanced over at Johari. "Has Celine left the city?"

She smiled over the menu at him. "Yes. It was a straight flight and she's called to let me know she made it to Miami."

He nodded. "That's good to hear." Then after glancing at his menu a few moments, he asked, "Do you see anything you would like?"

She smiled up at him and closed her menu. "I'm not a big eater so a bagel and cocoa will be fine."

Deciding since he was a big eater and needed more than that, when the waitress returned he gave her their breakfast orders. He saw Johari looking at him with a smile on her face. Automatically his gaze was drawn to her lips and remembering how perfectly they had fit his last night sent all kinds of sensations radiating through him.

He shifted his focus to her eyes, and with a slow smile he leaned over the table and asked in a low voice, "May I ask what you find so amusing?"

"Your appetite," she whispered, returning his smile. "You eat as much as my brother."

Rasheed arched a brow. "You have a brother?"

She said nothing for a moment while staring at the silver-ware, and he studied her, thinking that once again she had said something she would have rather kept secret.

He didn't intend to let her off that easy. "Jo?"

She lifted her head. "Yes, I have a brother, but I prefer not talking about him."

"All right."

She held his gaze for a moment. "Are you always this easy?"

Rasheed almost muttered at the absurdity of that claim because he was not an easy person by any means. Although most of the people of Mowaiti considered him a fair man, one who would go to any lengths for their needs, they knew on certain issues he could be as difficult as crossing the Sahara Desert. He had matured a lot over the past few years and was no longer the hothead that he used to be. The two things about him that hadn't changed were that he always put the people of Mowaiti first and he chose his friends wisely.

"No, I'm not always this easy," he finally said, laughing softly. "I've made you an exception."

"And I appreciate you for doing so."

Instead of responding Rasheed simply looked deeply in her

eyes as he took a sip of his coffee. When his carefully laid-out plans came to light he doubted that she would appreciate anything about him. He couldn't remember the last time, if ever, he had gone out of his way to pursue a woman. And the thought he was doing so now and the object of this mad obsession was the very woman he would marry added a degree of intrigue to the chase. And what made it even more tantalizing was that Johari had no idea she was game. What a pity.

The waitress brought their breakfast and when she began eating so did he, taking every occasion he could to look at her. Every time he did so he couldn't help but remember their kiss and couldn't help imagining how it would be to kiss other parts of her body. Specifically, he would love for her to bare her breasts with the sole purpose of him tasting them and could just about envision the texture of her nipples on his tongue.

And then there was the area between her thighs, which was considered a woman's hottest as well as her sweetest spot, and he would love for his tongue to enjoy her there, as well. He was having a challenging time keeping his hormones in check this morning and sooner or later he would have to do something about it. But then there was that promise he'd made to her that he would not forget she was promised to someone. Since that someone was him he doubted he would forget, so there was no chance of him breaking that particular promise.

And, he thought further, if she assumed remembering she was promised to someone meant he wouldn't be trying his hand at seduction, then she was sadly mistaken.

It took everything within Johari to sit and eat her breakfast without staring across the table at Monty, although she was very aware that he was staring at her. She could actually feel his eyes roaming over her.

A few times she had glanced up and seen the heat that was sweltering in his gaze. *Also in his gaze was another promise, one she hadn't asked him to make.* She had seen that look before in the eyes of guys around campus. Most of them knew she was a princess from another country and Saud's presence only made her a challenge to some of them.

When her bodyguard continuously foiled any of their zealous plans they had resorted to relaying their ardent desires through eye contact. She had dismissed the looks as a waste of their time and hers. But for some reason she couldn't do the same with Monty. It was as if his look had substance, a lot more confidence. His eyes didn't broadcast a look of what he wanted and could not have, but what he figured he would get eventually. In the meantime he would be content to patiently wait. All of that confused her since he had made her that promise and she believed he would keep it.

Now if she herself could remember she was promised to someone. Monty was making it very hard for her to do so. If she thought he oozed sexuality last night then he was really overflowing with it this morning. During the cab ride to meet him, she couldn't help wondering why he would want to spend time with her today. There was no doubt in her mind that with his worldly air and handsome features, he could have just about any woman he wanted. Even now, it didn't take much to notice the number of women around the room who couldn't eat their breakfast for looking at him, *checking him out,* as Cel would often say. And he was a man worth checking out.

"I thought we could spend a day at Coney Island. Do you feel up to it?"

She glanced up and met Monty's eyes. They were beautiful and the kind you could lose yourself in. He was wearing a crisp white shirt along with a pair of khaki pants. When he had stood as she had approached the table she had gotten a good look at his attire with his sexy physique. She concluded that he would look good in any clothes he put on his body.

"Yes, I'm up for it," she said. "In fact it was on my list as one of my things to do. It sounds like a place I'll enjoy."

He smiled over at her. "And we will make sure that it is."

As they walked on the boardwalk of Coney Island, Rasheed would be the first to admit that even he had had a great time today. They had gotten on a number of rides, had eaten a number of hot dogs and had taken off their shoes to walk on the beach. He had discovered Johari had nerves of steel when she had agreed to ride the Cyclone, but his greatest joy had come in seeing her ride the carousel as she tried time and time again to get the brass ring located in the center of the ride.

It was getting late and he wasn't ready for his day with her to end. He glanced over at her and slowed his pace. She lifted a brow when he stopped walking and he reached out and took her hand in his. "Would you have dinner with me tonight?"

She smiled wryly. "I would think you would have had enough of me today."

He fought back the temptation to say he hadn't gotten as much of her as he'd intended to get. He pushed from his mind the mental image of taking her back to his condo with the sole purpose of seducing her senseless and then making love to her.

"No, I haven't had enough of you today. I've enjoyed your company and hope we can spend time together again tomorrow."

He thought that by now she felt somewhat comfortable with him. He hadn't gotten out of line and they'd had a really good time. And he had kept his promise. "So will you join me for dinner?"

She gazed at him for a moment, breathed in deeply and then said, "Yes, I will have dinner with you."

Chapter 5

Johari stepped out of the shower and proceeded to dry off with the huge bath towel. She couldn't help the smile that touched her lips when she thought back on the day with Monty. He was an amazing man and incredibly easy to talk to.

She had enjoyed herself so much that for a little while she had forgotten she was a woman in hiding. But then she had been smart enough to put a smoke screen in place, thanks to one of her classmates and friends who lived in California. If everything worked out according to plan, anyone looking for her would assume she was somewhere in Los Angeles. Only a few close friends from school knew that Cel had rented a car and had driven them to New York.

She dropped the towel and stood in front of the floor-length mirror to examine her body. While around Monty her breasts had begun feeling achy and her nipples seemed sensitive against her clothes and even now looked slightly swollen.

Her gaze lowered past her navel to look at the feminine mound between her legs. It was the part of her body her mother had always referred to as a woman's most precious jewel, her ruby. That particular part of her body was smooth as a result of a Brazilian wax, and after twenty-four years her ruby was still untouched by a man.

She knew Sheikh Valdemon could not make the same claim in regard to his own private jewel when it came to other women. Lately she had begun feeling agitated regarding her country's double-standards policy and that agitation had become more prevalent over the past couple of days, mainly because for the first time in her life she had met a man she could say she truly desired.

She held her breath and waited for something to happen with that bold yet honest admission. She glanced up. The ceiling was still in place and did not appear ready to fall down on her head. Nor was the floor shaking beneath her feet.

She released her breath as she pushed her fingers through her hair, tossed her head and then watched how the curly strands fell about her shoulders. She smiled, thinking at that moment she looked like a sexy naked temptress and wondered what Monty would think if he were to see her now. Would he find her desirable?

She knew for certain she had aroused him the other night and had felt him when he pressed against her, hard and fully erected, while they danced. That had been the closest contact she'd ever had with an aroused man, and the feel of his shaft even through her clothing had sent heat escalating inside her.

Her mind started thinking about another type of fun she could have by playing a game she had never played before, and that was of temptress. How would Monty handle it and would he still keep his promise and stay in control?

She had seen Delaney tempt her brother and could recall Jamal's reaction. She had seen the same thing with her mother and witnessed how she could use her feminine wiles on her father to push through any agenda for the women of Tahran that she wanted to approve. She noted the same thing with her sister and brother-in-law.

Johari wondered if the man she married would allow himself to be so manipulated. Probably not, since he had more than enough mistresses to keep him happy. She could vividly recall a few years ago, overhearing her parents talking, where her mother was expressing her concerns to her father regarding Sheikh Valdemon's numerous mistresses. Her father had tried to assure her mother that in time he felt certain that the sheikh would put all those other women aside and be faithful only to their daughter.

Johari thought then the same thing she thought now, that the sheikh had no reason to send those other women away when he didn't love her and when she didn't know the first thing about pleasing a man. Once again the question flashed through her mind as to which a man would prefer—an inexperienced virgin or a woman who knew something about pleasuring him?

Deciding she didn't want to think about her fiancé any longer, her mind shifted back to Monty. She had trusted him enough to tell him the name of her hotel when his driver had returned to pick them up from Coney Island. Sometime during the car ride she had fallen asleep, and when she had awakened she had found herself cuddled in his arms with no idea how she'd gotten there.

She smiled as she moved away from the mirror and walked toward the bed where she had placed the outfit she would be wearing this evening. The dress wasn't as bold and brassy as the one she had worn last night, but was just as sexy. She wondered what Monty would think when he saw her in it. Did it really matter?

She smiled as she began to get dressed thinking that, yes, it did matter.

Rasheed leaned back against the seat in his limo while Ishaq drove through the New York traffic to pick Johari up for their dinner date tonight.

Surprisingly, she had offered no protest when he had asked for the name of her hotel so he could take her home after their day at Coney Island. In fact she had been so excited about their time together at the iconic amusement park that she spent most of the ride to her hotel reliving every moment.

She had laughed as she recounted her experience on the Cyclone and had hidden her face in embarrassment when he teased about how many games on the boardwalk she had nudged him to play. Due to a traffic jam on the bridge she had literally fallen asleep cuddled in a corner of the car. He had ended up pulling her into his arms and regretted the moment he had to awaken her when they had reached their destination.

He checked his watch. Unbeknownst to her they would be dining in his condo. The reason he had decided on that as the best choice was due to the number of celebrities in town attending Sterling's movie premier, and the media was sure to be out in full force. The last thing he wanted was for a photograph of him and Johari together attending a restaurant to be plastered in the New York papers in the morning. It didn't make a difference to him but he would do anything in his power to protect Johari's reputation.

He pulled his BlackBerry out of his jacket when he felt it vibrate. "Yes?"

"Rasheed, this is Jake. I called to make sure everything was all right. I hadn't talked to you since you had to leave Luke's wedding unexpectedly."

Rasheed smiled. Over the years Jake Madaris had become one of his closest and most trusted friends. The two were involved in many successful business ventures both in the United States and abroad. His circle of business contacts included men like Jake and Syntel Remington, wealthy oilmen, as well as a phenomenal woman by the name of Corinthians Avery Grant, whose skill and ability to find oil reserves had literally transformed Mowaiti from an impoverished country to one enjoying prosperity as one of the world's leading oil producers. Together they proved to be a formidable team.

"Everything is fine, Jake. With Alex's assistance Johari was found in New York," he said, leaning back in his seat. "In fact I'm on my way to her hotel to pick her up. We're dining together tonight."

"So the two of you have officially met? She knows who you are?"

"Yes, we've met, but she does not know my true identity."

Rasheed then told Jake of his decision to not reveal his identity to Johari. "And just so you and your family know," Rasheed went on to add, "I'll be using my Madaris name for a while.

"You're an honorary member of our family, Rasheed. My family will always be grateful for how you interceded to keep Christy out of harm's way, virtually saving her life."

Rasheed remembered that incident and was glad things turned out the way they had. He and Jake talked for a few minutes longer and then they ended the call. As he tucked his BlackBerry back in his jacket, the driver pulled in front of Johari's hotel. They had agreed to meet in the lobby and as soon as the car came to a stop and Ishaq had come around to open the door, Rasheed got out and swiftly walked into the hotel. He tried to ignore the fact that he was very anxious and excited about seeing Johari again.

Johari walked off the elevator and grinned when she saw Rasheed standing in the atrium. She was intensely aware of him as a man. There was something about seeing him standing there that stirred something deep inside of her. He gave off vibes that were powerful, dominant, so elemental male that she almost missed a step when she began walking toward him.

She recalled her naiveté as a young girl after being told of her future and the man she would share it with and how accepting she had been of the decision. It was a decision made by a grandfather who'd died only months after her birth. She had envisioned her husband-to-be would appear at some point in her life to assure her that as his wife he would love and protect her. That never happened.

It became obvious that although Sheikh Valdemon would obediently fulfill his grandfather's wish as she was doing with hers, their life together would not be the storybook romance she desired. And now as she gazed upon the man she had met only two days ago, who would be the only man she would consider suitable, she knew her parents would never accept him in her life. Her brother Jamal had already stretched the limits by marrying a Western woman. And although King Yasir loved his American daughter-in-law dearly and cherished the two grandchildren she had given him, Johari knew that when it came to her, he expected her to marry the person she was promised to.

As Monty moved to meet her, his strides were sure and confident, and the look on his face told her, even with her limited knowledge of men, that he would be the kind of man who, if he ever fell in love, would love hard and be a protector for life as well as someone who could be adored and admired. She felt envious of the woman who would claim his heart. And from the number of women who were pausing with their full attention directed on Monty as he made his way across the room, she wasn't the only one thinking that way.

When Monty reached her he took her hand in his and whispered, "Once again your beauty has taken my breath away, Jo."

She couldn't stop the smile that touched her lips from his words. "Thank you for the compliment, Monty. You look handsome, too." She meant every single word and wondered if *irresistible* was his middle name. Mainly because he was that and more.

Holding firm to her hand, he led her from the hotel to the private car waiting out front. The New York night was abuzz with energy. Flashing bright lights, the sound of car horns and people conversing while walking on pavement, she had only been here for a few days but whenever she came out at night the sights and sounds simply amazed her. There was nothing quiet and slow about this place, and as she slid into the back seat of the waiting limo, she knew there was nothing quiet and slow about the man who slid into the seat behind her.

If things were different and this was an ordinary date, she would want to know everything about him, and would want to share everything about herself with him. But considering the circumstances surrounding her particular situation, she could not. She would accept that whatever time she had to share with him was limited.

The sights and sounds of the night no longer held her attention once the driver closed the door, locking them inside. The interior smelled of leather seats and a virile man. And the man who was still staring at her had a quizzical look in his eyes. She couldn't determine if he was looking at her like she was a puzzle he wanted to figure out or a delicious morsel he wanted to eat.

"Do you always enjoy your trips to New York?" she asked, deciding she needed to say something. There was a lot of sexual chemistry flowing between them tonight. This was all new to her and she couldn't help but feel a little overwhelmed by it. As much as she talked about not wanting to marry an "older" man, it was an older man who had stirred feelings in her she had never felt before. Regretfully, it wasn't the one whom her hand had been promised to for marriage. It was the older man sitting beside her in the car who was still holding her hand firmly in his.

"I do." He paused and then said, "The media is all over the place tonight because a number of celebrities are in town for Sterling Hamilton's movie premier. Instead of going someplace where we'll get mistaken for some notable couple and get our photo plastered all over the newspaper in the morning, I thought that we might dine in my condo. I hope that is acceptable to you."

Johari swallowed deeply. She didn't want to think of the consequences if such a thing were to happen. It would definitely be a disaster for her as well as for her family. "Yes, it is acceptable," she said, knowing she much preferred dining with him in seclusion.

She glanced over at him, remembering how things were when she had been in his condo before. They had shared a kiss that even now could stir sensations within her at the memory. And the thought of being alone with him again was almost more than she could handle.

She pushed any apprehensions from her mind. She had only a few days left before she would be leaving New York and going to another city she wanted to see in the United States. The key was not to remain in the same place too long.

She stared out the car window at the flashing signs, bill-boards and skyscrapers they passed, fascinated by the number of people moving briskly along the sidewalk toward their destinations. She glanced back over at Monty and saw his gaze was on her. For a long moment their eyes locked, and something that seemed more powerful than just sexual tension flowed between them. She watched his gaze darken, saw the way his pulse was beating at the base of his throat and noticed the slight movement of his lips. Although his action was subtle, it seemed to start something churning deep in the pit of her stomach.

She didn't say anything, and neither did he. They just sat there and stared at each other while the air between them was electrified from an undeniable awareness of their physical at-traction to one another.

Johari didn't doubt for one moment that something tur-bulent and primitive was taking place between them. And as she continued to stare deep into his eyes, she began imagining all sorts of things. She wondered how it would feel for those same eyes to watch as she removed every stitch of her clothing, piece by piece. And as her gaze shifted downward again to his lips, she couldn't help but remember just how those lips had felt on hers, how that tongue in his mouth could illicit pleasure that had her pulse racing at the memory.

She pulled in a deep breath, trying to control her reaction to him. She tried to think about her fiancé, the man she was to marry, but the only visual that formed in her mind was that of the man staring back at her.

She blinked, noticing his lips moved, and realized almost belatedly that he had spoken. "Excuse me, what did you say?" she asked, once she found her voice to do so.

"I said we're here. At my place."

She looked out the window and saw that they had arrived at Trump Towers. Surprisingly, the driver had already parked the car at the curb and was opening their door. All of that had happened while she had sat there staring at Monty like a woman who'd lost it.

She couldn't help wondering if all women responded to him this way or whether it was her degree of inexperience that was bringing on these sorts of reactions.

Pushing all those thoughts from her mind, she climbed out the car still holding his hand. "I intend for you to have a marvelous time this evening, Jo."

She glanced up into his eyes and her heart pounded. Her gaze shifted to the smile on his lips which looked devilishly sexy. She had a feeling Monty didn't make promises he wouldn't keep. And as much as she wanted to experience more exciting things, she had a feeling that his ideas of a marvelous time was something she might not be quite ready for.

Rasheed glanced over at Johari as he took a sip of his wine. They were seated across from each other at the dinner table and had been engaged in intense eye contact all night. It was as if they were saying with their eyes what their mouths refused to say. They wanted each other.

To be totally honest, he had a feeling Johari didn't know what she wanted. She didn't want him to forget she was engaged to marry, yet he could read in her eyes a desire that could make his blood simmer.

She was a very beautiful and desirable woman, but he was discovering another side of her that she was slowly exposing to him. For years she had hidden behind the mask of being the perfect daughter of King Yasir and was never given the time or the chance to just be herself. For some reason he wanted to give her that time. Maybe then she would settle down and step into her role as his wife and accept the life they would share together.

"Of all the places you live, which one is your favorite, Monty?"

Her question pulled his thoughts back into focus mainly on her. He wished he could tell her Mowaiti was his favorite and that being around his people would always be special to him. But then over the years, in the United States, he had accumulated a number of friends he enjoyed visiting on occasion. And then there was his home on a secluded island between Brazil and Argentina near Rio de Janeiro.

"I commute to too many places to have what one could consider a favorite. However, I own a place in Brazil that I love to travel to and spend time there whenever I can."

She did not need to know that Raul Santini, the man being tapped as Argentina's next president, was a very good friend of his and a close friend of her brother, as well. As a teen Santini had also attended the private academy in France.

He leaned back in his chair. "Would you dance for me again tonight?"

He loved watching her move her lithe body and could vividly recall what seeing her on the dance floor—performing her mating dance—had done to him. Her eyes glimmered. "Are you sure that you want me to?"

"Yes, I am positive."

She smiled brightly. "I love to dance."

He figured as much, just as he assumed her dancing in public was probably frowned upon by her family. But he had no problem in her performing just for him. He watched as she pushed away from the table and he stood, as well. Taking his wineglass, he led her through his living room and then to the balcony.

The night air was warm, sensual; it pricked at the lust that had formed around his edges. The desire that was rousing his middle. Her scent added to the atmosphere and made him want her that much more.

He stood back and watched her slip out of her shoes before moving toward the console on the wall. The skirt she was wearing tonight was a little longer in length than her mini-dress so chances were he wouldn't see as much thigh. But he believed what he didn't see would tantalize just as much as what he did see.

When she indicated she was ready to begin, he flipped the switch for the music while taking another sip of his wine. She threw back her head as the upbeat tempo washed over her and then she began moving her body to the beat.

He stood there and watched as she once again danced to a different song but basically executed the same moves—one in particular that was calling out to him in a huge way. With every dip and roll she made, his lower body reacted accordingly. He was transfixed in place and knew that after they married, he would have her dance for him each and every night. Seeing the smile on her face, the laughter in her eyes, the sensuous movement of her body was simply priceless.

She closed her eyes, which he thought was a good thing. If she were to open them and look at him there was no way she would not detect the lust flickering in the depths of his eyes or the huge bulge behind his zipper. Neither was he trying to hide. Both were something she needed to get used to seeing if this was the type of dance she liked to perform. They were the kind that showed she was a woman who knew her body and was quite comfortable with using it to lure a mate.

Moments later when the tempo of the music slowed down, she paused to catch her breath. The timbre of her fast breathing exhilarated him even more. It was the same sound he would expect her to make after sharing a mind-blowing orgasm with him.

She opened her eyes and stared over at him. He met her gaze. Held it. At that moment something sizzled between them, something that he could no longer deny. With the ease of a man who knew exactly what he wanted, what he intended to do to get it, he placed his wineglass on the table and moved toward her. She had done something no other woman had done. She had stolen his soul.

Riotous curls framed her face and fell past her shoulders. Her hands were at her sides, her bare feet crossed at the ankles. From the look in her eyes he could tell she was nervous. Not fearful. Just nervous. He could also tell that she desired him and it wasn't the desire of a young woman who didn't know or recognize her feelings and emotions.

At that moment he knew he would have to rethink his reservations regarding the differences in their ages and her inability to pleasure him. She might be young but she was still a woman capable of handling him. Already she had successfully tied him in knots. None of his experienced mistresses had the ability to do that.

He came to a stop in front of her. "Do you know what type of dance you performed on the dance floor tonight and last night?" he asked.

She shrugged. "No, it's just a dance I've watched others do."

He nodded. "It's a mating dance, Jo."

Surprise lit her eyes. "A mating dance?"

He shoved his hands in his pockets or he would have been tempted to reach out for her. "Yes, a mating dance, and I'm answering the call."

She shook her head. "I didn't know. It was not intentional."

"Doesn't matter. I'm answering."

She took a step back. "But you promised that you would not forget that I have a fiancé, Monty."

He stared at her with a degree of restraint that surprised himself. "I haven't forgotten, Jo. However, I intend to make sure that you do."

Chapter 6

He was going to kiss her and instead of resisting when he began lowering his head, she leaned up on tiptoe and met him halfway.

The moment his lips whispered across hers, she felt something akin to pleasure creeping up in every part of her body, and when their mouths touched, her senses were overtaken and shattered. Immediately she dismissed the thought that she was promised to another.

It started out as a slow, deep and gentle kiss with him placing fingertips on her cheeks as if getting to know the texture of her skin, the shape of her face and the sound of her breathing. She automatically responded to his tenderness as desire thrummed through her, inflicting every nerve, every limb and every muscle. Then in a move that made her moan, his tongue lashed out and began stroking hers in a way that enticed hers to join in the play. Working solely on instinct, she followed his lead while at the same time marveling in his taste.

A multitude of feelings and sensations rammed through her, making her whimper. And then when he angled his head and deepened the kiss she shuddered and became ensnarled in a degree of desire that stunned her, had her moaning deep in her throat. This kiss was just as thorough as the one last night, but he had thrown in an element that once again displayed his skill and mastery at seduction. Each stroke of his tongue increased her torment, while at the same time enticing her to keep her lips locked to his.

When the intensity of the kiss increased, certain parts of her mouth seemed sensitive yet hungry for his, and she wrapped her arms around his neck at the same time he tightened his arms around her waist to pull her closer. Instinctively or purposely, the move made her realize the degree of his desire for her when his engorged erection pressed hard against her, sending a tingling sensation at the juncture of her thighs.

Heat was pouring through her, entrapping her senses with every flick and lick of his tongue. A need, as sensual and primitive as it could get, raced along her nerve endings, became absorbed in her skin, and weakened her knees while wreaking havoc on all her body parts.

His kiss had gone from gentle to deep to outlandishly greedy, and his mouth became even more demanding, stirring every sensation embedded within her core. Her rational mind pushed at her to stop this madness, but something refused to let her do so. She was driven by passion instead of logical reasoning and accepted that this wasn't madness at all but unadulterated gratification of a kind she'd never experienced before.

So instead of fighting it, she embraced the moment and decided to deal with the consequences later. She felt herself falling over the edge and there was nothing she could do to stop it. So she leaned in closer to his tall, strong form and continued to enjoy what they were sharing.

There was something about being in Monty's arms that made her feel feminine yet protected, but not in a suffocating sort of way, not overbearing. There was something comforting about his desire. The way he could stroke her wants and longings, fuel the flames, make her yearn for things she hadn't ever thought about. Make her want to do things she would never have considered doing until she met him.

For two weeks she had wanted to be independent, enjoy her life to the fullest. She didn't just want to be the youngest daughter of King Yasir or the future wife of Sheikh Valdemon. She had wanted to be Johari Yasir in a way she had never been before. She had wanted to do things she'd never done before without anyone watching, protecting and judging. For the first time, she felt a sense of freedom by stepping out on her own.

And then Monty had entered the picture. The only things she knew about him were that he was from here in the States, he was a highly successful businessman, he was wealthy, handsome and he wanted her. And she wanted him, as well. The man who was showing how much pleasure could be shared when two people's lips and tongues touched, stroked and entangled…like theirs were doing at this precise moment. The man who was showing just how she could feel his warmth and his heat from being held in his arms. Was it wrong to want, to desire and to experience this with him? To have, to hold and to pleasure?

When he slowly pulled his mouth back, ending the kiss, she automatically dropped her face upon his chest. His hands cupped the back of her head in a display of tenderness so profound she couldn't stop the shivers from moving through her body. His hands shifted and began to slowly caress her back as they both continued to pull in deep breaths. She closed her eyes, thinking the way she had responded to him was outright scandalous, totally outrageous. But she would do so again and again. She was filled with so many emotions, too numerous to name but all stirred by him.

"Jo."

There was something about the way he said her name that sent trembles rippling through her body, shivers of passion escalating through every limb. Instead of answering she leaned back and looked up into his face, met his gaze. What she saw was intense heat, blatant desire and everything else that told her she was a woman that he wanted. It was there for her to see. Unhidden. Blatant. His features all but spelled it out to her.

She had a feeling that it was his intent for that kiss to be just for starters. How could he want her so much? Surely he could tell she had no experience with this sort of thing and was merely following his lead.

"Yes?" she whispered, as sensations threatened to overwhelm her at the thought that he wasn't through with her yet.

She had a feeling there were more kisses in store for her and that he had no qualms about moving things to another level. She might be a virgin but when it came to what men and women did together intimately, she wasn't clueless. Although she had to admit this was the first time she had felt so much tingling in certain parts of her body, especially the area between her thighs. Monty had accomplished just what he'd said he would do, which was to make her forget that her future was already planned with another man. A part of her knew that everything she envisioned sharing with Monty were things that she should wait and share with the man she would marry.

Too late, she thought, as she traced her bottom lip with her tongue. She could still taste Monty there. It was a taste like no other. And then there was that steam of heat he emitted that seemed to touch her flesh, reminding her she was a living, breathing woman being sexually awakened for the first time.

He reached up to frame her face with his hands while staring deep into her eyes. "Come fly away with me. Let me introduce you to fun of a different kind. A very sensuous kind of fun," he whispered in a voice that intoxicated her senses.

"Fly away with you?" she asked, needing to make sure she had heard him correctly. She didn't repeat the words he'd said about introducing her to fun of a different kind. A sensuous kind of fun. The thought of that sent passionate shivers up her spine.

A heavy silence fell between them as she stared up at him with her heart thumping wildly in her chest. And then he spoke again, to respond to her question. "Yes, I want to take you away, Jo. Spend time with you. Do things with you."

She suddenly felt dizzy and her heart began pounding faster. She could imagine what things he wanted to do with her. He was a wealthy international playboy, whose business had him jet-setting all over the world. He was used to getting any woman of his choosing, and for some reason he had decided he wanted her. Why he had made that decision she wasn't sure when it was obvious she lacked the experience he was probably used to. Evidently he wanted a change of flavor and saw her as a novelty. But then, didn't she see him as a novelty, as well, after living such a sheltered life?

Sensuous fun.

The idea of engaging in an affair with him was shocking and she should be recoiling at the very thought. But if she didn't jump at the chance now, when would she have another opportunity? There was no doubt in her mind that Sheikh

Valdemon would only consider her as his personal possession. A woman whose main purpose was to birth his heir. She was someone he was to pamper, coddle and treat like the queen she would be. Her husband-to-be would not give her the consideration Monty was offering. He would have mistresses to perform that task. He would expect her to be happy and satisfied with a loveless and passionless union. But she wanted more. She wanted passion even if the thought of ever being loved by Sheikh Valdemon was hopeless.

"Would it sway your decision if I promise to let you decide what activities you would want to participate in?" he asked, reclaiming her attention.

She wondered if he considered sharing a bed an activity. "No matter what they are?"

He nodded. "Yes, no matter what they are." And as if he'd read her mind he added, "And when we're in residence anywhere, you will be given your own bedroom until you decide differently."

"And if I never decide differently?"

A smile touched his lips. "You will."

His statement, spoken with such confidence, pretty much said that he saw her as a challenge he intended to overcome. A woman he planned to seduce. "I just met you yesterday," she said softly, reminding him.

"And I just met you yesterday, as well. You've kept a lot of information about yourself private and so have I. If it will help matters I will tell you everything you want to know about me, but then I'd expect you to do the same. Otherwise, I'm Monty and you're Jo."

His hands then tightened around her waist. "I'm also a man who wants you but is willing to wait. A man who wants to take you places, will make sure you enjoy yourself immensely. I would never force myself on you, I would never take what you don't give, and I will keep you safe. So will you fly away with me?"

Instead of giving an answer, she moved away, crossed the room to look out the huge window that showed New York—The Big Apple. The same one she had taken a big chunk out of last night and today with all the excitement she'd had…thanks to the man who she knew was watching her closely.

When she heard him making a move toward her she quickly turned back around and held up a hand. "No, please stay over there, Monty. I can't think when you're near me."

A sexy smile touched his lips. "All right."

She turned back to the window frowning. She wondered if this was one of those times when Cel would have cautioned her about giving too much information. Possibly. However, in this case she couldn't help it since what she'd told him was the truth. She couldn't think when he was near her. And now the same man who could overpower her senses wanted to whisk her away in his private plane with a guarantee for some sensuous fun.

And she was leaning toward taking him up on his offer.

Would she accept his offer or would she turn it down?

That question ran through Rasheed's mind as he took a sip of his wine and glanced across the room at Johari as she stood at the window deep in thought.

As the future king of Mowaiti, his expectations for his future bride would be for her to turn it down. She had already violated protocol by even being alone with him, allowing him to kiss her not once but twice and being anywhere unchaperoned and without a bodyguard. However, he had an unsettling notion that she would accept. It seemed that she had no problem being rebellious, breaking rules and placing herself in situations he could only define as inappropriate.

But then on the other hand, a part of him, the part that was deeply attracted to her beauty and was lusting after her body, hoped that she *would* fly away with him. He was more than ready to introduce her to all those things he would have taught her anyway after they'd gotten married. Her defiant behavior as well as his intense desire for her made waiting for the wedding no longer an option.

He wanted her in his bed now.

"Monty?"

He glanced over at Johari again. Met her gaze. Felt her heat. Could almost taste it. He wanted to taste it. Intended to taste it. "Yes, Jo?"

He watched her breath in deeply. Watched how her breasts moved as she did so. An image popped into his mind of those breasts, uncovered, exposed, bare, and ready to be claimed, tormented and devoured by his mouth.

"I'll go with you but only on one condition."

He stared at her, slightly annoyed that she thought she could set stipulations. "And what condition is that?" he asked, taking another sip of his wine.

"That you teach me how to please a man."

He cleared his throat after nearly choking on his wine. "What did you say?"

She didn't speak for a moment. He figured she was trying to get past what was probably a shocked look on his face. "I said that I will go with you if you promise to teach me how to please a man."

He swallowed. That's what he thought she'd said. He had planned to do that anyway, but to hear her suggest it was sort of unnerving. Women groomed to be wives didn't ask such things. They didn't even think it. "Why?" he asked, slowly crossing the room to her, needing to look in her face when she explained herself.

He came to a stop in front of her. Her eyes were as bright

as the sun rising over the Persian Gulf and as serious as a heat wave in the Sahara. "I will be getting married soon."

He nodded, thinking that he of all people knew that. "And?"

She looked away briefly and then directed her eyes to him. "And the more I know, the more my husband will appreciate me."

His brows rose. "And why wouldn't he appreciate you? You will be his wife."

She hesitated before giving him an answer, and he figured she was trying to decide how much information to share with him. "It will be an arranged marriage, which is not uncommon in my country. The man I am to marry will be allowed to have a mistress, as many as he wants. Although it is our way, I'm too possessive to accept something like that. I thought I would be able to, however, I know I won't and unfortunately, it will cause problems with my marriage."

Yes, it will cause problems, he thought. It was on the tip of his tongue to suggest she get over it because he *would* have a mistress. In fact he would have more than one. No wife could compete with a mistress when it came to bedroom skills and shouldn't even try. Everyone had their roles. A wife was a wife and a mistress was a mistress. A man would not expect his wife to behave like a mistress.

"Do you want to cause problems in your marriage?" he decided to ask.

"No," she said, shaking her head. "But I can't settle for anything less than a man who will be faithful to me. That is why I want to learn everything I can."

He felt he needed her to understand. She was setting herself up for failure. "Even if I agree to what you're asking, you will never learn everything, Jo."

A determined look settled on her face. "As long as I know

what's important to him. It shouldn't be hard to keep him happy because of his age. He's old."

Rasheed raised a brow. "He's old?"

"Yes, he's fifteen years older than me, so I would expect most of his good days are gone already, over and done with. So I wouldn't have to know a whole lot to keep him happy. Just the *right* stuff."

Rasheed didn't say anything. He hadn't recovered from what she'd said about his age. "How old is he?" He knew the answer but asked anyway.

"Thirty-nine."

He shrugged. "I don't think that's old."

Johari wrinkled her nose. "I disagree," she said, as if she had made up her mind about it and it wouldn't be changed.

"If he's had mistresses for as long as I've heard he's had them," she went on, "then he's probably well worn-out by now, although I'm sure he probably doesn't think so. I need to convince him that he is and from now on, I will be enough for him. But I'll need to back up that claim with knowledge of the things a man would like."

Her voice had gotten stronger. Was filled with more conviction, he thought. He tried to keep the hard line from forming on his lips, but more than anything he needed to make her see reason. He had no problems teaching her anything she wanted to learn, but he didn't want her to be disillusioned and think for one minute it would matter in the bedroom. The bottom line was that he intended to keep his mistresses.

He pulled in a deep breath. It seemed that Johari was going to be more trouble than he originally thought. What she was thinking was utter nonsense, a waste of good time and energy…on her part but not on his. He would enjoy every moment teaching her things. But in essence it wouldn't change a thing, although she assumed she could wrap him in so much pleasure that he'd be convinced he only needed a wife and no one else. He shook his head. For the love of Allah, there wasn't that much pleasure in the world.

That realization played on his conscience. Could he let her believe that? He looked at her and decided, yes, he could. It would be a hard lesson but one she deserved for not returning home to plan their wedding. Had she done the right thing, neither of them would be here now.

"So that is my condition, Monty. Will you take it?"

Rasheed felt it was time he taught his rebellious fiancée a few important lessons and he would enjoy doing so. In the end, when he revealed his true identity to her, she would see just what a mistake she had made in thinking she was clever enough to outwit her family and outsmart him.

He met her eyes and saw the soft, innocent plea in their dark depths. She had no idea what she was asking for. He had to be certain. "And you're sure that is what you want?"

"Yes, I'm sure."

He waited for a few moments and then he said, "In that case, my driver and I will take you back to the hotel. I suggest you pack up your belongings and get a good night's sleep. I'll come to the hotel in the morning to pick you up at eight o'clock. We will fly out of New York by nine."

She nodded. "Where are we going?"

A smile touched his lips. "First stop is to my private villa near Brazil. And your lessons will start tomorrow."

"Thank you."

He blinked. She had actually thanked him. Did she not understand the seriousness of what she had agreed to do? What she had asked of him? He inclined his head. Out of curiosity, he decided to ask, "Won't your fiancé expect you to come to him on your wedding night a virgin?"

She shrugged. "Probably. But I'm hoping he will prefer pleasure over innocence. Wouldn't you?"

An easy smile curved his lips. "I refrain from giving my opinion."

And he thought, for her sake, that was a good idea.

Chapter 7

"Are your comfortable, Jo?"

Johari glanced over at Monty, who was sitting across from her in his private jet. She had flown in a private plane a number of other times since both her father and brother owned them. But there was something about Monty's jet that was unique in that it was larger and had a lot more amenities than any she'd ever flown in. When she had mentioned it to him he'd explained it was due to the amount of time he spent in the air.

"Yes, I'm fine. Thank you for asking."

She broke eye contact with him and glanced out the window, trying to recall every single detail of last night after they had agreed to have an affair. The thought made shivers run up her spine. She had just gotten kissed for the very first time two days ago and already she was looking forward to something more.

Johari turned back toward Monty and saw he was browsing through a stack of papers he had taken out of his briefcase. She could only vaguely remember leaving his condo to return to her hotel last night. He had walked her inside the hotel as far as her room door and then, doing nothing more than placing a soft kiss on her cheek, he had made sure she had gotten safely inside before leaving.

She settled back in the soft cushions of the leather seat and nervously licked her lips, thinking this was the day her lessons were to begin, but he had not yet shown any interest in starting them. He had picked her up at the hotel at exactly eight that morning. Before he had arrived she had taken time to make a call to Cel. Although her friend was out on international waters, Johari had left a message letting her know she was on her way to Brazil with Monty. In a way she was glad she had not spoken to Cel. Her friend would have berated her for acting so impulsively and going off with a total stranger. But for a reason Johari didn't understand and couldn't explain, she felt safe with Monty.

She had taken more time with her appearance this morning, deciding to wear a white sundress and, from the look he'd given her, she knew she had made the right choice. But that was all she had gotten from him so far—a look and several smiles. She wasn't sure exactly what she had expected, but to be ignored hadn't been it. Maybe she had counted on too much too soon or maybe she was just a little too anxious for her lessons to start.

She glanced back out the window as she tried to blot out of her mind an incident she had heard about from the whisperings of her parents' household staff. A sheikh who was to marry one of the daughters of a neighboring sheikhdom had ordered his bride-to-be to undergo a physical examination before the wedding to verify she was still a virgin.

When the examination showed she was not, the sheikh had called off the wedding and taken extreme measures to humiliate the woman before demanding that she be banished to Siberia. What if the same thing were to happen to her? What if Sheikh Valdemon got wind of the fact she had not returned to Tahran as expected and believed he'd been compromised by her behavior and ordered such an examination for her?

She didn't want to think about such a thing happening. She was depending on him not finding out anything until their wedding night, and hopefully, by then once she showered him with all the things she had been taught, she would be able to convince him that the loss of her virginity didn't matter. She wanted to believe that her future husband would appreciate a wife with exemplary bedroom skills. But still…

She drew in a deep breath, realizing it was too late to have second thoughts now since they were probably already halfway to Brazil. The sky was a beautiful blue and they were flying high above the clouds. A few moments ago the pilot had announced their altitude but she hadn't been paying much attention. Her focus had been on the man sitting across from her.

And speaking of Monty…

She glanced quickly over to where he sat to find him looking at her. She swallowed and tried to control the deep pounding of her heart. He was looking at her the same way he had last night, just moments before he kissed her.

"Come here, Jo."

His voice was deep, throaty, and she wasn't sure she had heard him correctly. "You want me to come over there?"

A sexy smile touched his lips. "Yes, I want you over here." He patted his lap. "Right here."

She swallowed tightly as she unfastened her seat belt. The plane had leveled off, which made getting out of her seat and walking the distance to him safe and easy. He unsnapped his own seat belt and then proceeded to shrug off his jacket and toss it aside. When she was within arm's reach, he placed his hands around her waist and tugged her down to him, snuggling her into his lap with her head resting against his chest.

The only time she recalled being held this way by a man was when she had nearly cried her eyes out as a child of three when Jamal had left home to attend school in France. Jamal had been her hero. Her protector. The brother she adored. She had thought her world had come to an end and her father had held her tenderly while she shed all her tears. And now she was in the arms of a man who definitely wasn't her father. In his tight embrace, she could feel the outline of his taut muscles. Hard. Firm. Masculine.

"Ready for your first lesson, Jo?"

The warmth of his breath fanned against her ear and she lifted her head off his chest to meet his eyes. "Here? Now?"

"Yes," he said, curling his fingers gently in her hair, guiding her face closer to his. His lips tugged into a sensuous smile. "And this is how."

Johari wasn't sure what to expect, but she didn't anticipate having her mouth made love to in such a way that turned her to complete mush in his lap. They had kissed before, but never like this. First he took the tip of his tongue and traced all around her lips, causing a sizzling sensation to stir throughout her entire body. Holding her mouth in place with his fingers resting on her cheekbones, with agonizing slowness he continued the process. His featherlight caresses were sending heated desire circulating all through her.

And when her lips parted on a moan, he inserted his tongue and curled it around hers, slowly and methodically taking a hold of it in a firm grasp. He began sucking on her tongue with a voraciousness that had her reaching out to clutch his shoulders when an incredible ache erupted inside of her. Dead center between her thighs. Waves of longing she had never felt before took over her senses and she could easily feel the engorged erection beneath her bottom and the solid hard chest pressed against her breasts

The muscles in his shoulders felt firm and hard beneath the grip of her fingers and she could only savor his taste while the mastery of his kiss rippled through her, stirred an absolute ache within her.

He slowly pulled his mouth away and murmured against her moist lips in a low, throaty tone, "A woman lets a man know how much she appreciates him by the way she kisses him. The most important elements in a kiss are taste and feel. Use your tongue to do both with the sole purpose of building a craving inside of him that is strictly for you."

"Strictly for me?"

Another sensuous smile formed on his lips. "Yes. Go ahead, Jo, and try it."

She wondered how he could entice her to do such a thing when so many sensations and emotions were running through her. Ninety percent of her body felt overheated and there was a throb in her center that seemed to have taken on a life of its own.

"I'm here to teach you everything you need to know," he said assuredly, as the warmth of his breath came in contact with her ear, sending a sensuous shiver through her.

She breathed in deeply. "What if I don't do it right?" she whispered in a soft voice.

"You will do it right because there is no right or wrong way. Just continue to grip my shoulders, lean close and go for my mouth the same way I went for yours. Feel me and taste me. Build a craving inside of me that is strictly for you."

She focused on his lips and her heart began racing in her

chest all over again. The tips of her breasts felt tight and achy and sensations were swirling around in her stomach. Her hands left his shoulders and clenched the front of his shirt instead. And then she leaned forward.

It took everything within Rasheed to just be a participant in the kiss and let her take control, be in control. His lips throbbed beneath the tip of her tongue as she traced his mouth from corner to corner with the lightest of strokes. The same way he had done hers. Johari was a quick study. She was also one very sexy woman. And the dress she was wearing looked stunningly feminine on her. There was just something sensual about white against brown skin.

A shudder rumbled through him. He could actually feel perspiration forming on his brow, and the erection behind the zipper of his pants felt helplessly engorged. There was nothing like being savored by a woman, having her tongue roam over your mouth, tasting you, feeling you, and destroying your ability to think straight. To think at all. When he parted his lips on a groan, she inserted her tongue to taste and feel some more, and when she did so he drew her tighter into his arms at the same time Johari deepened the kiss.

Desire answered the call of their mating lesson and he felt like a primitive animal being overpowered. Taken. He was the one being seduced. She was effortlessly sweeping him into a stream of heated lust and, when she sank her mouth deeper into his, he couldn't help the fingers that went through her hair to hold her mouth steady while images of what went beyond kissing filled his mind. This was pleasure as gratifying as it could get and he had been the one to show her how it was done.

"Please get ready for landing, Your—Mr. Madaris."

Rasheed was glad Johari was so focused on what she was

doing that she missed the almost-slipup by his pilot. She slowly pulled her mouth away, but not before taking the tip of her tongue for one final flick.

Oh, Allah. He breathed in deeply. His student had been extra, extra thorough, eliciting a response from him that he had felt all the way to his toes. A knot formed in his throat when she lifted her eyes to meet his. He was finding it a challenge to maintain control. The lust running through his body was about to kill him.

"I need to go back to my seat now, Monty. How did I do?"

He let out the breath he was holding. "If you do any better I won't be able to handle it."

He saw the way her lips tilted in a proud smile. "Thank you." She eased out of his lap. "Do we practice the kiss some more later?"

The eagerness in her tone touched a sensuous chord within him. Her innocence touched him, as well. It took everything he had to rein in his desires and any emotions attempting to overtake his common sense. He did not let women affect him. He affected them. "Yes, but we'll also move on to other things, as well," he finally said. "We have but ten days to cover everything."

He watched how she moved back toward her seat and appreciated the sway of her hips. That sundress was adorable on her and he was looking forward to taking it off her later.

With Monty sitting beside her in a car driven by Ishaq, Johari smiled as they made their way toward another airport, where a smaller plane would fly them to the island where Monty's villa was located.

As they rode across the scenic spans of the Costa e Silva Bridge, the largest bridge in the world that connected the cities of Rio de Janeiro and Niteroi, she was fascinated by everything she saw. All around was water bordering tall, magnificent buildings with mountains looming in the backdrop and all encased under the splendor of a beautiful blue sky.

This was her first time in South America and she thought the country was simply breathtakingly beautiful. She had been captivated from the moment she had stepped off the plane in Rio de Janeiro. Monty didn't let her tarry too long before he escorted her to the car that had been waiting on the runway for him. Ishaq had taken over as driver and now they were on their way.

She didn't have to glance over at Monty to know he was watching her. He was studying her intently and had been doing so for the past few minutes. She couldn't help but wonder why. Was she some type of puzzle he was trying to figure out?

She couldn't resist the temptation any longer and turned away from the window. For a long moment their eyes locked and no words passed between them, making her as intensely aware of him as he was of her.

And then an unexpected mischievous smile touched his lips as he picked up the car's remote and pressed a button for the power privacy divider to separate them from Ishaq. Window covers immediately rolled down, as well, shielding them from outside view. They were plunged into semidarkness with only a few accent lights around the mirrored ceiling providing illumination.

"Come closer, Jo."

"Closer?" she asked softly. In the dimness of the lighting, he appeared solid, masculine and so starkly handsome it almost made her mouth water.

"Yes. It's time for another lesson."

Her eyes widened. "There's time?"

He tilted his head to the side as if giving her his absolute attention. "For you we will make time."

The words, spoken so matter-of-factly and glistening with sexual tension, had the heat of arousal and were the reason the very air they were breathing seemed to drip in blatant hot sensuality. She had never experienced anything like this before. Living a sheltered life for twenty-four years had certainly made her miss out on a lot of things, especially men like Monty.

She was wasting time and she knew it. He knew it, as well. There was nothing about him that frightened her. Only the way he was making her feel, the emotions he could awaken. The man was so passionate, so sensual, he could easily stoke the flame of desire in any woman. But she also had that power on him. Whenever she came in contact with that certain part of his body, it didn't matter if they were standing or if she was sitting in his lap, his desire for her was evident.

She would have to say the feelings, the desire, were mutual because she wanted him as much as he seemed to want her. It was the novelty, as she had figured out earlier. It couldn't be anything else, especially for him since she was definitely not the type of woman he was used to.

Drawing in a deep breath, she slid across the leather seat to him, felt a tingling in her body the moment her thigh touched his. He was wearing a white dress shirt and a pair of dark slacks. But even sitting she could only marvel at his muscular body, fit and trim, wide shoulders, flat stomach, perfect abs. Her attention moved lower, specifically to his crotch, and the only words she could think to say were, "Oh, my."

He shifted so he could easily turn to look at her. "I love your dress. The moment I saw you in it this morning I wondered about a few things."

Johari felt the trembling in her body when he reached out and, with the tip of his finger, traced around the thin strap. She was trying to concentrate on the fact that the smock-styled sundress, with an empire waist and full skirt, really didn't reveal a lot. But she had known the moment she had seen it during one of her and Cel's shopping sprees that it was the dress for her. She had no idea at the time she had made the purchase that this was the man—this incredible caliber of man—she would be wearing it for.

"What did you wonder about?" she asked, as his dark eyes swept over her once again. Everywhere his gaze touched seemed to ignite something within her that made her pulse race.

"Your breasts."

It seemed that as soon as he mentioned that part of her body her nipples began to respond as if they knew they were being discussed. They suddenly felt sensitive against the material of her dress and she wondered if Monty knew she was not wearing a bra. This type of sundress did not show any cleavage so nothing would have given her away. Well… almost nothing. There was that telltale sign of those same nipples pressing hard against her dress, easily being seen.

"What about my breasts?" she heard herself ask, grateful that Ishaq was not privy to their conversation.

"I was thinking about how pretty they must be, how they would fit in my hands, how they would taste in my mouth, wrapped around my tongue, sucked, licked and devoured."

Johari released a slow, deep breath. She could only stare into Monty's dark eyes, speechless, and it didn't help matters that he seemed fascinated with her dress straps. His long fingers, caressing both the material of her dress and some of her skin, had sensations fluttering in her stomach, heat settling between her legs.

"Lesson number two, Jo, when it comes to a woman's breasts, when used correctly, they can bring a man to his knees," he drawled huskily.

Johari knew the look she gave him at that moment had to

be wide-eyed surprise. She knew men liked breasts but didn't know they could be that powerful. "Why and how?" she couldn't help asking.

He smiled as he continued fidgeting with her straps. "A number of reasons, but I think the main one is that it gives them such a warm, sexual feeling. Some men think they are the softest part of a woman, which is why they like to cuddle with them."

"What do you think?" she asked, trying to get her mind off the fact that his fingers were slowly working their way beneath the front of her dress as they talked.

"Personally, I think they are one of the most beautiful parts of a woman," he said.

"And personally," she decided to say, "I don't know what's the big deal."

She didn't want to come out as bitter, but she was one of those women who'd never been blessed with big breasts, and sometimes the significance a lot of men placed on them annoyed her. To some, the larger the better. She was far from being flat-chested, but now she couldn't help but wish they were somewhat bigger.

As if Monty had read her mind, had been privy to her every thought, he said, "Your breasts are perfect."

She looked him straight in the eye and said, "How would you know? You've never seen them."

"Because I know. And as far as seeing them…"

Before she could draw her next breath, he leaned over and captured her lips.

Never had Rasheed taken so much pleasure in kissing a woman as he enjoyed kissing Johari. There was just something about her lips, the way they fit beneath his, the way they tasted, their shape, size and texture. Everything about her lips was perfect, just like he knew her breasts would be. Just thinking about them made hormones that he had tried to control most of his adult life spring into action, threw his testosterone into overdrive and made everything male about him aroused and ready to go. He could not recall such a thing ever occurring before.

But there was something about this particular young and innocent tongue that was frolicking inside his mouth that had every cell inside his body thrumming to life, making him realize just how long it had been since he was pleasured by a woman, and just how much he wanted to be pleasured by one now. But he knew not just any woman would do; only this woman.

Amazing.

Another amazing thing was how right she felt in his arms, how warm, tantalizing and right. It was as if she was created specifically for him. He suddenly lifted his mouth from hers, thinking he was having a monumental lust attack to even consider such a thing. No woman, even the one he was destined to marry, had been made specifically for him and it was foolish to even let such a notion take shape in his head.

He studied her lips, which his mouth had just released, saw they were moist from his kiss and knew he wanted to sink his mouth into hers again, so he did while his hand reached out to cup the shape of her breasts through the material of her dress.

He absorbed in his mouth the moan she made in her throat and appreciated the way her body arched against his hand. Automatically and absolute. He would be a fool not to acknowledge the fact that she wasn't the only one nearly pushed over the edge. And while his mouth was still locked with hers, using skilled fingers, he eased down the straps of her dress.

With perfect precision, unerring timing, he moved his mouth from her lips to her breasts, immediately latching onto a nipple, liking the sound of her moan when he did so. The moment he drew it into his mouth and began sucking on it, he knew her taste would ultimately be his downfall. She was sweetness and temptation all rolled into one and he became fascinated by the feel of his tongue as it circled her nipple, enjoying the texture as well as her taste.

He released one nipple and before moving to the other he leaned up and gazed at her chest, and felt his erection harden even more. Her breasts were perfectly shaped mounds, the perfect size, the perfect weight. One nipple was wet from his kiss.

"I told you that your breasts were perfect," he whispered, leaning to capture the other peaked nipple between his lips. His tongue skimmed over it before he greedily sucked it into his mouth.

He could tell from the way she gripped the back of his head to hold him to her breast that she liked the feeling and that he was arousing sensations inside of her. They were sensations she had not felt before. But he didn't plan on stopping there. There was a direct correlation between a woman's breasts and that area between her legs, which was the reason she was shifting her legs back and forth. With every suck of his tongue, heat was gathering near her womb and spreading through all parts of her body. Her panties were getting wet and the feminine scent of her was flowing through his nostrils and causing him to devour her breasts with unrestrained hunger.

Needing to touch the wetness that had gathered between her thighs, he shifted and reached his hand under her dress while keeping his mouth firmly on her nipple, letting his tongue continue to drive her over the edge and showing her what a perfect multitasker he was.

His fingers moved past her panties and she automatically spread her legs. When he felt her moist heat, he was filled with a monumental need to taste her in that very spot. Stake his claim. It was a good thing that he knew they were less than five minutes from the airstrip, otherwise he wouldn't hesitate to lay her back on the seat and bury his head between her legs. But still, he intended to give her something to remember him by.

Giving her breasts a rest, he buried his face between them as his hands concentrated on letting his fingers pleasure her. She felt swollen, hot, ready, and he moved his fingers inside her, caressing the area he knew would stir a need within her, a need that only he could quench.

"Monty!"

Her crying out his name did something to him, and the sound was of an intensity he hadn't heard before. There was a sexiness in her voice and the more he stroked her the wetter she became. He could tell she was on the verge of the climax he was intentionally giving her.

And when her body moved in a fierce jerk, he knew she was about to let out a scream and he quickly left her breast to angle his head. He sank down on her mouth, tangling with her tongue the same way his fingers were tangling with the sensitive and beautiful blossom between her legs.

She was still quivering beneath his mouth, and his fingers were enjoying the feel of the aftershocks going on between her thighs. The air surrounding them had the fragrance of uncompleted sex. He breathed in deeply, absorbing it into this nostrils, pulling it through to his lungs.

"You came."

His words hadn't been sugarcoated. They had been as blatant as words could get, given his hand was still under her dress, not ready to let go. A satisfied smile touched her lips and she slowly opened her eyes and met his gaze. "Yes, I did, didn't I?" she responded breathlessly. Stunned, but totally without shame. "My first time."

A huge smile curved Rasheed's mouth. He hadn't expected

it, but it only gave credence to what a passionate being she was. She had held his head to her like mother would hold a baby and he had taken all she had offered, and she hadn't been ashamed to admit she had gotten an orgasm. Her first. Now was not the time to tell her there were many more where that one had come from.

He pulled his hand away and made sure she watched as he licked his fingers. "I can't wait to taste you there," he said, smiling over at her.

And then because he couldn't help himself, he leaned over and kissed her again, vaguely aware of Ishaq on the intercom letting him know they had less than three minutes before they reached their destination.

He pulled back from her lips but not before taking one final swipe with his tongue. He then leaned up and readjusted her dress, making sure the straps were back in place.

"We're sharing a bed tonight, Jo. If you have any objections you need to let me know now."

She nervously swiped her bottom lip with her tongue. He watched the movement and wished she hadn't done that. It was bad enough thinking about what would take place in his bed tonight.

"No, I don't have any objections."

He smiled. "I'm glad." *And only Allah knew just how glad he was.*

Chapter 8

Johari glanced around the bedroom she'd been given thinking of just how beautiful the room was decorated and the view she had of the Atlantic Ocean was stunning. It seemed there was a lot Monty hadn't told her, such as the fact that he was good friends with Raul Santini, the man who was making headlines for being a top contender as the next president of Argentina.

The size of his villa was another thing Monty hadn't told her. Situated between Brazil and Argentina, the villa was on a private island that Monty owned. When the small plane had landed she was speechless at the size of the estate that sat in the middle of the ocean with its own landing pad. Monty had explained the only mode of transportation to his island was either by plane or boat.

The huge multilevel villa was breathtaking in both design and structure and was surrounded by beautiful trees and lush grasslands. She doubted she'd ever seen so much greenery in her entire life. And there were the mountains in the background providing a picturesque view of turquoise blue waters and a sandy white beach.

According to Monty, he had purchased the existing island a few years ago from a member of Raul's family and came here whenever he wanted to rest and relax.

He told her about the tennis courts he had installed and the racetrack he had put in due to his love of auto racing. And because he enjoyed riding horses he kept several on the island as well as a catamaran he liked taking out on the water to fish on occasion.

She could only assume business for Monty was going well for him to be able to indulge in such luxuries. The staff had been glad to see him, had greeted him as Señor Monty, and she could immediately tell they respected him and he respected them. She guessed, from their easy acceptance of her presence, that it was not uncommon for him to bring a woman with him whenever he came to the island.

Johari drew in a long breath. Knowing such a thing should not bother her since she was nothing more to Monty than a woman he had agreed to teach how to please a man. She couldn't stop the blush from spreading over her features when she thought of what had happened in the back seat of the limo earlier that day. Her body was still tingling from the memories. If he could make her feel such pleasure with his fingers, she didn't want to imagine how things would be with him inside her body.

She heard conversation outside and moved across the room to the balcony. Monty and Raul Santini were standing downstairs on the patio carrying on a conversation. They were speaking in Spanish and whatever they were discussing had them in good moods.

She couldn't help studying the two men. Both were darkly handsome but it was Monty who was holding her attention. He had removed the jacket he had on earlier and was wearing a pair of dark slacks and a white shirt. He was more than just darkly handsome, he was sensuality and elegance all wrapped up in one. He was passion. He was pleasure. And no matter when she saw him, his appearance was immaculate. There was a cool assurance that radiated from him and drew her to him like a magnet.

He even had the ability to maintain that air of cool assurance whenever she was in his arms. Her heart began pounding in her chest when she recalled his mouth on her lips, her breasts and his fingers inside of her, stroking her flesh and making her feel sensations she had never felt before. Sensations that had singed her skin, shattered her nerve endings and made her come apart in his arms. He had proved all the things she had heard from some of the girls at school were true. There was power in passion. Power in persuasion. Power in pleasure.

And he had promised her more pleasure tonight. They would be sharing a bed and he had not hesitated in letting her know that. He was giving her just what she asked for—lessons on how to go about pleasing the man she would marry.

Why was the thought of being in the arms of any man other than Monty beginning to disturb her? Why was the thought of any other man tasting her lips, kissing her breasts, using fingers to stroke her into an orgasm beginning to bother her?

She let out a confused sigh and the sound must have carried because Monty glanced up and saw her.

Rasheed had stopped conversing with Raul Santini the moment he sensed Johari's presence. And when he had stared up and seen her standing on the balcony he had become speechless. She smiled at him and he felt a deep stirring in his gut.

Her hair, which she had tied back earlier, was now fanning her face, showing the beauty of her features in a way he enjoyed viewing. Even from a distance he could see the lushness of her dark eyes and perfect lips. They were lips he enjoyed kissing. His focus shifted to the sundress she still wore and he couldn't help recalling the moment he had lowered the straps, finding her braless and devouring her breasts, discovering her taste. He was getting aroused just standing there, looking at her and re-membering. He was tempted to go inside and—

"I see your future wife fascinates you, Monty."

Santini's words reminded him of his friend's presence. He had contacted Santini from New York and told him he would be arriving. He had also shared with his good friend everything. There were few men he trusted implicitly and Santini was one of them. He knew there was nothing Santini would not do for him and vice versa. In this situation, Santini had been placed in a precarious position, since not only was he Rasheed's friend but he was close friends with Jamal, as well, since their days as teens attending that private school in France. This was Santini's first time seeing Johari, although everyone had heard of Jamal's baby sister and his fondness for her.

Rasheed smiled at Santini's observation since it was right on target. "She does more than merely fascinate me, Santini. She fires my blood." His words were true and he couldn't help but look forward to tonight when he and Johari would move their relationship to another level. A very intimate level that had blood gushing through his veins in anticipation of it.

"I can understand why. She is a very beautiful woman. The kind that can leave a man breathless." Santini paused a few moments and then asked, "When will you tell her the truth as to who you are?"

Leave it to his friend to remind him of the farce he had orchestrated. "I don't know," Rasheed said. "We will share ten days together and then I will return her to New York. I will tell her then."

"And I will hate to be in your shoes when you do. She will feel betrayed."

Betrayed. At that single word Rasheed glanced back to the patio to find Johari was no longer standing there. He turned back to Santini and said, "*Betrayed* is a strong wrong, isn't it? Given the fact that she is the one out of place. She should be back in Tahran planning for our wedding. Instead she is here being seduced by a stranger. The way I see it, I am the one who should be feeling betrayed. I told you how I walked into that nightclub and found her dancing on the tables, Santini. That type of behavior from a woman who is destined to be my future queen is not acceptable."

"Yes," Santini said and smiled. "But when you saw her she evidently fired your blood. Even now you can't stop looking at her. I couldn't help noticing."

Rasheed frowned, slightly agitated. "You notice too much."

"Yes, but in this case I couldn't help it. And I still say that she will feel betrayed."

Rasheed shrugged. "Then she will just have to get over it. I would not have taken such drastic measures had she followed protocol. As far as I'm concerned, whatever happens she has brought on herself."

"So a wedding will take place regardless?"

"Yes, a wedding will take place regardless," Rasheed said. He would marry Johari. Once she discovered his true identity she would feel the sting of betrayal, but like he said to Santini, as far as he was concerned she had brought it on herself. She would be sharing a man's bed. She had been given her first orgasm by another man. It meant nothing that the other man had been him. The bottom line was that Johari didn't know it. And how she would feel once she found out the truth didn't matter to him. She had initiated this mockery; however, he was more than happy to bring it to an end, but not until he had his way with her. He would gladly prove to her that no matter how experienced, a wife and a mistress were two separate entities and as far as not being able to accept him having a mistress, she would not have any choice in the matter.

"I wish you luck, Monty."

He glanced back at Santini. "Luck?"

"Yes, because you're going to need it. No matter what brought this on and no matter how she might have contributed to it, she will resent what you're doing. She is not just one of your other women."

Rasheed chuckled. "No, she definitely is not that." His mistresses weren't exactly the innocent types. The last one he brought here had liked wearing next to nothing and hadn't minded flaunting her attributes in front of him, Santini or anyone else caring to look. But Johari was different. Even his staff had noticed the difference the moment Johari had entered his home. She had greeted them with kindness, and she possessed an air of innocence that any woman he dealt with before could not come close to claiming. For Pete's sake, she was still a virgin. When was the last time he had bothered to rid any woman of her virginity? Anyone who knew him knew that he much preferred experienced women.

And another thing Rasheed was sure his house staff had noticed was the fact that Johari was a lot younger than the women he usually had affairs with. Another giveaway was that he'd asked that she be given a separate bedroom. Juanita, his housekeeper, had stared at him in surprise before escorting Johari up the stairs to one of the guest suites.

"Will you be staying for dinner?" he asked Santini.

Raul Santini smiled. "Thanks for the invitation, but I have a strong feeling that you would like to be alone tonight with your future wife."

"Johari, have you lost your mind?"

Johari placed the phone from her ear, convinced Cel had burst her eardrums. "No, my mind is very much intact," she responded.

"Then what are you doing on some island off the coast of Argentina instead of back in New York where I left you?"

Johari sighed deeply. "I told you why."

"Yes, you explained your reasoning but I'm not sure what you're doing is going to work. What if Monty teaches you all that you want to know and your future sheikh still wants a mistress?"

"Then I would have accepted that I had failed."

"You would not have failed. You need to just sit down before the wedding and lay down the law to him and—"

"Cel, I've told you. In my country a woman does not lay down any laws. She accepts any that her husband has made for her. That's why, knowing what I know, I have to do whatever I can before the wedding."

"Yes, but you're supposed to be enjoying the sights, having a good time, not spending your time worrying about how to please a man, who in my opinion would be a total jerk to take another woman in addition to you. Experience or no experience, it just wouldn't be right."

Johari heard everything Celine was saying. And she *was* having a good time. That day she had spent with Monty at Coney Island, dancing those times for him in his condo, the plane trip across the ocean where she had sat in his lap while he had kissed her senseless, and even now being here on this island with him. And Monty had suggested that they do a picnic tomorrow.

"Don't worry about me, Cel, I'll be fine."

"I do worry about you. Promise you won't do anything foolish."

Johari considered Cel's words and wondered if sleeping with Monty fell within that category of foolish. In that case she would indulge in a lot of foolishness tonight.

"I need to get ready for dinner. Do enjoy the rest of your cruise." She quickly hung up the phone before Cel could start preaching again. She checked the clock on the nightstand. She needed to shower and get dressed for dinner. Anticipation was flowing through her veins at the thought of seeing Monty again.

Chapter 9

Johari sat across from Monty at the dinner table, fully aware of everything about him. His every movement, no matter how slight, tightened her nerves, had heat blazing through her veins and made awakening passion flow down her spine. She had struggled through the entire meal trying not to stare but, more times than not, hadn't been able to help herself. He was such a handsome man, strikingly so.

When she had arrived downstairs for dinner he had met her at the bottom stair. He had showered and changed into another outfit like she had done and from the way his gaze had moved over her beneath long, shuttered lashes, she had known he liked her choice of outfit—a gauze skirt set in bright geo print. It added a flare to her that he hadn't seen before in any of her other outfits. She liked the way the top hung off her shoulders and the skirt ruffled around the hem.

He was casually dressed in a pair of dark slacks and a white shirt. It was simple enough attire, but the magnitude of his sexuality hit her hard the moment she saw him. All her senses had been on alert and the moment he'd taken her hand in his, she had to steady herself to keep from passing out. The man transmitted sensuality with such an intensity that it slammed into her head-on, made her wonder how she would be able to handle such a man in or out of the bedroom.

"Would you like anything else, Jo? Dessert perhaps?"

The sound of his voice—deep, authoritative, yet considerate—made her look up from her dinner plate to meet his dark eyes. Her response almost caught in her throat from the intensity of his stare. She noticed how, ever so slowly, subtly, yet very thoroughly, his eyes would scan her face, linger on her lips, making them throb under his scrutiny.

"No, I don't want anything else. Thank you."

He smiled before nodding at one of his household staff members standing not far way. Within minutes the table before them had been cleared. "Would you like to join me for a glass of wine in the ocean room?"

"The ocean room?"

He smiled as he stood on his feet. "Yes."

Intrigued, she stood, as well, and when he walked around the table to her and took her hand in his, she felt a tingling sensation all the way to her toes. She tilted her head and looked up at him, already regretting the time when they would part. In just a short while she had grown to feel close to him, felt protected by him. She couldn't help wondering how it would feel to be loved by him.

She wasn't into masochism by any means, so why would she even go there and imagine something that would only cause her heartbreak and pain? Monty was what he was, a jet-setting playboy, a wealthy tycoon. When it came to mistresses, he was probably in the same league as the man she was to marry. The same league Jamal had been in before he'd fallen in love with Delaney.

She might be naive in some things but she was smart enough to know just what short-term affairs were about and what was expected. She knew Monty was getting something from it, as well. When it ended, and Monty returned her to New York, he would be on his merry way, ready for the next willing conquest. She was determined not to let the thought that she was just one of many bother her. Things were as they were. She only had his company for two weeks, not enough time to start something that could never be.

As they left the huge dining room and continued walking along the foyer that led to several rooms, Johari was amazed at the beauty of the paintings on the walls, the intricate wood carvings that adorned several mantels. When he pushed open a set of double doors and they walked into the room, her breath caught. The symmetrical room was perfect in design and furnishing, and completely glass all around. One section of the room stretched out as a long glass-enclosed deck that extended out over the Atlantic Ocean.

It was late evening and the sun was just going down on the horizon. The sight was breathtaking, truly magnificent. Monty released her hand to move across the room to the bar and she turned around in a circle to take it all in. Glass everywhere. The ocean everywhere. She quickly moved toward one of the windows when she noticed a school of dolphins in the waters below.

She couldn't help the excitement that shone on her face when she turned back around to Monty and he handed her a glass of wine.

She smiled up at him. "Oh, Monty, do you see them? It's simply wonderful! I can't believe this place and I'm so glad you brought me here."

He returned her smile. "I'm glad I brought you here, as well. At night when the lights are darkened and you stare out over the ocean it's even more beautiful beneath the moonlight," he said, speaking smoothly.

Johari sighed deeply. She couldn't wait to experience something like that. She took a sip of her wine, noticing just how close Monty was standing to her. She became intensely aware of him, not that she hadn't been aware of him already. But suddenly something was happening as they both paused to take sips of their wine while staring at each other. She could feel it and knew that he could feel it, as well. Once again she was feeling a rush of desire for him that was so keen and deep that her pulse rate quickened. She stood there staring into his eyes, slipping under his spell as sexual tension shimmered between them.

"In addition to the picnic on the beach tomorrow, I thought we would go out on my boat," he said, as he continued to stare at her.

"Sounds like fun," she found the words to say, not sure if he could even hear her through her suddenly tight throat.

"And I intend for it to be."

Her gaze fell to his lips, the same lips that had devoured hers in the car earlier. He had such a robust and manly flavor, she was certain she could still taste him on her tongue. "I admire the person who built this place."

Monty broke eye contact with her to turn a smiling gaze to where the dolphins still played in the water. "When Santini's father was an Argentinian ambassador, he had it built for Santini's mother. They both died the following year unexpectedly in a car accident and Raul wasn't interested in keeping it. He knew how much I liked it and offered it to me and I bought it. I love it here."

"And I can understand why."

"Do you?" he whispered in a raspy tone.

"Yes. You are a private person and being here gives you the privacy you crave when you desire it."

He studied her intently for a few moments and chuckled and then said, "You are right. Few people know how to figure me out."

And few people could get next to her as he was doing so effortlessly, Johari thought, as she continued to feel the warm fires stroking within her at his nearness.

"I never did give you an official tour of my home," he said, placing both of their wineglasses aside and offering her his arm. He led her toward the door. "We'll return later, after it becomes dark," he whispered as they left the ocean room.

She took deep, calming breaths as she walked beside him while inhaling his sensual scent. There was something about Monty that had disturbed her senses from the very beginning. And now after meeting him in a New York nightclub a few days ago, she was here with him on his own personal island.

He escorted her around the various wings and she truly believed he enjoyed seeing the astonished look on her face with every room they toured. Her pulse increased as they headed up the stairs.

"So tell me something about you, Jo, that no other living soul knows," he said as they continued up the stairs.

She fought back saying, *I think I'm falling in love with you against my better judgment.* Instead she smiled and said, "I can tell you something that very few people know, and that is I have a baby."

She couldn't help but smile when Monty nearly lost his step. He stopped walking and stared at her. His mouth, full sensuous lips and all, dropped open in shock and the sharp cut of his eyes wiped the smile from her lips.

"You have a child?" he asked in a low, hardened tone.

"Not a human child," she quickly said and regretted that her words had not come across as the cute joke she had intended.

"Not a human child?" he asked, repeating her words with a confused look in his eyes. "Is there any other kind?"

Her smile returned. "For me there is. I own a puppy that I consider my baby, because he definitely acts like it sometimes."

He lifted a dark brow. "A puppy?"

"Yes, but no one knows about him but Cel and another friend from college. I heard him crying one night and when I investigated he was outside the condo where I lived. Someone had thrown him and four others in a nearby Dumpster. The moment I held him in my arms I fell in love with him. He was barely a few days old and was so tiny and I knew I had to take care of him."

"What kind of dog is he?"

"The vet said he is part Yorkie terrier. He is still tiny and the most he will weigh is four pounds. He is being kept at Cel's parents' home. I'm hoping once I'm married my husband will allow me to bring him to my country. I named him Copper and he means a lot to me."

Monty nodded before they resumed their walk up the stairs. "Is there a reason your husband wouldn't let you own him?"

She met his gaze, realizing he was probably not familiar with her country's customs and said, "Yes, in my country a dog can't be housed in the main living quarters, but I'm hoping my future husband will agree to let me keep him at a kennel somewhere close by where I can visit him on occasion."

"And what if the man you marry isn't easily persuaded?" he asked in a thoughtful voice.

When they reached the landing, she turned to him. "Then I need to persuade him to indulge me on this one thing, because…"

"Because what?" he asked softly.

She drew in a deep breath, held his gaze, smiled and said in a compelling voice, "Because I'm worth it."

Because I'm worth it…

Rasheed fought to keep from frowning at Johari's words. The woman was not low on confidence by any means. Did she honestly think that the man she would marry, just because of his wealth and position, would indulge her in such a rebellious thing?

He shook his head as he continued to walk beside her. Where in the world did she get such a stubborn streak? He then remembered Jamal from their days together at the private school as teens and his rebellious escapades. But that was then and that had been Jamal. Besides, Jamal was a man and Johari was a woman. He glanced sideways and his gaze swept over her. Yes, she was definitely a woman. A woman determined to be defiant and unruly.

A woman he couldn't wait to bed.

Besides her belief that she was worth her husband giving in to her unorthodox whims, what made her think for one minute that she could persuade him to do such a thing? And how could she assume that she would learn in ten days all there was to know about pleasuring a man to the point she would become an ace at it? Didn't she understand all he could do was introduce her to the basics and that the skills would have to be perfected over time? Did she not know the use of sex whenever she wanted anything amounted to nothing more than manipulation? If she thought for one minute that she could learn to control his physical desire to the point where she could use it to have her way then her way of thinking was preposterous.

Rasheed berated himself under his breath for getting worked up over Johari's foolish notions. That was the main reason women had husbands to keep them safe, protected and, in Johari's case, out of trouble. He decided to put what he thought of his future wife's behavior out of his mind for now and shift his thoughts to something else. Specifically, what her role would be to him not once they got married, but beginning tonight.

He gave her a tour of the upstairs quarters, showing her how each room had a view of the ocean. When they had left one of the guest rooms, she glanced around. "It's seems awfully quiet all of a sudden. Where is everyone?"

He caught her eyes as he led the way to his bedroom. "They are gone."

Johari's eyes widened. "Gone?"

"Yes." Rasheed kept walking.

Johari stopped. "Gone where?"

Rasheed stopped and turned to look at Johari. "I sent Ishaq back to the States and the others to the mainland."

She stared at him. "Why?"

"So we could be completely alone."

Johari suddenly felt dizzy and seconds later she felt an intense flutter in the pit of her stomach. Other strange sensations began to claim her, play havoc with her mind, body and senses. Her lips, which seemed to be holding his attention, had begun to throb and there was a deep pounding in her chest.

They were on the island alone. That realization was unfolding a mirage of emotions in addition to the sensations she was feeling. She nervously chewed the underside of her lip as she stared back at Monty. He smiled and the sexiness behind the smile was so blatantly predatory that she had to fight to catch her breath.

"It's time for another lesson, Jo," he said quietly.

When she didn't say anything he leaned back against a wall. "Are you having second thoughts?"

Her brow rose. "What gave you that idea?"

He chuckled. "You've been standing in the same spot now for over five minutes."

Johari swallowed. Yes, she had.

"Come here, Jo."

Her lips curved into a nervous smile. "You want me over there?"

"Yes. For now. But I'm sure you know I do have other plans for you tonight in my bedroom."

Her heart rate increased at the thought of what those plans were. Did he have to be so brutally straightforward? She began moving, closing the distance separating them as she pondered that question. By the time she stood directly in front of him, she still didn't have an answer. He was so tall that she had to tilt her head back to look at him, stare into his dark piercing eyes and become the recipient of his heat.

"I'm here now," she said, when he just stood there staring at her. She swallowed again. The look in his eyes was so intense, it was beginning to awaken things in her that had been dormant for twenty-four years.

"Monty, I—"

The words were basically lost when he leaned over and swept her into his arms.

Chapter 10

Carrying Johari in his arms, Rasheed crossed over the threshold of his bedroom. He glanced down at her and thought that she looked adorable when she blushed. It was a pleasure to see that his rebellious, unorthodox fiancée did have a shy side.

Rasheed was aware of his own vulnerability as he carried Johari to his bed. He was fascinated with this young wisp of a woman who just wanted to experience life. Unlike what she evidently thought, what was about to take place between them would bind them together forever. One day she would become his wife. She was to be his life.

He continued walking until he placed her on his huge bed and then he took a step back. He saw her glance around. He saw the look of appreciation and admiration in her eyes at the magnificence and splendor of his furniture, the high ceiling in the room, the chandelier and the wood-grained moldings, a decor in rich colors of red and gold. It was a room fit for a king…and his queen, and they represented both.

"This room is simply beautiful, Monty," she said in whispered enchantment. The splendor of his room mesmerized her and she continued to glance at the furnishings, but his eyes were transfixed on her. He thought that she was beautiful. She was on her knees in the middle of his bed. Her thick shimmering mass of hair fell about her shoulders and the outfit she had on looked simply gorgeous on her. But he was ready to remove it. He wanted to see her naked. He wanted to see those breasts he had tasted earlier. He wanted to see that part of her where his fingers had been. He wanted it all.

He was aware of the moment she stopped glancing around the room to return her gaze to him. He noticed the slight tremor of her body as his eyes swept over her. He watched the way she nervously licked her lips. For a long moment their gazes locked as heat passed between them. Sexual desire and a fierce, deep need also swirled in the air around them.

At that moment Rasheed knew what he wanted. He wanted to make love to her and not just have sex with her. He didn't want to teach her any lessons tonight. For their first mating he wanted her to know him, know his body. One day she would discover that he was the only man she would ever intimately know.

"Come here, Jo."

He held out his hand and watched her stare at it for only a second before scooting across the bed to him. The moment their hands joined, something akin to fire touched him, blazed inside of him. He heard her sharp intake of breath, heard the deep breathing forced through her lungs. Her reaction to him fueled his fire even more. Made his desire for her stronger.

The atmosphere in the room suddenly thickened with sexual tension and he was unable to take his eyes off her. He tightened his hand on hers and gently pulled her closer to him. When she was so close that her chest pressed against his and he could feel the tight buds of her nipples, he studied her lips. They had to be the prettiest pair he had ever seen on a woman. Struck with an intense urge to taste them again, he touched his hand to her cheek, leaned closer and sank his mouth into hers.

Something flared to life within him the moment their lips touched and when he deepened the kiss even more, the primitive male inside of him took over, and he wrapped his arms around her, taking the desire within him to new heights. When she released a deep moan, his mind toyed with the idea of abandoning any foreplay. He could strip her naked, spread her thighs and sink his body into hers with the same intensity he had taken her mouth. But something held him back. He broke off the kiss and leaned slightly away from her. This was her first time with any man, her first time with him. He had a feeling that with this woman, he could develop an insatiable appetite when it came to lovemaking and he didn't want to frighten her.

But he did want to convey to her just how much he wanted her and prepare her for what was to come. "I want you." He leaned back in and whispered the words against her lips just mere seconds before his mouth covered hers again, lightly at first, using his tongue to do a thorough sweep of her mouth, flickering over certain parts he'd discovered that when touched could make her moan. So he touched them, laved them with the tip of his tongue in a sensuous assault. And when she moaned so deeply in her throat that he could feel the vibration of it in his, he felt his manhood throb in a way it never had before.

He deepened the kiss, unable to do anything but that, communicating with his tongue just where he intended for this kiss to go and that he was ready to take her there. So he continued feasting on her mouth with the intensity of a starved man. And when she returned the kiss, the power of her passion infested his brain and he felt the rumble of desire escalate all through him, nearly driving him out of control.

He pulled his mouth away from hers and she slumped against him, her head falling on his chest while he wrapped his arms around her and silently counted to ten to calm the raging fires within him.

"Why do you keep stopping, Monty?" she lifted her head to ask.

He looked down at her. Stared into the darkness of her eyes and nearly lost control again. He had to maintain his senses to recall just why he had stopped kissing her that time. Something elemental, compelling and powerful was waging a battle within him and he was losing the fight. There was so much that she didn't know. So much he wanted to introduce her to.

Before he could respond to her question, she reached up and placed her arms around his neck and pressed her hand against the back of his neck, forcing him to bend his head while she leaned up and met his mouth halfway. The moment their lips touched he stopped thinking and began reacting. He responded to the way her tongue immediately latched onto his, kissing him in the same manner, with the same intensity that he had kissed her several times.

Rasheed wasn't sure just how she had managed to catch on so quickly, but there was nothing subtle in the kiss. It was all fire and passion. The way she was taking control of his mouth was a daring feat. He was beginning to realize his future bride had mastered the ABCs—audacious, bold and courageous—incredibly quickly.

He pulled back a little just so his teeth could nibble passionately on her lips, brand them his, while his tongue lapped at them from corner to corner.

"Monty."

She said his name in a voice that sent shivers all through him, made his erection seem to expand ten times, made him want to touch her everywhere and then follow the trail of his hand and taste her everywhere, as well. Without stopping what he was doing to her mouth, he reached out and grabbed hold of her skirt, bunched the gauzy material in his hand and slowly raised it past her thighs to her waist.

He knew the moment the cool air touched her skin. She tried to pull her mouth back, but he had an intense lock on it, determined to intoxicate her with as much pleasure as he could. And before she could react, he quickly moved his hand toward her center, slid his fingers beneath the band of her panties and touched her at the same time his mouth slanted deeper over hers.

But that didn't stop her moan, throatier than the last, from spreading to him, causing an avalanche of desire and passion to consume his mind and every part of his body. And when his fingers tested her wetness, felt it, penetrated the air with her aroma to tease his nostrils, something tore through him, made him burn for her in a way he had never burned for any woman. It was as if his entire body was on fire with a different kind of need.

Unable to prolong the moment, he pulled his mouth away and her protest came out in a whimper that only fueled his hunger. He clenched his teeth, trying with all his might to retain control, but every time he inhaled her scent he was filled with a need that was as primitive as mankind, and the only thing he wanted to do was to make love to her. The thought of being inside her body sent blood surging through his veins. She had no idea what he was going through that very moment. She was young, innocent, and didn't have a clue that intimately touching her, watching her reaction to his fingers moving inside of her, was strumming his senses. She was totally different from the experienced women who graced his bedroom; lovers, mistresses and courtesans who knew what to do and were proficient in their skills. But this was a difference he enjoyed, a welcome change from any woman before her.

He slowly pulled his hand away and licked his fingers, tasting her on his tongue. He saw how her eyes darkened as she watched him. "I want to give you a chance to change your mind, Jo," he said in a deep husky tone. "If you decide this is what you want, I will be your first and I'll make sure it is an experience you won't forget. I intend to introduce you to numerous sexual pleasures."

He saw the frown that crinkled her forehead when she looked at him and said, "But I don't necessarily want to know how to receive pleasure. I need to know how to give it. I want him, the man I will marry, to only want me and no one else. Please help me make that happen, Monty."

Her words shook him to the core and he fought back the feelings of guilt that were trying to stir inside of him. Even now she was thinking of *him*. She had no idea that his pleasure would come from him pleasing her. There was no way he could receive pleasure without giving it, as well. To have a woman moan from his skillful touches, to have her reach an orgasm from his mouth on her breasts—like Johari had done earlier that day—only made him want her more.

For the first time since he could remember, a woman was causing mixed emotions to run through him. How could he agree to something that he knew in the end she would fail at? How could he explain that one woman wasn't capable of fulfilling all his needs, all of his pleasures, and that although he would always place her above all others—as his queen and his wife—that there *would* be others? It was a way of life and she needed to accept it.

"Monty?"

He heard the plea in the way she said his name. He saw it in her eyes. "Yes, Jo?"

"Will you help me make that happen?"

At that moment he could not refuse her anything, but he couldn't totally lie to her either, so he said, "I can't make you any promises, but I will try."

He studied her features, literally held his breath, waiting, watching and wondering if his response would be enough. Would it satisfy the part of her that was determined to accomplish an impossible feat? She held his gaze and something, he wasn't sure just what, tugged at emotions he wasn't used to encountering. They were emotions he couldn't even put a name to. And they were so strong he almost took a step back. But then she spoke, and he couldn't move, not even an inch.

"I know considering everything, Monty, how we met, what little we know about each other and the reason I am here with you now, there is something about being with you that seems right. It's as if you were meant to be a vital component in this part of my growth as a woman. Yes, you will try and that is all I can ask."

Something inside Rasheed crumbled. He reached out and ran his palm down the side of Johari's face then leaned in and, knowing how imperative it was to live up to her expectations, lowered his mouth and captured her lips.

For a woman who hadn't been kissed by a man before, Johari felt she was making up for lost time each and every time Monty joined his mouth to hers. He was a skillful kisser and she couldn't help the slow heat that was consuming her body at that very moment. This kiss was deep, drugging, and she could even taste herself on his tongue, which added a bit of daring that tormented her senses.

Giving in to an impulse she didn't quite understand, she wrapped her arms around his neck and pressed her body closer to his, needing the contact of her breasts pressing against his chest again. Pleasure gripped her when his tongue began toying with hers in an intimate play that made the area between her legs feel consumed with heat.

And when he finally pulled his mouth away, but not before nipping gently at the corners of her lips, she could only sigh in contentment. "Did you like that, Jo?" he asked her in a low, husky voice, as he unbuttoned his shirt.

"Yes, I always like your kisses, Monty. From the first," she responded, being completely honest with him, although doing such a thing might make her look a little forward.

The smile that touched his lips indicated he was pleased with her words, which had been the truth. She would always remember their first kiss, the one they'd shared right after she had danced for him that first night in his condo.

Once he had unbuttoned his shirt he slowly removed it and she feasted her eyes upon his broad hairy chest and abs that were so tight she figured he had to exercise several times throughout the day to be in such perfect condition. She didn't see an ounce of flab anywhere on his body.

"Now for your blouse," he said.

Reaching out, he touched her blouse, and then slowly slid the buttons free. Seconds later he tossed her blouse aside and she could feel the heat of his gaze centered on her bra. "I've tasted your breasts before and want to do so again," he said, reaching behind her and unhooking her bra.

And when he removed her bra, baring her fully to his eyes, she felt the increase in her pulse rate the moment he lowered his head and flicked his tongue over her breasts. "I want you totally naked before I finish devouring them again," he said, easing her down on the bed to remove her skirt.

It didn't take Monty long to dispense of her skirt and she watched as he stared at her body, keeping his gaze trained on what was being uncovered with the removal of her skirt. And when she reclined on the bed before him with only a pair of panties covering her body, she knew it wouldn't be long before those were done away with, as well.

But it seemed Monty had other ideas, because he kicked off his shoes and eased onto the bed with her. She felt her heart slamming mercilessly against her ribs when he leaned back on his haunches and his gaze traveled the length of her body and zeroed in on the area between her legs that her panties shielded from view.

"Are you going to take them off me, Monty?" she asked in a whisper. The way he was staring at that part of her nearly stole her breath right out of her lungs.

"Not yet," he said as he continued to stare at her. "I want you wet some more."

As if his words had the ability to turn her on like a faucet, she felt that area get wetter and wondered if he'd known that it would. He must have since he inhaled deeply and said, "Your hot scent is driving me crazy, Jo."

At the next moment he was there over her and with the tip of his tongue, beginning at her lips, he began devouring her, lapping her up, using his tongue to trace hot trails all over her.

"Monty." She closed her eyes and whispered his name, feeling electrified every single place his mouth touched. And when his mouth reached her breasts, she almost screamed. He had no idea how he was making her feel. He didn't have a clue that she didn't want him to stop, and how she adored the way his tongue was skillfully feasting on her breasts. It seemed every pull of a nipple into his mouth was causing a contraction in her stomach that was pumping out moisture between her legs, and sending all kind of sensations ripping through her nerve endings, especially those in her center.

Maybe he did have a clue, which was the reason he finally moved from her breasts and began a slow trek downward, laving a path to her belly, where he greedily licked the area around her navel. She couldn't help the moan that escaped her lips when his teeth gently nibbled around her hipbone, as if branding her in some way. And then as easy and as carefree as anything she had ever seen, she watched as he lifted her hips and eased her panties down her legs.

After tossing her underwear aside, he resumed licking all around the curves of her hips and thighs before returning to her navel, as if cherishing that area of her. "You taste good," he whispered. "The texture of your skin, your taste is wonderful to my tongue. You are becoming addictive."

She was developing an addiction, as well, but she couldn't tell him that. The only thing her mouth was good for at the moment was groaning out her pleasure as every part of her seemed poised, ready for something she wasn't sure of and couldn't identify. And when he began to suckle the area around her navel, causing sharp explosions in her stomach, the only thing she was aware of was the sensuous awareness tearing behind her closed eyelids and the sensations that were causing her stomach to flinch in response to his tongue and mouth.

She didn't feel his tongue moving lower until he was there, right at her center, with his head between her legs. She felt his hair on her thighs. Her eyes flew open the exact moment he opened her up with his fingers and captured her precious jewel, her ruby, into his mouth, sending pleasure tearing through all parts of her body.

The intense hunger in the tongue devouring her could be felt all the way to her womb and in response she arched her body, lifted her hips and reached down and grasped a lock of his hair and held on to it as his mouth became a sponge to absorb all the wetness between her legs. Her body shivered, sending tremors beneath his mouth, but he didn't seem to care. The only thing he seemed interested in was tasting her to a degree that had sharp explosions radiating through her from every angle. Her ruby began to vibrate with every lap of his tongue and when he continued to consume her she moaned in pleasure as her hands pulled at his hair.

The sounds he was making, not of pain but seemingly of pleasure, were primitive, primordial and primal, and they sent sound waves crashing through her nerve endings. The more of her wetness he pulled in the more drenched she became, but he didn't let up, suckling her ruby as if his life depended on it. It was as if he had been starving for her for such a long time, and that tasting her in this particular way was the most elemental thing in his life at the moment.

Then something, that same exquisite feeling that had capsized her earlier that day in the back of the limo, took control and although she tried to fight it, it descended on her nerve endings, took over every cell in her body and a sensation similar to an earthquake shook her, followed by an explosion that tore into her.

She screamed as a degree of pleasure she didn't know could exist invaded her mind, rippled through her body, slammed into her senses. Her thighs began shaking something fierce, but Monty would not release her. He continued the exhilarating assault with his tongue, probing her tightness, stirring all kinds of naughty pleasures in her wetness, and in such a way that had her releasing his hair and grabbing hold of the bed coverings. It was either that or she would have pulled every single strand of hair from his head.

Release flowed through her. The room began spinning and she couldn't stop it. It was as if she was under some sort of spell that was pushing her closer and closer to the edge. Monty wasn't through with her yet. Whatever he had planned was far from over.

And when he finally lifted his head and stared down at her, she knew what he had just done was only the beginning.

Rasheed stared down at Johari almost in a daze. There was something about the sight, scent and the taste of her that had him off balance. When she had come in his mouth, he had been overtaken with pleasure in a way he hadn't known was possible and his body was still responding to it.

His erection felt engorged and he knew the only way he could find release was inside of her. He needed to feel the essence of her femininity wrapped around him, pulling him in, holding him in tight, her inner muscles flexing to milk him dry. His shaft began throbbing at the thought of that happening.

Without saying anything, he eased off the bed to remove his pants, meeting her gaze as he slowly slid them down his legs. Next came his briefs. The moment her eyes lowered to his midsection to take in his size, he saw the look of both admiration and uncertainty in her expression. "I won't intentionally hurt you," he said, knowing he had to assure her. He would not lie and tell her there wouldn't be pain when more than likely there would be. However, he didn't want her to worry about it. Either way, sooner or later, he would make her his in every way possible and he wanted it to be now.

"I believe you, Monty."

He could not help the fact that he became even more aroused by the blatant look of desire in her eyes. There was also a degree of trust, which he knew, considering everything, he really didn't deserve.

He forced that thought to the back of his mind as a shudder of desire rippled through him as he moved back toward her and she automatically crossed the bed to him.

Rasheed reached into his nightstand and pulled out a condom box. Rasheed knew Johari was watching him with keen interest as he tore open the box and pulled out a condom packet. Moments later he covered his aroused shaft in latex, which wasn't an easy thing to do.

"May I do it the next time, Monty?" she asked in a soft voice.

He glanced up at her and smiled. "You certainly may."

And then he reached out and slid his arms around her. And when she tilted her head back, he captured her lips and they both went tumbling back onto the bed.

Johari glanced up at the man who was kneeling over her, straddling her hips with his thick thighs. She took in the dark hair that covered his chest, perfect abs and a handsome face. He was breathtakingly aroused, and just to think she was the one to fill him with such a physical need sent desire riveting all through her body.

His closeness, his position over her, was creating an intense ache between her legs and the way his gaze held hers caused stirring sensations in the pit of her stomach. He slowly lowered his body to her and she breathed in sharply when the length of his shaft pressed close, right at the juncture of her legs, her ruby. It felt like a thick rod of heat touching her, yet at the same time it sent all kinds of emotions rumbling through her.

She loved him. Johari could no longer deny that. And for

now she wouldn't. When their affair ended, she would return to her home, marry the man her family had chosen for her, live with him in his sheikhdom, bear his children…and live the rest of her life with these memories.

And when she felt him push forward into her tightness, instinctively she wrapped her legs around him. She was wet for him, which made things a little easier as he continued to push inside of her. She swallowed tightly against the pain, thinking there was no way he would go inside of her all the way.

He stopped moving and leaned down and placed a kiss on her forehead. The tip of his tongue lapped off her sweat. "You're okay?" he asked in a husky tone.

"Yes, I'm okay. But I don't think it's going to work."

He lifted his head slightly to smile down at her. "It will. Relax and open your legs a little wider. Inside of you is my home. Let me come home, Jo."

His home. She thought those words coming from him had to be the most romantic a man could say to her. The thought of it sent pleasure racing through her. And when he lowered his head and captured a nipple in his mouth and began sucking on it, her body automatically did what he wanted. On their own accord her legs spread and she could actually feel the increased wetness of her hot, swollen, inflamed ruby. Her inner depth craved relief that only he could give, but first, he had to move past the obstacle of her tightness.

He was trying to be gentle, but she needed him now. Needed to have him fill her to the hilt, needed to know he was deeply embedded inside of her all the way. Needed to know he was home.

"Please do it, Monty. I can't stand to wait any longer."

"I don't want to hurt you," he said in a rough growl, pushing a little more, his hands cupping her bottom tenderly.

"You're hurting me by not making me yours."

He went still and too late she realized what she'd said and just how it sounded. She was well aware it was not his intent to make her his. Their time together did not have the same significance for him as it did for her. To him this was just a sexual act, a way to pass time. To her, it was a whole lot more.

She swallowed, wondering what she could say to retract her statement. "Monty, I—"

Before she could finish what she was about to say, he sank his mouth down to hers, stealing her words at the same moment he pushed the remaining length of his erection inside of her, swiftly, quickly, absorbing her cry of pain into his mouth as he made it home. *Home.* She grabbed hold of his broad shoulders, tightened her legs around his waist when he gave her body a chance to absorb the impact of his invasion.

And then he began to move and it seemed when he began pumping in and out of her, gentle at first, she could feel every cell in her body become fragmented, and when he pulled his mouth away her whimper was one of both protest and pleasure.

"I want to look into your eyes when you come this time, Jo," he whispered softly as he continued to thrust in and out of her, letting her feel his heat and at the same time absorb his hardness. She arched her back, lifted her hips each time he came down, went inside of her slowly, easily, penetrating her deeply. And when he pulled out, she tightened her legs around him and gripped his shoulders to make sure he returned.

He always did and the feel of him moving in and out, back and forth, sent sensuous shivers of pleasure all through her. Instinctively, her inner muscles clenched, pulled, milked, needing something from him that she knew would push them over the top as well as over the edge. With each downward thrust her body stretched for him, then automatically tightened, the rhythm inflaming her senses. He continued thrusting with slow, easy strokes and then suddenly the tempo increased and she held on.

"Ahh."

His long and deep, satisfied growl radiated through the air surrounding them, and automatically her hips arched upward when he moved to the hilt.

And then another hoarse moan tore from his lips at the exact moment his body bucked in an explosion that triggered her own explosion.

She screamed, her control shattered, overtaken by ecstasy. The only thing that ruled her mind was pleasure, pure unadulterated pleasure, as her body shuddered with the force of her orgasm.

Her hands dug into his shoulders and when his mouth lowered to hers she knew she would love him forever. No matter what.

Chapter 11

Rasheed eased out of bed and, without bothering to put his clothes back on, strolled over to the window. He always thought the ocean looked beautiful at night but glancing back over his shoulder at the naked woman asleep in his bed on top of the covers, he quickly came to the conclusion that nothing looked as beautiful as she did at that very moment.

She had been an innocent yet, in her very own way, a natural. It seemed that Johari and everything about her had been created just for him. She had responded to him in a way no other woman had before. He had been the one who was supposed to teach her a few things and in the end, tonight, she had been the teacher and he the student.

A frown dented his brow at the memory of the exact moment he had gone inside her body, the brave look in her eyes when he had done so, the flash of pain that crossed her face, which she had tried to hide, and then the look of pleasure that had infused her features. That look had been his undoing. It had touched him in a way that even now he hadn't recovered.

He breathed in deeply as he turned to look back out the window. His jaw tensed at the thought that, with one single act of lovemaking, Johari had stolen his soul and now at that very moment was working on his heart.

He momentarily closed his eyes against the thought of anything so foolish as that happening. His heart, he tried assuring himself, had nothing to do with it. What he'd done for the past hour or so was solely about the physical. It didn't connect emotionally to his heart, just a certain other body part that even now was throbbing with wanting her again. But that wasn't the point. His erection had throbbed before, several times for other women. It was a primal habit. No big deal. Nothing more than an automatic reaction to the sight of a nice and enticing piece of feminine flesh. But why was something as basic to him as sexual satisfaction, something that had never caused him pause before, something as natural as eating or sleeping, now consuming his mind?

And why was a twenty-four-year-old woman who had never been touched by a man before responsible?

He was smitten with everything about her—her taste, her scent, her voice, even the sounds she made when he was tasting her captivated him. He wanted her again and the intensity with which he did stunned him. He turned again and stared at her for a long moment before finally turning once again to stare out the window.

Rasheed was not at all happy that he was letting such a thing get the best of him, letting what happened in his bed rule his senses. He was irritated, slightly perturbed, but not angry. He couldn't imagine gnashing his teeth about something that even now had his entire body thrumming with anticipation of her waking up so that he could make love to her again. The eagerness and the hunger were things he could handle. The thoughts swirling around inside of him, thoughts that were messing around with emotions he'd never felt before, were sentiments that he could not handle.

He heard the sound of a body shifting and turned around. His gaze connected to Johari. Suddenly, he felt them again, those turbulent sensations he was trying so hard to fight, trying with all his power to resist. He breathed in deeply and made a frantic attempt to stay in control, but she seemed hypnotic, drawing him in.

Rasheed moved toward her, not accustomed to giving in to any woman's wants and desires. But tonight was an exception. Johari was an exception. Tonight her unexplainable hold on him was too strong and there was no point trying to fight it. And if he were to be totally honest with himself he would admit he had no desire to fight it. As he moved closer to her, he watched desire light her face, shine in her eyes and the sight made his heart beat faster in his chest. He inwardly told himself that it was all right to want her this much, that the novelty would wear off soon and she would be nothing more than the woman he was destined to marry. Her place was by his side as his queen, to bear his children. There would always be other women for him to indulge himself, and nothing she said or did would change that. And for now he was satisfied just to want her. But no matter how intense the wanting, it would not complicate the issue.

That thought was solidified in his mind until the moment he slipped into bed beside her and she willingly came into his arms. Her body felt undeniably right. Perfect in every way. And when his passion once again flared to unprecedented heights, he captured her mouth and for the faintest instant, he imagined he was in a world where only he and Johari existed.

* * *

For the first time in her life Johari awakened in bed with a man. But not just any man, he was a very naked man. But then she was naked, as well. And her body was spooned to his in a way that the back of her head rested against his chest. One of his legs was entwined with hers, his hand resting on her stomach, and her backside was fitting snug against his front. She could feel him. He was long and hard, yet the sound of his even breathing warm against her neck indicated he was sleeping. Was it normal for a man to sleep aroused? Was he really asleep?

All she needed was to tilt her head to find out, but she didn't have the inclination to do that right now. All she wanted to do was to lie there and relive the pleasures of last night, every wonderful moment. Even now her breasts felt tender from his mouth being on them so much and the area between her legs was still sore from his kisses and his thrusts. And considering his size, she had wondered if she would able be able to walk again. But miraculously they had fit, and so perfectly it nearly brought tears to her eyes thinking about it. And once the pain had passed, the pleasure began and it had remained constant, throwing her into one orgasm after another until she had finally drifted to sleep.

Monty was a very gifted, skillful and considerate lover who had made her first time very special. After their first joining, he had gone into the bathroom to return with a washcloth and basin of warm water to soothe away her soreness. It had been a very personal act, a very intimate one, and it had made her so aware of what a wonderful and caring person he was.

She closed her eyes when the full reality of her situation pressed down upon her. What had she gotten herself into? And more importantly, how was she going to get herself out of it? But the main problem was that she didn't want to get out of it. As crazy as it sounded, she had fallen in love, but not with the man she was destined to marry.

Sadly, Sheikh Rasheed Valdemon was not the one responsible for the warm rush of total feminine satisfaction she was now feeling, or the glow she knew was probably showing in her features. It was a man she had miraculously met, a man who not only was showing her how to have fun but had introduced her to a world of pleasure, as well.

Any woman would be overwhelmed by the essence of his sensuality. He was a man that dreams were made of—handsome, wealthy, powerful and, she thought with a smile, almost sexually inexhaustible. A man who even now was sharing his heat with her, holding her close to him while he slept so she could be right there with him when he woke up.

She felt secure and protected and at that moment would give anything to feel loved by him. She knew that was asking for a lot. To be honest it was asking for the impossible. She shuddered at the tongue-lashing she would get when she returned to Tahran. Her father and brother would ask questions, demand answers. But she would tell them nothing, especially about this. This part of her life would be always be her secret, to keep her warm during those cold nights when she shared a bed with a man who would not have her heart.

"Cold?"

The murmur of the warm, sexy voice broke through the silence of the night, the stillness of the bedroom. The sound was a balmy stroke against her neck. "What makes you think I'm cold?" she asked quietly, when at that very moment heat was flaring through her, along every nerve ending she possessed. She decided not to turn around and look at him now. She would probably burn to a crisp if she did. Whether he had wanted to or not he had made her his in a way her future sheikh could not.

"You shivered. That's how I knew you were awake. I've been waiting for you for almost an hour now."

She raised an arched brow. So he had been awake. And as to the reason he had been waiting for her, she didn't have to ask, especially when the erection resting snugly against her backside began to get larger, harder, hotter.

She flipped on her back the same exact moment he leaned up to support himself on his arm to look down at her. Her heart caught in her chest as she stared into a pair of beautiful dark eyes. An unruly mane of hair, just as long as her own, flowed around his shoulders and the depth of his handsomeness actually shook her senses, sent a throb through her body and intensified the strong emotions that had settled deep in her heart.

The thought that she was probably just another in a long line of conquests he had made didn't bother her, although the fact that the next nine days were all they had left together actually did.

But she would survive.

Chapter 12

Over the next week Monty discovered that Johari had a way of getting to him on every level. She had an innocence about her that he found totally refreshing and a sensuality he could not ignore. Nor had he wanted to.

She had the ability to make him smile, laugh and have fun in ways he'd never had fun before. They played checkers, chess and strip poker. They went swimming together every morning and took walks every afternoon. On occasion they would go horseback riding or play tennis and he even showed her how to operate his race car…within limits.

Another thing he discovered was that she had a sophistication far beyond her years and an ingrained sense of what was fair that some people never grasped. Over the dinner table they talked endlessly on many topics, always careful not to divulge too-personal information about themselves. She would tell him about her childhood but kept from providing specifics.

He knew that although she had defied her family's wishes by not returning home after she'd graduated from Harvard that she was close to her parents and totally adored her brother and sister and thought her sister-in-law was simply fabulous. Johari had admitted that as the youngest sibling she had been pampered. Yet he could tell from their conversations that she had a respect for mankind and humanity.

They had left the island off the coast of Brazil and had flown to Vanuatu, a beautiful island in the South Pacific. They would be staying here for several days before flying to his villa in the Greek Islands. Once there he intended to take her shopping in Athens and cruising along the waterways.

Nothing had changed since coming to Vanuatu. He continued to enjoy Johari's company immensely both in and out of bed. He looked forward to their nightly bedroom lessons and how proficient she was in everything he taught her. Just as he'd done before arriving in Brazil, he had notified his household staff and instructed them regarding what to call him while he was there. Under no circumstance did he want Johari to discover his true identity.

Considering everything, he couldn't help wondering how she would feel once she discovered the truth. Was Santini right? Would she feel betrayed, used and taken advantage of? Before, he had dismissed Santini's words as irrelevant but now the thought of her feeling that way bothered him more than it should have.

Yet, despite his concern for her feelings, he couldn't bring himself to tell her the truth. He intended to stay with his original plan and tell her when they returned to New York, just before putting her on the plane that would return her to her family.

He stood at the window in his bedroom in Vanuatu, glancing out at the beach in deep thought. The view outside the window was breathtaking. He had bought the villa a few years ago for that very reason. Even with the waves pounding the seawall, giving it one fierce beating, the view always managed to bring a tranquil calmness to his world.

His estate sat on a high cliff, which proved to have the fortitude of a fortress. It would not have been an easy task to invade his private sanctuary because of the seawall, not to mention the wrought-iron gate surrounding his villa. It was impenetrable against all intruders.

A smile touched his lips as he immediately recalled that one man *had* done the impossible and invaded the grounds of the villa, going over the seawall and bypassing the security of the gates...and all in the name of love. Alex Maxwell had shown just how far a man would go for love when he had come here to rescue Christy Madaris. It had been a daring, dangerous and very successful undertaking.

Rasheed knew at that very moment that if Johari had been Christy Madaris and placed in harm's way, as Christy had been, he would have done everything in his power to get her back safely. He would have turned this world upside down in his search if he had to. But it would have been possession and not love that would have driven him.

Just then, Rasheed turned at the sound of his bedroom door opening and couldn't help the smile that touched his lips or the unexplainable joy that filled his heart when Johari slipped inside and closed the door behind her and leaned against it, looking more beautiful than any woman had a right to look. She was perfect in every way and possessed a body that had the ability to arouse him no matter what she was wearing.

Today she was dressed in a blouse that hung off her shoulders and a full-length skirt that flowed to her ankles. The print of the outfit was multicolor and gave her an exotic look. With her hair flowing around her shoulders and a beautiful white orchid in her hair, she could pass for an island girl—a very sexy one at that.

She had spent the morning in his private spa, pampered by the best masseuse and spa staff that money could buy. He could just imagine all the wonderful things she'd had done to her body. She looked relaxed, rejuvenated and totally sexy.

Shoving his hands in his pockets, he simply stared at her. The eyes staring back at him were filled with a degree of desire that sent a rush of heat through his body that made him want her right then. Right there. At that very moment. Regardless of the fact that it was the middle of the day and his staff was in residence. What mattered to him was that he had put that look in her eyes.

He had been the one to initiate her need. Intensify it. The one who over the past several days had taught her a number of naughty things, things that made his erection engorged just thinking about them. Under his teachings she had become a temptress, a seductive vixen. A woman who was learning how to please a man and getting very good at it.

A woman he wanted.

His nostrils flared. Hot blood rushed through his veins. And without further thought, he began removing his clothes. She took his cue and began removing hers. But there was something about her movements—the way she shimmied the skirt past her tiny waist with little modesty, baring hips he had ridden last night—that caused him to pause, freeze in place and just watch her. An intense shudder passed through him, and he felt it all the way to his core. He swallowed. Mesmerized.

She dispensed with her blouse and her hands went to the front clasp of her bra. Before he could blink her twin mounds were freed from confinement. He studied her nipples, watched them harden before his eyes. He could imagine his fingers moving across them, his thumb touching them lightly, and followed by the touch of this mouth, the heated tip of his tongue licking them gently before his mouth began sucking, taking them with a hunger he felt all the way in his gut.

As some of the potent arousal pumped through his bloodstream, he tilted his head and a guttural groan eased from his lips. Even from across the room he could feel her responding to his sensuous mating call and her body answered in the most provocative way. While her gaze held his she eased her last remaining piece of clothing, a pair of black panties, down a pair of gorgeous legs. She moved her legs apart in a stance that was as tempting and as sexy as anything he had ever seen.

And the area between her thighs was as sexy as anything he'd seen, as well. It was beautiful, smooth, deliciously waxed. At that moment he couldn't think, he could just feel, and what he was feeling was a need so gigantic and voracious, it was growing hard and fast, which was why his swelled shaft was pressing hard against the zipper of his pants.

He resumed the process of removing his clothes, thinking he couldn't get down to his bare skin fast enough, and when he finally did he released another guttural groan as he crossed the room to her.

She met him halfway and he knew there was nothing he wanted so badly as Johari at that very moment. Every part of him was hypersensitive, awareness was so keen even the hairs on his chest felt receptive to her very presence. And when he reached her and swept her into his arms and carried her over to the bed, a burning need took over his entire body and soul.

Not for the first time he asked himself what was there about her that made him want to be unrestrained, want to package the pleasure they shared as theirs and theirs alone? Making love to her again was all he could think about at that moment, getting deep inside her body where they were as connected as any two bodies could get. And as crazy as it sounded, he wanted to release his seed inside of her. Here. Now. He wanted to get her with child and not wait until the wedding. He planned on moving the date for that up anyway. He intended that there be a wedding as soon as she returned home.

"Monty?"

He was on the bed with her beneath him, the softness of her body under the hardness of his. His thighs were pressing into hers and her scent had him staring at her with sensually aroused eyes.

"How do I have the ability to pleasure you so? Make you want me this much?" Johari said.

Wonder. Astonishment. He heard both in her voice and knew why she was asking. In the days they'd spent together since leaving New York, all it took was a look or an innocent touch from her to send blood pounding through him with a need and desire that left him shaking. He was breathing harder just thinking about it. Multiple orgasms were common for them and when they occurred he didn't hesitate to let her know how he felt as he was buried deep within her body. He would let her know just what she was doing to him. Just how much she was pleasuring him.

That was information he would not have shared with another woman, but he felt right in sharing it with her. She needed to know and understand when the time came after their marriage and he did take a mistress it had nothing to do with her, but that was just the way things were.

Knowing he had to be as honest with her as he could in answering her question, he pulled in a deep breath. No other woman had ever asked him such a question because no other woman would have dared. But he wasn't dealing with any woman. Johari was someone who'd proved she didn't adhere to protocol. Nor did she stick to doing what most would consider politically correct. And because of it, he would tell her things he had never told another woman.

"Because the moment my tongue tasted your breasts, the juncture of your legs as well as your lips, I knew that I had to have you. I had to be the one to spread your thighs and go inside you, give you something you've never had before." And there was no need to tell her at the same time she had given him something he'd never had before, as well. Her absolute trust. She had trusted him, a total stranger. A man who wanted her so much he ached.

"You wanted me to teach you how to pleasure a man, Johari, but in the end such an instruction wasn't needed as you have a natural instinct, an ingrained ability to give pleasure without even trying," he whispered in earnest.

"You and you alone have the ability to make a man want you and not disappoint him when he gets you," he said as his hand gently gripped her hip.

"And when I eased inside of you," he said, letting his shaft slide easily inside, nearly moaning in pure pleasure at the feel of her hot wetness, gritting his teeth to keep from thrusting deep so fast. He wanted it slow and all the way to the hilt. "I'm at a place where no other woman has taken me," he muttered, leaning down and brushing his lips over hers, plying the corners of her mouth with butterfly kisses.

"I was supposed to be teaching you a few things but in the end you taught me," he whispered against her lips, before opening his mouth fully on hers and all but sucking her tongue inside.

Her soft moan was something he couldn't ignore and as his mouth mated hungrily with hers, he pushed his erection deeper and deeper inside of her, feeling himself getting larger with every inch he took.

And when she wrapped her legs around him to hold him inside of her, he lost it and began thrusting, pounding her like there was no tomorrow, as if their time together was almost at an end, and in a way it was. But until the day he returned her to New York, he planned on rocking both their worlds, getting inside her body every chance he got, make her scream with pleasure while at the same time allowing her to push him over the edge of ecstasy.

Like she was doing now.

Each time he thrust, her womb was like a vacuum, sucking him in, holding him tight between clenched muscles. She was hot, wet and the feel of being inside of her, getting everything he had pulled out of him, was driving him insane. And each time he pulled out, sliding through her hot wetness to do so and then plunging back in, impaling her, taking her with a force that had her moaning his name, he felt he was in a world created just for the two of them. At this moment, this was all he needed.

She was all he needed. Now and always.

That realization caught him unawares and at the same time an explosion within him erupted and shocks of pleasure ripped through him, pounding his veins, blasting through his entire system. An upsurge of blood seemed to collect at the head of his erection and the detonation was like nothing he had ever felt when his body kept releasing inside of her, shooting his semen inside her womb.

"Monty!"

He tightened his hold on her at the same time his hips shifted slightly, wanting her to feel his hot release everywhere and he could tell by her whispered moan that she did.

This was too much pleasure. Almost more than he could bear. He felt the lower half of his body, straining, pushing forward, trying to get even deeper inside of her and in sweet agony discovered that he couldn't. He was as deep as he could get. At that moment with their bodies connected it was almost impossible to tell where one began and the other ended. But he didn't care. The only thing he cared about was the woman in his arms. The woman who had come to mean so much to him. The woman he was destined to possess.

Johari felt every bone in her body shiver in pleasure. Even after enjoying an exhilarating orgasm together, Monty hadn't stopped, too intent on stroking her right into another. How could one man have so much stamina? How could one man deliver so much pleasure?

He was inside of her. Deep. Hot. Expanded. He was making her use muscles she had never used before she had made love to him. And she was feeling things she had never felt before. And his words earlier, telling her she had a natural skill to please, had touched her in a way she could never forget.

She stared up at him, saw the way he was looking down at her, the intensity, the full-blown sexuality that was outlined in his features, in the eyes staring back down at her. Her legs were wrapped around his hard, thick muscular thighs and he was thrusting inside of her at a pace that almost had her purring, took her breath away, had her lifting her hips to receive his every plunge inside of her. Over and over again.

She was feeling every inch of him and at that moment she felt something with him she had no right to feel. Possessive. And she began using her internal muscles to once again milk everything out of him. A hard shudder tore through her the exact moment that he screamed her name. And then while he continued to thrust inside of her, giving her everything she wanted, he took her lips with a greed that had her trembling, exploding in her own release, while her ruby continued to clench him, hold tight to the full length of his erection. Force another full release from him.

And then he screamed her name and she felt another release shooting within the depths of her and she thought this much pleasure just had to be uncommon. But it was always the case with Monty, passion and ecstasy of this mind-jarring degree.

She suddenly felt exhausted, limp, and when he eased off her but held her in such a way that kept their bodies intimately joined, she moaned as she rested her head against his chest. She felt his arms tighten around her and she snuggled closer to him.

And when she felt the gentle kiss he placed on her forehead and the words he whispered telling her to rest, she opened her eyes slightly to stare at him, love rising in her chest, in all parts of her body, and she heard herself whisper words to him before drifting off to sleep.

Rasheed lay there and watched Johari slept. He had not meant for her emotions to come into play. He had not meant for her to fall in love with him. Yet those were the very words she had spoken before drifting off to sleep. She had whispered she loved him.

She was to marry one man but had fallen in love with another. But then, he had to remind himself, although she didn't know—she didn't have a clue—he was one and the same.

He rubbed a hand down his face. What had started out as a way to teach her a lesson about being rebellious had back-fired on him and in a big way. It seemed he was the one who had been taught a lesson. No two women were the same and, as far as he was concerned, Johari was in a class by herself. At twenty-four, a virgin, she had made him feel things no other woman had. And he wasn't sure just what he would do about it. A wife was not supposed to make her husband feel these things and to this degree.

And he wasn't sure he wanted a wife to love him. Obeying him would have been enough. Women in love got possessive toward a man when it came to other women. She had already made it clear that she wanted to be the only woman in her future husband's life and didn't relish the thought of him having mistresses. If she fancied herself in love with him that would only make matters worse.

Now he was faced with the problem of what to do. Tomorrow they would leave Vanuatu to spend their remaining days on his Greek island, then they would return to New York. He would not be completely satisfied until he watched her get on a plane headed for the Middle East and then later get a call from Jamal informing him she was safely back in Tahran.

Chapter 13

"**Y**our secret is out, Monty. I know where you are from now."

Monty's hands paused in midair. He lifted his head and glanced into Johari's eyes. She was lying on her stomach on a blanket as he leaned over her and rubbed lotion onto her back. They had arrived at his oceanfront villa on the Greek island yesterday and had spent most of today outside on the beach. He had requested that none of his staff be present when he arrived so he and Johari would have the small island to themselves.

She was smiling and his breath caught as he inhaled deeply before moving his hand again, his fingers coming into contact with the smoothness of her skin. He loved touching her. He loved kissing her. He loved making love to her. But most importantly, he loved being with her.

"And where do you think I'm from?" he asked, his eyes never leaving hers as he continued to stroke her back.

"From here. I heard how you converse with the people at the airport. You were comfortable with them. Comfortable in being here. You are from here. You speak Greek too fluently not to be."

The tenseness flowed from his body and he couldn't help but chuckle at her reasoning. "I speak several languages fluently," he said honestly.

She shifted her body, flipping onto her back to stare directly into his face. "Are you saying you are not Greek?"

Was that disappointment he heard in her voice? "Do you want me to be Greek for some reason, Jo?" he asked, and then held his breath awaiting her response.

He watched as a smile touched her lips, beginning at the corners and then spreading before she said, "It doesn't matter to me, Monty. I enjoy being with you. Your nationality is of no concern. What matters is that you are a good person, someone I trust. Someone I love being with. I've had such an amazing time with you."

She lowered her head and he watched as she then lifted it back up while drawing in a slow, deep breath. "And I don't look forward to my time ending with you. I will think of you every day of my remaining time here on earth."

He could feel his heart pumping fast and furious and knew he needed to help her understand why she couldn't feel that way about him—especially not as the stranger who had entered her life, swept her off her feet, seduced her mercilessly and had somehow captured her heart. He had to make it real for her now. Allow reality to set back in. They had only three more days to spend together.

"And how do you think your fiancée will feel about that?" he asked, staring deeply into her eyes. "Will you ever tell him about the time you've spent here with me?"

Holding her gaze, he saw how her entire body responded

to the reminder that she was engaged to marry another. "No, I won't tell him," she answered somberly. "I'm sure he will come to our marriage with secrets of his own. Secrets he won't have any qualms about not sharing with me. So it will only be fair that I keep a few of my own, as well."

He nodded, thinking he could accept her reasoning considering her ingrained rebellious nature, a trait that was beginning to grow on him. It kept him on his toes and his body aroused. "And after you are married," he ventured on to say, "if our paths cross and the opportunity presents itself, will you become my lover again if I can discreetly make it possible?"

He watched as pain settled into the depths of her eyes before she shifted her body to sit up. She then reached out and touched his face. "Please, Monty, don't ask that of me, for I cannot. I am here with you now, but this is all there can ever be for us. Once I commit my life to my husband I could not and will never betray him, no matter what. Not even for you. I will be committed to my marriage vows."

He stared at her. "Even if he refuses to give up his mistresses?"

He saw the grief in her eyes when she said, "Yes, even then."

She then leaned up and placed her head against his chest. When he felt a tear touch his skin he fought everything within him to tell her the truth right then and there. But at that moment he could not risk seeing what he knew was love in her eyes turn into hate. And when a whimper eased from her lips he tightened his arms around her.

"Shh. It's okay, Jo. Forgive me for bringing *him* up," he whispered close to her ear. "I, too, will cherish these days, these moments and I, too, will never forget."

And he would not, especially when she discovered the truth of his duplicity. There would be hell to pay and he had a feeling she wouldn't forgive easily and that's what bothered him the most. He was silent and so was she. His hands stroked her back and he wondered at the situation he was now in. It was one of those where his friend Jake would laughingly say the hunter had gotten captured by the game. And so it was.

He had always appreciated women. He thought they were boxes of jewels filled with surprises, excitement and pleasure. A few he had decided were challenges, especially those who thought they could capture his heart, tame his soul or make him vulnerable to their lovemaking skills. But he knew now, could easily admit, the woman he held in his arms was different. She had taught him that there could be more important things to share with a woman than endless passion, unspeakable pleasures and never-ending sexual gratification. There were things such as companionship and contentment. Johari's willful, rebellious and defiant nature challenged him in more ways than one. In the bedroom she'd had an innocent thirst for carnal knowledge and outside the bedroom she was still everything he would want in a lover, and he would even go so far as to admit that she was everything he would look forward to having in a wife.

She lifted her face from his chest and pushed her fingers through her hair after quickly wiping away the last of her tears. "I'm sorry. I did not mean to become emotional. I am here to have a good time." And then in a soft voice, she added, "There will be no regrets, Monty."

He reached out, captured her chin in the palm of his hand. He was silent for a long moment as he studied her features, immersing his vision in every single detail. He knew at that moment his only regret would be when the truth was brought to light and she assumed the worst. But then hadn't the worst been his plan all along in order to teach her a lesson? A lesson she rightly deserved to learn?

He could feel himself floundering in that regard, going so

far as to consider having a change of heart. But a part of him, the part that refused to give in to emotions of any kind, stood fast, unmovable. So here he was fighting for a sense of balance and logical thinking where she was concerned and wasn't doing a good job of it.

At that moment he didn't want balance or logical thinking. He wanted her. And he wanted her in a way he'd never wanted a woman before and on his secluded Greek island underneath a beautiful June sky. Here out in the open. No restraints.

"I want you, Jo."

He leaned over and captured her mouth, sliding his tongue into it at the same time he lowered her back onto the towel. Those four words were ones he had found himself saying a lot lately and each time he'd said them, he meant them.

There was an intensity in their kiss, a countdown of the days they had left. Not many of them. And a promise to make the rest of them special, more than significant in some way. He wanted to remember every detail of her mouth, every single inch and how it felt to use his tongue to taste her, make her groan and whimper as he raised the level of pleasure for both of them.

He felt her hands gripping his shoulders and then they wrapped around his neck when he took the kiss deeper still. She was as desperate to taste him as he was to taste her and it showed in the way she was responding. Her taste was erotic. It fired his senses, escalated his arousal and made him want to get inside her something awful.

He pulled back and breathed in deeply. It didn't take much time to dispense of her skimpy bathing suit or his swimming trunks. The earth seemed to tilt the moment he rose above her. Naked. Hard. Ready. He stared down at her as desire vibrated through him, in every single pore of his body. Instinctively, she raised her hips to him and the feel of her heated flesh on him sent shivers down his spine. When he slid inside of her, a maelstrom of pleasure, as deep as it could get, ripped through him.

When he began to move, his senses exploded in a need so strong he had to fight to retain control. But moments later he lost it when her inner muscles began stroking him, pulling him in, taking everything he had to give, increasing his hunger for her that much more.

His greed was reflected in his deep penetration, his downward thrusts. Her body deserved satisfaction and he was giving it to her in every way he could. And when an orgasm struck, a rumbled groan erupted from his throat the moment he felt himself go up in flames. Profound rapture, as intense as it could get, shot through his system.

And seemingly spontaneously, she was consumed to the same degree of pleasure. She screamed his name as the lower part of her body held on to him, clenched him tighter within her, gripped his shaft with her inner muscles, holding it hostage until the very last of the semen was drained from him.

It was only then that he bent his head and captured her lips, licking and nipping at the corners before thrusting his tongue into her mouth, tasting her with a voraciousness that made him pull his mouth back and growl out his pleasure.

At that moment he knew that she had drawn more out of him than his seed. The feel of her chipping away at his guard, the security net and the safety shield he had kept for thirty-nine years around his heart, nearly broke his control. The very thought that she had accomplished such a thing sent shock waves through him and he felt consumed by her in a way he had never felt consumed before.

And for the first time in his life more than lust was driving him. And when he stared down at her, held by the depths of her incredible, beautiful, dark eyes, he knew Johari Yasir had done the impossible. She had captured his heart. Totally. Completely. Exclusively.

He heard his own sharp intake of breath at that admission and didn't want to think about what that meant and how such an emotion thrown into the mix now drastically changed his plans. He no longer wanted to humiliate her before putting her on a plane bound for Tahran by telling her how he'd intentionally set out to seduce her just to teach her a lesson.

He forced those thoughts to the back of his mind to deal with them later. Right now the only thing he wanted to concentrate on was the woman beneath him whom he wanted to make love to all over again.

"More." That one word flowed from his mouth in a ragged and rough tone, and he watched her gaze darken with renewed desire the same moment she licked across her bottom lip with her tongue.

Without giving her the chance to drive him any further over the edge, he leaned down and captured her lips at the same time he began moving inside her. The one word that suddenly flared to his mind was *mine*.

And he knew at that moment that Johari was truly his.

Chapter 14

Exactly two weeks after their first meeting Johari stood on the balcony of Monty's condo in New York and stared down at him. He was standing below on the sidewalk talking to the man who had picked them up from the airport yesterday.

Ishaq's appearance was a stark reminder that her time with Monty was up and he would be taking her to the airport. She had called and spoken to her mother and, surprisingly, no questions had been asked. Nor had her mother seemed surprised that she would be flying out of New York and not California. But she could tell by the exuberance in her mother's voice that she was glad she was coming home. A private plane would arrive at the Kennedy Airport for her around noon today.

Johari had then placed a call to Cel, who had agreed to bring Copper to the airport so she could cuddle him one last time before she left the States. She didn't want to think about when and if she would ever see her puppy again.

The sound of a car horn blasting broke into Johari's thoughts and she watched as Ishaq walked toward the limo he'd been driving, leaving Monty standing alone. He was extremely handsome and elegantly dressed in a tailored business suit. His attire was another stark reminder that her carefree days had come to an end.

She left the balcony to return to his bedroom to continue packing. She would not only miss this place but all the other places she had been with Monty. When she had arrived in New York two weeks ago she had figured she would mostly stay in her hotel room and venture out in late evenings in time to enjoy the nightlife as she sought out lively entertainment. She'd had no idea that a handsome stranger would whisk her away to three different islands where she would spend time with him and indulge in fantasies she had only dreamed about. He had given her enough exciting moments to last forever.

After arriving back here yesterday they had spent most of their time in bed, ordering room service when the need for food had overtaken their need for each other. That hadn't been often. It was as if they needed to store up all the passion they could, knowing it would never come their way again. At least she doubted it would come her way. There was no doubt in her mind that once she was gone Monty would replace her with someone else. A part of her could not get angry about it, because she'd known he was a sophisticated, experienced and worldly man, a jet-setting playboy. But that knowledge hadn't kept her from flying off with him. Nor had it stopped her from falling in love with him.

At the sound of footsteps she turned toward the open door and seconds later Monty walked into the room. His presence caused her heart to begin pounding in her chest and sent a stirring in the pit of her stomach. She would miss him. Oh, how she was going to miss him.

"I'm almost packed," she said when she met his gaze and saw intense heat lodged there.

"No hurry. Ishaq is early. We still have time." He hesitated for a moment and then said, "Come here, Jo." He then reached his hand out to her. "I want to hold you for a while."

Without any hesitation, Johari crossed the room and placed her hand in his. He swept her into his arms and carried her over to the love seat and sat down with her in his lap.

For a long moment neither of them said anything. In essence there was nothing left to say. In a few hours it would be time to part ways. Since she wasn't sure whether or not Jamal would be on the plane sent to get her, she had asked Monty not to be seen with her once they arrived at the airport. She needed to walk in alone. He had reluctantly agreed.

She lifted a smiling face up to him. "I talked to Cel and she will have Copper at the airport so I can give him one final hug before I leave the States," she said to break the silence.

"That is kind of her to do so."

"Yes, it is," she agreed, aware of the sexual tension building between them. She then added, "I'm sure Copper will be well cared for."

"I'm sure that he will be."

She nodded. "I wonder if he will miss me."

"Yes, he will miss you. I will miss you."

She felt his hands tightening around her waist and felt the huge, hard bulge beneath her bottom. They had made love that morning, a number of times. Greed and a need for memories seemed to have overtaken their senses.

She twisted around in his arms, needing to see him, to feel his heat one last time, to fuse to her mind his perfect features. Beautiful and flawless as anything she'd ever seen. When he darted his tongue out to lick the corner of her mouth, she became breathless, had to force herself to take a deep intake of air.

"Last night you proved just how resourceful you are in putting all your new knowledge to use."

A blush crept across her face with his mention of what she had done last night. In a surprise move she had pushed him onto his back and, before he could stop her, she had gone down on him, taken him into her mouth and made love to him that way. She had known from his groans and the tight hold on her hair that his enjoyment was just as deep as hers. And when she finally released him and lifted her head to smile up at him, the satisfied pleasure she'd seen in his eyes touched her in a way that made her pulse race.

"I had a great teacher. Thank you," she said, trying to get her breathing under control at the feel of his hand reaching out to cup a breast through her blouse. The pad of his thumb then stroked the nipples that were pressed hard against the silk material.

"It was my pleasure."

And then he leaned in, sank his mouth onto hers and, on her breathless sigh, his tongue entered her mouth, claimed possession and stirred a magnitude of erotic sensations all through her body.

Moments later he pulled his mouth away and gazed deeply into her eyes. "Do you want to share pleasure with me once more? Before you leave?" he asked huskily.

"Yes," she responded, not once thinking of turning him down and not caring how little time they might have.

He stood with her in his arms and she knew at that moment that no matter what the future held for her back in Tahran, Monty had given her memories to last a lifetime.

"Drive around the airport for a while, Ishaq, and pick me up back here in around twenty minutes."

"Yes, Your Highness."

Getting out of his car, Rasheed watched from a distance as Johari was first greeted by her friend Cel, who was holding a cute little puppy. He saw the joy on Johari's face when she took the puppy into her arms. Her happiness at seeing the animal touched his heart. He continued to watch as the two women chatted endlessly and entered the airport terminal. He and Johari had said their goodbyes in the car since he had promised her that he would let her walk into the terminal alone. But he had not promised her that he would not follow at a safe distance to watch her finally leave the country to return home.

He felt a tightening around his heart upon thinking of how bad things were going to look when the truth was revealed to her. He had thought about speaking to her a few times yesterday and this morning but each time he'd tried he had not been able to get the words past his lips. The thought of her despising him for playing her for a fool was something he would not have been able to handle.

And then he was burdened with the thought that he had placed himself in the precarious situation of having to compete against himself for his future wife's affections. But it was a situation he intended to work out and would do everything in his power to convince her that, whether he was Monty or Rasheed, he was the same man whose heart she had captured.

He paused when a uniformed guard approached her and then she and Cel were led through a long corridor for private international flights. This was a section of the airport he knew well. He continued following at a discreet distance and flashed a uniformed officer his special credentials when he was approached.

He had made it to the glass window when she returned the puppy to Cel and then gave them both a final hug before watching them walk away. And then as if she'd known there was no way on this earth he would have let her get this far away from him, she scanned the terminal until she saw him.

Rasheed drew in a sharp intake of breath and it took every ounce of his control to not cross the floor to her. He knew he was in enough trouble as it was. So he stood there and stared at her.

For a long, silent moment across the wide expanse of space they continued to stare at each other. Suddenly she made a move in his direction. Seemingly out of the blue, a man appeared at her side, touched her shoulder and claimed her attention.

"Jamal!" Johari threw herself into her brother's arms, glad to see him. And when she glanced back to where Monty had been standing just moments ago, he was gone. She glanced around the terminal but didn't see him anywhere. At that moment she couldn't stop the tears gathering in her eyes. She was choosing duty over love.

"Johari, are you all right?"

She glanced up into her brother's concerned face and forced a smile to her lips. "Yes. I'm fine and I'm ready to go home now, Jamal. Please take me home."

He wrapped his arm around her shoulder. "Come on. Delaney is waiting for us in the jet. As soon as they finish re-fueling, we'll be ready to go."

Chapter 15

One week later

Johari had wondered how long it would take for her father and brother to finally summon her to meet with them. Everyone had avoided asking her any questions and she hadn't offered them any information. There was nothing that needed to be said.

Evidently after a week they now felt differently. As far as she was concerned she wouldn't provide any more information today than she would have last week. She might regret causing them undue worry, but there was no way she would regret meeting and subsequently falling in love with Monty.

Monty.

She missed him so much she actually ached. And each night she dreamed he was there with her, holding her in his arms while she slept, only to wake up in the light of day to find herself alone. But she had stored up plenty of memories of the time they had spent together and all the things they had shared. These memories would sustain her.

And…there was a possibility she carried his child. She wouldn't know for another week or so, but that was the reason she had not brought up any discussion regarding moving ahead with her wedding plans. Luckily, that was one subject her mother hadn't broached either.

The guard standing outside her father's door nodded and then opened the door wide to announce her. "King Yasir, Prince Jamal. Princess Johari has arrived."

She slowly walked into the room and glanced around, trying to recall how infrequently she visited this room where her father conducted most of his business matters regarding the sheikhdom. It was a huge room and one she used to like to play in when she was younger.

She approached her father, who sat in a chair behind a huge desk. Jamal was sitting in a chair at his right. "Yes, Father," she said quietly. "You sent for me."

Her father stared at her for a moment and said, "It's been a week, Johari, and now it is time to address your act of disobedience. Not only did you cause me and your mother undue worry, but Saud was taken to task for failing to keep you under his watchful care."

"But it wasn't his fault. I—"

"Outsmarted him. We know, so he was not held at fault," her father said, shaking his head. "Playing hide-and-seek from your bodyguards was all for fun and games when you were younger, Johari, but your actions are unacceptable now. You are twenty-four, a woman promised to a man who will be king of a very important country."

"I didn't hurt anyone by having some fun," she said, lifting her chin and meeting her father's direct gaze.

"Whether you hurt someone is a matter of opinion, one we will let your future husband decide," her brother spoke up to say.

She turned her head to where her brother sat. "What are you talking about, Jamal?"

"What Jamal is talking about is the fact that once you became missing it was imperative to notify Sheikh Valdemon immediately," her father responded in a rather tired voice.

She frowned. "Why? It didn't concern him. I only prolonged my time in the States. A big deal should not have been made of it."

Now it was her father's turn to frown, and the one masking his face was considerably fiercer than the one on hers. "How can you say such a thing, Johari?" he asked in an angry voice. "You were missing for two weeks without a proper chaperone and bodyguard. The man who will be your husband had a right to know. And based on your actions, it would have been within Sheikh Valdemon's rights to cancel the marriage contract between the two of you. If he had taken that option, it would have brought much shame on this sheikhdom, and all in the name of you wanting to *have fun.*"

Johari couldn't do anything but lower her head. It hadn't been too often in her life that her father had been upset with her. Now, not only was he upset but, she could tell by the tone of his voice, he was disappointed, as well.

There was no need to tell him or Jamal how she had needed that time to herself before marrying a man who would not love her. A man known for his numerous mistresses. How could she explain that she didn't want to endure a loveless marriage and that she wanted to be loved and cherished the same way her father loved and cherished her mother? The way Jamal loved and cherished Delaney. And the way Prince Shudoya cherished and loved Arielle.

And…there was no need to tell him that if it was determined she was pregnant there would not be a wedding and she would accept her banishment to another continent if that was to be her punishment. She was not worried about being shipped off somewhere to live away from her family just as long as her child…Monty's child…was with her.

"He will be here tomorrow to meet with you," her father said.

Johari snatched her head up. "Who will?"

"Sheikh Valdemon." Now it was Jamal who was speaking. "I spoke to him this morning and he wants the marriage to take place as soon as possible, so there will be a private ceremony here tomorrow night. A wedding celebration will be planned at a later date."

Johari was taken aback by her brother's statement. She was certain the color completely drained from her face. "Marry? Tomorrow night? But that's not possible."

"It is possible, Johari, and if that is what the sheikh wants then we can and will accommodate him, considering your willful behavior," her father stated adamantly.

"I need to speak with the sheikh privately before I will agree to marry him," she said.

Her father's frown deepened even more. "Agree? There is nothing to agree to, Johari. Need I remind you it is your duty? There *will* be a private ceremony here tomorrow night. Unless, however, you can show just cause why there shouldn't be."

Yes, there is just cause, she wanted to scream. *I could be pregnant with another man's child and I won't marry him until I am sure that is not the case. So there is no way I can marry him tomorrow.* She could easily recall when Jamal was destined to marry Princess Raschida and how he had discovered the princess's devious plot to hide her pregnancy by another man from him, trying to pass off the child as Jamal's. Johari would not do such a thing to Sheikh Valdemon.

"Johari? Is there a reason why a marriage between you and the sheikh should not take place?"

It was Jamal who was asking the question. She met her brother's gaze and for some reason she felt the brother who knew her well, at that moment, realized there was something she was not telling them. She lifted her chin and said, "I won't answer that, Jamal. I need to meet with Sheikh Valdemon and I will let him decide."

Without saying anything else, she quickly left the room.

Upon awakening the next morning Johari received word that Sheikh Rasheed Valdemon had arrived at the palace and had agreed to meet with her. It seemed the entire palace was buzzing and all the young female staffers were whispering about how handsome the sheikh was. She ignored their chatter, not at all impressed and thinking no man could possibly be more handsome than *her* Monty.

She deliberately stayed in her room most of the day, even taking her breakfast and lunch there. Her mother paid her a visit when she was eating lunch and Johari couldn't help noticing the excitement that was shining in her mother's dark eyes.

"You don't appear to be excited about this being your wedding day, Johari."

She stopped eating to look up at her mother, fairly certain her father had shared the details of yesterday's meeting with her. "I'm sure you're aware, Mother, that a wedding might not be taking place." Johari was grateful her mother did not ask her why she felt that way.

She had showered and dressed in a skirt and blouse when she received word that Sheikh Rasheed Valdemon of Mowaiti was ready to hold a private meeting with her. Instead of meeting with her in one of the conference rooms in the same wing as her father's office, as she'd assumed, she was told he would meet with her in one of the entertainment rooms in a wing of the palace that was seldom used. Johari was further surprised when she was informed there would be no chaperone for this particular meeting.

Just as well, she thought as she walked the long corridor to where the meeting was to take place. The fewer people who knew of her predicament the better. She intended to tell the sheikh everything, including the fact that she was in love with another man, and like she had told her father, the decision as to whether there would be a wedding later today would be his.

The room that had been selected for their meeting was usually kept private except for when her father entertained dignitaries from neighboring sheikhdoms. One of the features in the room was a huge fountain in the center of the room that had been sculpted in the shape of one of the Egyptian waterfalls.

She knocked on the closed door and a deep, husky voice speaking in her native tongue indicated she could enter. Taking a deep breath, she opened the door and walked in, closing the door behind her. She could not recall the last time she had been in this room, not since she was eight or nine. But just like all the rest of the rooms of the palace, it was richly decorated in colors of red and gold. Another thing she noticed was that the blinds hadn't been opened, which gave the room a dark effect except for the few wall lanterns that were lit and shining brightly.

Her gaze swept the room and then she saw him. The sheikh's back was to her as he stood staring at the huge waterfall. He was wearing royal sheikh attire complete with his native headdress.

Even with his back to her he emitted a power that she couldn't help but feel. She knew this was a man who issued orders that were obeyed. He was also a man who over the past six years had taken an impoverished country and turned it into a thriving one.

She found herself clearing her throat and then saying in her native tongue, "I am here for our meeting, Your Highness."

Instead of turning around to acknowledge her presence, he responded likewise in their native tongue. "You wanted to meet with me before the wedding, Princess Johari?"

She was slightly annoyed that he hadn't turned to look at her, and wondered if the reason had anything to do with his disgust with her behavior in the States. If that was the case then he was about to become more annoyed with her. "Yes," she said. "I need to advise you of some developments."

"Such as?"

She paused for a second and then decided to just get it out. "While in the United States, I met someone. A man I fell in love with. And I think you should know that we were intimate and I could be having his child."

That confession should turn him around, she thought, and when it didn't, when he just continued to stand there silently with his back to her, she was puzzled. "Your Highness, did you hear what—"

"Do you know for certain that you are pregnant?"

She stared at his back, more confused than ever. He was asking the question as if a pregnancy was something he was anticipating happening. "No, but if you marry me tonight without knowing for sure then you could possibly claim someone else's child."

"Not necessarily. In fact, I know not."

It was then that he slowly turned to face her. She frowned

at the dark eyes staring back at her and when he reached up
to remove his headpiece, her head began spinning and she
thought she was going out of her mind. Her breath caught and
the name she had held to her heart slipped from between her
lips. "Monty!"

Rasheed stared across the room at the woman who had
been in his dreams each night, the woman who was on his
mind each day. The one and only woman who had captured
his heart. She stood staring at him, speechless and as beautiful as he remembered.

"Monty, I don't understand. What are you doing here?
And where is Sheikh Valdemon?"

He slowly crossed the room to her. "The reason I am here
is because I am one and the same. My friends know me as
Monty. To others I am Sheikh Rasheed Valdemon of Mowaiti."

He watched as it slowly began to dawn on her what he'd
said and what his admission meant. And he was very aware
of the exact moment the surprise in her eyes turned to anger.
"You deliberately misled me into believing you were someone else," she said in an accusing tone. "That night in New
York, when you first approached me at the club, you knew
who I was, didn't you?"

Rasheed saw no reason to be less than honest with her.
"Yes. In fact, my only purpose in coming to New York was
to find you and send you back to Tahran."

She lifted her chin in a defiant manner. "And just how did
you manage to find me? Everyone else was looking for me
in California."

He nodded. "Yes, you deliberately sent them to the wrong
area of the country. However, a friend of mine is an ace when

it comes to tracking people. I hired him to find you and he did so within forty-eight hours without falling for your false leads."

"And once he found me, you decided to make it all fun and games?" she snapped.

He crossed his arms over his chest. "At the time I figured why not, since you'd made a point that you were looking to have some fun anyway. In fact when I walked into that nightclub you were dancing on the tables."

He noted the embarrassment that stained her features. "Yes, I wanted to have fun but it wasn't my intent to be used!" she shouted angrily.

She turned to walk away, intent on leaving the room. He reached out and grabbed her hand and pulled her back to him. The moment they touched, sensual sensations that they had previously experienced raced through their bodies.

He pulled her close to him so she could look directly into his face. "And tell me, Johari. Just how did I use you? Did I force you in any way? I don't recall kidnapping you any of those times you were on my jet or when you went to my islands. In fact you seemed rather happy to be there. To my way of thinking, I kept you out of trouble. And also to my way of thinking, I gave you everything you wanted."

Another blush stained her features. "And you were probably laughing behind my back while doing so."

"Trust me, the only laughing moments are those we shared together. Otherwise, the tone between us was serious, pretty intense and sexual if you were to ask me, or if I need to remind you."

She glared at him. "Well, I'm not asking you nor do you need to remind me of anything," she said. "In fact, I don't want to have anything to do with you!"

"That's not possible with your admission of two things tonight. You love me and there's a possibility that you might be pregnant with my child. Make no mistake about it, Johari. I want both. I intend to keep your love and I want you to have my baby. If I didn't want those things then you wouldn't be in the predicament you're in now. I was well aware of each and every time I made love to you without protection."

Shock showed on her face. She would have stumbled back if he did not have a firm grip on her arm. "Are you saying you deliberately tried to get me pregnant?"

"What I'm saying is that I deliberately didn't use protection. It felt better that way inside of you and since you were going to be my wife anyway, I decided it wouldn't bother me in the least if you were to have my child."

"Because you had me no matter what! And you led me to believe you were American and then Greek. You made a fool out of me!"

"I never said I was American, nor did I say I was Greek. You assumed those things because of my fluency in both languages, but like I told you I can speak several languages," he said fiercely. "So you were wrong about my nationality just like you were wrong about my age. As you can see I'm not an *old* man after all, Johari. Most of my good days are far from being gone."

He knew his words made her recall just what she'd said and in anger she tried pulling her hand away, but he only tightened his grip.

"I told you all my secrets regarding my upcoming marriage when the marriage was going to be to you," she said with hurt in her eyes. "You deliberately maneuvered me into bearing my soul. You were teaching me ways to please my future husband, who conveniently happened to be you. You played me well and I won't forgive you for doing so. There is no way I will marry you now."

A heavy frown settled on Rasheed's expression when he saw the tears forming in her eyes. "We *are* getting married tonight, Johari."

She crossed her arms over her chest. "No, we're not."

"Yes, we are."

She glared at him. "You can't make me."

He couldn't restrain his smile. "Yes, I can and I will. Have you forgotten that I have a knack when it comes to seduction? I will keep you in here and by the time I'm finished with you, you will agree to just about anything."

She narrowed her eyes. "My father and brother will not let you touch me."

A smile touched his lips. "Your father and brother are probably aware that I've already touched you. They knew I was going to use my resources to find you and they were told the moment you were found. So they know you were with me the entire time, the majority of those two weeks."

She snatched away from him, livid. "Which means, considering your reputation with women and my naiveté, that they knew I was in your bed."

"And with my full intent on marrying you, no matter what."

She threw up her hands. "Why? Why do you want to marry me when you know I will cause you nothing but trouble? I refuse to compete with your mistresses. I couldn't tolerate being with you knowing others have been with you, as well."

"So you've told me, several times, and that is something you don't have to worry about. There won't be anyone but you."

Johari rolled her eyes and nearly laughed out loud at the same time. "And you expect me to believe that?"

"Yes, I expect you to believe that and you can believe this, as well. I love you and I don't intend for any other man to have you or our baby."

He saw the stunned look on her face. "What did you just say?" she asked him in a shaky voice.

Rasheed had no problem repeating it. In fact he would shout it to the entire world if he had to. "I said that I love you, Johari, and I don't intend for any man to have you or our baby."

She lifted her chin. "That's not love. That's possession."

He couldn't help but grin. His future wife was a spitfire and there would not be a dull day around her. "Actually, it's both," he decided to clarify. "But love has the higher percentage. I, Rasheed Amin Valdemon, have never loved a woman until I fell in love with you. I had no desire to love one or a need to love one. But my need for you, my desire for you, Johari, leaves me vulnerable to things I've never experienced before."

Rasheed paused, knowing he had to make her not only understand but believe. "When I see you, I am filled with exceeding joy, happiness, so much it is staggering. And when I'm with you intimately, inside of you, making love to you, you pleasure me more so than any woman. That includes any woman before and there will be none after, because you've taken away my desire for any others. I only want you. I love you."

He could tell by the look in her eyes that she wanted to believe him but still wasn't fully convinced. Probably because of his past reputation with women, she couldn't imagine such a thing as being true. But he knew he had spoken the truth. She was the only woman he wanted. Now he understood what his good friend Jake Madaris meant when he'd said that although he hadn't been interested in having a wife, since marrying Diamond he couldn't imagine his life without her.

Rasheed could admit that he felt the same way about Johari. He couldn't imagine a life without her. He couldn't bear it if she was not by his side, in his bed, the mother of his babies. His queen.

He reached out and captured Johari's wrist and gently pulled her to him. "I am possessive with you so I know you will be possessive with me. I have no problem with that. In fact, I want exclusivity. Totally. I haven't touched another woman since meeting you and before I landed back in Mowaiti a few days ago, I had my secretary call my mistresses and dismiss them all. They are no longer needed. You are the only women I want, the only woman I need. During those days you were with me, you wrapped me in pleasure so tight I couldn't imagine having any other woman in my bed but you."

"Are you sure?" she asked, seemingly through a forced breath.

Rasheed saw the ray of hope that glimmered in her eyes but she was still holding back. "I'm sure, Johari. I am positive. I want the type of marriage with you that will last forever." He reached out and placed her hand on his chest, right on his heart. "Every beat is for you and will be always. This has been the longest week but I knew I had to give you time to adjust to being back home before I stated my plea to your father. I have to marry you tonight, Johari. I can't live another single night without you."

His gaze burned into hers when he added, "You are my heart. You are my soul. You are my woman. You will be my queen. Please say that you will be."

More tears came into Johari's eyes, but Rasheed knew these were tears of happiness. She shifted her body to wrap her arms around his neck, held his gaze and said, "Yes, I will be your queen. I want to be your everything."

A satisfied smile touched Rasheed's lips. "You are already that, sweetheart."

And then he lowered his mouth, sank down into the pleasures he knew awaited him there. Her response was immediate, her passion quick. He kissed her like a starving man. A man who needed this and her to survive. And she clung to him, returned his kiss with the same fire and passion he was displaying. The same pleasure.

Reluctantly, he pulled his mouth back and smiled down at her. "Now you understand why I wanted to marry you tonight? If there was a bed in here you and I would definitely be in trouble. I can guarantee you that we would have fun."

She threw her head back and laughed and tightened her arms around him. "Oh, Monty. I love you so much. I will have plenty of fun as your wife."

He liked the sound of that. "So you are in agreement. We marry tonight to make things legal and then six months from now we have a huge celebration in Mowaiti and invite others."

She nodded. "Yes. The only problem with that is if I am pregnant now, I will be very much pregnant at our celebration. What will everyone think?"

"That I am a man who's found favor with Allah." He then lowered his head to reclaim her mouth once again.

Epilogue

"Your wife is a very beautiful woman, Rasheed."

Rasheed smiled up at Jake Madaris. A number of his American friends and those he considered family had traveled to Mowaiti to attend his wedding celebration.

He followed Jake's gaze and saw Johari as she stood talking to Jake's wife, Diamond, his sister-in-law, Delaney, her friend Celine and several other women. Jake was right; Johari was beautiful and the six months since their wedding had been the best ever. She hadn't gotten pregnant during their New York adventure but she had awakened him that very morning with the news that they would be expecting their first child, so he had double the reasons to celebrate.

"Thanks, Jake, and you are right. She is very beautiful."

Rasheed continued to stare at her, thinking of all the happiness she had brought to him. All the wonderful moments they had shared. "Excuse me a moment, Jake. I need to grab my wife for a moment."

He moved in her direction, ignoring the interested looks other women were giving him. There was only one woman who had his heart, body and soul. And now she had his baby growing inside of her, as well.

Johari turned and smiled at Rasheed. She'd known he was headed her way. It was as if certain parts of her body were like radar and had honed in on him. Already she felt the tightening of her breasts and the sensitive nipples pressing against the fabric of her gown.

She studied him as he made his way toward her. Studied him and appreciated him as a man. He had the ability to steal any woman's breath away, just as he was doing now.

Instead of wearing his native garb, he was dressed as she had seen him that first night in New York in a business suit tailored to his body. Broad shoulders. Muscular arms. Firm thighs. Flat abs. She knew just what good shape he was in, both physically and mentally. And to think she had thought her life was doomed being promised to an *old* man. She had to take power naps during the day just to keep up with him at night.

"May I steal my wife away from you ladies for a moment?" he asked the group of women when he finally reached her and placed his arms around her waist.

She felt him inconspicuously give her stomach a gentle rub in the process. Their eyes met and held and she knew what he'd done was his way of communicating with their child. They hadn't announced news of her pregnancy just yet, deciding to keep it to themselves, basking in the knowledge that together, with their love, they had made another human being.

Firmly holding her hands in his, he led her away toward an area where few people were standing, so they could converse privately. She looked at him as he gazed out at the crowd. "I see you have just as many American friends as I have," he said.

She couldn't help but smile. She had met the Madarises, the family that had made her husband an honorary member of their clan. He had told her why and she had been proud of how he had helped to save Christy Madaris Maxwell's life. She had met the woman earlier, along with her husband, Alex, and thought they were a beautiful couple. Rasheed would be taking her for a visit to Jake Madaris's ranch in a few months, where Jake and Diamond would host a party in their honor. She was looking forward to meeting Corinthians Avery and her husband, Trevor. Corinthians was the woman Rasheed credited as the person responsible for determining the location of oil in Mowaiti.

She then glanced over at the group Rasheed was speaking of specifically, the ones she considered as *her* American family, the Westmorelands. A number had flown in to share in the celebration. They had become her family when Jamal had married Delaney and she adored each and every one of them.

She then looked up at her husband and smiled. "Now we have reason to visit the United States every chance we get, Monty. And who knows, when our daughter gets older, she may decide she wants to go to school there."

She laughed at the expression that appeared on his face at the thought of that happening, especially if their daughter was as rebellious as she had been.

"Our *son* can attend school there, but forget the thought of any daughter of mine doing so. She might want to pull something like you did."

He leaned over and placed a kiss on her lips and then said, "Come on, I want to show you something."

Taking her hand again, he led her away from the crowd and through a beautifully landscaped area not far from the palace.

She'd always thought the grounds of her family's estates were beautiful until she had seen the palace where Rasheed lived. In addition to the palace, there were several surrounding villas, all breathtaking. She had lived here close to six months and she still hadn't seen it all.

Rasheed stopped her in front of a beautiful two-story villa with a picket fence. The grounds were immaculate. He turned her to face him. "This is my wedding gift to you, sweetheart. It's within walking distance of the palace and someplace you can come when you want privacy and solitude. To read, knit, write and whatever else you want to do."

He leaned closer and whispered, "It's also the place I will visit with you on occasion to make babies."

She couldn't help the smile that touched her lips. He had presented her with her very own private castle. She reached out and gave him a hug. "Thank you, Monty. It is more than I expected."

He chuckled. "I hope not, because there is more."

Her eyes widened. "More?"

"Yes. Let's go inside and see."

He opened the gate and they walked inside and she could tell that the villa had recently been renovated. Everything looked new and fresh and then when he opened the door to let her inside, the sight before her nearly took her breath away. The villa was huge, spacious and…she thought, fit for a queen and her king. A beautiful romantic hideaway to make babies.

"So what do you think?"

She glanced around. The furniture and the decor were simply elegant. So much so that it nearly brought tears to her eyes. She could see herself spending her time here. "It is beautiful, Monty. Thank you."

She leaned up to thank him but he pulled back. "Don't thank me yet. There is more."

She raised a brow. "More?"

He smiled. "Yes. Something that will be kept here at this villa for you to enjoy whenever you want."

He then led her through the front portion of the house to the bedroom and stood back. Not knowing what to expect, she glanced at her husband bemusedly before surveying the room. And then she saw what he intended for her to see in front of the fireplace.

"Copper!"

She raced across the room to her puppy the moment he saw her. Dropping to her knees, she removed him from the crate and hugged him until she remembered he was so small and she couldn't hug him so tight. Tears she couldn't contain streamed down her face. She had missed him so and wondered how often she would see him. She and Monty had visited him once on their trip to the States and it had been hard telling him goodbye again.

Johari turned eyes to her husband as she placed her dog back in the crate. She stood when Rasheed crossed the room to join her. She wondered if he had any idea how happy she was at that moment.

"But how? Why?" she asked, looking up into his face with what she knew was love and deep appreciation shining in her eyes.

He held her by the waist and pulled her to him and, just before capturing her mouth with his, he leaned down and whispered, "Because, sweetheart, you *are* worth it."

* * * * *